Lost on Dark Trails

Rukis

Lost on Dark Trails

Published by FurPlanet
Dallas, TX
http://www.FurPlanet.com

ISBN 978-1-61450-220-3
First Printing, January 2015

Cover art by Rukis

Table of Contents

What came before:

Lost on Dark Trails is the direct sequel to *Off the Beaten Path*. This is the story of a bobcat female of the Katoshen tribe, who was sent by her family to be married to Methoa'nuk, a bobcat warrior of the neighboring Anukshen tribe. Methoa'nuk was a cold and abusive husband. He forced himself upon his wife until she conceived. However, the son she bore him was frail, and Methoa'nuk declared him unfit, the result of his wife's infidelity.

The tribe performed a cleansing ritual intended to punish the infidelity and purge the evil spirits. It was a ritual she was not intended to survive, and which her son didn't. Having been saved from death by her spirit animal the vengeful Crow, and rescued from her grave by the hunter-trapper coyote name Ransom, and his companion the disavowed shamen Puquanah, or Puck, she took the name Shivah as she embarked on a quest of vengance against her husband.

After the ritual cleansing, Methoa took up with a band of imfamous raiders lead by the otter Rourke, who have been terrorising the settlements for a number of years. Shivah, Ransom and Puck fell in with a band of Marshals from the government, led by the husky Grant Wickham, tasked with hunting down and eliminating Rourke. They met in a disasterous encounter at the village of Serahaven, which was suffering from an outbreak of Seer's Feaver.

This story picks up immediately after the conclusion of *Off the Beaten Path*, as Puck, under threat of torture from Rourke's band of raiders, took Len'sal berries which induced a state of unconsciousness nigh indistinguishable from death. Ransom, devastated at what he believed to be Puck's death has fled, while Shivah and the Marshal Grant set out to get Puck to a physician who can heal him before it is too late...

CHAPTER ONE
Return to Crossroads

The nearest healer with any real skill was the Physician in Crossroads, who was nearly a day's ride away. I knew I needed to get Puck there, as fast as possible. How to do so, however, was the question.

Even if he didn't understand what I knew about the Len'sal berries, it didn't take long for Grant to accept that Puck was in fact alive. Especially after he heard his heart beat for himself, and we realized that some of the shallowest wounds, the small lacerations from being cut up as he was dragged were healing.

But it was too early to celebrate. We'd barely treated Puck when we'd found him, since everyone had assumed he was dead. His wounds had been left to bleed... Which in retrospect, should have been another sure sign he was alive, but I wasn't a healer, and Grant's limited knowledge included field dressing wounds, and little else.

Many things should have occurred to us earlier. I should have thought of the Len'sal. I had thought from the moment I saw the fox—had simply assumed because of his terrible state—that he'd been dead. I'd been sure of it. I could hardly fault Grant and his men for failing to detect the signs of life in the fox, either.

Being in denial about death is one thing, but questioning whether or not a corpse is a corpse is quite another. And I, of all people, should have. I'd been buried, and was still walking the earth today.

I'd thought it would be a hard thing to ask to pull Grant away from his duties to get us back to Crossroads, but he agreed to it without a second thought. I suppose Connall and the men had the fort held down here for now, and while it might have been irresponsible for Grant to leave them, I wasn't about to question it.

Puck's body was in a deep, cold sleep. Even if he wasn't dead yet, that didn't mean he couldn't still pass. He'd been badly hurt, to what extent we didn't even know. The Len'sal had slowed down his heart, which for all I knew was doing him even further harm. Didn't a person need the heart to beat quickly in order to live?

I didn't know what to do for him, save wrap his wounds and pray, and get him to a real healer. So that's exactly what we did. We didn't even go to meet with Connall before we left, a fact which honestly I didn't mind. I didn't need to explain all of this to him, and I suspected he wouldn't have been entirely agreeable about Grant helping us 'lesser creatures' with our crisis.

We did meet briefly with Laesom, who'd only returned to Serahaven today from his post at the river and was horrified when we related the events that had happened in his absence. The man was quiet as ever, but he agreed to return to town on Grant's orders and help keep the villagers safe while we were gone. He and the two Marshals with him had seen no action whatsoever at the river post, so at the very least Connall would have three fresh men.

My earnest hope was that Rourke was simply done with this town. We'd done all we could do for them and more at this point, and now I had to devote myself to my friend.

Friends, if one counted Ransom. But I still didn't know where he'd gone, and now with Puck alive the urgency to find him was overwhelming. As soon as I got Puck to someone who could resuscitate him, we had to find the coyote—before he did something stupid, and possibly deadly.

I found Molly left in the barn where we were keeping Helios and all of the other horses, and that only deepened my fears. Wherever Ransom had gone, he hadn't even taken our mule, or most of his supplies. And at this point, he'd been gone for almost a day.

All the man had had on him when he'd left had been the few things he kept on his person, and his weapons. A man out in the world with money, alcohol, and weapons—nothing else—could have no good purpose.

Grant saddled up his horse and I the mule. The husky was going to have to keep Puck with him, which meant there was no room for me. But it was about time I learned how to ride, and this would have to be a crash course.

As it turned out, domestic animals generally just followed one another when you took them on the road, and Grant assured me the mule would be no different. Just to be certain, we kept a lead tied to Helios for the first hour or so, but when we seemed certain the animal would simply follow on her own, we untied her so that the both of us could pick up the pace.

Riding an animal you didn't need to control wasn't nearly as hard as it would have been if I were on my own, but doing so at the pace we were taking, with my body already failing from exhaustion proved trying. I got my strength from seeing Puck's unconscious form tightly held in Grant's one free arm ahead of us. Every time I felt sleep and weariness trying to claim me, I simply looked to him, and remembered the grief I'd felt when I'd thought he was gone. That kept me going.

Grant had been awake and active just as long as I, and I couldn't imagine how physically taxing it had to be holding the fox against him throughout the entire ride. Small or not, Puck was entirely dead weight at the moment, and the husky had to both support him and hold him in the saddle. We had no other option, after all. A wagon would have slowed us down.

We stopped only twice, to water the horses, and ourselves. Both times, Grant and I looked over Puck's wounds and at least tried to make sure his bandages were still on correctly, and checked for signs of life. They were as faint as ever, but they didn't seem any worse than they'd been at the outset. At least, we hoped so. It was so hard to tell…

He was cold, and getting colder. That was the one thing we noted. I wrapped him in my Dyre hide cloak over his own, hoping it would help some, but that was all I knew to do. The winds were growing icy and strong, and the first few flakes of

11

snow had begun to fall by the time darkness threatened the sky. The storm brewing in the mountains was opening its maw, and judging by the fact that it was snowing this far down from the pass already, it was going to be a bad one.

It was nearly morning the next day by the time the distant lights of Crossroads came into view, and by then even the sight of Puck was barely enough to keep my body awake. The mind was willing, but my structure was falling apart. As soon as we saw the blazing watchtowers of the fort, Grant turned to me, and shouted through the darkness, "Do you know where the Physician is?"

I nodded. "Puck took us there. I remember."

"Then catch up to me!" Grant said, tugging the fox in close and kicking his horse into a gallop, taking off down the road.

Molly couldn't follow as quickly, but I had some rudimentary knowledge of how to handle the reins now, so I made the rest of the way into town on my own. I watched Grant and Helios's silhouettes disappear into the dim morning light down towards the city from the trail head, cheering for them silently in my mind, willing them to make it in time.

As it turned out, I didn't remember the way to the Physician's as well as I'd thought. I still didn't know Crossroads well, and all of the town streets tended to look the same in dawn's light. To make things worse, commerce was beginning by the time I made it there, so I had to navigate a place I didn't know well, with an animal I couldn't control well, through crowded streets—on nearly three days of no sleep.

By the time I found the small, familiar residence, I was falling off my feet dragging myself through the door. But I saw Helios tied out front, and as soon as I made it into the main room, I saw Grant standing near a small desk, speaking with a portly Otherwolf woman with white, curly fur. They both turned to regard me when I entered. I must have looked worse even than I felt, because the woman's first words to me were, "Oh good Lord!"

Grant looked about the worst I'd ever seen him as well, and I was about to comment on that fact, when my knees decided they wanted to get friendly with the floor.

Both the woman and Grant were at my side immediately, the husky wrapping an arm around my midsection to try to help me slowly to my feet. But my body said, 'no, no, this isn't happening again' the moment I tried to put weight on my feet, and my knees just gave out again as soon as I was up. Thankfully this time, I had a husky.

"Good God," the woman said, worriedly, leaning over me and blinking her large brown eyes down at me. I mumbled something about Puck, but she was fussing with putting on some kind of apron or smock over her strange white, functional-looking dress. "Marshal, this woman needs to be seen!"

"I wouldn't want to summon the doctor from the fox—" Grant objected, tiredly.

"And you as well!" the woman chided, taking hold of the man's bruised jowl with her thumb and forefinger, pointedly, the husky wincing in pain. "You can't ignore a cracked tooth. That has to come out."

She began heading off through the small room towards a hallway behind the desk, motioning for us to follow. Grant stooped enough to pick me up entirely, lifting me into his arms.

I swear, I almost fell asleep right then and there. I could have gotten used to this.

"But the doctor—" Grant insisted, as he walked with me towards the room.

"Oh don't you worry, handsome," the Otherwolf woman snorted, like she was using the term to mock him. "I'll be the one extracting it."

I swear to you, even drifting towards unconsciousness, I thought I heard the husky whimper.

"Stop being a child…" were the last words I heard the Otherwolf woman say, and then everything else was a muddied garble, and I fell asleep.

I woke slowly, reality taking its dear time to come into focus amidst a wash of exhaustion and disorientation. I was alive, and warm. That much I was certain of.

I shifted beneath a particularly soft, cozy blanket and blinked at the colorful tapestry of squares that made it up. Such a silly-looking blanket, but it sure was comfortable.

The room was dark, but there was a window covered by a drape nearby, and as my eyes began to adjust, I was able to pick out something of my surroundings. The room was small, and neat. There was a long cabinet on the adjacent wall with some odd implements in several glass jars spaced evenly across one side of it, as well as some carefully-folded linens and blankets visible up on the shelves above.

And the sound of heavy, deep breathing was coming from the end of the bed, where my eyes finally settled. And there I saw a husky.

The man looked about as haggard and terrible as I'd ever seen him, and the position he'd fallen asleep in suggested he'd had to have been beyond exhausted. He was—mostly—sitting in a chair at the end of the bed, but at some point he must have leaned forward to lay his elbows down on the bed beside me, because he'd fallen asleep that way, his muzzle buried between his arms.

He'd taken his vest off at some point. I saw it draped over a nearby chair. A few bloodstains down the front of it suggested it hadn't come off entirely for comfort's sake. His gun belt, gun and sheathed knife were hanging over the same chair, along with whatever few possessions he kept on his person. A pouch that likely contained his coin, whatever else he owned of value, and some kind of metal pendant, hung by a tarnished chain.

The husky's fur was rough and unkempt, for about the first time ever, and he looked particularly vulnerable. He couldn't possibly be comfortable like that. He must have only fallen asleep that way because he was exhausted.

I shifted up slowly, trying to get a gauge of how I was feeling. Of course the answer was still worn and tired, but I felt as though I'd slept for some time. I was replenished, at least somewhat—enough that I wanted to be awake right now. Enough that I wanted to know...

Puck! What had happened to Puck?

I hated to wake him. The man looked so tired, but I had to. Slowly, gently, I leaned over and shook the husky's shoulders. It took a considerable amount of time—and shaking—before he actually came to. And when he did it was with a start, his blue eyes blinking open, unfocused and wild for a moment, as he half-stumbled out of his chair.

I knew the moment he started to move that something was off about the man, but I equated it to exhaustion, at first.

"Sh... ivah..." he said at length, blinking his eyes blearily down at me, before thumping back down into his chair, heavily. "You're awake..."

"I am," I said quietly. "You don't look good, Grant..."

"Bloody barber surgeon..." the husky groaned, pressing a palm over his cheek and giving a long hiss through his teeth. "I'm still tastin' blood."

I winced. I'd thought that blow from Connall might have done more damage than it seemed on the surface. I vaguely remembered that woman mentioning something about a cracked tooth. It must have been from the back of his mouth, because I couldn't see one missing.

"Are you alright?" I asked, as the man stumbled back up to his feet and unsteadily navigated his way over to a nearby small table, where a pitcher and cups had been left for us. He poured himself a glass of water, spilling about a third of it, and not seeming to care. He drank the water with a grimace, then began pouring another glass.

"What's wrong?" I asked, concerned.

"Whiskey..." the man muttered at length, before using the table to support himself as he unsteadily handed the second glass to me.

15

"Why were you drinking?" I asked, confused, but taking the glass from him appreciatively. I gripped the man's arm as he made his way back to his chair and settled back down, heavily.

"Because she pulled a sodding tooth out of my face, that's why!" the husky exclaimed, before clutching at his jaw again, in pain. He gave a growl, then muttered between his teeth, "S'the strongest thing they 'prescribe' here for pain."

"Here…" I murmured, getting up on my knees to lean over the bed to the small table, which was more easily reachable for me, and poured him another glass of water. I handed it to him. "Keep drinking," I said softly. "Ransom always drank a lot of water when he'd had too much to drink. I think it's important."

The husky went through about three more glasses of water before he seemed done, leaning his head back at length, closing his eyes, and slouching uncharacteristically in his chair.

I let him relax for a few more minutes, but I didn't want him falling asleep again, not just yet.

"Grant," I said at length, "do you know how Puck is doing?"

"Physician said he's out of the woods," the husky murmured, without opening his eyes. I felt the tension inside me begin to uncoil at his words. I could finally breathe.

"I guess somethin' about th'berries… actually helped with th' wounds. Kept him from bleedin' out," the husky murmured. "But he still said… 'e was a fool for takin' 'em. Them things can kill you, if yer already in a bad state."

"I doubt he had much of a choice in the matter," I said, giving an exhausted smile. "But we can—we can ask him, when he wakes."

"Doc says he's gotta sleep it off…" Grant muttered. "We ain't s'posed to disturb'm."

I nodded, leaning back against the bed's headrest and going silent for a few moments, as the husky's breathing evened out slowly. But he didn't look asleep again just yet. He was still wincing every few moments. I could only assume his jaw was throbbing. I'd had a tooth pulled once before.

"You sound like Ransom when you're drunk," I noted, with some amusement.

"Oh God, don't say that," the husky grumbled.

"I don't mind the twang on you, actually," I assured him.

"I worked hard t' git rid of it," the husky sighed, then opened one eye lazily, to look at me. "Don't tell me you got a thing for it."

I laughed. "No, no. I just meant... It's good to see what's beneath, sometimes. Actually, I'd rather not be reminded of Ransom by someone who's 'courting' me, if you must know."

"I never even took you out for a drink..." the husky muttered regretfully, with a sigh.

"I think you've had enough to drink."

"No shit," the man grunted, putting his paws up on the bed and stretching his legs out, running a hand down one of his thighs and rubbing at the sore muscles beneath his dusty, dirt-caked riding pants. His paws looked similarly dirt-caked and worn from the last few days of hell we'd endured.

I flexed my own toes, my own paw-pads feeling raw and dirty. I was filthy, as well. I could feel the dirt in my fur, the tangles in my mane, and every second I was fighting the urge to lick at my paws or my arms and clean myself at least a little. If I'd been alone, I wouldn't have fought the urge. But a previous incident in the camp with Ransom had taught me that apparently licking oneself in public, especially around men, was not as acceptable amongst canines as it was amongst felines. Go figure.

"I need a bath," I said with a sigh, slumping back.

"Not nearly as badly as I do," the canine said, sounding disgusted.

"I don't think you smell bad," I tried to assure him. "It's almost comforting to see you're mortal like the rest of us."

The Otherwolf actually laughed, then gave an 'Ah!', and gripped at his jaw. "Damnit, woman," he chuckled, "don't make me laugh. And I like t'be clean. Dirty huskies ain't near as handsome."

17

"You're always handsome, Grant," I said softly.

The man opened his light blue eyes slowly to regard me. After only a few moments lingering on my gaze, though, he dropped his head slowly.

"Pity that's all I've got goin' for me anymore," he murmured, bitterly.

"We aren't done with this yet, remember?" I tried to remind him. "I have to find Ransom, first, but... Once I do, I'll meet back up with you and your men at Serahaven. You can head back first thing once you're better, and begin the hunt again—"

"I ain't welcome back in Serahaven," Grant said suddenly, his voice almost too quiet to be audible. I thought I'd misheard him.

"Your men aren't welcome in the town anymore?" I asked, confused.

"No, I ain't welcome," the husky stated. "Why d'you think I was able to leave my men at all?"

"I thought..." I trailed off. What had I thought?

The husky gestured towards the chair where his things were, pointedly. "Look on over there. D'you see a badge?"

"No," I said, suddenly noticing the lack of it.

"Connall took it," the man muttered, bitterly. "Took me off the payroll."

"How can he do that?" I said, shocked. "Weren't you the Commanding Officer?"

"What d'you think 'Paymaster' means?" the husky sighed. "I was in charge o' the mission. Which failed—spectacularly. I lost almost every man under my command. Man was in his rights to strip me."

"What happened in Serahaven wasn't your fault!" I said, outraged now. I was mostly upset at Connall, but I was somewhat concerned that Grant hadn't told me all of this in town. He must have known as soon as he came back to find me in the Shrine.

He'd been trying to tell me, I realized suddenly. But then, everything with Puck... He'd been holding this in this entire

18

time? And he'd helped me anyway. I'd been so focused on my own problems, I hadn't even thought…

"Grant…" I said, softly, leaning forward to move towards the man.

"It's over," the husky said, his elbows resting on his knees, his hands knitted, eyes on the floor. "It's really over for me now. He don't want me anywhere near the mission. He told me just to go back to Headquarters, or… quit the force entirely. They'll probably boot me off soon as I go home, anyway."

"How can he do that, though?" I insisted. "If it's your mission, you're in charge—"

"Of everythin' but hiring and firing," the husky said, impatiently. I was somewhat taken aback by the snap in his tone as he looked up at me. "That's what a Paymaster does. Gives the men someone to hate an' fear other than their C.O. Keeps 'em in line without havin' the resentment put on the man in charge of the task at hand. You got me? And that means Connall can fire whomever the hell he wants. Includin' me."

"Well then he's in charge," I said, emphatically. "So why shouldn't some of the blame in all of this be his?"

"Because I made the calls!" the husky said, his voice escalating to a yell near the end, and I wasn't certain if the anger in his voice was directed at me, or at himself. Either way, it was alarming. I wasn't accustomed to seeing Grant angry.

"I followed the leads that led us here," the man said, his voice gone hoarse and tinged with pain, likely from his jaw. "I hired Gabriel. I insisted we go to Serahaven!"

"And if we hadn't, all of those people would be dead," I reminded him. "Grant, even if things at Serahaven went badly, they didn't go as badly as they could have. You made the right choices, but sometimes things happen we can't control… Men like Magpie are masters of deception, and men like Rourke are vicious and brutal. We can only do as well as we can against people like that! You don't have to make a mistake for something to go wrong. Sometimes things just go wrong."

The husky's head remained hung, and he looked so weak, so defeated, in that moment. I sunk to my knees in front of him and wrapped my arms around him, tugging him forward. He didn't put up much resistance, just leaned his head against my shoulder, clutched at my waist with one hand and leaned against me. I held the conquered man against me for as long as he needed, wrapping my arms entirely around him eventually and running a paw gently down the tousled, ragged fur along the back of his neck softly, trying to be of any comfort I could.

"Connall should be ashamed of himself, putting this all on you," I said angrily, against the man's fur. "I wish you'd told me back in town. I would have had a few choice words for the man."

Grant was silent for a long time, and I gave him all the patience he needed, sitting with him and not letting him go. It was painful to see him defeated, but… I was glad he wasn't afraid to show it to me, finally.

At length, the question of the hour had to be asked. I waited until he leaned up on his own, his tired gaze settling back towards the window, where enough light was filtering in that I could tell it was probably… dusk? Dawn? Who knew anymore? It had been a trying few days.

"So, what will you do now?" I asked softly.

"I don't know," he said with a shuddering sigh. "I'm just a civilian now. If I were to continue after Rourke, it'd be as a bounty hunter. There's nothin'—legally speakin'—more that I can do here." He turned his gaze back to me. "Helpin' you get the fox here was the last bit'o good I could do."

My gaze softened. "You have no idea how grateful I am for that, Grant…"

His eyes narrowed, but not in anger, in frustration. "I just… I don't understand it," he said, his tone lost. "I just wasn't ready for this. Why'd they give me a chance at somethin'… somethin' I wanted t'be so badly… if they were just gonna take it away?"

He looked back up at me, and I wished I had answers for him. "I tried, Shivah. I bloody tried. But they gave me Rourke. For my first damned mark! So many men've died trying to bring in that monster. How the hell was I supposed to be any better than the ones that failed?"

"We haven't failed yet," I said, determinedly.

"I can't hunt him anymore," the husky growled, gritting his teeth despite whatever pain I knew him to be in. "Not legally."

I reached forward and took his chin gently in my palm, lifting it so that he'd have to look me in the eyes. He did, albeit hesitantly.

"Grant," I said, meaningfully. "Answer me something. Does that matter to you?"

He was silent a long while, and I knew there was an inner struggle there I'd never truly understand. I'd not lived his life, not served the Otherwolf country. I'd not made the oaths he had to his laws, and his society. But I also saw a determination there I recognized, and that gave me hope.

"No," he said, at length, in a hard tone. "It doesn't. Takin' that man down before he murders again matters more than the law."

I nodded slowly. "Then you don't need a badge to keep doing what you set out to do. And you won't be alone."

I released his chin, leaning back and carefully considering something before I said it. It was something I'd been considering for a very long time, and now, I thought it was about time I made a final decision on the matter.

"You said before," I said carefully, "that you'd rather take orders from someone else. Is that still the case?"

"I never wanted a command position," Grant admitted. "I was just thrust into the role. I tried to take to it, but…"

"Would you take orders from a woman?" I demanded.

The husky got the strangest expression for a moment or so, before giving a forcibly-subdued smile, like he was trying to

21

cover how much the idea pleased him. "Yes... yes, I would agree to that," he answered.

"Good," I said, firmly. "Then from this point on, I'm in charge. Understood? No more complaints about your decisions making or breaking us. It's on me now, alright? I can bear it. You just do as I say from here on out."

"Yes, ma'am," the man replied, a little hazy-eyed.

I sighed. "And first thing, get in bed. You're about to fall asleep in your chair again."

That seemed to snap Grant out of it. He considered the bed for a few moments, uncertainly, before murmuring, "I—I don't know if I should—"

"We're going to focus on finding Ransom when you wake," I stated. "I need him, and so does Puck. I need you at your best, and you're not going to be anywhere near that without rest. Are you really going to decline the first thing I tell you to do?"

"N-no," the husky stammered, "I just..."

I rolled my eyes. "Do I have to sleep on the floor to assuage your fears of not being a perfect gentleman?"

"No, no," the husky said quickly.

"Good," I said, "because Ransom is a dumb bastard, and I just know tracking him down is going to be hard, and I still need more rest."

Apparently seeing I was serious, Grant forced himself back up unsteadily, and unceremoniously got into bed in the way most drunk men do—awkwardly.

As soon as I'd actually gotten him to lie down, though, it was clear he wasn't going to remain awake for long, regardless of his scruples. He gave a long groan as he stretched out his legs and his back, and I ran a paw up over his head, sighing.

"Rest," I murmured, stroking my pawpads softly through his fur, until I heard his breathing begin to slow.

I awoke somewhat alarmingly entangled with the man I'd fallen asleep next to. Apparently, either I or the husky—or both of us—were prone to nuzzling up in our sleep. The way things ended up, I rather expected it had been both of us. It honestly wouldn't have bothered me, except the woman who worked here was the reason I'd woken, and she was none-too-pleased.

"None o' that ungodly behavior here!" the curly-furred, middle-aged Otherwolf woman shouted, waking me from my sleep with a start. Before I could even begin to really rouse, she was literally beating on the both of us with a pillow, and Grant was so startled he twisted free of me and fell out of bed.

The woman stood over him, hands on her wide hips, glaring down at the husky like one might a child they'd caught stealing food. "Marshal, honestly ah'm ashamed for you!" she chided.

"It's not—" Grant stammered, "we weren't doing anything untoward—"

"I'll believe that when the sun don't come up tomorrah," the woman huffed, batting at him once more with the pillow before she set it down on the counter, near the fresh blankets that had been left the night before. "Now git, the both of you. We need the room."

She hustled off after that, leaving Grant on the floor to clutch at his jaw, which was clearly still paining him… and me to ruminate on how nice those few seconds I'd woken in the husky's arms had been.

I finally caught sight of the elusive Physician when he made his way out of Puck's room to speak to us. He was a tall, thin, wire-haired Otherwolf man dressed in crisp black and white attire, who seemed to be middle-aged and a bit stooped in the shoulders. He also didn't look particularly friendly, but then… I found it hard to read the expressions of some Otherwolves, especially those with mustaches of fur along their muzzles.

"He's awake," he said to us, in Otherwolf. Well, I should say, he said to Grant. He didn't seem to be sparing much in the way of regard for me. Honestly, I didn't care. So long as he'd done his job.

He and Grant shared a quiet conversation that I tried to make out, but my 'Amurescan' was still far too spotty. I understood that the man expected to be paid for his work, though. I couldn't blame him. I still had no coin. I had my turquoise, though, and I didn't care if I had to part with all of it. It was worth it to have saved Puck.

Before I could so much as interject myself into the conversation, Grant handed the man a few silver coins, and the Otherwolf said something along the lines of, "He has the bed for a day more," and left.

"Grant, you didn't—" I began.

"Please, just don't fight me on it," the husky said with a sigh. "Let me feel a little better about all of this, alright?"

I didn't. I probably would have protested more, but perhaps in an attempt to avoid that, the husky opened the door at that point. I hurried in behind him to see my friend.

It was, and would always be, one of the most triumphant moments of my life, seeing Puck perk his head towards us as we entered the room, and blink those big pale eyes at me again. The only other time I remember feeling so happy was the day my son was born.

I bounded across the room and paused only when I was nearly atop the small fox, remembering he was still injured. I wrapped my arms around him gingerly and slowly, but with no less joy.

"Puck…" I sobbed, burying my muzzle against his soft, warm fur. He was warm. His body was warm.

He was here. Alive. Everything that I'd thought impossible, not a day ago.

"Shivah," he said softly. He sounded so tired, but he wrapped one small, exhausted arm around me, all the same.

24

I'm not sure how long we just held one another. I could have done so forever, after I'd so nearly lost him. The only thing that made me part eventually were the myriad of questions I had. I pulled away from him finally, not far but just enough that I could speak again.

"You scared me so much!" I said, crying again. My poor eyes were still sore from the grieving just a day ago, it felt like reopening a wound. But I couldn't help it.

"I'm so sorry, Shivah," the fox said, his eyes drooping and his tone quiet and subdued, like someone half asleep. I remembered what it had felt like, being under the effect of the berries. And I'd only had the draught made from the ripened ones. "I... didn't have a choice," he said, "I knew he wouldn't stop until he'd killed me. So... I had to make him think he had."

"The Physician said the combination of your injuries and that poison could have killed you," Grant said from over my shoulder. "Or the raiders might've just finished you off to be sure. That was a hell of a risk you took, fox."

"Given the circumstances," Puck murmured, then gave a shrug and the slightest of smiles, "I didn't have many other options..."

Puck patted my arm, gently. "It's alright, Shivah," he murmured. "I'm still here."

"What did he want?" I asked, even though I knew. I wanted to hear it from him.

"The villagers," Puck said, closing his eyes for a moment. "He wanted the villagers. I kept telling him they were in the grain cellar. I was just... hoping to buy time... but they couldn't get in to the grain cellar."

"Why?" Grant asked, his own curiosity clearly peaked. "They burned the Mill. They must have thought they were in there, in the end. How did you—"

"The door was reinforced, so it seemed like it'd be a good place to hide people... from the outside, anyway," Puck said, with some difficulty, clearly fighting off the effects of the Len'sal, still. "That's why I told them we couldn't use it. Too obvious. We broke… a key off in the lock, though. Before we left. So they'd think we were barricaded inside. But she… she thought I was lying…"

" 'She'?" both Grant and I said at once. Then, a few seconds later, I murmured, "Who, Puck?"

"Shadow…" Puck said, barely above a whisper.

The room fell dead silent. I could feel the shock from Grant beside me, and I scarcely knew what to think of the revelation, myself. As a woman, let alone a woman warrior, I should never have allowed myself to be so prejudiced, but I had never for even a moment considered that one of the raiders might be a woman, let alone their assassin.

"It isn't what we've all thought, all this time," Puck said, blinking his eyes blearily as he spoke. "Rourke… the man who tortured me…"

"You're certain Rourke was there?" Grant pushed.

Puck nodded, slowly. "She called him by name. Several times. And he by hers, once. Just once, but… I caught it."

"What do you mean, not what we've thought?" I asked, not wanting to push the fox too hard, but he was literally the only survivor of these monsters now, and what he knew could be paramount to hunting them down.

"Rourke is just… a raider," the fox said, wincing as he shifted against one of his injuries. "Like the others. He doesn't lead anyone—at least none of the raiders who were there when he found me. And he is mad, Shivah. The way he talks… repeats himself in circles and speaks intermittently to questions no one has asked… He's seeing things no one else can. I think the man's had the fever. But I'd… I'd have to see his condition better to confirm it."

"A madman hasn't been eluding us for years…" Grant murmured, as realization snuck up on us all.

"Shadow," I said softly. "They're led by a woman?"

Puck nodded, slowly, then swallowed. "I think… Rourke is important to whatever it is they're trying to do. Someone amongst them knows a lot about the disease. Or maybe they just use him to torture people. I-I don't know…" He shook his head, clearly trying to stay awake. "But that woman… she's in charge. She was even snapping at Rourke."

"You're absolutely certain she was a woman?" Grant asked, still disbelieving.

"I heard her voice," Puck murmured, "but she masks her scent with a strong pine oil, so… It would be hard to notice. I think she's covering the fact."

"Ransom saw her once," I pointed out, "and he referred to her as a man. But he also said she covers herself—or himself—entirely, so…"

Puck gave a soft sigh. "Is he too angry, or too cowardly to come in and see me? My bet is on angry."

I blinked. Oh god, he didn't know.

"Puck, he's…" I leaned forward, and took his hand. "He's not here right now."

The fox's expression shifted immediately to fear. "Is he alright?" he asked.

"I… I don't know," I admitted at length. "He was alive and… not well, but alive the last time I saw him."

"The last time you saw him?" Puck said, his voice sounding more and more alarmed. "Where is he?"

"We don't know," the husky said quietly from behind me.

"He…" I sighed, threading my fingers through my mane, slowly. "He thought you were dead, Puck. We all did."

"What?" the fox exclaimed, struggling to push himself up in bed. "B-but I… I left the Len'sal scattered on the ground, where they were hurting me. You didn't see them?"

"There was a massive fire," I said, inwardly cursing myself for not realizing this sooner. "We… Ransom found you… in the state you were, and… we all thought you were dead for nearly a day, before I realized what had happened."

"Ransom thinks I'm dead?!" the fox repeated. "Oh god…" he gasped, struggling out from underneath his blankets, despite the obvious pain he was in. He was still covered in injuries, and his chest had been wrapped to cover the two

27

largest puncture wounds. What's more, there looked to be a cast over one of his legs. I put my hands on his shoulders, trying to stop him. But he was fighting me with remarkable strength for someone so weakened.

"Puck, you aren't well enough to move!" I insisted. "You need to—"

"He's going to kill himself!" the fox cried, suddenly.

I was taken aback by his words, but perhaps not as much as I should have been…

"He wouldn't—" I attempted to insist.

"He told me he would!" the fox shot back, before I could even finish my thought. "Before I went into the Mill. He told me if I let myself die in there, he'd have nothing left."

"I'm with her, actually," Grant said from behind me. "I don't know the man as well as the both of you, clearly, but I've known the types of men who are likely to put a gun in their mouth. He doesn't strike me as being that cowardly. I think it's far more likely he's off somewhere in a bottle. We might even find him in town."

"Or off hunting Rourke," I said. "To even the scales—"

"You're thinking like you, Shivah," Puck insisted. "I know Ransom. I know him better than he knows himself. And when something's too painful for him, he doesn't get angry. He gives up."

I leaned back, considering the fox's words, and chewing on the back of one of my knuckles as they sunk in. I'd been assuming all this while that Ransom would go out after Rourke, to avenge Puck, because that's what I would have done.

But Ransom and I weren't that much alike. We dealt with many similar demons, but I lingered on mine. He'd pushed his away so much, he honestly didn't seem to remember them. Puck might be right.

"Where's he gone, then?" I asked myself, my voice fading off as I considered the possibilities. Even if the coyote was on a path to self-destruction, I didn't believe for a moment he'd just eat his gun. He was too stubborn, too proud to go out that way. But Puck was right. If he'd gone off to pursue Rourke, that would be like admitting what happened to Puck. He'd end this some other way.

"What did he say, Puck?" I asked, taking the fox's hands. They were shaking. He looked up at me, lost. "What did he say, before you went in the Mill?"

"Just… just what I said," Puck replied. "I was so angry at him for putting all that weight on me, I didn't really…" His voice trailed off a few moments, then his ears snapped up and he gripped my palm, tightly. "The last thing he said, was… if I died in there he'd meet me on the mountain."

"On the mountain?" Grant asked, puzzled. "Is that a tribal phrase? For the afterlife?"

"No," I said, confused. "Do you think he meant—"

"The pass," Puck said in a soft-spoken moment of complete clarity.

All of us, even the blind fox, looked towards the fading light filtering in through the small window in the room, towards the great mountains, and the storm rolling in.

CHAPTER TWO
The Mountain

"Are we certain about this?" Grant asked nervously, as the server at the inn we'd chosen to get our final meal at dropped off our drinks. Something called 'beer' for him, milk and tea for Puck and I.

"No," I said softly, looking down into my cup. The milk smelled amazing, but even it wouldn't ease my worries right now. "But it feels right. And Puck thinks so, too."

"I don't need the Spirits to tell me where Ransom's gone," the fox said, sorting through the pack I'd returned to him and producing some kind of wrapped, crushed herbal mixture, before carefully pinching some of it up between his thumb and forefinger and sprinkling it into his tea.

"What are you taking?" I asked, curiously.

"It's a mixture of willow and birch shoots and bark shavings," Puck muttered, as he mixed it into his tea. "It helps with pain."

I winced. The fox was still covered in injuries and really should have been in bed. But he'd insisted on leaving the Physician's, despite all of the man's warnings.

The fox had a splint over a fractured leg and could barely walk, even with help. He had two bad stab wounds to the ribs that he couldn't even remember receiving. I suspected they'd been Rourke's attempt to ensure he was dead, when the Len'sal had taken effect. And he had more superficial injuries than I could count, which while not life-threatening, had to be awfully painful to endure.

They'd pulled out several of his claws—pulled them out.

"You should have stayed in bed, Puck," I said with a sigh.

The fox just shook his head, determinedly. "No, I'm going with you."

"That's—you can't possibly—" Grant argued.

"I will go alone, if you won't take me with you," Puquanah snapped, looking up and somehow managing to stare the

30

husky down, despite the fact that his pale eyes couldn't even focus on the man. "I'm not arguing this out with either of you."

"Puck, I only just got you back," I said softly, frightened.

The fox turned to me, his tone losing some of its hard edge, but it was clear he was still firm on the issue. "Shivah," he said, "I appreciate our friendship, and everything you've done for me. You saved my life. I want you to know... I value how you feel." He took my hand, and squeezed it gently, "But," he continued, in a soft tone, "I love him. I have to find him."

Both Grant and I fell silent. Even the husky, whom I knew to be at least mildly discomforted by the knowledge of the two mens' relationship, had a lot of respect in his eyes in that moment.

"You don't need to come either, Grant, you know," I pointed out to the man, even knowing what he'd say.

The Otherwolf just gave a determined smile. "Shivah... where you go I go."

"Not if I tell you not to," I replied, crossing my arms over my chest.

"You're going to need my horse," Grant pointed out. "We'll make better time mounted. At least until we get to the highest elevations."

"I could just take your horse," I threatened, although I didn't mean a word of it. I was honestly uncertain how far I could push the man, and it was fun finding out.

"Helios won't budge without me at the reins," the husky retorted, stubbornly. "Besides, how would you stop me from following you after you left?"

"I could tie you up."

Grant paused, at that, looking uncertain. "You'd do that?"

"Okay," the fox interrupted. "As amusing as it is listening to you two engage in completely bizarre foreplay, we need to talk about gearing up. I don't believe for a second that Ransom took to the trail with any supplies, seeing as he left them all in Serahaven. Which means he has, at most, his waterskin, his

31

weapons, and whatever bits of trail rations he had on his person, and nothing else."

"Gods," I breathed, "his skin won't even last him the trip up…"

"He doesn't care," Puck said, concern laden in every word, "he went up there to die."

Again, silence fell. But this time, Puck broke it quickly, in an authoritative tone. "But we're not," he said, "so we need to supply ourselves well, and bring enough for four, for when we find him."

"Five," a deep, older voice spoke from behind us. It startled the hell out of Puck and I, but when Grant's head snapped up and he looked over my shoulders, a smile split his muzzle.

"Laesom!" the husky said in a somewhat relieved tone, standing and pulling out a chair. "Good God man, what are you doing here? Are the men back in town?"

The wolf moved around towards the husky and slowly sat down in the offered chair, gripping his knees as he did, and rubbing at one of them as he settled in. The man had to be in his fifties. I was amazed he was as active with the Marshals as it was.

"I'm afraid not," the wolf said at length. As usual, his tone was hard to read, he'd never displayed much in the way of emotions that I could see. He just seemed to be a very mild-mannered, quiet man, but then I'd heard wolves, especially lone wolves, often were.

"What are you doing here?" Puck suddenly asked, and I didn't miss the suspicion in the fox's tone.

"Aye," Grant said, confused. "Shouldn't you be back in Serahaven—"

"Connall… relieved me of my duties," the wolf stated, quietly. "Permanently."

Grant's eyebrows shot up in alarm. "He took you off the force?"

"I never had a badge," Laesom stated, calmly. "But he made it clear that my skill set was no longer of use to him. He also got rid of Ethridge. I got the distinct feeling his sudden disinterest in keeping us on may have had something to do with our ancestry."

I blinked. That's right, the mink. He didn't speak Katuk, so we'd never spoken, but he often traveled with Laesom, likely by design. Keep the non-Otherwolves together.

I could almost feel Grant's disappointment and anger from across the table. The husky sat down heavily, brows knitted, muzzle tipped down.

"That rutting bastard," he muttered, bitterly. "The second I'm off the squad, he de-integrates it."

"It's just as well," the wolf murmured, still almost irritatingly calm in tone. "I only would have stayed in Serahaven long enough to ensure the town was safe, anyway, and he's bringing in men from the garrison for that. I can't work under that man."

"So then what are you doing here?" Puck repeated, warily. "And why were you listening in on us instead of just announcing your presence?"

The wolf looked across the table to the fox, his golden eyes taking the small creature in for a moment, before he replied, "Believe it or not, of late, I've been having trust issues."

"I believe it," both Grant and I muttered.

"I trusted Magpie," Laesom admitted, quietly. "I still don't understand why he did what he did. I just wanted to be sure you weren't all also..."

I narrowed my eyes at the wolf. "I would never work with that monster!"

"No, your current quest seems something else entirely," the wolf murmured. "And I'd like to help."

"Why?" I pressed.

The wolf didn't respond for a long moment, but then, at length, he did.

"Because my mate," he murmured, "was beaten nearly to death by men who thought he was an aberration. His own countrymen. His friends. People who should have respected him for who he was, but couldn't."

He looked up, slowly, and I saw his jaw tighten. "And I wanted to follow him, into the afterlife. But he told me to stay here, do whatever good I still could with my time. And I've been trying."

No one said a word. Puck looked sympathetic. Grant just looked shocked, his eyes unfocused, as if he was lost in thought, or a memory. He must not have known. And he'd been traveling with Laesom for quite a long while now, if what I understood was true.

"I know if I were to help you find your mate," Laesom said quietly, to Puck, "he would be happy that I helped two young people who walked the same path we once did."

I looked to Puquanah. This decision fell on him, ultimately. I wasn't entirely certain I trusted the wolf, and we'd had a lot of issues knowing who to trust of late, but it was hard to doubt the pain in the wolf's voice. It was the first time I'd ever heard any kind of emotion in him, and it sounded genuine. I'd always thought the wolf's oddly subdued, mysterious demeanor was just a trait of wolves. But the man's silence, his unsocial demeanor, the fact that he'd never once spoken about himself to me, or apparently even much to Grant, who really seemed to value his friendship.

A lifetime spent hiding…

"You have a horse, right?" Puck asked, finally. "Because we're going to need two."

The storm was already on top of us by the time we made it to the trail head, which meant somewhere, Ransom was in the thick of it. To our best estimation, he had about a two to three day lead on us, but that was only if he'd gone directly there. It was possible, although unlikely, he might have actually stopped to supply himself in Crossroads. Puck thought not, and I was forced to agree. If the fox was right, and Ransom wasn't planning a return trip…

There was still the hanging thread of doubt about our entire assumption, of course. Puck might have been wrong. Ransom might have gone anywhere in the world. We couldn't know for sure.

But what he'd said about the mountain… The more I thought about it, the more I could almost see it playing out in my mind. I couldn't help but remember the look in his eyes when he'd been in the peaks, when we'd learned the Wraith Lion was near the trail this year. It wasn't so much the intensity of a hunter I'd seen there, but a twinge of madness. This was an obsession, for Ransom. One I had no doubt he'd die for. And if he was truly looking to die, what better way?

I was terrified for the coyote—terrified and angry at him. Yet gods, my feelings were in such turmoil! I knew the helplessness, the feeling of loss he was facing now. I'd thrown my own life away by attacking Methoa in a vain attempt to save my child. Could I really judge him?

I couldn't even imagine how frightened Puck must have been, but the fox wore his troubles bravely. And that was especially impressive, considering he was taking to the trail with terrible injuries, a few days after his own hellish ordeal.

Having Laesom along proved useful within the first few minutes of setting out. The man had a horse, which as Puck had correctly surmised, we needed. Grant and I could ride Helios, but if we'd not had another mount, I would have been forced to walk so that Puck could travel. Laesom had offered to let the fox ride with him right off, solving that issue. And the wolf apparently knew the trails in the area so well, he'd promised us he could shave some time off our route.

Indeed, over just the first day of travel, we'd cut through several properties and all but ignored the roads, meeting the trail head in nearly half the time it had taken us to travel down. Grant told me to trust the wolf, and I'd been dubious when we'd taken some particularly overgrown, neglected game trails, but Laesom seemed to know precisely where he was going, even when I felt entirely lost. There was something to be said for age and experience, especially when you'd lived in one region your whole life. I'd always respected my elders, but it had been because I was told to. I'd rarely had a chance to benefit from their wisdom in such a direct manner, unless you counted learning how to weave baskets.

We made camp only in the darkest hours of that night, and slept for a scant few hours. We had to make ground while the going was still moderately easy, and before the worst of the storm moved in. For now, the snow was falling in gentle flurries, but I knew when I couldn't see the mountain peaks the next day that the storm had settled in, and if the dark horizons were any indication, it was only going to get worse.

That first day on the trail, the drop in temperature was the most startling thing we all had to endure. The climb brought us not only deeper into the storm, but into the frigid winds blowing down from the peaks. And the temperature naturally dropped the higher we went, as it was.

We didn't speak much throughout that day. We all knew what lay in one another's minds, and we were trying to ignore it. Going into the pass in the midst of a storm was suicide. This is how men died. And this could all be for naught. Ransom could be dead already. Ransom could be elsewhere. We just didn't know. Yet we were still doing this. It was madness.

But if anyone had doubts, no one voiced them. And we survived that first day with little more than chapped noses and aching bones.

The cold just sapped everything out of your body, especially when you were already pushing it. It was like moving against water sometimes, with the winds buffeting us, our muzzles tucked into our cloaks, gripping at the beasts we were riding and hoping all the while that they could endure.

Both Grant and Laesom knew their animals well, though. They knew when to push them, and when to rest them. Several times we took shelter under rock faces or in heavy pine thickets, just to let the animals rest. They were both traveling horses, not lacking in endurance, but the trail, even as well-hewn as it was, was steep and trying in places, and both animals were burdened with more weight than they were used to carrying.

It was lucky at least that Puck and I were both small people, or we'd be testing their fortitude even more. As it was, both Grant and Laesom had lightened their saddlebags before we left, which gave us precious little in the way of emergency supplies, but we had enough to make it up and back down. We hoped.

By the second day, the snow was beginning to accumulate to a noticeable degree, and again, I would have worried about us getting lost, but Laesom always seemed to know the way. Once or twice we'd stop and he'd take a few moments to look around at the landmarks, before silently gesturing for us to follow him atop his speckled horse. And then, inevitably, we'd find the trail once more.

Cynical though I was, I was hard-pressed to believe the man's motives in all of this were anything but what he'd told us. And that was just very sad.

Almost everyone who walks this earth has, or will, lose someone they love at some point in their life. For me, it had been my son. For Laesom, it had apparently been a lover. And I wasn't even certain how long ago he'd lost the man, but to be honest, I hoped it had been recent. My own pain over the loss of my son was still so sharp, I couldn't imagine living an entire lifetime with it. I hoped to die young and rejoin him soon, and I suspected I would. Crow had all but promised as much. Oddly, it was almost comforting to know. I didn't want to grow old without my child.

I didn't, and would likely never, know this wolf's life story. But I could see how tired he was. The weariness in his every feature spoke of a very deep sadness, but resolve to continue living. And if he felt as I did, his only reason to continue on now was to do as he'd promised to his loved one before he died.

I understood that feeling. But I'd only endured it for half a year, now.

It was an odd thing to say, because I honestly wished the wolf no ill will, but I rather hoped his suffering would come to an end, soon. It was a mercy I would wish for myself someday, as well. Once my task was done.

By the third day, the skies had grown dark and we were forging into the thick of the storm. It was both majestic and terrifying. The world beneath us seemed to disappear, the haze of snow flurries whipping through the winds diminishing sight to as little as twenty feet in front of us. We'd been making good time until then, but now, things began to get truly frightening. The knowledge was with all of us that if we veered even slightly off the trail, we could lose it entirely.

We tried to put our faith in our guide, but even he had begun to take longer and longer to get his bearings. Up until now, we'd made very good time, but the elements were battering us back. And somewhere, up there ahead of us on the trail—alone—was Ransom.

We got our confirmation on that third day. Despite the storm, despite the seeming impossibility of picking out anything in the sharp, cold winds assaulting us, he caught a scent. And it led us to a small, abandoned campsite, nestled into the tight crevasse between three massive, flat slabs of boulder that had fallen together to form a small pocket of safety just off the trail.

"We found this place," Puck said softly, as we all stood beside the doused fire and the remnants the coyote had left to burn. Amidst the ashes were several things I knew to be his. His water skin, for one, which I could only hope he'd at least bothered to drain, first. Several snuffed cigarettes, and several more that he hadn't even bothered smoking… and his harmonica. It sat in the center of the ashes, charred and blackened almost beyond recognition.

He was destroying everything. Gods, this didn't bode well.

"Three years ago," Puck said in a soft, hoarse voice. "We found it when we took the trail too soon. We had to hunker down here for two weeks straight. He spent most of the time complaining about the weather..." he gave an almost pained smile, "but, honestly I'd never been happier. It was just us. We were safe here, you know? To be who we were. No one could bother us. Even he seemed to relax. We just... we were just together for days..."

Of all of us, it was Laesom who offered Puck a gesture of comfort in that moment. The old wolf put a paw on the fox's shoulder and rubbed it gently. A small thing, but somehow, it meant more that it had come from the stoic wolf than I knew it would have meant if it came from me. I may have known the fox better, but I didn't know this flavor of pain.

Puck dropped his muzzle, closing his eyes, but he didn't reject the gesture. The two men barely knew one another, had barely ever even spoken, but I saw the birth of a bond there. Even if it was an unspoken one.

"Don't die on me," Puck murmured, like rhetoric, like it was a prayer. I knew he'd probably been saying it every few moments in his mind, over and over again, because I had been as well.

"Don't you die on me, Ransom."

The fifth day brought us to the peak, and into the roiling clouds of snow tossing about on the winds like smoke from a fire. There was no staying on the trail any longer, even Laesom could barely pick out landmarks amidst the blizzard. We knew at least that we were near the halfway mark, where Grant's man had seen the Wraith Lion and where we'd found its tracks. Any more than that, we couldn't be certain of.

And wherever Ransom had gone from here, we couldn't possibly know. There was no tracking any beast, coyote or lion, in this storm. All we could do now was search on foot.

It seemed impossible that we'd find anyone in this storm, but it had also seemed impossible that we might make this seven day journey in five, through a blizzard. Yet we had. And we hadn't lost the horses. None of us had every skill necessary to survive this ordeal, but together—together, we were managing.

Grant had the sheer endurance to keep the pace, and still keep watch at night while we slept. I'd seen that endurance aid him before in running through the mountains, and it helped see Puquanah to the Physician, which likely saved his life. And now, he was our protector.

Laesom knew the trails better than any of us, and was primarily the one responsible for shaving so much time off of our trip. We may have even caught up to Ransom. It was impossible to know. The coyote had a hell of a head start on us, but he had no horse, and likely hadn't been eating.

And Puck had been indispensable in keeping us and our horses alive through the conditions we were enduring. He knew when it was best to eat to keep our bodies from tiring, had a salve for our noses and pads as they began to crack and bleed from the freezing winds, and had brought some kind of tea mixed with orange peel and several herbs I didn't know that would hopefully keep us from contracting an illness of the lungs in this frigid cold. And if we found Ransom, I knew he'd be in even worse shape than we were.

And my time was to come now. With Ransom gone, I was the only remaining tracker. He'd taught me almost everything I knew. And I was going to use it to save him.

We'd established a small base camp wedged into a rocky area with some little shelter. We'd taken a scant few hours to sleep, and only because we'd been falling-down tired. But when I woke, Grant was already preparing our things to move out. I rather wondered if he'd slept at all.

"I've ventured only to within fifty paces or so from the camp," he said, as I approached the fire, pulling my quiver strap over my Dyre-hide cloak, which I'd all but lived in for the last week. "But I think," he said, as he traced something on the hard stone slab our camp was atop with the burnt, charcoal tip of a stick from the fire, "I know where we are. Do you remember that small divot we found in the earth, when we were up there? The one that formed sort of a bowl, like, ah, like a miniature valley?"

I nodded. I remembered searching it. I had a few important memories from that night. It had marked a shift between Grant and I. One I was still trying desperately to make sense of. The confusing feelings I had for the man nipped at the fringes of my consciousness even now, as he looked up from the crude map he'd drawn to regard me, with those blue, blue eyes.

Tired blue eyes. No matter how resilient the man was, I could tell the last few days had taken a heavy toll on him. When this was all over, one way or another, I wasn't entirely certain how I'd thank him. But I'd find a way.

I heard Puck and Laesom approaching us from behind, and as a group, we all settled in to listen to what Grant had to say. It looked like he was right. We were actually in the miniature valley we'd found that night, if the tail end of it. We simply hadn't realized it with the storm raging around us. At least not until he'd taken the time to take careful stock of the terrain.

That gave us a starting point, at least. If we'd gotten our bearings, there was a good chance Ransom had, as well. He'd obviously gotten here ahead of us, the question at this point was really only by how long—and how far he might have gone towards the peaks to pursue the lion.

Through the storm, somewhere higher in these mountains than any man, tribal or no, had ever gone, was the mother's spine. That was where the lion had remained hidden for so long, one could only presume, and it was likely where Ransom had headed. Determined or no, he'd never be able to climb the spine. Just the fact that he might try could very well be enough to kill him. The elements alone right now could accomplish that task. The lion herself would not be necessary.

Our best hope was that he'd exhausted himself so thoroughly getting here, he'd be slow-going. And no matter what, he'd be losing tracks. In a storm like this, they'd disappear quickly, but it still gave us a chance, if he was anywhere near.

41

"Our biggest fear should be losing contact with one another," Laesom said evenly, his worldly eyes flicking up to mine as he spoke. "The most important priority in saving a life is ensuring you do not lose another in the process."

"The storm is slowing down some," Grant said with a sigh, glancing out past the pines that sheltered our rocky abode, "but still, it's going to be all too easy to get lost in this."

"And we have to spread out to look for him," I murmured, concerned.

"I can't go alone," Puck said quietly, like he hated admitting it. I looked sympathetically to the fox. He was right, of course. There were sheer cliff faces, dangerous dips in the terrain and possibly even predators out here, and his senses were of little use to him in this storm. Not to mention, he was barely walking on his fractured leg.

"I'll go with you," Laesom promised in a gentle tone, putting his hand on the fox's shoulder. Puck gave him a tired smile. The two seemed to be building a fairly strong rapport already.

Grant cleared his throat, glancing away. I wasn't entirely certain why Laesom seemed to make him uncomfortable when Puck and Ransom rarely had, but it was undeniable at this point. Perhaps because he'd known the man for longer, and the wolf had hidden his preferences from him this whole time?

"It's probably best if you and I split up," I said to the husky, bringing his attention back to the matter at hand. "We'll at least cover the North, South and West, that way. The East leads back towards the trail, and Crossroads, so I think we can at least conclude he's not gone back that way."

I gestured to Grant's crude map, in the direction of the West, towards the Valley. "You keep to the trail, Grant," I instructed. "You're the most likely to get lost and be unable to find your way back, but Ransom may well have headed down-slope, if he thinks the lion may have gone down recently to hunt. The legends said something about her moving in storms, so—who knows?"

42

"No offense taken," Grant said, anticipating me. "I'm no tracker, I know. And you're right, he may well have headed down towards the Valley."

"Laesom, you're to the South," I continued. "The terrain there's less rocky, but it's also shapeless, in all this snow. I'm hoping you'll still be able to find your way, since you know this land far better than I."

The wolf simply nodded. He never seemed to speak unless he felt he had something important to say.

"And I'll go North," I said with a deep breath, "towards the Spine. I really hope he's not that stupid, but we have to cover it. At least I can pick my way through the rocks in the steeper areas without much trouble."

"Aye, your paws make mine look clumsy in comparison," Grant said with a lopsided smile.

I smiled back, and tried to look confident for them all. I was rather liking being in charge, I was finding day by day. There had been so many times in the past I'd wanted to be the one to corral the chaos amongst my comrades, to ground the menagerie of rowdy, strange men who'd become a part of my life into something more orderly. And now, I could.

"If you become lost," Laesom said, "stay in place. Don't wander further."

"And let's use a callback system of some sort," Grant added. "If you're in danger, lost, or if, God willing, you've found him… give a long, loud call. Something that will carry. We used to use callbacks in the Road Wardens, when we were out seeking a lost traveler or a lost child. We all know where we've gone, so if we've head in your general direction, we'll eventually catch the sound. Just keep calling until you're found."

"And no matter what, we meet at dusk, here," I said with a meaningful look to the men. "No heroics."

We readied ourselves, fed our fire to keep it burning as long as possible, in case Ransom might find his way to it—even though we all thought that unlikely, there was always hope—and headed our separate ways.

Or at least, we were supposed to. Puck and Laesom were quick to move out, but I lingered long enough to stoke the fire and feed it the wood we'd dried while we slept, and after a few moments spent stirring the ashes up, I realized Grant had lingered, as well.

I turned to regard the Otherwolf. He looked like he very badly wanted to say something, or do something. And I knew, but yet couldn't really grasp a hold, of what it was. So I said nothing, just looked down, away from his eyes, into the fire.

"Please be careful," I heard him say, at length.

"I will," I murmured. "You as well."

"I'll be fine," he responded, quietly. "I'll be taking the trail." There was a long pause there, before he moved forward a few steps towards me, murmuring, "Shivah…"

I kept my eyes averted from his. I knew I was once again about to do something dangerous, incredibly dangerous, most would say. And we were on that precipice where one was supposed to say things they normally wouldn't, because there was a chance their time was limited. But everything from the last few months of my life was a tangle of confusing and conflicting purpose and desire. I couldn't even begin to make sense of what I wanted from the Otherwolf, not until I had some closure in at least one of the chapters of my life.

And even then, what could I possibly expect? I was on borrowed time, and not only because of a wrathful spirit who'd threatened to recall me to the next realm if I didn't remain focused on the task he'd given me. It was my task. It was my purpose. I'd prayed for the chance, and that chance had been given to me. It was the only reason I was alive, walking the earth. And when it was done, I could finally be at peace.

That peace would only come from seeing Methoa dead. Anything else I found along the way that brought me pleasure was a fallacy. I'd never really be happy until I'd avenged my son's death. And after that, I'd… My train of thought stalled there. I'd what? What if Crow's words were only metaphor?

What if he left me here, alive in this world, even after I'd taken Methoa's life? What then?

It seemed somehow impossible to think past the end of my quest. It was like I hit a black wall of nothingness in my thoughts when I tried. Like there simply wasn't anything there. Perhaps that was Crow's way of confirming that would indeed be the end of my time here. When Methoa died, I would die. My task would be done. My time would be over.

And for the first time, I really thought about that. And I began to question everything. Why would Crow want my life linked to Methoa, even to the bitter end? It seemed unfair. Almost as unjust as being forcibly married to him, forcibly tied to him. I was, in essence, free from him now. Why would my guiding spirit want to tie me so inextricably to him again, even in death? Couldn't I ever escape this man? Couldn't I ever be happy again? The way my son had briefly made me?

I'd never known love until I'd held my child in my arms. Not from my parents, who saw me as a burden, or the man who married me, who saw me as property, or even the tribe that I married into, who saw me as a lesser unless I could prove myself in their eyes.

But my boy had loved me. And I'd loved him. And everything about it had been perfect. It was like, for that brief time, I'd finally known what living was meant to be.

And this burning fire, this rage did not make me happy. All there was, every day in and day out, was this aching, bitter anger. It pushed me. It gave me strength. It had shaped me into a powerful woman. There was no denying that.

But peace?

I looked down into the fire I'd been stoking. The crackling kindling I'd fed beneath the new logs was curling and blackening, as the fire popped and snapped its way into the new wood, hungry and roaring steadily stronger. Every day I spent obsessing over finding Methoa, I was feeding that fire. I'd seen it in Crow's eyes. He'd fed it into my soul. And over time, it had

45

dimmed, then roared to life again, whenever my conviction waned or grew stronger.

One thing I knew for certain was that Grant, and my friends, quieted that fire. And with it, my conviction. My anger. And sometimes I wanted to give in to that. So badly. But did giving in mean giving up on hunting Methoa? I just—I wasn't certain any more. Crow had warned me against distractions, and the Otherwolf was certainly that.

But so were my two companions from the Valley. In fact, here I was helping them. Doing something that had taken me far from Methoa, could cost my life, could mean I would never complete my quest. And I'd not questioned it. Not for a second. Months ago, perhaps, I would have. I would have prioritized going after Methoa when I knew I was close. Even if it was foolish to do so alone. Even if he and the raiders had just proven they were deadly, clever, and able to evade us at every turn.

The reason I had never questioned this decision was Puck. Neither Crow nor my quest had been able to stop me from admitting I cared about, even loved, the fox. His spirit was too overpoweringly good to question my feelings for him. He was my first real friend.

And Grant was something else. Something far too complicated for me to have come to terms with yet. The sort of pain I had associated with men had no bearing on the relationship between Puck and I the fox had never felt threatening to me in that way. But Grant…

Puquanah—even Ransom—were, first and foremost, my friends. But Grant was… a man to me. At some point I'd accepted that friends fit in to my life, could even be essential to my quest. But a man…

The only man in my life right now was still Methoa. My purpose in life right now centered around him. And that realization both disgusted and confounded me, because whether or not I wanted that place in my life filled by Grant—or hell, even empty!—I just didn't want it controlling me anymore! I was growing angrier by the minute at Crow as it sunk in. The spirit wanted my every thought fixed on my goal. Whether or not it intended it, it had leashed me to Methoa, had me living for Methoa again!

I felt Grant's hand on my shoulder, and slowly looked up. The husky's gaze had switched from one of uncertainty to concern.

"Are you alright?" he asked quietly.

I looked him in the eyes, and he seemed briefly taken aback by the intensity of my gaze. But he didn't avert his eyes. He just waited, silently, for me to say something. He was deferring to me. He was on the same precipice as I, but he'd been there for longer, and unlike me I don't think he'd ever been uncertain.

But he never overstepped his bounds. He was, always and ever, waiting for me.

I still wasn't certain what I wanted. But I knew one thing. Crow had given me life, and had entrusted me with my task. If he trusted me, he was going to have to trust from this point on that I was going to do things my way. And whatever or whom-ever my life from this point on involved, it would be my choice. I wasn't going to live in fear of the spirit any longer.

"Thank you for everything you've done for me, Grant," I finally said, softly. "Your friendship, and Puck and Ransom's friendship, has made me a far stronger person than I would have been alone. And I want you to know how grateful I am, because I don't show it as often as I should."

The husky was silent for a few moments, then gave a slow nod, and the faintest of smiles. And I could tell he was sitting on so much more, but I think we both knew now was not the time.

"Let's get that bastard back, then," Grant replied, pulling his duster closed and buttoning the heavy fabric down the front flap, preparing himself for the storm outside. "So you can remind him why throwing his life away was a shitty thing to do to his friends."

"Trust me, I plan on it," I growled. We clasped our hands together with a firm squeeze, and then the husky headed off for his horse.

And I made my way into the whiteout on foot.

I spent over half of that day pressing through the storm, towards the Spine, calling for my lost friend. The winds tore at my cloak and bit at my nose and ears, ice caking on my brow. I had to squint through the worst gusts to see even far enough ahead just to choose my footing. The terrain here was broken and rocky, full of steep drop-offs and icy slopes, and I knew if I was having trouble negotiating it, Ransom would be, too.

If he were even here.

But as time began to fade away, as the cold wracked my body with quaking shivers and my breathing became labored, I somehow felt I knew where to go.

It was an impossible feeling to describe. Even my dreams with Crow couldn't compare, because I was conscious, now. I was in full control of my body, and yet not. My footsteps were compelled by something else entirely. One could argue I was only searching randomly, anyway, so I might have been imagining it, but it really did feel as though something were guiding me.

The shift had taken place slowly. First with fatigue. As my body grew more and more exhausted, my motions were compelled more by my will than my strength. The utter and complete white surrounding me, broken only occasionally by dark rock, by flashes of the sky above, of dark roiling clouds, the fact that at times, I often could not tell the ground from the air, made me feel as though I were no longer in the real world. It was like I'd truly entered another realm while awake—impossibly.

And my senses had gone almost entirely blank. I could smell nothing, hear nothing, and see little but white. All I felt was cold, and the pounding of my heart. The totality of it all sent me into a trance-like pattern of movement.

Step... step... step... call out for Ransom... my voice echoing through the impossibly silent, white world... answered back only by my echo. Step... step... step.

At some point, I couldn't say when, I felt as though my body and my mind had become disconnected. Like I was watching my life through the eyes of another. I had transcended. The feelings of my body were muted, subdued, but something else, something greater, was taking over—a sense of the world surrounding me.

The elders called this a vision quest. The men would starve and exhaust themselves, often for days, then take to the wilds with nothing, not even water, and the deprivation would push their spirits away from the shell of their bodies. And then, and only then, could they feel the world. Then and only then would they travel in the spirit realm.

I felt both blessed and terrified to have received such a gift, but now that it had come, even if by accident, it could not be fought. The elders said when your vision came, you mustn't fight it. You must ride the currents, like a canoe along the river. It would bring you back to the safety of your body in time, unless you fought it. Men who fought it would never be able to return.

Trust the currents. Do not fight them.

I closed my eyes, or I saw myself close my eyes, as I walked. I was not afraid that I'd fall or lose my footing, because I could feel the spirits of the mountains around me, walking beside me. They were everywhere, even in this storm. I could feel the spring, sleeping beneath the blanket of snow, trembling for its chance to awaken. And each and every pocket of moss, of the mountain seeds and grasses waiting to burst to life, knew the way. They had felt another walk this way, as I had.

Seeking something.

I could feel the hawk spirits that circled these peaks, watching the skies while their flesh and blood brethren slept and waited to hunt again. They were the true sentinels of this mountain. The eyes who knew all. They had seen every soul who had come over the pass, had seen the passing of all those who had been lost... and he was still amongst the living.

But he wasn't seeking something alive. He wasn't hunting Her. They knew Her. She was here, in the storm. She was guiding another. But he had not come here seeking Her. No... He was seeking something dead. Buried, beneath stone.

The stones told me that. The mountains themselves, they knew what souls lingered here. They knew what poisonous demons they hid inside of them. And he was there somewhere, festering, like a wound closed over. The stones concealed him, kept him here. Kept every trace of his evil away from the rest of the world. They were strong. They would always endure. They would lock him away, for all time—this dead, angry, festering spirit.

A sudden, sharp, blinding pain cut through the distance between my soul and my body, pulling me back towards it, like water rushing quickly towards the edge of a falls. I felt a wrongness creeping into me, a sense of foreboding, as what felt like blood trickled slowly down my muzzle. A sense of desperation, of pain, of wrath built slowly and over time, boiling inside, growing with each and every wrong endured.

I saw eyes, flickering at the edge of my consciousness. Yellow and leering, watching me in the darkness. Always there. Always waiting to seize upon my every moment of weakness, reminding me I would never be safe.

And then, a scream. And I couldn't be sure if the eyes were Methoa's, or if they belonged to another—or if the scream was mine—or belonged to another.

My eyes snapped open, and I sucked in a deep gasp, coughing up snow as I did and clawing at the ground for purchase. I'd fallen somewhere. I'd passed out, or the spirits had brought me here, wherever 'here' was.

It was darker here. That much I knew. The storm was quieter here, in the shelter of a great, imposing rock face, flat and high, and ringed by the small pines that grew at these heights. I'd fallen down a steep hill of loose rock and snow that led to this hidden place—this haven from the elements.

Yet despite the reprieve from the winds and the snow, this place did not feel inviting. It felt dark, more than just visually. Colder. The cold here sunk into you like heavy earth, like you were slowly being buried in it.

Death. This place felt like death.

But no fear, no sense of foreboding, was going to stop me from continuing on now. Because there in the snow, not ten feet from me, at last I saw footprints.

I shoved myself shakily to my feet, stumbling up and taking another deep breath of ice cold air, forcing it painfully through my lungs. I mentally willed my body to move, and as always, my willpower won out. I followed the footprints through this strange, dark crevasse, nearly walking in them, in some absurd fear that I might lose track of them in this still, sheltered place.

I felt something warm sliding down my muzzle, and ran my pawpads up over it. I'd cut my muzzle open on something when I'd fallen, which had likely been that sharp, slicing pain I'd felt. I ignored it for now. I'd tend to it later.

I walked along the crevasse for some time. I could see quite far in here compared to my vision in the unsheltered storm outside this enclosed world.

Enclosed. Buried.

That feeling of wrongness crept into me again, and this time it grew stronger the further I walked. It reminded me of the stench of a corpse, if one could feel something like that in their soul, warning my instincts not to come any closer. Something terrible lay ahead—something dead, yet still very much alive in this place. It lived on, as a spirit. A malevolent presence, kept from the rest of the world in this tomb of rock, buried deep here in the mountains, where it could not escape.

Where it couldn't hurt anyone ever again.

At first, I'd thought the silhouette in the distance was just another fallen rock, covered in a light sheen of the powdery snow that dared trespass this place. But then he moved. He moved, ever-so-slightly… a statue come to life from cold, dark mountain stone. I knew when I saw the notch in the ear that I'd found him at last.

Ransom. He was simply sitting there, at the foot of the collapsing crevasse, where the peaks above gave way into a frozen rock slide of broken, crumbling boulders. This place was slowly collapsing in on itself, from this one point. Even though all was still now, it was clear the walls here would not long hold. The mountain storms were eroding the earth, reducing the walls to piles of rock and earth, filling in the crevasse. Like even the mountain wanted this place gone forever.

I'd seen him move, so I knew he was alive. And that sped my pace beyond even what I thought myself capable of at the moment. Exhausted though I was, I ran. I ran down the last length of the dark crevasse, towards the mountain of rock Ransom was crumpled beside. I ran until my breath was ragged.

I could tell he'd heard me, but he was slow to regard me. When he did finally turn, it was done in such a staggered, weak motion, I almost feared the wind alone was responsible for moving him.

But then his eyes slowly focused, and I saw some clarity return to them. And I crashed into him, flinging myself around his shoulders and gripping him, tightly, screaming his name as I did.

He was so cold, so terrifyingly cold. That alone brought me entirely back to the realm of reality, and I wrapped my Dyrehide cloak around the both of us, keeping my arms around the coyote tightly, and trying to give him what little heat I had. He had his own cloak here, which meant he'd worn it at least this far, but it was discarded on the ground beside him. He'd purposefully stripped himself down to his thin cotton shirt and battered old leather pants.

He really had been trying to die. And he might still succeed.

"You stupid bastard!" I cried, even as I clung to his shoulders and buried my muzzle in his fur, squeezing him tightly and trying to rub as much warmth back into his shuddering form as my own shivering hands would allow. "How could you do this to us?"

The coyote seemed to ignore my question entirely, but he did, at length, look me in the face. And his gaze looked far gone already distant, lost. But he was looking at something specific. Something I'd been ignoring.

"He got you too, did he?" he asked in a strained, hoarse voice. And then, of all things, he gave a dry, humorless chuckle. "'Course. Stupid of me t' think death would stop 'm..."

"What?" I asked, confused and concerned the man was delirious. "I-I don't—"

Slowly, like it ached for him to do it, the coyote lifted his arm, and swiped his thumb over the scar across his muzzle. And after a few moments and a knowing look from him, I did the same, and came away with blood. My injury.

"When tha' heals," the coyote rasped, "if it looks like a knife wound, I wouldn't be surprised."

"Ransom," I murmured softly, finally seeing what was really clouding the man's eyes. He wasn't delirious. He'd been crying. I had never, in all the time I'd known him, seen him cry.

"Dominick," he said around a swallow, as his eyes swept up over the pile of collapsed rock and snow, "died here. Somewhere beneath all that. We used t' camp here, when we came into these parts. Good shelter here. And none o' this rock had fallen then..."

He looked to the pile. "I couldn't... couldn't... bury him. Th' ground was frozen. I jes-jes sorta'... left him. Looks like th' earth did the deed for me."

His gaze fixed on a spot, beneath all the mountain stone, that only he could see, a place buried not only by rock, but by time, and denial. What he was seeing, I would never know. But the fear, the terror I saw there, told me all I'd ever needed to know.

I'd always known, I think. Victims know their own. I'd just never been willing to accept it, knowing the man he'd grown into. The strong, masculine, defiant man, who was never a victim.

But he'd been young, once. Young, and trusting, and vulnerable. Just like I'd been.

"There are demons in th' world, Shivah," he breathed, his voice barely audible, it was so harsh and quiet. "Demons tha'... get into the hearts of men. Turn them wrong... make them capable of things no person with a soul should be."

"I know," I said softly.

The coyote licked at his ice-caked muzzle, his breath coming out in thin wisps of steam in the air. "Y' can't reason with 'em. Y' can't love them, or they'll use it against you. All you can do, Shivah... all you can do... t' make them stop... is kill them."

I looked out over the crumbled remains of the chasm walls, caved in specifically in this spot.

A tomb. For a demon.

Ransom was shaking, almost more so than before. I knew from his fall into the river that that could be a good sign, but it could also have been because of something else entirely. Anger. Fear. Grief.

"When did you remember?" I asked at length, wrapping my arms more fully around the coyote from behind, so that his body was covered more by my cloak than even I was.

"Started comin' back slowly, b'fore I even met you..." he murmured. "I don't know, maybe it's always been there," he admitted after a further few moments, his muzzle dropping. "It feels like I always remembered, just didn' want to think about it."

I nodded slowly, leaning my nose against his shoulder.

"Started gettin' real bad... lately," he said, and now his body was almost shaking mine. "Seein' what," his voice cracked, and he closed his eyes, dropping his head entirely, "what tha' man did to you. That husband o' yours. I'm sorry I treated you so bad tha' first month, Shivah. I didn'a even want t' pull you outta the earth, when we first found you," he

54

blurted, running through the words quickly, trying to stifle a sob. "It just… brought back so many damned things… things I didn' want to remember. The dreams kept gettin' worse… I'd see him sometimes, when I slept. Crawlin' in beside me, puttin' his…" he swallowed heavily, "his hands on me. And then when I… when I hurt Veronica, tha' night at the Barrel… I-I just… it all came back. I thought he was there, Shivah," he said his tone haunted. "I thought… I was a kid again, and he was there, in that bed with me… and he was touchin' me the way he used to…"

He leaned his head back slowly, dragging in a deep breath as he looked heavenward, his body giving a long, deep shudder. "You have no idea how much faith—how much love—I had for that man. I wanted him to be my father. I wanted to be him. I gave up my family, because he told me he'd show me how to be a real hunter, like my ancestors."

I held him tightly, knowing it was all I could give. I wanted so badly to take this all away from him, somehow—to change things. Step back in time, and just make this not happen.

Sometimes, I really hated the world.

He shook his head, slowly, but again and again, like the memories were water he was trying to shake off.

"He didn't even wait a day," he half-growled, half-sobbed, "a day away from my home before he did it th' first time. And after that, after he knew I couldn't stop 'm, it never bloody stopped! Not until I sunk that fuckin' knife into his gut! I tried everythin', before then. I pleaded with 'em… I tried acceptin' it, I tried… gettin' used to it. But there ain't no gettin' used to it! You can't ever! It just gets worse, every fuckin' time, cuz I knew… I knew it was gonna happen again. And if I fought… if I fought, he'd just beat me bloody 'til I couldn't fight back no more!"

I remained silent, but I was swallowing back my own tears. I needed to be strong for my friend right now.

But I remembered those nights, too. Remembered how he'd overpower me, or simply strike me until I didn't remember where I was. You learn not to fight back, quickly. The fear begins to control you, and then it's just easier for him to do it again.

"I was twelve," he whispered, after a very long pause. "When it started. Twelve. I didn' even know what was happenin'. I just knew he was hurtin' me. And I thought I did somethin' wrong… for a long time… a long time…"

He lifted his eyes slowly to the pile of rubble, and then suddenly, he ripped away from me, wrenching himself to his feet and grabbing one of the rocks near us as he stood. He flung the stone violently at the pile, and the fragile slate shattered against one of the heavier boulders, creating a resounding crack that echoed through the chasm.

"Why'd you make me do it, Dom?!" he demanded in a hoarse scream. "I told you to bloody stop! I told you I'd kill you if you didn't fuckin' stop!"

I stood quickly, to catch him as his body gave out, and he crumpled back down to the ground. All I was able to do, ultimately, was slow his fall and help him to his knees. Realizing I could do more than just share my cloak, I grabbed at the one he'd discarded, and tried to put it around his shoulders. But the coyote shoved it away, almost as soon as I tried to cover him with it.

"Leave me alone, damnit!" he snapped. "I came here t' end things on my terms. Alone. I wanna die with some goddamned dignity."

"There's nothing dignified about killing yourself, Ransom!" I bit back.

"Better this way than drinkin' myself t' death in a ditch, or eatin' my gun. A' least here, ain't no one gotta see," the coyote rasped, dragging a long breath through his nose. He didn't sound like he was breathing well. "Dom and I can jes… fade outta memory, up here. Ain't no one ever gotta know we lived, or what a waste we was. Better that way."

"Don't compare yourself to that man," I said, insistently.

"We belong t'gether," Ransom spat, bitterly. "Two rotten bastards who didn' ever take care o'the one... the one person who ever actually gave a damn about 'em."

And that seemed to do it, for him. The anger fell out of his tone, entirely, and the man just hung his head. One long tear traveled the contours of his scarred muzzle, finding its way to the ground, between his knees. Every ounce of life, of that strong, fiery, defiant man I'd known, seemed gone. The man was nearly a corpse already.

"Ransom..." I said softly, gingerly putting a hand on his shoulder and trying to keep my tone gentle, but earnest. "Puquanah is alive."

The coyote shoved my hand off of his shoulder, weakly, but I let him. He turned to regard me, a bitterness flashing through his eyes. "Don't you torture me, Shivah. If you got any decency in you... jes' leave."

I put some strength into my words, standing my ground. "I'm not lying to you, Ransom! I came across half a bloody mountain to find you for him, and I am not letting you stop me! Now get up!"

"I saw him! I held him!" Ransom cried out, his voice cracking. "You ain't gonna fool me into comin' away! Jes' let me rest, damnit!"

"Even if he was dead," I countered, trying to argue a point I might actually make. "Do you really think you'll ever see him again, if you die in this place? Do you really think you'll find him in the afterlife, if you're trapped here? With Dominick?"

As I'd hoped, that actually did seem to stall the coyote in his thoughts. I saw the look of momentary panic and realization come over him, and I seized upon it.

"You don't deserve the same fate as him, Ransom," I said, in a quieter, calmer tone. "You're too strong to let him pull you down to his depths. You're too good a man for this."

"I murdered him..." the coyote said quietly after another long pause, his voice breaking.

I took a deep breath, knowing somehow that the words I was about to speak, I would have to live with, myself.

"There is a difference," I said softly, "between murder, and defending yourself."

"I just wanted it t' stop, Shivah, " the coyote gasped.

"I know," I murmured against his brow, holding him tightly, and trying to grip one of his hands in mine. His fingers felt stiff, ice cold.

"Gods, this all messed me up so bad, inside," he said through grit teeth. "I fucked up everythin' good that ever came my way. Nothin' felt right anymore, after him. Everythin' good felt dirty. Even..."

He went rigid in my arms, suddenly. I lifted my head from his shoulder, and followed the line of his neck to his eyes. They were wide, staring past me. Above me. I turned slowly, and followed his gaze.

At first I almost didn't see her. It's true what the legends all said. She was the same color as the snow, fading seemingly in and out of sight with the whipping winds of the storm... like her very visage was flickering.

The massive beast stood at the precipice of the chasm, overlooking us, near another collapsed-in rock slide. She was standing almost entirely still, and easily several hundred yards away, but all the same, I could feel her eyes on us. Even from here, her predatory gaze was piercing. Terrifying, but mesmerizing.

I had never seen a saber lion before, but I couldn't imagine they were all so large, or so beautiful. The two long fangs from which her kin got their name could have easily been the length of my forearm, and her tail swept back half the length of her body, the long white fur along it trailing in the wind. Her fur was thick and elegant, lending her an even more bulky appearance than her imposing figure already gave.

I thought for a moment that she might have been a figment of my imagination, carved by my exhausted mind out of rock, or tree boughs, but then I saw her turn her head and look behind her. The motion was so natural, it couldn't be denied. She was alive, and she was real.

I slowly, shakily pulled an arrow from my quiver, gripping my bow tightly. Beautiful or not, this beast was enormous and dangerous, and we were weak and alone. I had to-

"No," Ransom barely breathed from beside me, putting his hand on my arm as I tried to nock an arrow. I looked to him, disbelievingly. His gaze was fixed on the beast, his jaw open, expression fixed in one of awe. I slowly lowered my bow, uncertain what he wanted me to do. Could we afford to lower our guard?

She wasn't coming for us, though. She seemed poised on the cliff face, no longer looking our way, but behind her, to something else distant that we couldn't see. But then, she turned again, and looked to us. And I saw Ransom stare straight back at her.

"She..." the coyote said softly, "she was never the monster I was looking for..."

The imposing, beautiful beast moved, suddenly, walking slowly and purposefully along the cliff face, closer towards us, but not coming down.

And behind her, I finally saw what she'd been looking towards. Or who, rather.

The silhouette of a canine, wearing a thick winter cloak, and holding another, far shorter figure at his side, came into view past the edge of the rock slide, peering down into the canyon past whipping winds and snow. I knew he'd seen us immediately, and knew with the wolf's long mane tossing in the wind, and the smaller figure clinging to a gnarled walking stick, it could only be—

Ransom struggled to his feet beside me, as the men's distant, wind-muffled voices carried down the small canyon. And then he pulled away from me, wrenching himself entirely to his feet. I let him go.

I saw Laesom's distant figure stoop, and he hefted the small fox, lest he try to get down the rock slide himself with a fractured leg. The rocks would have been hard enough to trespass for the old canine normally, but carrying someone... I don't know how he did it. I ran towards them myself, but the crevasse was long, and by the time I'd gotten anywhere near, or even caught up to Ransom, Laesom had somehow managed to traverse his way almost entirely down the canyon to the bottom.

Puck started limping his way across the rocky debris field almost the second the wolf set him down. Both he and the coyote were barely in any shape to move, let alone run, but they tried. It was like watching a man claw his way towards life again. Every step took pain and tremendous effort... but this was their final bridge to cross, and I wasn't going to stop either one of them.

A desperate sob tore its way out of Ransom's chest, like a guttural howl, when Puquanah collapsed against him. The coyote pulled the small fox against his body, tightly, holding fast to him like he had the ice in the river, like he needed to hold on to him to breathe.

I made my way up behind the two men, desperately trying to catch my breath, and feeling a real sense of joy and relief wash over me, for the first time in weeks. Seeing them hold one another again was one of the most beautiful things I'd ever seen in my life, regardless of the circumstances, or the terrible condition the both of them were in.

"How?!" was the first thing I caught from Ransom, as he ran his frozen paws over the fox's head, gently pushing back his cloak to look at him.

Puck gave a shuddering sigh, and I could tell he was exhausted, but he looked so happy. "Len... sal..." he said, at length, as he struggled to catch his breath. "I took Len'sal... so they'd think they'd killed me..."

"I thought they'd killed you, damnit!" Ransom exclaimed, almost laughing between his sobs.

"I'm sorry, I-I'd run out of more clever ideas..." the fox said, shaking his head. "I just did the only thing I could..."

The coyote just cut him off by pulling him in closer and holding the fox's muzzle beneath his, tucked under his chin. He rocked on his knees, slowly, but seemed in no danger of collapsing entirely. Not with the fox in his arms.

"You are a clever little bastard," the coyote said hoarsely. "I'm just not that bright." He tipped the fox's muzzle up, finally, and looked him in the eyes. "But don't you ever do this to me again, you hear? Not the Len'sal, just... everythin' that happened in Serahaven. Next time, I don't care what you feel you gotta do... You do it, but I go with you. I don't care if it's treatin' some plague, or... throwin' yourself off a bloody cliff. You go, I go. You got that?"

Puck nodded, sniffing and wiping his pale eyes with the back of his sleeve.

"And," the coyote nosed him, gently, "in case I die, somehow... in th' next few minutes..."

He pressed his muzzle softly to Puck's, and the fox went limp, his small ears tipping back. Ransom's hand curled possessively against the nape of the fox's neck as they kissed.

And when they pulled back, Ransom murmured, "I love you," against his muzzle, and then they were kissing one another again.

I'd have felt self-conscious about being witness to the scene, except that Ransom had clearly made his admission loud enough to be heard by me, the meaning of which was not lost on me. And judging by the joy the fox was expressing through that kiss, it hadn't been lost on him, either.

Still, I left them be for a bit, and moved slowly towards Laesom. The old wolf was sitting now, stretching out one of his legs and rubbing at his knee, while he rested. He was watching the couple, though, and smiling. And I got the feeling that smile was a rare one.

"Are you alright?" I asked softly, sitting down next to him and resting my own sore feet.

"Nearly took a spill coming down here," the wolf said with a gruff chuckle. "But yes, I seem to be in one piece."

We were silent for a bit, still watching the two reunited men. It was hard to express how happy I was that they were happy. It felt like seeing this all end the way it had was reaffirming something I'd given up on, long ago.

"How did you find us?" I suddenly asked, realizing how far off-course they must have become to be here.

"We'd circled around back to camp," Laesom said, sedately. "The storm was worse where we were looking. No rocky terrain to break up the winds. I knew we had little hope of finding anything out that way, but the fox wanted to continue, and we were trying to decide what to do when we saw her..."

I followed his eyes back up to the cliff face, where the Wraith Lion stood. She was still just watching us, as if she were standing sentry.

"I knew she was a spirit when first I laid eyes on her," Laesom said reverently, as he looked on the distant beast. "I have always wanted to see a spirit. Today is a blessed day."

I smiled. "It really is," I agreed, softly.

"She led us here," Laesom murmured. "Always at a distance, but always within sight."

"I can't believe Puck agreed to follow her," I murmured. "You know he doesn't believe in spirits. He thinks she's just an animal."

"He may well have lost his faith long ago. Faith is a fragile thing," Laesom said, before giving me a serene smile. "But I think some days, when we are at our most desperate, even the cynical amongst us put our trust in faith. I choose to believe his prayers were answered."

"You think she's his spirit?" I asked, moving my eyes from the lion, to the two men, who seemed all but oblivious to her presence, anymore.

"I think she is their spirit," Laesom said sagely. "And the spirit of this mountain. Here to guide all when they are lost."

"Ransom saw her after he..." I paused, "after something terrible happened to him on this mountain when he was young. Or so he claims."

"I have no doubt he did," Laesom nodded, then stood, slowly. "Perhaps she even led him then, as she led us today."

I stood with the wolf, my gaze sweeping back up to the cliffs. But she was gone.

I thanked her, silently, and hoped my prayer would reach her ears.

"Grant!" I said suddenly, blinking. "Oh hell, he's still out there. We need to let him know we found him."

"We've kept in touch," Laesom said with a mild smile. "He is near. It's close to dark. He's been working his way back to camp for several hours, now. I've been calling to him since we made our way back. It can take a few moments for it to carry, but…"

The old wolf climbed atop a nearby flat boulder, spreading his feet shoulder-width apart to plant himself firmly in-place, then pushed back the hood of his cloak, slowly, and looked into the sky. The winds were lessening, the clouds were still thick in the sky, but the snow was coming lighter, now. We might well have finally been on the tail end of the storm.

And then the man tipped his head back, and he howled. I had only ever heard a wolf call from distant mountains, before. The eerie song of the wolf tribes carried through our valley every now and then, and sometimes when I'd been young, I'd tried to listen, tried to hear what they were saying to each other. I'd always found it hauntingly beautiful.

But I'd never actually heard or seen a wolf howl right beside me before, and it was breathtaking.

He didn't stop for a full minute, save to breathe, or to shift in pitch. And when he was done, and the crevasse fell silent, I barely breathed. I could tell he was waiting for a reply, I could only imagine, but—

My ears twitched, and there, at length, I heard it. Distant and muffled by the winds that remained, but I heard it. Higher in pitch and far more of a 'woo' than a true howl, but… it was there.

Laesom gave a soft chuckle and held out a hand for me to help him down.

"He's nearer than before," he said, as he stepped down. The old man looked almost mirthful. And that was so unusual for him, I had to ask.

"Is something funny?" I queried, confused.

"Ah, not exactly," the old wolf chuckled, "I just... You would have to be a wolf to understand." He turned to smile at me, "The way huskies and most Otherwolves howl is amusing, like listening to pups when they're first learning. Except they never grow out of it. Don't ever tell Grant I said that, though. He'd be mortified."

I gave a lopsided smile. "Well, we wouldn't want that."

"We need to get him back to camp," the wolf said, looking to Ransom a bit more seriously. "His fingers are in bad shape, and it's getting dark. It's only going to get colder. And this place is..." he glanced around, uncomfortably, "evil. I can feel it in my bones. We need to get him some place safe, or we could still lose him."

I nodded, looking to the two men. They were still holding one another, neither saying a word, but so many things were passing between them. Things they would probably need years to fully say.

"I think he'll be all right," I said quietly, and hopefully. And I really believed it.

We can't overcome evils we never confront. They just stay locked away, festering inside of us. Ransom had finally found his monster, and that was, at least, a beginning.

The fight was hardly over, but at least now, we could help him.

CHAPTER THREE
LETTING GO

Ransom was in terrible shape, as were we all, but we forged back to our camp that night nonetheless, knowing we'd need the shelter, the fire, and our supplies. Fortune was with us that night in droves, so it was arrogance to expect anything more, but fate, it seemed, remained on our side for once. Our fire was still simmering by the time we made it back, and it proved easy to stoke. Within minutes of returning, we were able to huddle around that life-saving warmth again.

And the storm seemed to be dying down! Not gone, not even close to gone yet, but visibility had improved, the winds were lessening, and in the shelter of our carefully-chosen campsite, sequestered between a miniature pine forest and two imposing rock faces that had tipped together over time to form an almost triangular cove, it finally felt survivable, up here. Still bitingly cold, and the snow still fell outside, but here, here we were safe and together.

All of us together, once Grant returned, which was not long after we did. He was exhausted, just as we were, but he didn't seem in the least frustrated or bitter that his own searching had borne no results. We'd found Ransom, and he was alive. The husky seemed just as happy to see the man as we all were. They even embraced one another.

But soon, Puck took the coyote away, retiring with him to their tent to see what could be done for the man's obvious frostbite, and whatever other terrible conditions he'd become afflicted with up here. It sounded like he had a chest-cold and he was certain to be starved and dehydrated, as well. The fox had no easy task ahead of him in treating his beloved patient. But I knew if any healer could restore the coyote to wellness, it would be him. All we could do now was give them time.

As Laesom began to set up his own tent and it became clear we were turning in for the night, I stood and finished the last of the tea I'd been drinking. We'd all eaten what was left of our best jerky. Even Ransom ate, which had been good to see, and with a full stomach, a lighter heart, and an overwhelming sense of belonging amidst this small group we'd founded, I realized that, even if it was just for tonight, I felt at peace and happy.

It seemed almost impossible, but tonight I didn't give a damn about Methoa'nuk, the raiders, or anyone who had ever wronged me. I simply didn't care enough to spare my thoughts for evil men and women. They couldn't take this moment from us. This incredible, peaceful, amazing moment in time. It was all ours. We'd earned it.

And tired though I was, I wanted to enjoy it. So instead of going right to sleep, which my body should have yearned for, by all rights, I wanted to stay awake a little bit longer, and just feel this contentment. Bask in this night, for all it was worth.

I found myself wandering towards the edge of the camp, where the rocky crags that formed the little niche we were camping in came together into a slim passageway. Beyond it lay a small stretch of flat rock, on which snow had piled and lay pristine, white and undisturbed in the quiet lee of the stone faces. Twenty paces out was a sheer drop, but for all its danger, it afforded a magnificent view of the mountain stretching beneath, and the other side of the valley.

For the first time since we'd been forced to endure its trials, I saw the storm for its beauty. It had coated the mountain in white, and with the moonlight just beginning to sift down through the clouds, it lit the world up like it was all aglow. The clouds curled overhead in the sky in shades of deep blue, and the tossing rivulets of snow on the winds danced like distant butterflies in the night sky.

When I'd been a young kitten, I'd run through mountains like these, on the other side of the valley, chasing butterflies, beautiful yellow butterflies that fed on the fragrant mountain flowers, some larger than my hands. I'd stalk and pounce after them, pretending they were game and I was a proud, noble hunter taking care of my tribe—and not just by weaving baskets or cleaning clothing. I'd always wanted to do something more adventurous with my life. And now, even if it had been in the wake of terrible events, I was.

But when I was a young girl, I never really tried to catch the butterflies—even if I had one cornered, even if I knew I could have caught one. I never wanted to actually touch them, because they were fragile. I'd killed one once, and it had felt so terrible.

So I just chased, because the chase was what made me feel like a hunter. I never wanted to be a killer. I just wanted to be chasing something beautiful.

My body ached, but my feet felt lightened by the sheer joy of the night… so much so, that I couldn't help but bound forward at one of the drifting flakes, laughing at my own childishness as I leapt to bat at it. I'd lost touch with that little girl I'd once been so long ago. It was strangely cathartic to feel connected to her again, even if I was far too old now to be acting this absurdly silly.

Well, it was alright. So long as—

A deep chuckle from behind me confirmed my greatest fears. I'd forever ruined my stoic, intimidating persona with one of my friends.

And gods, did it have to be Grant?

I dropped my ears, glancing over my shoulder guiltily. The Otherwolf was leaning up against the stone face behind me, regarding me with a lopsided smile. I was simultaneously embarrassed and considering not giving a damn. What did I care about intimidating this man anymore, really? When I'd first known him, I hadn't trusted him, and I'd felt it necessary to frighten him off, to keep him at a distance.

I didn't know what I wanted from him anymore, but I didn't want him at a distance. If anything, all I'd wanted over the last few weeks was for he and I to be closer. And whether or not that really was just because I was in heat, or because I held some honest affection for him before all of this, after the

68

last few days, that affection was completely real. Very few people in my life had ever done so much for me, for so little reward.

What did it all really mean? Where did it come from? What did I really want from him, in the end?

I still didn't know. Methoa had so confused what should have been my natural inclinations where men were involved, I wasn't certain I'd ever be able to regard them in any normal way, ever again.

But the better question was, why did it matter why I felt the way I did? No matter why I was fond of the man, I was fond of the man. It wasn't worth denying that any more. It was actually a lot of work, actively frightening him off every day, and it always dismayed me when I actually succeeded. Why was I sabotaging myself? I liked being near him, liked speaking to him, liked being touched by him. And I almost never enjoyed being touched! Especially by a man.

I didn't want to intimidate him anymore. I didn't want him to see my 'persona' anymore. I wasn't ashamed of showing him who I was. And what happened from here... I didn't know, but it seemed worth finding out.

So I looked across the rocky clearing towards him, and then, I just smiled, and bounded towards another dancing snowflake, batting it out of the air. I heard him laugh.

"You almost got that one!"

"The really big ones are slower," I said, between another jump, "like... big fat hares. Easier to catch."

"They don't stand a chance, you vicious predator," the Otherwolf remarked with obvious amusement.

I was out of breath by the time I made my way back towards the rock face, and the husky who'd been watching me. By all rights, the last thing I should have been doing tonight was bounding around in the chill night air even more than I had already, but I just felt so exhilarated, so childishly happy, I couldn't bring myself to care. Grant didn't question me, or chide me about my antics, he just smiled softly down at me when I joined him, leaning my back against the mountain stone, and giving a happy heave of a sigh.

"I came out here to see where you'd gone, and ask how you were feeling," he said with a smile down at me, his blue eyes catching the moonlight, "but I think I can deduce."

I gave a breathless laugh, smiling and staring up into the sky. I could almost see stars through the gaps in the clouds. It felt like the whole world was laid before me, and for once, I couldn't wait for tomorrow. We had beaten death. We had endured the storm. We were standing at the top of the world, and if we had come this far, I was convinced there was no further obstacle we could not overcome.

"My chest feels fit to burst," I said, turning my eyes towards the husky, "I'm so happy. It's been so long since I've had hope."

The man looked down on me softly, and gingerly, always hesitant, always careful to ensure his gestures were welcome, he slipped a paw down my cheek, curling his fingers gently through a few locks of my mane. I pressed my cheek into his palm and nuzzled it, to show him just how very welcome the gesture was, right now. He ran his thumb gently over my cheek, and I breathed out softly into his palm. I knew I was purring, felt my face flush, the warmth from the simple touch seeping down through me like sunlight cascading over my body. And for once I didn't fight any of it, didn't question it. I just basked in how good it felt, how right it felt.

"You are so beautiful when you smile," the man said in a hazy, entranced voice. Having moved to stand before me now, I was able to look him directly in the eyes when I opened mine. We were no longer at a respectful distance. I could have admonished him for being less than gentlemanly, and a few weeks ago, I would have.

Tonight, though, I stopped questioning the urges I'd fought for so long, and I just grabbed at the man's travel-worn shirt wherever I could find purchase, leaned up, and kissed him. And it was so easy. It was so simple, and uncomplicated, and nothing like what I'd thought it would be. No lack of experience, or loss of innocence, or fear, or awkwardness mattered. In fact, I stopped thinking about just about everything.

Grant returned the gesture all but immediately, after a second or two of shock. And then I hardly needed to know what I was doing, because he clearly did. The far taller Otherwolf leaned his muzzle down into mine, and braced himself against the rock wall behind us with one hand, while his other moved down from my cheek to my shoulder, and ran the length of my arm, all hesitance gone from his touch, finally. It felt as though I'd broken whatever bonds had been holding him back, at last.

I'd never even kissed my husband. Our marriage ceremony had necessitated no such pleasantries, and he'd never wanted them. So I hadn't even known what to expect with another feline, let alone a canine, but it was so much gentler, and softer, and yet so much more intense than I'd thought it would be. There was something so indescribably intimate about feeling someone else's breaths, about having your nose pressed into their fur, of having your senses entirely overwhelmed by them, and only them. I don't even know how long that first kiss lasted, but by the time I had to part to take a breath, I knew I wanted to do it again.

I could tell Grant was about to say something, but I didn't let him, I just kissed him again. He gave a soft, breathy groan against me as I pressed my muzzle to his, but it didn't sound like an argument. I clung tightly to him, not really certain where to put my hands, only knowing I wanted them on him.

I felt the man's paw move down to wrap around my waist, and I didn't fight it when he pulled our bodies closer together. If anything, I pulled him in even closer, until we were all but flush to one another. My blood was singing through my ears in a pounding rhythm, and I felt so warm. I wanted that heat right now. I'd been cold for so long.

Grant wasn't wearing his coat. It had almost been too icy to remove when he'd gotten back, and it was defrosting in front of the fire, now. So it only made sense to me that I share the blazing warmth he was creating within me, and I tried to do just that. I kept as close to him as possible, running my hands down his back, slowly. We'd barely embraced in the past, but I found it hard to believe I'd never realized how strong the contours of his body felt, before. Or how very much I'd always wanted to move my fingers through the thick fur at the ruff of his neck, or touch his ears, or feel him pressing me back against this stone wall. How did I get him to do that? Did I ask?

How did you even ask something like that?

When I opened my muzzle just barely into the kiss to try and take a breath, I felt the tip of his tongue brush against mine, and... gods, I wanted that, I wanted more of that, and I wanted it now.

The frustration I was contending with was our height difference. My toes only took me so far towards him, and he still had to stoop, even with his muzzle leaning down into mine. I clutched at his shoulders, my fingers furrowing into the fabric of his worn cotton shirt and vest, and when I felt the soft, wet warmth of his tongue slipping over the tip of my muzzle again, I tried desperately to cling at his shoulders enough to lift myself more fully into the kiss.

And that's when I had a brilliant idea that suddenly, and irrevocably, shifted the entire mood of the moment.

It was like an instinct. I didn't even really consider it before I'd done it. But as soon as I realized I could lift myself against his body by holding fast to his shoulders, my feet left the ground, and before I could stop myself, I'd wrapped my strong legs around his waist—

And then he pushed me up against the rock wall, just as I'd wanted. And it was every bit as satisfying as I thought it would be. The entire weight of my body was pinned between him and the stone, and I was finally entirely flush to him, chest to chest. I could feel every contour of his body in contact with mine, could feel the warmth of him beneath his shirt. I curled my calves around his lower back, his tail brushing against my paws as it swayed back and forth.

I wrapped my arms entirely up around his shoulders, thrilled to be at the same level as him, finally, and I shared a long, deepening kiss with the man that made the warmth in my body blossom into something outright fiery.

I'd never have imagined kissing could involve all of this, but maybe it was a canine thing. I wasn't really sure, but I wasn't arguing. Between kissing me, he'd even gently lick my muzzle every now and then, and the soft, warm, provocative sensation made my heart leap in my chest, and my pulse quicken. My body was beginning to quiver, and it wasn't from the cold. Every second of this was building this strange, but exciting tension in me, and I thought the more we gave one another, the closer I might come to somehow alleviating it. It was a familiar tension, one I'd been contending with for weeks now, almost since I'd first met him. And for all it was frustrating, I didn't exactly want it to stop, either.

I couldn't have possibly fought back the urge to purr right now if I wanted to, but the deep thrumming seemed only to spur him on, so I held nothing back. I finally was able to release my hands from his shoulders, now that he was holding me against him, and that freed them to travel up through the soft ruff of fur along his neck. I cupped one of his ears and ran the velvety texture between my paw-pads, and I felt him groan against my muzzle. I just smiled and purred in return, stroking his ear gently as my other hand traveled his back, feeling his shoulder-blades shift reflexively when my fingertips ran down his spine.

Every little thing I did evoked a response, and it was completely fascinating to discover. I'd never known men could be like this. And I'd never known kissing could be so... playful.

That tension was still there, though, and now that I could feel his body so close to mine, I could feel it in him, too. We were coming up to breathe less and less often, our joined breaths when we remembered to have them were coming faster... We were nearly panting into one another's muzzles...

On some level I think I realized a certain amount of restraint had been lost, but I didn't care.

At one point when we pulled away to breathe, I nuzzled beneath his chin, burying my nose in his soft neck ruff. He smelled of ice and trail dust, but also his own mild, foreign musk. Again, I didn't question myself when an urge struck, and I pressed my muzzle into the soft skin beneath his fur, and gently lathed it with my tongue, like I would were I cleaning my own fur.

The man sucked in a sharp breath at that, and with a suddenness that felt like it was almost instinct, his hips pressed hard into mine. But just as soon as it had happened, his eyes snapped open, he was tipping his muzzle away from mine and loosening his hold on me, and the both of us took a moment to catch our breath.

I'd felt why he'd stopped.

In the blissful exuberance of the moment, I'd somehow managed to forget Grant was still very much a man, and men got a certain way, when a woman let them touch her. And that would be much different than the playful kissing we'd been enjoying. That would be something else entirely. That would be… what Methoa had done.

But it would have to be a little different, with a different man, wouldn't it? It couldn't be nearly as bad. Grant cared about me. Of that much at least I was certain. We weren't husband and wife, but Methoa had been, and that certainly hadn't made it any better. Even though everyone had told me it would.

Gods, was I really thinking about this? Why was I thinking about this? Hadn't the kissing been enough?

Why was I making excuses to let him do what he'd been good enough to stop himself from doing? Grant was a decent man. He would never require it of me. We could just kiss. Kissing had been nice. I'd been pleased by it, he'd seemed pleased by it…

But that coiling, nagging need was still inside me, and now, it was turning into a sharp feeling of frustration, like a dull ache. I hadn't wanted to stop what we were doing. I couldn't exactly blame Grant for halting everything. He'd done so for my benefit, I was certain, but it was still—frustrating.

"We should really..." the husky mumbled, in an almost delirious, breathlessly low voice, "ah..."

He reached down to run his paws over my thighs, and ease them down. I slowly released them, sliding my calves down his until my feet hit the ground. My legs felt shaky, so I remained leaning against the stone wall. But Grant was still leaning against it as well, so apparently, I wasn't alone.

He at least wrapped his arms around me again, which I was immediately grateful for. I tried to tug his body towards mine again, so that I could at least have that contact again, but this time he resisted, giving a gruff sigh.

"Just give me a moment..." he murmured.

I nodded, pretending I understood. I did, to some extent. It's just that Methoa had never actually stopped, once he put his hands on me. It looked like it might have been difficult, even for Grant. And the man had amazing self-restraint.

"I'm sorry," I said at length, not certain what else to say.

"Oh my God please don't be," the husky said with a hoarse laugh. "Please. I don't ever want you to regret any of that. I plan to repeat it, and I'd rather you be just as exuberant then."

I gave a small smile. "Then I will be."

"We probably should have showed a little more self-control," the husky admitted, straightening the collar of his shirt some. At some point I'd managed to yank it pretty far out of place. "Or rather, I should have. Apologies, it's just I've been..." his eyes turned to mine, "wanting this... for some time, and you were incredible."

"I think we're both to blame for letting that get away from us," I said with a mildly embarrassed smile. "I really enjoyed myself, too."

The man looked on me blissfully for a further few moments, before leaning in to kiss me once more, softly. He pulled away too quickly for me to relish it as I had the ones before, but it was just enough to make me want more, again. I found myself chasing his muzzle with mine, and he let me, for a few moments, but then he spoke again.

"So," he said in a low, husky voice, hopefully, "does this mean…?"

I paused for some time, before murmuring, "I don't really know what it means, to be honest. I wasn't thinking into it too much."

The man was silent for a moment, then he just smiled. "Alright, then," he said with a nod, "maybe that's for the best, for now. We have time. Let's not over-think it just yet. We'll get it sorted out when the time's right."

He nuzzled me, softly, and I tried to kiss him again, since he'd given me the opportunity. He let me, but pulled away far too quickly for my liking to speak again.

"Even if we're not… exactly courting," he murmured, as one of his broad paws swept over my head, cupping one of my ears. "I'm very much in love with you, Shivah. I hope you know that."

I pounded a fist against his chest, startling him. "You can't just say that out of nowhere!" I said, exasperated. "What happened to not over-thinking?!"

"I'm not!" he insisted around a laugh, trying to defend himself against my mock blows. He gripped my fists, and opened them gently, guiding my far smaller fingers through his. He looked me in the eyes, and despite my annoyance with the man's entirely too free emotions, I couldn't look away.

"That was from the gut," he said, earnestly. "I swear. And it's not new. I've had a very high regard for you ever since I first met you. But these last two weeks…" he looked down for a few moments. "You've seen me through some very hard times. I'm used to being the man who has to handle everything. Keep it together, keep my family afloat, and then… leading my men…"

he gave a sigh. "Everyone relying on me." His eyes moved back up to mine, slowly. "Except for you. I love that you can handle yourself, without my help, if that makes any sort of sense."

"I suppose," I murmured, trying not to show how flattering that statement truly was.

"I know that even if I fail, you'll manage," he said softly. "And for a man who's had to contend with so much responsibility that is immensely satisfying. It doesn't mean I'll stop trying to do everything I can for you," he assured me, as though I needed that assurance. "I just—I know you can stand on your own—"

"Grant," I interrupted him with a sigh, and cupped the man's cheek with my palm. "It's alright. I understand what you're trying to say. And I don't doubt that you're speaking from the heart. You're just very… free with your heart. And I'm…" I glanced away. "I'm not."

I'd looked away because I didn't want to see it when I upset him. But when I finally moved my eyes back to his, I saw only the same peaceful expression I'd left him with.

"You're not upset," I noted.

"In all the time you've known me, have you ever seen me give up, just because I was rebuffed?" the husky countered. "At least this time you didn't implicitly say 'no'. Or growl at me."

"I did sort of hit you," I mumbled, embarrassed.

"I'll recover, I think."

"I like being with you, Grant," I said with a soft sigh. "And I liked… what just happened," I said a bit more quietly, my fingers toying at the collar of his shirt.

"And if that's all it ever is, that's fine by me," the husky replied, simply. "I'm not a complicated man, Shivah. We don't need to make this complicated, if it makes you uncomfortable. But no lack of courtship, or ceremony, or commitment is going to stop me from feeling the way I feel. When I first started realizing my feelings for you were deeper than just a surface attraction, I contended with a lot of realities, right away. And one of them was that this would never really be traditional. For reasons that actually have little to do with you."

I blinked, realizing what he meant. Amidst my own inner turmoil at allowing someone this close to me, after all I'd endured with my husband, I'd forgotten that we were crossing into dangerous territory between our cultures, here. Amongst the mountain tribes, it was forbidden for Otherwolf men to even see tribal women, and though that hardly mattered for me anymore, being as my tribe was almost entirely gone, it would likely mean I could never rejoin a tribe in the future, if Grant were at my side.

Was I really considering a future with him? Just a few days ago I'd been certain my future ended with a vengeful spirit and the death of the man I was hunting. And while that hadn't been pushed entirely to the back of my mind, I really was starting to hope this could somehow all still fit into the same life as my quest.

If this wasn't a 'distraction', I didn't know what was. But Crow hadn't shown himself to admonish me lately, not even in my dreams. So maybe he was neutral concerning all of this? Maybe he approved of Grant because the man was following me, now, and we were still planning to pursue Methoa?

Maybe we could make this work, after all.

But what Grant was referring to, I was certain, were his own people's prejudices and social stigmas against my people, let alone any kind of union between us. He worshiped an entirely separate God. Would the spirits even recognize him? I highly doubted his God would ever recognize me.

We couldn't ever marry. We certainly couldn't ever have children. His family might never accept me, his peers would shun him because of me.

Would we go to different places when we died?

It was all a tangle of unknowns. And one he'd clearly been considering for some time now, all on his own... and had apparently decided was worth risking.

I wasn't sure yet.

"So, whatever we have, it's enough," the husky said, softly. "I'm just happy to be with you. Happy, and honored."

He leaned in and kissed my brow, softly, and I looked up to him, feeling very small in that moment. It's not that he made me feel diminished. It's just that sometimes, the man's openness, and acceptance, made me remember a younger time in my own life, when I'd questioned things like affection and love less than I did now. It was both an admirable and dangerous character trait. Dangerous because others could seize upon it and take advantage of it. And I didn't want to be the person who embittered him.

"I care about you, Grant," I said softly. "Is that enough, for now?"

The man smiled, contently. "Yes."

"Are you…" I paused, glancing down. "are you feeling any better?"

He blinked. "Oh. Oh. Yes, some," he said, clearing his throat, and readjusting his belt.

"Good," I said, "because I'm actually getting cold, and we both still have tents to set up."

"Ah…" the man hesitated just enough that I knew there was an issue. "Actually, I'll be sharing a tent with Laesom tonight."

I arched an eyebrow. "Why?" I asked, mystified.

Grant sighed, gesturing towards the camp. "Because one of the things we cut down on, to keep the load on the horses lighter was tents, and bedrolls. They're very heavy, and we thought we could do with one less. Laesom and I have shared a tent before. We'll be fine."

I glanced back towards camp, uncertainly. "Are you certain?" I asked. "Because you seemed uncomfortable when he admitted his preferences to us, over dinner that night before we left."

"What? Oh-no, no," Grant insisted. "That's not—I already knew he was… I've known for years now."

I blinked, confused. "But you seemed so shocked."

Grant sighed, softly, putting his hands on his hips and turning to look out over the horizon. "It wasn't over that."

I remained silent. I could tell he was eventually going to speak again. Although whatever this was, it really seemed to be bothering him.

"I think I knew his mate," he murmured, in an oddly sad tone, for the usually jovial man. "I just never knew he was his mate. Which I suppose makes sense. They wouldn't have wanted anyone to know. But they were close. I should have seen it."

"You didn't know he'd died?" I queried, softly.

"No, I knew he died," Grant shook his head. "And the way that he died, it was just as brutal as Laesom said. I guess I just finally put two and two together."

He hung his head for a few moments, his ears tipped back, eyes narrowed at the horizon. At length, his paw settled over his holster, and the weapon there. "His name was Holt Easton. He gave me this gun. And he taught me almost everything I learned on the Wardens. He was a good man. Hard, not exactly what you'd call congenial, but a good man. I really respected him."

"You can still respect his memory," I insisted.

"I do," he said, turning to regard me, and by the slight snap in his tone, I knew he wanted me to know he was being honest. "I could never disrespect him. And I don't care if he and Laesom were…" he gestured at the air, uncomfortably. "That didn't change who he was. It's just odd that I never saw it, is all. Hard to put all of that into the context of the man I knew."

I nodded. "I went through that with Ransom," I admitted.

"The men I'm angry at are the ones who killed him," the husky said, his muzzle twitching. "I wasn't with him on patrol when he died. But I'd always been told he was killed by the Seccoa Bandits. But Laesom said he was killed by his friends. Which would mean…"

I took a breath, realization dawning. "The other Wardens?"

"I need to speak to Laesom about this. At length," Grant muttered. "I need the whole story. I wish he'd told me ages ago, but he probably thought he was sparing me, or something along those lines. He worked closely with the Wardens, and with Holt and I, for many years. He took it hard when Holt died. I never knew just how hard."

"Talk to him, then," I said softly.

"Not tonight. I heard him snoring before I even came out here," Grant said with a sigh, shaking his head and clearly trying to shake the memories off, at least for now. "I'm not going to disturb him after the day we've had."

"Then you probably shouldn't go clambering into a one-man tent with him," I pointed out.

"He managed to share it just fine with Puquanah on the way up."

"Yes, but Puck is itty bitty," I said with a bit of a laugh, making a gesture to indicate the fact with my hands. "You two are both huge. You're going to be mashing into one another all night. It's going to be all legs… and paws, flung everywhere."

"Well, what else am I supposed to do, Shivah?" the man asked, exasperated.

I knew he'd seen the smile I was trying to cover, when his face fell, and he put up a hand.

"No," he shook his head, immediately. "Bad idea, Shivah. Very bad idea—"

"We've done it before," I pointed out.

"We were both exhausted then, and I was drunk."

"So now you'll be sober, and even more gentlemanly," I said, taking his paw in mine, and trying to tug him towards camp. "Come on. It makes a lot more sense than you cramming into a tent with a full-grown wolf."

Grant gave a ragged sigh, looking terribly torn. "This is bad, dangerous territory, Shivah," he insisted, not budging just yet. I was wearing down his defenses, though. I could tell.

I blew out a breath of frustration, gripping his hand tighter and trying to make him look me in the eyes. "Come on, now.

Why not? We're both adults with… moderately good self-control."

The man slowly arched an eyebrow at me.

"We'll just sleep," I insisted.

Grant rolled his eyes. "You know as well as I do that won't be the case, Shivah."

"So you're going to be uncomfortable all night, and inconvenience a friend, because of what might happen?" I stated.

"No," the man replied. "I'm going to be uncomfortable all night and inconvenience a friend because of what almost did happen, just a few minutes ago. And that was in the elements, shoved up against a rock."

I glanced away at that, a smidge guiltily. I suppose I had been the one who'd escalated that.

"You stopped when things got out of hand," I pointed out.

"Shivah, I'm a mortal man," Grant sighed. "There are limits to what I can endure. Look," He moved up to me, putting his paws on either of my shoulders and looking me in the eyes. "Emotions are running very high tonight, and I'd rather we not make a mistake. Especially not in a one-person tent, with our friends not five feet away," he said pointedly.

I suppose he expected that would end the conversation. But I'd never been one to back down.

"So, that will be all the more incentive for you not to misbehave," I countered, and the husky opened his mouth to object, but I cut him off. "I could just order you to do as I say, you know."

Grant gaped at me. "That is an abuse of power, Shivah," he said, so aghast that it almost made me laugh. "A C.O. can't just order their men into bed with them."

"Just tell me you don't want to, Grant," I said, getting to the point. "And I'll let it drop. I've heard a lot of excuses, but nothing about your not wanting to."

"What I want is beside the point," the husky insisted.

"I think it's exactly the point," I said, softly. "Grant, I'd like it if you'd stay with me tonight. It's cold and I like being near you. I don't feel unsafe with you. It seems like an obvious choice to me."

The man regarded me a moment more, before taking a deep breath. "Alright," he said at length.

I smiled, and took his hand again. He clasped it back this time, and we began to head back towards camp. I chuckled softly as we walked. "You have a lot of trouble saying no to me," I pointed out, more than a little mirthfully.

"That's precisely what I'm worried about," the man replied, dryly.

I woke the next morning to an extremely pleasant sensation I'd almost forgotten I could feel. I was overly warm. That was likely because I was nestled, if not entangled, with my tent partner. Apparently his fondness for nuzzling up at night was not in fact tied to pronounced whiskey consumption.

I wasn't arguing. Last night had been, honestly, very pleasant, but the time I'd spent conscious had been woefully brief. After we'd set up the tent and crawled our way inside, the events of the day, and the week preceding it, had finally caught up with me, and I'd been about as tired as I had been the night in the Physician's office. And we'd fallen asleep about as quickly. So I'd inadvertently kept to my word. All we'd done was sleep.

It was almost disappointing. It wasn't that I didn't respect the husky's wishes, I'd just honestly hoped there'd be a bit more of what had happened on the cliff, once we turned in. Even though he'd warned against it, I felt I could control myself. And if I could, he could.

I was no naïve young thing. I knew what the natural conclusion to such escalating affections would inevitably be. And eventually, I'd probably decide to allow it, if only to make him happy. I was a strong woman. I'd endured it many times before, with a man I loathed. I was certain I could endure it again, without letting what had once hurt me affect how I felt about Grant. Even if it hurt, again. I'd gotten remarkably good about dealing with pain, of late. I'd be fine.

At least that's what I kept telling myself.

Last night had been a surprise. I'd never known kissing, or touching a man, could be so pleasant. I'd enjoyed it enough that I'd even dreamed about it, and was looking forward to him waking, so that we could kiss one another again. It was rather unfortunate that the things I'd enjoyed doing with him elicited the response from him that they had. But I could hardly blame the man. Men liked to mate. The act was made to please them.

If I need endure it at some point in the future—for Grant—I would. He, at least, would be gentle. And he'd never force it upon me. Really, I couldn't ask for more. I would just have to try very hard not to let it sour how I felt about him. I could do that. I really hoped I could do that.

At the very least, perhaps it would alleviate the symptoms from my heat. I actually wasn't certain it would, but any shot at relief right now might be worth taking, just so I'd be able to tell if my physical attraction to the man was genuine, once I was entirely back to my senses. The thing was, Grant wasn't feline, so I wasn't even certain everything would work the same. That in particular had been a subject of my curiosity... and my dreams. Which made me blanch just thinking about it, now that I was drifting slowly into full consciousness.

I pressed my muzzle up the man's chest, towards where the collar of his shirt had been unbuttoned, and buried it in his fur, closing my eyes and tugging myself in tighter to him. His breathing was still steady and even, and he showed no signs of waking any time soon. The man had a lot of sleep to catch up on, after all.

I took the rare, quiet moment to take stock of the canine I'd allowed—alright, all but forced—into my bed. I'd spent so much time now trying not to let myself get drawn in by the man, I'd never really considered him as a mate in any physical sense. Back amongst the valley tribes, men would show their prowess and their strength at ceremonies, or in dances, paint-ing their bodies and adorning themselves with feathers and elaborate horn jewelry. Even if it wasn't entirely our choice in the end whom we married, a lot of more desirable women from more powerful families, or who were exceptionally beautiful, might actually have their choice from several suitors.

But if those women were to be believed, by our tribe's standards, Methoa'nuk had been highly desirable. I'd never had the chance to decide for myself whether or not I was physically attracted to the man, because his very presence had intimidated and frightened me from the first time we'd met, and the first night he'd had me, I'd made the mistake of being less than cooperative in our marriage hut, and he'd hurt me. After that, I could only see him as a monster.

I suppose at some point, I'd lost touch with the part of myself that was supposed to find men attractive, or desirable. But Grant had certainly ignited something.

I hadn't really ever considered until this moment that it was strange—my people would say unnatural—for me to be drawn to a canine. Maybe it was because he was so different than Methoa that I was able to find him attractive. Maybe I'd never find another feline desirable, thanks to that despicable man.

But then, maybe I wouldn't have to.

There were a few basic physical differences I'd have to contend with, several of which I'd already run into. The man was, far larger than any bobcat man I'd ever known, both in height and weight. His presence dwarfed mine in our shared tent, but I rather liked that I could so completely nestle into his chest. Methoa had only barely been a few inches taller than I was, and only a bit heavier. Grant was twice my weight, easily. And strong. The man wasn't all taught sinew and hard edges, like a tribal warrior would be, like Methoa had been. He was younger, and probably far more well-fed.

I suspected he was far stronger than any tribesman from my tribe would have been, but his strength was more natural than honed. His primary asset in the field actually seemed to be his endurance and durability. Grant was a tough man, but he would have made for a poor hunter, by my tribe's standards, except perhaps to run something down.

I toyed with the edge of his cotton shirt. It was un-tucked, for once, a rare occasion to be certain. That was another difference between the Otherwolf and a tribesman, and one that was becoming frustrating to me. The Otherwolves covered themselves so completely with their strange clothing, all I'd ever seen of the man was from the neck up, his paws, feet, and tail. He even wore something that covered most of the arch of his paws! It was madness. He had thick fur, he didn't need so much clothing. Even I didn't cover my arms most of the time, and once summer came, I'd be wearing far less. And I was a woman!

I didn't even know what color his fur was beneath it all. And I know that was a small detail, but it was just SO strange not knowing. I'd know what a bobcat's pelt would look like everywhere. But Grant was a mystery. A mystery I very desired to unwrap, already.

My paw-pads lingered at the edge of his shirt, and I briefly wondered how much I could get away with while he was still asleep. I fought back a pang of guilt for my mental wanderings, but really, after everything I'd been made to endure, wasn't it finally my time to take something enjoyable out of my time with a man? It's not as though it would hurt him…

I slipped a few fingers beneath the hem of his shirt, and gingerly tugged it up just enough that I could see the fur along his hip. Red. Alright. And it looked like it faded to white along his stomach. So the two-color pattern pretty much just seemed to continue. Curiosity assuaged.

There were probably other shapes formed by the two colors, over his chest, and his arms, though. I knew at least that his paws and hands were white.

His fur was so much softer along his abdomen. I just wanted to pet it for a bit.

A hazy mumble shocked me out of my secretive thoughts and forbidden touching, and I yanked my hand from beneath his shirt, flush with embarrassment.

87

"Mnhnever pet a husky's stomach… less you want' m' to follow you around forever," Grant said in a drowsy, lazy tone. His drawl seemed to emerge whenever he was half-asleep, as well. He had one blue eye cracked partially open, and was regarding me with a sleepy smile.

"I… that… I wasn't—" I stammered, cursing the fact that I was so terrible at lying. I felt like a child who'd stolen food.

"I didn't say y' had to stop," the man murmured in a low, husky tone.

I probably should have, anyway. I probably should have questioned his lucidity, or mine, considering we were both still mostly asleep. I probably should have done a lot of things.

But instead, I just pushed my palm up entirely beneath the man's shirt, and ran my fingertips through the soft fur along his abdomen, and over the strong contours of his body beneath. The man gave a deep, satisfied sigh, and I'll admit, so did I. I pulled myself in a little closer to him, and we shared a long, drowsy, contented kiss. I'd realized by now I could breathe through my nose when I kissed him, and since that meant I could do it for longer, I fully intended to spend the next—hour or more, if I had my way—doing just that.

For the moment, Grant didn't seem to be putting up any resistance to the idea. I needed to catch him when he was sleepy and uninhibited more often.

I curled my legs through his, and pushed myself close to him in the warmth and comfort of our small, shared space, and things rapidly began to intensify just as they had last night.

Except this time, it was our companions who brought a halt to everything. Inadvertently.

Someone had dropped something, likely a cooking pot, by the sound of it, outside, and the sharp noise brought to focus the other sounds of our friends moving about in camp. I heard Puck's distinctive voice speaking to someone who sounded like Laesom, and one of them chuckled.

It snapped us both back into reality fairly quickly, Grant almost moreso than me. The husky blew out a breath through his nose and disentangled himself somewhat from my legs, stiffly pushing himself up with one hand and running the other through his sleep-tousled fur.

I sighed, and flopped back down onto the bedroll, letting him go. The husky looked down at me sympathetically, before reaching around blindly for something. His vest, as it turned out, and tugging his shirt down with his other hand.

"Like I said last night," he murmured. "Bad idea."

I ran my palms over my face, and nodded. And then I let him get re-dressed, because only one of us could at a time. We'd both slept in most of our clothing, anyway. It didn't make much sense to undress on the trail, for one. For two, that was a line we'd yet to cross.

By the time he'd gotten dressed and equipped for the day and had headed out into the sunlight beyond the tent flap, I knew by the playfully mocking voice that greeted him outside that Ransom was awake. I took a little extra time getting ready for the day, just so I didn't have to be a part of all of that. I brushed my mane, for one. It was in terrible need of it, after the week we'd had. I even took the time to re-braid and re-bead some of the strands, and I washed up a little, as well as I could with my tongue alone. I needed to find a stream.

By the time I'd emerged into camp, things had grown quiet again. The fire was crackling pleasantly, and Puck was leaning over it, pulling some kind of poultice out of a boiling pot. His ears twitched my way as I emerged, and he gave me a friendly smile.

"You slept late," he noted. "Feeling well-rested, at last?"

"At last," I nodded. "I needed it."

I looked up between the rocks when I felt something warm filtering through, and for the first time in nearly a week, I saw blue between the clouds. I smiled to myself.

"The storm is passing. Finally," Puck said with a sigh, as he gingerly handled the hot, grape-leaf wrapped poultice he'd been preparing, opening it and shifting back his cloak, to the two still very obvious puncture wounds along his chest. They looked a lot better than they originally had, but the sight of them still made me cringe.

The fox expertly applied the healing paste over the wounds, his muzzle only twitching now and then as he did so. I would have to commend him later on his tolerance for pain. I'm not sure I'd be able to treat my own wounds the way he was able to.

"How is Ransom doing?" I finally asked the obvious. I'd heard the coyote, but I couldn't see him at the moment. Or either of the other two men, for that matter.

"I'd be fine t' move out today if the fox wasn't bein' such an old biddy about it," the coyote's voice cut through the camp, and I turned. Apparently, he'd been in their tent this whole time. He had the flaps open and was leaning his arm over a knee, regarding me with a cocky smile.

Almost despite myself, I couldn't resist smiling back, "Near-death can't keep you down, I see, Ransom. Same as ever."

"I'm a 'yote, darlin'," the man smirked. "Tough as nails."

"Shut up, you imbecile," Puck muttered. "He almost lost four of his fingers. Don't let him fool you, Shivah. He isn't moving for at least a few days."

"I'll be fine by tomorrah! I'm fine now."

"You are not fine," the fox stated, in a very matter-of-fact, no-nonsense tone. "You're dehydrated, malnourished and recovering from frostbite. And stay under the blanket!"

"How in the bloody hell did you know I took it off?!" the coyote said, disbelievingly.

"Fox magic," Puck muttered sarcastically, focusing his attention on finishing treating his own wounds.

"Y' know, sometimes, I wonder," the coyote muttered, suspiciously, and grabbed at his discarded blanket. But instead of pulling it up, he just pulled it around himself and clambered out of the tent, meandering towards the fire wrapped in it, and getting comfortable on a bundled horse blanket.

I'd noticed immediately that he'd sat right next to the fox. Considering the distance the two men had kept before, even when they were just around me, it was a change worth taking note of.

"So," Ransom muttered, as he reached into a nearby pack which very clearly wasn't his—it looked to be Grant's—and fished around until he pulled out a wax-wrapped hunk of cheese. He gave it a curious sniff for a moment, before shrugging and unwrapping it. I made a mental note to admonish him another time when he wasn't recovering, even though I was fairly certain Grant would have parted with all of his food to the starved coyote if he'd just asked.

"So?" I asked after a few moments, wondering where he'd been going with that. But now he was muzzle-deep in cheese, and apparently enjoying it, because he'd eaten half of it by the time he chose to speak again.

"So," the coyote said at length, after swallowing a particularly large bite, and licking his muzzle. "I'm wonderin' if the husky and I need t' have a little 'talk'."

I just gave him an odd look. "Well that's up to you, I suppose..." I said, confused. The men talked often, so far as I'd ever seen.

"Oh," Puck paused in what he was doing, and wiped his hands, turning his muzzle Ransom's way. "That talk?"

"Thinkin' so."

"They're just sharing a tent because we're short one, Ransom," Puck insisted. "It might be a bit premature for 'that talk'."

"Is this some kind of language barrier?" I asked, frustrated and confused. "Because I don't understand what you're talking about."

Ransom just gave a smirk. "The 'c'mere, boy, and let me tell you how much that girl means t' me' talk. The talk where I'm jes' conveniently cleanin' my rifle the whole while. And Puck's... I dunno, cleanin' his walkin' stick?"

"I don't need to threaten anyone with physical violence," Puck said, deadpan. "I know sixteen different lethal poisons that are both flavorless and odorless."

"Don't you dare!" I said, in sudden realization. "Either of you! Grant doesn't need to be threatened. He's a good man, he'd never treat me poorly."

The two men looked between one another, and Ransom grinned suddenly. I sighed.

"Well, guess we just confirmed that, then," the coyote said with a chuckle, leaning back against the rocks behind him.

I glared at them both. "I never judged the two of you, you know."

"I ain't judgin', darlin'," Ransom replied. "But we are gonna have that talk, now. Less we're already too late."

"Grant's been a perfect gentleman," I assured him, with another glare. "And Puck's right. We're only sharing a tent because we're missing one."

"Right, right," the coyote said with a snort. "I forgot it was you, Shivah. You got that, like… aura surroundin' you where men just don't get laid."

Puquanah, of all people, broke down laughing at Ransom's comment, and I turned to regard him, aghast. He was trying to cover it, to no avail.

"Puck!" I exclaimed, shocked. "How can you laugh at that?!"

"I'm sorry," the fox apologized, between another bout of laughter, trying to cover his muzzle. "It's just so true!"

I pushed myself up and grabbed at my traveling pack, trying not to act too upset by the two men's comments. They were clearly in good spirits, for the first time in a long while, and I ought to be able to take some good-natured teasing. I suppose my presence amongst their group had sort of made their intimate moments together more limited—especially when they'd been hiding it from me.

But the fact was, it was all hitting a little too close to home, considering the events of late, and what had been on my mind since last night.

"Hey, where're you goin'?" Ransom called out mirthfully as I went to put my cloak on.

"Giving you two some privacy," I replied. "And I'm taking my 'aura' with me."

"Shivah!" Puck called out, still chuckling, as I headed out towards the cliff. "I'm sorry I laughed, don't go!"

But I'd stepped out into the open air of the cliff-side I'd been on last night by that point, and in the daylight, the view was breathtaking. I gave a deep sigh and leaned back against the stone face, basking in the sun that was cutting through the clouds, and looking out over the lands splayed below. I could almost see where the edge of the storm had hit, from here, where the snow fall faded off into a mottle of browns and pine green, in forests beyond that had remained untouched.

My palms spread over the rock, running over its solid, ancient surface. And even when I was trying not to, even when I was trying to absorb myself in the beautiful surroundings, I couldn't stop thinking about the night before. About how this very same rock had felt, against my back...

I gave a frustrated noise in the back of my throat, and looked down at my pack. Maybe some breakfast would distract me from my mood, and this line of thought.

I was midway through an unappetizing bite of hard tack when I heard someone approaching from the campsite. By the sound of his footsteps, I knew it had to be Ransom. The fox was much quieter.

I didn't even look up when he moved out into the sun and leaned next to the wall beside me. I heard him resettle his blanket around his shoulders, and he let out a long breath, resting against the rock wall beside me silently for some time, as I finished my breakfast.

"Y' know we didn't mean nothin' by that, right?" the coyote asked at length.

"I know," I confirmed. "Don't worry."

The coyote nodded, clearly just as willing to let the whole thing drop as I was. He was easy like that. But I knew why he was out here. There really wasn't any point in dancing around it.

"How do you get past it?" I murmured, flexing my toes in the moss beneath my feet. Most of the snow up here had already melted, thanks to the afternoon sun. The ground was damp and beginning to reveal the beautiful quilt of mosses and lichens that I'd seen my first time up here.

"I don't know," the coyote admitted. "Forgettin' it didn't work for me. It's always there, even if you convince yourself it ain't. Comes up and bites you whenever y' least expect, like a snake hidin' along the trail. Specially likes t' come up when things remind you of it," he murmured, tipping his muzzle down and dragging in a deep breath through his nose. "And it makes you question a lotta things. Am I doin' this for the wrong reasons? Am I any better than he was? Shit like that."

I looked up to him, narrowing my eyes in concern. "You can't honestly think that, Ransom."

"I do. All the damn time," the coyote admitted, with some difficulty. His muzzle twitched, and he gave an irritated sigh, then spit on the ground beside him. "Am I just th' way I am 'cause of him? Am I just tryin' to make up for all the hell he put me through by doin' it to someone else? Am I really any different than he was? He was my cousin, y' know. My spittin' image. Makes you wonder if it all jes... runs in the family..."

"You can't possibly compare what that man did to you to what you and Puquanah have," I insisted, emphatically.

"Why not?" the coyote countered. "Same basic act."

"Because it's not the act that matters!" I said. "It's the intent! It's your regard for one another."

The coyote looked down at me, meaningfully. "Exactly."

I looked at him a further moment, then turned my gaze out slowly over the vista beyond us. And after a good long while, I gave a sigh.

"So this whole conversation was for my benefit?"

"I don't haf ta' make a point around you, Shivah," Ransom said. "You're better at it. All I gotta do is get you to listen to yourself, sometimes."

"I can't not think about Methoa, whenever..." I murmured, letting my words trail off. I closed my eyes. "I just... it's hard not to be reminded. I don't want what happened before to mix with what's happening now."

"Pushing it away don't work," Ransom said, flatly. "Take my word for it."

I nodded, not questioning the man, or his life experience with denial. "So what does?" I asked.

"I don't rightly know the one answer to that," the coyote said with a sigh. "I'm only just startin', myself. But," he looked to me. "talkin' helped. Felt like vomitin' somethin' really sick inside me up, finally. Like I needed to get it outta me. T' be honest, I already feel a little better."

I knitted my fingers together over my waist, murmuring, "Have you and Puck spoken?" I asked.

"All night," Ransom said, quietly. "But I could never get it out to him, before. I think because I didn't want t' burden him with it. I know how stupid that sounds, but it's like he's been through enough already, you know? It was just this whole new horror he's never had to endure, and I didn't think he'd really understand, or be able to handle it. T' be honest, I didn't feel safe sayin' anythin' to anyone about it... 'til you."

I looked up at him, and realized he was looking down at me.

"Feels safer, somehow," he said quietly, "talkin' about it to someone who's been there."

The corners of my muzzle twitched up into the ghost of a smile, when I realized what he was offering.

"So," the coyote murmured, "you wanna talk?"

Laesom and Grant had apparently decided to go out hunting that day in an attempt to replenish our dwindling food supplies. I highly doubted they'd find much of anything up at these elevations. I suspected it had been an excuse for the two of them to talk.

Yet nonetheless, they returned with a small ground pheasant, some ramps, and an assortment of edible nuts. I had no doubt most of the hunting and gathering had been done by Laesom, but Grant didn't look displeased. Serious, but not displeased, so I hoped it had been a productive day for him, too.

The pheasant shared amongst five people didn't make for much of a meal, but even a little fresh meat was welcome. I stowed the feathers to use as fletching material later. We chose to make a soup out of it, with the ramps, while we all picked at the nuts. I wasn't full when we were done, but I was full enough. And the air amongst our small group was warm and happy. Despite the lean provisions, it was one of the most pleasant meals I'd ever shared.

I knew eventually we were going to have to discuss our path from here. What we were going to do when we headed back towards the Crossroads, what we were going to do about Rourke, Methoa, Shadow, and the rest of the raiders. Though tonight there wasn't any point. I'd learned long ago, on this very mountain in fact, that along the road towards an unknown, it did no good to torture oneself over that unknown. We would find the raiders when we could find them, and we would face them when we could face them. What we needed to do now was rest, recover our strength, and stay warm.

Despite the peaceful atmosphere, I sensed that something very intense had happened between Laesom and Grant. I knew, of course, what he'd wanted to speak to him about. And while I wasn't worried about Grant, (the man had shown himself to be far too resilient against sadness in the past) Laesom's quiet demeanor concerned me some. The wolf had said nothing since he'd returned, and his gaze drifted, often. I knew when someone was lost in memory.

So, when dinner was over and we'd settled in for the night around the fire to talk and relax, and I noticed that Laesom was gone, I went looking for him.

There were very few places near the campsite he could have gone. Our camp was between two enormous rocks, so he either went back out towards the trail, or more likely, to the cliff-side. I guessed the latter, and that proved to be correct.

I found him standing near the edge of the rocky cliff, staring out over the other side of the valley. The wind had picked up tonight and was tossing his long, beaded mane over one of his shoulders. The man's gray fur looked blue in the moonlight, lending him an almost eerie quality, like he was a spirit, or a specter.

I knew he heard me, but other than seeing one of his ears tip back, he didn't regard me at first. And I thought I knew why.

"I understand," I said quietly, not approaching the man just yet. "I understand… how it feels…"

The wolf finally turned to look towards me, his eyes catching in the moonlight. It was hard to really make out his expression. He'd always been a hard man to read.

"I won't judge," I said softly. "I know how painful it is."

The wolf seemed to consider my words for a few moments, before he turned around entirely to address me.

"What do you mean?" he asked, in a level, but curious tone.

I blinked. "Well I just meant…" I stammered, now mortified I might have been wrong. "You were standing very close to the edge."

The wolf tilted his head at me a moment, and then, of all things, he gave a low chuckle. "You have me quite wrong, miss."

"Oh gods, I'm sorry," I said, quickly.

Laesom took a few long-legged strides towards me. The man moved with a certain grace and fluidity to him that I'd only seen with wolves. Even despite his age, that ancient majesty hadn't faded. Many tribes called them 'the old people', because they had been the pioneers of many areas. It was said if a wolf tribe could not prosper somewhere, the land was too wild for any tribe to make their home.

When he came near me, I was forced to recognize just how much larger than me the man was. Aged or no, the wolf was taller than me by a head. He was slim, almost as slim as Ransom, but tall and long-limbed. I'd almost never seen him with a weapon, save an old bow and quiver that he rarely seemed to use, but this close, he was still intimidating.

"Why would you think something like that?" he asked me, softly.

"I just," I stammered, feeling terribly awkward now. "I know what Grant wanted to talk to you about, and h-he told me… about your mate…" I faded off, not really certain what to say. What did I really know? I had a name, and I knew how he had died. But really, I knew very little about this man's story, or his pain. I suppose I had jumped to conclusions a little.

Laesom considered my words silently for a few moments. I hated that I could never tell what the man was thinking. But after a while, he turned to look back out over the cliff, and spoke again.

"Holt's death was hard," he said, quietly. "Harder still because of how it happened. It was painful for me. It still is. The death of someone you love is never easy to endure. He was not the first person I've cared for that I've lost, and I doubt he will be the last."

He turned back towards me.

"But that doesn't mean I wish to die," he stated. And then he gave a mild smile. "Life is a trail, miss… a trail I have been walking for some time. I've been fortunate enough to live a full and eventful life, but just because a man I loved is no longer here doesn't mean my path is at its end. I'll re-join Holt in the next life, as well as many of my loved ones, and other comrades I have lost along the years. It hurts me deeply," he said softly, his gold eyes slipping partially closed, "that I cannot share my remaining years with them. But none of the people I loved were my reason for being alive. They were just a wonderful part of it."

I looked down, suddenly guilty at what my own thoughts had been for so long now. But, those thoughts only led me back to memories of my son. Of his cries, when Methoa had taken him away from me for the last time...

"How do you live with it?" I asked aloud, without even really meaning to.

"You live," Laesom said, simply. "And look ahead. No matter how terrible the road seems, you've nothing to lose by walking it for another day. It all ends eventually, one way or another. No reason to rush. There's always more you can do with the time you have."

As he said that, he looked past me towards the break in the rocks that led back towards our camp. And I soon heard why. Ransom was singing.

I stood in shocked silence, listening to the coyote's distant voice, filtering through the night air, deep and melodic, and steeped in emotion. I wanted to hear what he was singing. The words sounded like the Otherwolf tongue, but I'd learned enough by now that I might be able to make sense of them, if I were closer.

I looked to the wolf, who was just smiling.

"I hope they find some peace together," he murmured, contently.

"We might never have found him without your help," I said, gratefully. "Thank you."

The wolf's eyes moved back to mine, and he nodded. "Always more you can do with the time you have. Take an old man's word."

Laesom chose to remain on the cliff after our short conversation, but I returned to camp. I wanted to listen to Ransom sing.

When I returned to camp, Ransom was seated near the fire, wrapped in his cloak, and leaning up against the dark mountain stone. Puquanah was lying curled up beside him, with his head in his lap. The coyote's hand was threaded gently through the soft fur along the arctic fox's neck, stroking him softly. And he was singing to him.

He looked up briefly when I entered the campsite, but he seemed to be finishing his song. The man gave me a smile when he saw me, but then he returned his attentions to the fox, and he began to sing again.

I sat down beside Grant, who also seemed to be listening, albeit from across the campsite, clearly giving the two their space. When I joined him, he smiled softly to me, and when I sat beside him, he ran a hand gently over my lower back, and held me loosely. We both listened.

From birth
I've known little but pain.
Each footfall I've put on this earth
Takes me farther from ghosts that I've slain.

O'er mountains and rivers, my trail
This path I have beaten alone,
Circles round to the past, without fail.
Ever darker and more overgrown

The mountains can't come between memories.
The rivers can't wash away hurt
And fighting this thicket inside me
Left me broken, face down in the dirt.

But one day our paths crossed ways
And in you I could see the same ache
The same will to forge on in your gaze
But the same beaten path in your wake.

Now I can't say the past don't still pain me.
But in some ways I'm starting to mend.
It ain't that loving you's changed me.
I'm just finally rounding the bend.

We'll claw at the world together.
We'll reap a clear path when we're pressed.
I know our journey can't last forever
But now you'll be there when I rest.

The coyote's voice was haunting, deep, and soulful—just as Puck had always said. It was almost hard to believe he'd had this ability inside him so long, knowing the man that I knew. And yet somehow, it entirely fit him.

By the time he'd finished his last song, and the fox had leaned up to nuzzle him softly against his collarbone, I got the feeling it was time I left the two alone. Grant seemed to realize it as well, and was already collecting his things. We both wished the men a good night and made for our tent, Grant ducking in after I did.

He unshouldered and discarded his coat almost immediately, folding the stiff duster as well as he could and laying it at the foot of our shared bedroll. He got to his knees and undid his gun belt next, setting his weapons aside carefully, while I did the same. The tent really was close quarters for two people, but we'd managed just fine last night.

Ransom had begun another, far lower, deeper song outside by then, and Grant paused as he tugged his chain out of his pocket and set his tarnished locket aside. He gave a somewhat amused smile.

"What?" I asked, curiously. I couldn't make out most of the words in these songs. They were all in Amurescan.

"The coyote's a bit of a romantic, is all," Grant said with a low chuckle. "They're all trail songs, but not the sorts I'd imagined him for."

"What was that one he sung just a few moments ago?" I asked, curiously. It sounded familiar.

"'A Beaten Path'," the husky said, after a moment's thought. "We've played it together before, although he only used the harmonica then. I wish I had my guitar. We'll need to play and sing together once we get back to Crossroads. Man has an astonishing voice. Who'd 've thought?"

I smiled, watching the husky unbutton his vest. When he'd gotten it entirely undone, I crawled forward and helped him tug it over his shoulders and down his arms, a bit of a difficult feat in our short, crowded tent. He glanced back at me, somewhat surprised by the assistance, but didn't object.

"I… had a bit of a talk with Ransom today," I said softly, folding the Otherwolf's vest in my hands and looking down at it, moving my thumbs gently over the foreign, deep blue fabric, and one of the silver buttons. It was so odd, so almost otherworldly, to think I was this close to a man who, a year ago, was from a people as unknown to me as the spirit world. I still tripped over the realization every now and then, trying to put together all the events that had led to my growing close to this foreigner, from his foreign world, so far and so different from everything I knew. But then I'd see him looking at me, and feel perfectly comfortable, moreso than I'd even been around my own people.

I wasn't certain I loved him. And it's not as though I hadn't felt love before. I just… perhaps I hadn't known him long enough. Perhaps we honestly just were too different for one another, or we simply weren't completely compatible. Perhaps in time, we'd mutually discover that. He seemed intent on winning my heart now, but that could change as he came to know me better.

But I did trust him. And I believed that he cared about me. And I knew he'd never hurt me.

"Hmm?" the man hummed back curiously, as he undid the ties on those odd coverings the Otherwolves liked to wear over the arches of their feet. 'Spats', someone had called them. I remembered because it was such an odd word.

Gingerly, I slipped my palms up his back, then looped them loosely around his waist, and leaned my muzzle against the back of his neck. That seemed to get his attention rather

102

quickly. He turned, shifting one arm to collect me against his side, and looked down on me, concerned.

"Shivah?" he murmured, running his thumb over my cheek. "What's wrong?"

I dropped my cheek to his chest, my voice slightly muffled when I spoke. "I've had," I murmured, "a lot of confusion about men, for a long time now. If I'm being honest, probably my entire life. So much of what I was supposed to do… what I was told… is just so at odds with what feels like it should be."

Grant gave a soft sigh, and pulled me in a little tighter. "Shivah, I'm sorry," he began to say. "Is this because of last night? I didn't mean to bring all of this up—"

"No," I insisted, looking up to him. "No, I'm glad you did."

The husky blinked down at me, confused.

"Everything I thought I knew was wrong," I said, letting out a breath on the last word. "I thought being married, I'd learned all there was to know about belonging to a man."

Grant got an oddly angry look at that. "You never belonged to him, Shivah. And he certainly didn't deserve a woman like you."

I couldn't help the playful retort. "And you do?" I asked, with half a smile.

"Well," the husky stammered, "I'm working on it."

I gave a breathless laugh. "You're doing well," I assured the man, which earned me a smile. "But I-I was so… I don't know, afraid of you, for a while. I treated you far worse than I would have most other men."

"Why?" Grant asked, bewildered. "I mean, not to say you weren't warranted. You were understandably defensive when we first met, and I've never questioned why. We didn't know one another well, but…" his ears actually drooped somewhat, "Why did I scare you?"

"Because I was attracted to you," I admitted, with a soft sigh.

The man's brows came together at that, and a hopeful smile tugged at the corners of his muzzle. It was such an innocent expression, I wanted to kiss him right there and then.

"But that was the problem," I murmured, almost ashamed of myself at the admission. "I didn't want to be. Even when you'd given me no reason to be cruel to you, it was just frustrating to me, and I took it out on you. I don't know how to put together being attracted to a man with my past experiences." I shook my head. "It's like trying to convince myself night isn't dark. Everything with Methoa was so terrible. I thought I'd have to contend with all of that, just to enjoy the good parts with you."

"I would never—" Grant gave a frustrated noise, then averted his eyes, clearly trying to subdue his irritation and anger. "I'm sorry," he said quickly, "I'm not angry at you. I'm angry at this man. I swear to God, when we find him, I'm personally saving a bullet for him. I don't know if this is an insensitive thing to say, but I don't care if your traditions allowed him to do what he did. Men who treat women like refuse, who hurt women, deserve the gallows."

He took a deep breath, and looked down, eyes distant. "Knowing there are men in the world like that makes me frightened for my sisters."

I gave him a sympathetic look, and rubbed his shoulder. "Well, the oath of vengeance is very sweet of you, but I don't need a man defending my honor," I said, with a mildly amused smile. "I'd rather do that myself. But anyway, that isn't entirely what I meant. I never thought you'd hurt me just because he did, Grant. I know you're a better man than that."

"Then," he paused, "I don't understand—"

"The," I paused, awkwardly, "the physical parts. I can handle myself in almost every other walk of life. I'm fairly certain I could even kill you, if I had to defend myself. You're clumsy, and I'm faster than you."

The husky cleared his throat. "Comforting..." he muttered.

"The mating, Grant," I finally managed to say. I don't know why it had been so hard to get out. "That part."

The husky tipped his ears back. "Oh," he murmured, after a few moments. But then he just got a stern expression, looking

104

to me. "Shivah, that's not… " he sighed, running a paw up over his head and scratching at the back of his neck, squinting his eyes closed for a moment like he was considering something very difficult. "I mean, I hesitate to say I'd want to go forever without—"

"The fact that you can even try to say that after last night is admirable," I said with a soft chuckle.

The man gave me a measured expression, before letting out a breath he'd been holding. "It's not as though a man can't control himself, Shivah. And any who tell you that are lying. Any man with a shred of decency can stop himself from doing something indecent. I could tell last night that… We'd gone too far," he said softly. "So I stopped. I'd wait years for you. I'd wait until we could find a priest to marry us, under whatever god will have us, if that's what you wanted. But I have to be honest… a lifetime?" He sighed. "I-I don't know. That might have to be another one of those things we figure out in time. But I understand why it frightens you. I want you to know that."

I nodded, turning my muzzle into the worn cotton of his shirt. "I liked kissing you." I said quietly.

He smiled affectionately down at me, and ran his fingers through my freshly-brushed mane. "I enjoyed that, as well. Immensely."

"But it leads to, well…" I murmured against his chest, "It leads to what nearly happened, last night."

"You don't even know how nearly," the husky said with a sigh.

"I could tell," I pointed out. "Trust me."

The husky looked away, guiltily. "Well kissing doesn't have to—we got unusually carried away, Shivah."

"I didn't want to stop," I admitted.

The husky looked down at me like I was stepping on his tail.

"That's what's been so confusing for me," I murmured, slipping in closer against him and moving a hand up his chest, near where I had my cheek pressed against him. I felt his chest move reflexively against my touch. "I thought," I spoke softly, "if I wanted to be affectionate with a man like that, I'd have to just endure the part afterwards, for his sake. And I'm fond of you, but I was afraid that bit might ruin it all."

"Shivah," the man said, stroking my head softly, "I know your experiences have been poor, but it's not supposed to be unpleasant. It's not supposed to be something you endure."

"That's one of the things Ransom and I talked about," I said, feeling less awkward about admitting it than I thought I would. Honestly, the talk with the coyote had quite possibly been the most relieving, most informative half hour I'd ever spent in conversation with anyone about the subject of my marriage bed. The man had listened to me. Really, just let me talk. And then he'd dispelled every single thing I'd ever been taught wrong, matter-of-factly, and without ceremony. His bluntness and willingness to listen to my experiences, all without mockery or judgment, had been so enlightening, it had made me angry about all the lies I'd been told in the past, and all the gaps my own parents had left.

Everything made so much more sense, now. How I could ever want for something now that, in the past had been so horrible, had always confused me. Ransom had compared it to living on a diet of spoiled food one's entire life, only to realize there were other meals to be had that wouldn't poison you. He'd said, when he'd found Puck, it was like realizing he didn't have to eat poison, just because he was hungry. It was an odd metaphor, but it made a strange kind of sense.

Methoa had been poison. Methoa had hurt me. But this could be done right, provided the coyote had been right about all of this. But there was really only one way to test that.

"Oh," the husky murmured uncertainly, like he wasn't certain whether or not that was a good thing. "Well," he said at length, "did talking about it help, any?"

"Immensely," I said with a nod. Then, considering something, I looked up to him and asked, "Would you have preferred I come to you?" That actually hadn't even occurred to me.

"Honestly, Shivah," Grant replied, "it doesn't matter to me whether it's me or someone else you trust. I'm just glad you were comfortable enough to talk to someone. I know you and the coyote have shared a lot..." he cleared his throat, "and I'm not particularly worried he'll steal you away from me."

I chuckled.

"So if he was able to help you, I'm glad," the man said with a soft smile. "I probably would have been awkward, and fumbling over every other word, and not much help. I'm decent at running, riding, and shooting... and not much else. Especially not deep-thinking like this."

"I think I've done enough thinking today," I said with a breathy chuckle against his chest.

"Agreed," the husky murmured, likely referring to his own talks with Laesom. He hadn't spoken about what they'd said yet, so I could only assume it was not meant for my ears. And that was fine. It was personal to them, just as my conversation with Ransom had been personal to us, and I'd learned about all I'd ever need to know about the wolf's lover, (and life in general) from the wolf already, tonight. I'd learned a lot today.

"Are you going to be alright?" Grant asked gently, leaning down to brush my ear with his muzzle.

"I'll be fine," I replied with a soft purr. I nuzzled up under the man's chin, and felt him give a content groan in the back of his throat at the gesture of affection. He just really seemed to love it when I purred.

"That's all I needed to know, then," Grant murmured peacefully. "We'll figure everything else out as we go."

He finally leaned down and kissed me at that, and I pressed up into his muzzle, happily returning the gesture. I curled my arms around the man's broad shoulders, pushing my fingers softly through the fur along the ruff of his neck with one hand, while the other just held tightly to his cotton shirt. He moved his muzzle softly against mine, and we teased one another for a little while, drinking in the moment in blissful ignorance of the time passing by.

I honestly wasn't certain how long we just kissed one another like that, but at some point, the husky let his body slump back into the bedroll, and I was all too happy to follow suit, atop him. He loosely wrapped his arms around my waist, one of his broad palms rubbing gently at my lower back, as our legs entwined.

We could have lain there, sharing soft affections late into the night, but he felt so warm, so solid, so good beneath me—I was feeling emboldened.

I decided to be the first to lick softly at his muzzle this time. He was all too eager to return the gesture, and before long, I was tasting him again, and he I, and we were sharing long, deep kisses that quite literally stole my breath away.

I inhaled his scent and trapped it inside my memories, wanting to remember him, just as he was now, on this night, for as long as my mind would serve me. He smelled like the mountain, like snow and fresh earth from the trail, and the scent of the both of us was beginning to co-mingle in his fur, and I loved that.

But most of all, I loved that he didn't smell like my husband. Methoa's scent was always strongest when he brought me to our marriage hut to perform my marital duties, and nothing had stuck in my mind more than the smell of him. I'd thought then that it was just the smell of men. But it wasn't. Just like his cruelty, it was unique to him, and something Grant didn't share.

I wasn't really certain how far I was going to let this go, tonight, but I still didn't want to stop, and I was just trying to trust in what felt right. That was another one of the things Ransom had said. All of this felt very right—extremely right.

I ran a hand slowly down the man's chest as we slipped our tongues over one another's, and gods, his was so smooth... how did he clean himself? But it felt amazing against my muzzle, and I knew I wanted more than that, but I wasn't really certain what or how. So I moved my own muzzle down to his neck, and rushed into the barrier we'd hit last time, gently lathing at him where I could feel his pulse beneath my tongue.

Amongst felines, licking one another was just how we showed affection, and how we cleaned each other, and ourselves. But it did something to Grant. The man gave a rumbling, almost helpless-sounding growl and tipped his head back, letting me do as I pleased without stopping me, this time. I nipped softly at him and ran my paws up over his shoulders, nuzzling up beneath his ear, before nipping at it, as well.

I wasn't even certain why I was doing what I was doing. I just wanted to, and he was letting me. He was enjoying it, as far as I could tell, so I let any concerns I'd had drift back into the haze of contentment being with him brought on, and just let go.

The man tried to kiss me every now and then, and I let him, but the first time he returned my own gestures, I got a taste of what I'd been doing to him, and it was nothing like just casual grooming, or casual affection. I wasn't certain what made it so much different right now, with him, but it was different.

His muzzle pressed into my neck, pushing up beneath locks of my mane. I felt his canines there for a moment, and it almost frightened me, but then he was just lathing that broad tongue against me, softly, and nuzzling at the sensitive edge of my ears, his breath making them twitch and quiver. I couldn't even explain how it made me feel. It made warmth blossom down my body, it made me feel too hot for my skin. I felt heavy, like I wanted to push closer to him somehow, even though that was practically impossible.

One thing I knew for certain was that I wanted to touch more of him. Enough of this.

I gasped against his chest, and suddenly pushed myself up from him, looking down into the bemused husky's far-too-blue eyes.

"I am tired of your shirt," I announced, matter-of-factly.

"What…" the man looked up at me, hazy and lost, "What now? What do you have against my shirt, exactly?"

I rolled my eyes, and just slid my hips down his body so that I could reach the edge of the offending garment, and began tugging it free from the waistline of his pants.

"Oh. Oh," Grant said, in realization. He got that look like he was going to object, even if he wasn't fighting my efforts just yet. He also wasn't helping, and I knew I'd never get this thing off of him if he didn't get up, at least a bit. "Shivah, we still shouldn't—your companions are right outside—" he whispered, desperately.

I didn't want to take the time to explain to the man what my plans were, so I just brought out the lure. "Yours comes off, mine comes off," I stated simply, sitting up and crossing my arms over my chest. And I waited.

It didn't take him very long to decide. Apparently the man's convictions weren't as ironclad as he'd led me to believe, when inducement came into play. He shifted up into a mostly sitting position. I still had his legs pinned, after all, and there really wasn't any room for me to move. He tugged the worn, white cotton shirt up over his head, over the thick musculature in his shoulders and arms, and tossed it aside. And made me a very, very happy cat.

He was good enough not to look at me expectantly when I stalled, but I wasn't stalling because I was hesitant to fulfill my promise. I just really wanted to look at him.

But at length, I remembered myself, and tugged the old shirt I wore beneath my leathers up over my head, with very little ceremony. It was an old shirt of Ransom's I'd taken apart and managed to cut down to make smaller for myself. All I really used it for was to wear it beneath my leathers (and only sometimes, like when it was very cold) and to sleep in.

And I hadn't wrapped my chest today.

Grant let out a breath I hadn't realized he'd been holding, and I glanced aside for only a moment, trying to fight back those familiar pangs of fear that came from being exposed.

110

This wasn't the same as then. I'd chosen this. This wasn't the same as then.

The husky gently pressed his muzzle into the fur along my clavicle, and wrapped his arms around my waist, tugging me slowly back against him. His ears tipped back, and he gave a long, shuddering breath against my chest.

I ran a hand over the top of his head, down his neck, and stroked him gently at the base of his ears. "Are you alright?" I asked at length. He'd yet to do anything other than press his muzzle against my chest.

"Mnnnhhhh…" was his only response, uttered somehow between a contented groan and a growl.

I almost giggled, and that was saying something. I never giggled. I smiled, stroking his ears softly in both hands now, while he ran his broad paws gently over my hips, and up my lower back. I decided immediately that I liked it when he touched me, too.

"I had no idea your chest was spotted, too," the man admitted, nosing softly along my breastbone. "God, you're beautiful."

I wasn't really certain how to compliment a man, so I didn't. But in any case, I doubted Grant needed me to. The man had always seemed well aware that he was attractive. It rather went without saying. But in all honesty, though his looks had initially caught my attention, they'd been, if anything, more a detriment to his pursuit of me than anything else. The Otherwolf's immaculate grooming, exotic pelt and striking eyes only served to point out how very different we were, and reinforced the distance I tried to keep from him.

If there was one thing I took a secretive, almost lurid pleasure in, it was the very thing that had made kissing him so difficult that night on the cliff. I liked that Grant was a much larger person than I was. I liked it, because despite it, I knew I could still conquer him.

I wasn't too proud to admit it to myself, either. It made me feel confident, empowered, nothing to be guilty over. I'd be lying to myself if I said my attraction to a man who deferred to me the way Grant always had didn't have a lot to do with my previous experiences. But I emphatically did not want to think about Methoa right now. And besides, with the exception of the brief chat I'd had with Ransom, I couldn't really be the one to lead, tonight. I was still hoping he'd know more than I. I had a better idea now, but still…

The husky had lowered himself down onto his back again, since he could barely stoop in a sitting position in our small tent, and I hesitantly followed suit, stretching out lithely atop him and trying to act confident, all while continuously reminding myself not to panic about the fact that I was bare from the waist-up. This wasn't like before.

At the very least, I didn't seem to have to worry about acting alluring, or whatever it was caught the interest of men. I couldn't even begin to guess at what Otherwolves found attractive, save those horrific 'bodices' I'd seen at the Cock and Barrel. Amongst my tribe, it was our manes, and our obvious, more womanly assets.

I had no idea what it was that enticed Grant, but apparently, I was doing it right. Or it was just me. Aside the fact that the man had been pursuing me since he'd met me, there were other more obvious signs of his physical desire, pressed up against my belly. And this wasn't the first time I'd felt the man's desire to mate against me. I think he thought he'd gotten away with that night on the mountain, a month ago. He hadn't, but I'd let him keep thinking he had.

The husky still had his muzzle pressed into the soft fur along my chest, and was nosing at me, gently. The male fascination with a woman's chest was, I suppose, something that remained, regardless of species. Mine was unimpressive, to say the least, but I didn't care if he didn't. It made it easier to bind for archery.

I ran my own paws softly down the Otherwolf's exposed chest, exploring the man's strong anatomy beneath all that soft fur. I loved that he wasn't all hard planes and unforgiving,

112

dense sinew. He was clearly an active man, but his body still had give, possibly just because he was still young, or ate better than my husband had. I felt like I wanted to melt into him, or feel him over me. I hated that I was still thinking of Methoa, though. How did I make that stop?

The husky did the trick entirely unintentionally, when his muzzle moved to the peak of one of my breasts, and he lapped it gently with his tongue. I forced my muzzle shut when the steady purr I'd been affording the man for his ministrations became a gasp. I gripped at the canine's hip, perhaps a bit too tightly, and muffled myself by pushing my muzzle into the fur along the back of his neck.

The man curled his thick arms around my midsection and held me, running his hands slowly up and down my back, and over my hips. He set to teasing my chest the same as he had my neck, and I just tried to focus on being quiet, but gods, it was hard. What was he doing to me? It was such an odd thing to do, and I'd have called him strange if he'd told me he was going to do it before he had. But the sensations he was causing were just making things rush inside me. That's the best way I could think to describe it.

Of course, that statement suggested I was thinking at all at the moment. And I couldn't. I was trying at least to remember where I was, and that my companions were right outside, but...

But my body was pressing into his, fur to fur, and I could feel the contours of his abdomen, and his waist, against mine. And his claws were moving over my spine, joining the shudders he was causing with his tongue, and I just wanted—I just wanted.

I nuzzled his neck, helplessly, trying to communicate how I was feeling somehow. But I just didn't know how. So I let my instincts do as they willed, instead, and I arched my back, pressing my chest wantonly against his muzzle, and rubbing my hips to his.

The man gave a deep groan that broke into a low whine, and his muzzle parted from my chest long enough for him to breathe hotly against it, "Nnhhh… Holy hell! We need to stop, love, this is going too far…"

I leaned down and recaptured his muzzle against mine, sharing a long, deep kiss, before whispering back, in a tone that didn't invite an argument. "We aren't stopping."

The husky gave a frustrated groan, and nuzzled me with a desperate sigh. "Shivah, I want to give you this if it's what you want, but I mean we literally can't. There just isn't enough bloody room. I'm afraid I'd knock over one of the tent poles, or bring the whole thing down. And they will hear us."

"I've seen them doing worse," I assured the man, with a huff, ignoring his arched eyebrow and the mild look of horror that followed. I'd tell him about shooting Ransom some other day, when it would be less mood-ruining. "Besides," I continued, "I didn't intend that. I-I…" I gave a soft sigh.

The husky looked at me, expectantly.

"I was hoping you'd just know what to do," I admitted, at length. "This is embarrassing."

"Never be embarrassed around me, Shivah," the husky said softly, running his hands up my back again. I shivered.

I gave another long sigh, trying to remember the brief conversation I'd had with Ransom on the subject of how I'd been feeling lately.

"You make me feel very warm. And coiled up," I said. "Frustrated. Ransom said that's normal, and you can feel better, if you're affectionate to one another. Without mating. Just… touching."

The husky blinked at me in what I thought was confusion for a few moments, and I began to panic. But then he spoke, in the tone one used when they'd come to realize something.

"You want to just fool around?" He asked, sounding as though he wanted to be certain.

"Yes?" I answered, uncertainly.

The Otherwolf gave a sort of lopsided smile, but he put a hand up, hesitantly. "You're certain? I honestly thought you'd be a much more traditional girl. But…"

114

I gave a ragged sigh. "I'm tired of feeling frustrated around you, Grant."

"You and I both."

I gave a hopeful twitch of my tail. "So you… know what he was talking about?"

"Sweetheart, I'm from the slums," Grant said in a rare moment of drawl. "I'm no choir boy. I just put on a good act." He glanced around us for a moment, then leaned back on his elbows.

"Enough room?" I asked, unable to gauge for myself. What little Ransom had told me could be accomplished just as we were now. Very little movement necessary.

"More than enough," he confirmed with a smirk, before dropping his brows in a moment of seriousness. "Are you—"

"Stop asking for permission," I insisted. "It's getting old. I'm willing. Wanting, even. Stop stalling."

"Yes ma'am," the man responded, in a far lower tone. And then, quite suddenly, he rolled me over.

It came so suddenly, I wouldn't have been able to fight back if I'd wanted to, and that was probably for the best. Being put under a man was one of the moments I'd most worried would cause me to panic. But it had come and gone, and I felt alright. Briefly a bit wary, but the memories were nipping at me less and less, tonight. Grant's presence was just too calming to frighten me.

Especially since he kissed me again, as soon as he was above me. And the way he held himself over me, without putting his weight on me, reminded me that he was actually concerned for me. Even if I sort of wanted to feel him atop me a bit more right now.

There was a secondary purpose, though, which I soon felt. His paw was moving softly down over my chest, and one of my hips. He was holding himself over me so that he could touch me. And I wasn't going to argue with that. His thumb ran softly over my belly, and circled gently over the arch of one of my hip bones. The way he touched me when we were like this

115

was so light. It wasn't like anything I'd ever felt before. It made my fur stand on end wherever he touched, in the best of ways, prickling at my skin and causing me to shiver. And that only intensified when his muzzle found my chest again. The combination of both sensations were a little overwhelming, actually.

And none of this was helping my frustration. It was just making that inner tension worse.

"Grant…" I panted softly.

The Otherwolf didn't stop, but he did lift his muzzle enough to speak, against my stomach, as his paw slipped down to the hem of my britches. He ran a claw gently beneath the edge, pausing where my lower belly sloped down to the dip between my legs. I tried not to flinch, but I did, my legs closing inward some.

"Trust me?" The man asked in a soft tone.

I nodded, because it was hard to say 'yes'. But I wanted to.

He leaned up to kiss me again, and I tried to focus on it, to distract me from the fact that he'd undone the tie on my britches. He spent a good deal of time just running his pawpads softly over my lower belly, and then gingerly stroking them down between my legs, over the cloth still covering me there.

Even with my clothing still on, feeling the man's touch there was startling, but not entirely in a bad way. There was that familiar rush of memory, amplified in that one moment because of where he was touching me, but similarly, I was able to remind myself that I wanted this… because of where he was touching me.

After a few moment spent reminding myself that I was strong, that he wasn't Methoa, that this was different, I was able to focus on other aspects of it. Like the fact that, for the first time, I didn't actually mind being pet there. It could just be like any other touching we did—like being stroked anywhere else.

Trying to assure myself of that was rapidly proving fruitless, though, because even if this wasn't like it had been with Methoa, it also most certainly was not like being stroked on the head, or even how being touched on my chest had felt. The paw pads along the man's fingers were only rubbing at me through the cloth, but even this way, I wanted to press up into his touch. The soft pressure, the slight friction he was causing. I wanted more of it, and I couldn't even say why.

And my clothing was rapidly getting ruined. I didn't want to mention it, but I knew the man could smell my arousal, if not feel it by now. I was trying not to be embarrassed, and trying not to look. But eventually, I did. I wanted to see how he was regarding me right now. I guess I sort of needed the assurance.

The husky was nuzzling at my chest again, softly, and much to my relief, he actually looked extremely pleased. Almost drunkenly content, actually.

He finally hooked both hands in the hem of my britches, and made it clear he meant to remove them. I did what little I could to help from beneath him, lifting my hips so he could slide the final garment off of me.

"God help me. You're not wearing anything beneath those, are you?" the husky said with a hitched breath, as he dragged them slowly down my legs.

"N-no... Why would I?" I queried, uncertainly. "They cover everything I need covered."

The man just gave a throaty, ragged noise in the back of his throat at that, which I took as an agreement of some sort. But then his muzzle had found my chest again, and he was far more hungrily setting to task there. And gods, I could get used to that tongue.

When he slid a paw-pad down towards my nethers this time, I parted my legs just a bit for him, because I knew it was coming, and I wanted it more than anything else right now. And then he was touching me, and I wildly clung to his shoulders, holding fast, because I hadn't been prepared for how it was really going to feel.

"Calm down..." the man murmured softly against the nape of my neck, nuzzling into me gently as he stroked me along my crease, and gave a soft rumble of approval. Then a moment later, a soft chuckle. "You really have been wanting. "

"How... What are you doing?" I tried to ask, between soft pants.

"Very little, actually," the husky remarked with a mildly amused smile, "You're going to spoil me, if this is all it takes..."

I crooned softly and pressed my hips up into his touch, and he briefly slipped one of his thick fingers deeper inside me. I squeezed my eyes shut, forcing back the urge to wrap my legs around him and force him to do that again, as much as I wanted to. I had to keep reminding myself that he knew what he was doing.

But if he did, why was he teasing me like this? I didn't want him to stop, not exactly, but every second of this was making that tension coil tighter inside of me... making it worse. And yet, I wanted it. Frustrating though it was, it felt so damn good. Like the pleasure I got from taking a deep breath, being touched and feeling loved, all at once. My heart was literally pounding. I could hear my pulse in my ears, quickening, and my body was quivering in eagerness for every new stroke of those pawpads.

I almost hadn't realized he'd been lapping softly at my chest again, but the combination was just beginning to prove over-whelming when his muzzle parted from me, his touch against my nethers stilled, and I had a brief reprieve. I used the chance to catch my breath, dragging the air in and out of my lungs and wondering when my body would similarly have a chance to exhale. And then things got strange, but just outright wonderful.

If he'd told me in advance, I probably would have balked. But he'd asked me to trust him, and I had, and perhaps wisely, he hadn't warned me this time. I'd enjoyed his tongue on my own, had enjoyed it even on my chest, so I should have expected it below as well, but I really, really didn't.

The first long, soft, hot lathe against my nethers nearly made me kick the tent... or him. But he was holding me down by the thighs, and saved us both the humiliation. I threw my forearm up over my muzzle to muffle the cry bubbling up in my throat, and nearly bit into my own skin to keep quiet. His paws slackened their grip on me and ran softly down my thighs after my first, panicked reaction had passed. One of his paws slid down my shuddering calf and stroked down the length of one of my paws, his touch calming my nerves wherever it lingered.

No calm would stick, though. I was past overwhelmed. I was euphoric, and going mad, all at once. Every hot, soft lap was blissful torture. I didn't understand what he was doing to me or how, but I felt like I couldn't possibly survive it much longer. And despite that, the last thing in the world I wanted was for it to end.

I sucked in a breath, as something inside me shifted, and everything just sort of rushed together. It was like a culmination of every moment of frustration and pleasure we'd shared so far just snapped together into place, finally. And finally at long last I had my relief. And I had never known such relief.

I gave a soft, breathless cry into the night air, which I could only hope later my companions had somehow—impossibly— not heard. And Grant gave an answering noise of satisfaction, although his more resembled a possessive growl.

In the wake of it all, I forgot to breathe for a good long while. I arched my back, rolling my hips up into the Other-wolf's final, gentle nuzzle against my nethers with an utterly contented purr. I was barely conscious for a good long while following that, all of the overwhelming sensations and realizations that came along with them blending together into a pleasant blur.

It was hard not to feel like this was some kind of a victory. My competitive side, at least, chose to see it as one. Whatever it was that had just happened between Grant and I, I felt certain it would forever mark a change in how I felt about exposing myself to a man this way. Like the very first time I'd struck a target with my arrow. The past had all been wrong. This was right.

I felt Grant shift back up over me, and lay to the side of me. My legs were still somewhat entangled with his and I liked it that way. I felt strangely weak and hazy, but it wasn't exactly unpleasant, just strange. And I didn't mind being vulnerable beside him, right now.

"I like fooling around," I said finally, when I was at last able to speak.

Grant outright laughed, then spread an arm slightly to the side and bowed his head, managing to look gallant despite his tousled fur and one partially flopped-over ear. "My experience in sinful behavior is at your full disposal," he said with a hazy-eyed smirk. "You've at last hit on one other thing I'm good at. It's a minor skill, but…"

I shifted to my side and lazily curled my arms up over his shoulders, leaning up and kissing him softly for a good long while. When I at last pulled back, I murmured quietly, "It wasn't minor to me."

The husky gave a very genuine smile, and kissed me again. And I pressed myself in close to him, wanting to be as close to him as possible in that moment, which served to remind me of something.

For one, he was still partially dressed. For two, well…

My own urgency had finally begun to fade, and that was immensely relieving. But also emboldening. I felt less panicked. Less harried. And increasingly, my fear was being replaced with curiosity.

Gingerly, because my experiences in the past were limited to being thrust down beneath a man and closing my eyes until it was over, and I didn't really know what to do besides that. I ran my paw down the husky's hip, and spread my palm over his lower abdominals, stroking the soft fur there for a time. He didn't seem to realize my intent at first, just closed his eyes partway and gave a soft rumble, his tail thumping once or twice against the bedroll.

Eventually, though, I worked up the courage to run my thumb down the hard ridge between his legs, still trapped by the constraints of his riding pants.

The Otherwolf gave a heady growl, and took a deep breath, murmuring in a thick tone, "Shivah. I'm not going to tell you to stop, but please, I'm begging you..." he gave an almost hoarse whuff, his hips shuddering. "Don't start this unless you intend to finish it," he pleaded. "Please."

I set my jaw, and said nothing. Instead, I just reached down and unbuttoned his trousers. I was thankful it was a simple button, I wasn't really good with Otherwolf clothes.

The man shifted at that, and reached down to finish the job himself, unbuttoning another strap over his tail that kept the trousers held closed over it. He rolled onto his back to kick off the dusty, weathered riding pants himself, giving a long sigh when he was finally free of them. Last came the smallclothes... a sort of undergarment male Otherwolves... and occasionally Ransom... chose to wear. I guess for men, especially men who rode, a bit more protection was necessary.

I put my paws over his when he began to tug his underclothes off. I wanted to remove that last layer between us. I'm not certain why. But he seemed to sense it was important to me, and withdrew his hands, allowing me the privilege of pulling the thin cotton down his hips.

I took a nervous breath when I saw the whole of him. On one hand, it felt like I was completing something, seeing him entirely uncovered. I'd wanted to for some time, if I was being honest with myself. And it's not as though I hadn't seen a nude man since Methoa. Puck and Ransom were both fairly shameless about being naked. It had never bothered me.

But Grant wasn't just nude, he was aroused. Because of me. The fact that I'd affected this change in him was simultaneously flattering and intimidating. And despite all of my bravado, this was the point where the fear really hit me. It's not that Grant frightened me. It's not even that I was really thinking of Methoa specifically anymore. It's just that...

If there were a crude analogy for it, this one part of a man's body was the weapon that had been used to hurt me, so many times in the past. And if one thought of it as a weapon, Grant was better armed. But I was only touching him, now. And I was suddenly grateful for that, because I wasn't certain I'd have been able to do any more, had we had the opportunity tonight.

The husky watched me, quietly, but intensely. His blue eyes were sharp, almost hungry... I was almost afraid I was going to do something wrong, until he spoke. And as always, he alleviated my fears.

"Relax, love..." he murmured softly, reaching down to run a paw up over my head and through my mane. "You need some help?"

I was glad at least that he didn't ask me again if I was certain about this. But I nodded eventually in answer to his question, and he slipped a paw down to mine to move it slowly up his thigh towards where his length rested against his stomach. When I reached it, I ran my pawpads softly up from the edge of his surprisingly soft sheath to the thick, warmer pink flesh of his root itself, which was pushed—I could only hope—almost entirely free, by now.

I shifted forward curiously, watching him as I slipped my hand entirely around him. The husky's blue eyes, bright somehow even in the dark, slipped almost entirely closed. He blinked heavily, visibly fighting back a growl and letting it boil down into a soft whine as I ran my thumb up over his tip. He showed me just enough of what to do with one guiding hand, it seemed fairly simple, before letting his hand, and consequently his head, fall back onto the bedroll.

And then I was on my own. But there was nothing frightening about this. If anything, I was intrigued. Every little touch, every small motion of my paw, made the man shudder and whine, everything I did evoked a surprising response. When I somewhat timidly ran my thumb and forefinger beneath his length, to the soft, round sack of fur beneath, he gave a particularly vulnerable-sounding noise, and I didn't fight back the amused smile that tugged at my muzzle.

I rolled to the side of him, so that I could more easily touch him. I nuzzled up beneath the Otherwolf's chin and purred, contently, and he gave an answering half-groan, half-growl. I felt his hips push a bit against my hand, and I smiled against his collarbone as I took a better hold of him, and did as he'd shown me. It honestly made a lot of sense, when I stopped to think about it. All of this was just mimicking what we'd eventually do when we mated, so it probably felt similar.

Well, what he'd done to me had felt in no way similar to how mating had ever felt to me. But I'd yet to mate with him, so maybe—maybe that's what it was supposed to feel like.

The Otherwolf uttered a word I wasn't familiar with, but it sounded like something profane Ransom had said several times in the past. He was thickening in my palm, and I could feel his pulse. I wondered if what he was feeling was similar to what I'd been feeling. I wished, momentarily, that I was able to be as good at this as he, but then he gave a whuff of a groan, and mumbled in a feverish exhalation, "Ain't gonna take much more, t'night. God…"

"But I haven't done the second part yet," I stated, confused. Was he trying to tell me it was time to move on? We needed to have a long talk about this, when we were done. I didn't like that I didn't know what to do, or when, or really how… Maybe I'd talk to Ransom again. Get the coyote to be more specific.

"Huh… ?" Was all I got out of Grant, his voice muffled somewhat from having his muzzle pressed into my mane.

Well I was an independent woman. I'd figure it out on my own.

I shifted, stilling my paw on him, and slipping down the large Otherwolf's body. I heard him giving a confused groan, and felt his eyes following me. He seemed to realize my intent eventually, and gave a sudden huff of realization. "Shivah, you shouldn—"

But at that point I lapped at him gently for the first time, and the man's body tensed and arched back into the bedroll beneath me, and he uttered, "Mother of God!" and gripped at whatever his large paws could find, which ended up being his discarded duster, and my shoulder.

I'd been somewhat concerned a feline tongue might be different for him, but after all, I used it to clean myself, so I'd known at the very least that it wouldn't hurt. Still, I went gently, and that seemed to have been a wise decision, because the smallest lathe was making the man whine like a pup. Again, I didn't fight back a soft smile, I just leaned forward to take hold of him somewhat, and renewed my efforts. I didn't really know how to do what he'd done, so I just licked. His musk was stronger here, and I rather enjoyed that fact, truth be told. It only served to remind me, again and again, how different he was from what had come before.

He kept to his word, though, intentionally or no. I'd not been at it very long before I felt his body, and most especially his abdominals, tense beneath me, and the man gave a strangled groan and spilled on his own stomach. It was impossible for me to entirely avoid it, but I didn't so much mind… I was more distracted by the odd bulge at the base of his root that had slipped free of his sheath near the end. I ran my fingers over it, gently, feeling the contours of the canine's anatomy just to assuage my curiosity.

Well, every species was different, I suppose. It wasn't so far from what I knew that it was bizarre, but it was definitely interesting.

"Nnhhhuhhhhh…" the husky groaned, helplessly, his body still shuddering from time to time, as I stroked up his length with my thumb and forefinger. How exactly was this going to go back in with the bulge there?

The man gave a long, deep, shuddering sigh, and let it out, closing his eyes and letting his head flop down onto the bedroll with a heavy thud. I remembered that feeling. I smiled and gave him a final lick to clean his tip that made him twitch. He'd have to handle what he did to his fur. That was a little much for me.

His hand lazily moved up over my head and stroked down through my mane, and I shifted up, lying my cheek against his chest. I didn't want to interrupt his moment of peace. The man looked so content. But eventually, I had to ask.

"Are you alright?" I murmured, inquisitively.

The man nodded, still not opening his eyes, taking another long, deep breath. "I am very, very alright," he confirmed, his voice thick and heavy.

I was silent for a little while, running my paw over the man's chest in a small circle, trying not to seem impatient.

"When can we do that again?" I finally asked.

The Otherwolf just gave a breathless laugh.

CHAPTER FOUR
Some Measure of Justice

"Good God, Wickham, did you get any sleep?"

The question came from a particularly jovial, leering coyote, who judging by the sharp-toothed smirk, already knew the answer.

Grant blinked awake, his muzzle very nearly dunking in his own coffee. He cleared his throat, then blinked blearily at Ransom, mumbling, "Hmm?"

"Sleep," the coyote chuckled. "Y' know, th' thing the rest of us was tryin' to do. Manage any?"

The husky just gave a blissful smile. "No."

Puck actually made an awkward noise, and continued at what he was working on, looking as busy as he could sorting through his herbs. I was trying to do the same, fletching an arrow.

Laesom seemed out of the loop, which I equated to the older wolf's hearing fading. Thank the gods for small miracles.

"Would you prefer I share a tent with the young lady tonight, then?" He offered, congenially. "You'll need your rest before tomorrow, and I don't mind sleeping in cramped quarters—"

"No," both Grant and I said in unison.

"So Puck's caught me up on what happened in Serahaven," Ransom said rather out of nowhere, and I mentally reminded myself to thank him, later. I think he'd sensed the teasing had hit a point where I was getting uncomfortable. For such a rough, abrasive man, he was proving to be remarkably empathetic.

The coyote picked at his claws as he spoke. "Sorry about yer employment there, Wickham. But I never much liked the pit bull, fer the record. Grated on me somethin' fierce. Mosta' the men out there tha' gave me tha' much guff are huggin' the earth real tight right now."

"Connall's not the enemy," Grant said with a sigh, leaning his elbows over his knees and staring into the fire. "Rourke is. And this Shadow."

"Tha' bastard showed 'is face?" Ransom snorted. "I thought all he did was creep about'n hunt down stragglers."

"Her face," I said quietly, slicing my knife down the shaft I was working on.

Ransom looked surprised enough that I caught on that Puck must not have told him.

" 'Her'?" he queried, confused. Then irritated. "Shit. Little bitch got up on me without my even knowin'. I just figured it had t'be a damn good hunter. These ears don't miss much."

I flashed a look his way, lowering my brow. "Are you saying women can't hunt?"

The coyote snuffed, averting his eyes from mine. "I didn' say that…"

"I wanted to spare your ego, Ransom," Puck said quietly, his attention still fully focused on his work.

"Well hell, it ain't like it changes much, but I would've found out eventually, fox," the coyote insisted, gesturing out towards the east. "We're goin' after them. We're gonna get th' bitch eventually."

"There isn't any need for that," Puck murmured quietly, sighing.

"Like hell I'm lettin' em get away with what they did t' you!" Ransom replied, sharply. "No. They went and made this personal." He looked up, and nodded to me. "Cat, whatever you got planned… We're in."

"You're just arbitrarily deciding things for me, now?" The fox said, narrowing his eyes in the coyote's direction.

"Neither of you need to help me," I tried to insist, putting a hand out. "Especially after everything you've just been through—"

127

"But you're goin' after them. Ain't you?" The coyote asked, and I knew it wasn't a question. He knew the answer.

I leaned back, and felt Grant's broad palm move gently over my back. I closed my eyes for a moment, so incredibly glad for the contact. This was a conversation I'd known would come, eventually. We'd been so safe, happy and warm in our little bubble of comfort here in the mountains, but the reality of what lay beyond this place was catching up with us. And the most difficult part wasn't going to be marshaling the nerve to pursue our enemies. It was deciding whose lives I was willing to put at risk.

Grant had his own reasons to pursue Rourke, and some very new reasons to help me, so his presence during the hunt wasn't in question. But Puck and Ransom…

They'd endured so much already, and come out together in the end. The last thing I wanted was for my quest, for these enemies that had little to no role in their lives before they'd met me, to be their undoing. They deserved to be happy, now that they at last had a chance.

"Yeah, that's what I thought," Ransom nodded. "I ain't lettin' you do this alone, Shivah. Them boys are owed some pain from me."

"None of you need to go!" the fox tried to insist, dropping the herbs he had in his hands in frustration.

"Maybe you can join us in the hunt in a little while," Grant tried to reason, ever the mediator. "I doubt very much that we'll find a fresh trail as soon as we get off the mountain. They may have even moved down-river again. It took me two years to get as close to them as we did this season. This could be a lengthy undertaking. Maybe take some time to get your bearings, heal up, we could meet with you in a few months, and then you can decide if you'd still like to—"

"You ain't even got a badge anymore, Wickham," Ransom pointed out, stabbing a finger at the man across the campfire. I saw the husky's ears drop, and felt a sudden surge to defend him. "So you're doin' this… what? As a bounty hunter?"

"There isn't an active bounty on Rourke anymore," Grant insisted. "I'm not doing this for money—"

"That makes it even more illegal though, don't it?" Ransom persisted. "If the state ain't even willin' to pay men to hunt this bastard anymore, we as citizens are breakin' the law by goin' after 'im."

"Connall's the man in charge of the hunt now, by default," Grant attempted to insist. "He's not going to waste his time going after us. He's as committed to finding Rourke as I was."

The coyote narrowed his eyes. "You sure 'bout that, Wickham?"

That got my attention. I knew Ransom only got that one of voice when he was about to point out something I, or someone else, had gotten wrong. Like whenever I forgot to stand in the right stance to aim.

"What is it?" I asked, leaning forward.

The coyote leaned back, crossing his arms over his chest beneath his blanket. "Just that I don't think the rat did it, is all," the man muttered. "I don't buy it."

"Why?" I queried.

"Because..." the coyote gave a long sigh and glanced aside, clearly remembering something that bothered him. "When I was outta my mind, after I left Serahaven."

I saw Puck's ears tip back, and the fox shifted forward onto his hands and knees and crossed the foot or so that separated him and the coyote, moving in beside him as the man muscled through the next few words. The fox's presence at his side seemed to help.

"I went back up through where we'd been, thinkin'... I dunno," the coyote said with a sigh. "Maybe that I'd find some of 'em that did it, and get some blood. But I didn't find none of the ones that were in town. Just the camp we'd already found. And it was in cinders. Rat did what he said he was gonna. All the boats was pulled into th' center of camp with their supplies, and burnt up. Must've taken a good long while to do it, too. They had a lotta shit up there."

"What about the man we left knocked out up there?" Grant asked. "Connall had only just sent a few men to investigate the mountain camp when he told me to leave. I never found out what became of everything up there. The one we left alive might have had more information, though…"

Ransom shook his head. "Gutted. And not by the rat. The way he was cut up was just like…" I saw his eyes drop down to the fox, and he seemed unable to continue. The look of pain that flickered over his features was a stark reminder of how devastated he'd been on that day. Even I had to swallow back a painful lump in my throat, at the memories—the feeling of loss.

Puck leaned his muzzle against Ransom's shoulder, and I felt like I needed to see it as much as Ransom needed to feel him there, confirmation that the worst had been averted. Puquanah was still with us.

"We don't need to be discussing any of this," Puck said softly, but insistently, running his small paw over Ransom's scarred arm. "Really. Let's just get on with our lives."

"I can't so long as those men still draw breath," I said, coldly. "I'm sorry, Puck. But they need to die. This isn't even just about Methoa anymore. I saw what those men could do… What they've been doing, over and over again. Do you really want to see any more towns suffer what befell Serahaven, when we could have stopped it?"

The fox gave a conflicted expression, looking down.

"We've already stopped it," he murmured.

"We only protected Serahaven," I insisted. "There will be others. If there haven't been already. They've been doing this for years. Whatever their ideology, they're not going to stop."

"Stop acting like this is something you're doing out of charity," Puck said, narrowing his eyes, flicking his ears between Ransom and I. "Both of you. You're both just out for blood."

"Damn straight," Ransom growled, unashamedly.

"Puck, I'm not going to force either of you to come," I tried to assure the fox.

130

"You're not denying what I'm saying!" the fox pointed out.

"You've always known what my main goal in all of this was," I said severely. "But there really is more at stake, now. What does it matter why I'm doing this? The end result will be the same."

"The end result could be some, or all of us dead!" Puck replied, harshly. "Are you ready to live with that, Shivah? These men are murderers. If we find them, Len'sal isn't going to save us. We've been lucky so far. Let's leave this to the lawmen, and enjoy the lives we wrested from the edge of oblivion."

I tried to bite back my frustration at the fox, reminding myself that he's just nearly lost his, and his lover's life.

"I hear you, Puck," I said in a measured tone. "That's why I'd never ask either of you to accompany me. Go. Live your lives. Head back into the valley for the year to hunt—"

"Puck, damnit, I ain't lettin' her do this alone—" the coyote snapped.

"She won't be alone," Grant spoke up, trying to sound firm and assuring. But the two men were caught up in their own argument now, and his words were barely heard.

"She shouldn't be doing this, either!" Puck snapped right back at the coyote. "This whole thing is beyond us. It's too dangerous, and unnecessary, besides that!"

"How can you abandon her?" the coyote demanded. "After everythin' she's done for us? You'd've been buried alive if it wasn't for her. I'd sure as hell be dead. We wouldn't be sittin' here to have this argument. I ain't castin' her off just when she's goin' into the mouth of hell. It ain't right. We owe her."

"Justice always finds people like that, eventually," the fox persisted. "One way or another."

"And how many people have to die before 'justice' catches up with 'm?" The coyote barked.

"You didn't care about those people before! You just want vengeance, now. Just like her!"

"And what the hell's so wrong with that?" Ransom finally demanded in a raised voice, real anger in his tone, now. "Men gotta make their own justice sometimes, Puck! We can't all just sit around and accept the way things are—"

"I don't want to lose you again!" The fox shouted right back. And the camp went silent.

Even Ransom shut his muzzle, looking down at the fox with a conflicted set of emotions filtering through his gaze.

"I don't want to lose any of you," the fox said, vehemently, trying to 'look' around the clearing at all of us. "These people are murderers. It is all they do. We only just escaped the jaws of death. This isn't just about Ransom and I! This isn't worth anyone dying for!"

Grant, of all people, gave a troubled-sounding sigh, and replied, "I think it is, actually… I wouldn't have taken on this task when I was first hired if I hadn't already weighed the possibility that I might lose my life to it. I decided a long time ago that it was worth it to me. And just because I no longer have a badge doesn't mean I don't still take the oath I made to the people of this country seriously."

"We've all seen what Rourke, Shadow and their men can do," I said, purposefully not mentioning Methoa. I tried to keep my tone soft-spoken, because I really did understand the point the fox was trying to make. But I doubted anyone in the camp would agree with it. Even Laesom hadn't taken Puquanah's side. "Someone needs to stop them," I continued, "and the Marshals didn't have much luck before, when they had more men and specialized hunters. I know the danger, Puck… I think we all do," I said, looking around the camp. "But Ransom's right. You can't always just accept the world as it is, or wait for the gods to even the balance. Sometimes we have to make our own justice."

"I didn't stop you when you wanted t' help those people in Serahaven, Puck," Ransom said, meaningfully. And rather than being obstinate, the coyote reached down and took the fox's far smaller hand, gripping it tightly. "I trusted you weren't gonna let yerself get sick, in the end, even if I rankled against it. Well, this's something I've gotta do. And yeah, my reasons ain't

132

exactly all about lendin' aid to the downtrodden, but... It's still bloody important t' me."

"It will work itself out without any of you needing to throw your lives away..." Puck said, so quietly it was almost beneath his breath.

"No one's gonna expect you to kill folk, Puck," Ransom assured him. "You just be there for us, and stay outta it-"

"Damnit, just stop!" the fox suddenly shouted. He so rarely used profanity, it had its desired effect, garnering him the complete silence and attention of the entire camp. "And stop treating me like I'm some fragile, docile pup to be protected. I took care of those people, alright? None of you need to do anything!"

I looked to Ransom, confused. But even the coyote looked baffled. Whatever Puck was talking about, he'd clearly not even spoken to the coyote about it before now.

"The people in Serahaven?" I asked, finally, uncertain what he meant.

"The raiders," Puck said, snarling. "Well, Shadow, but she should be enough. I know she was the one leading them. I heard her giving orders. She's the one who ordered..." he sighed, half-closing his pale eyes, "ordered the two people I was trying to get to safety... shot."

"What?!" I asked, shocked, my sentiment echoed by every party around the fire. Even the coyote was staring at Puck, aghast. "How?"

"She was the one who first grabbed me," Puck murmured. "I had two sick people with me, so... I tried to defend myself. I stabbed her with one of my surgical blades. I don't think I would have managed if she hadn't been so arrogant, but she left herself open. Probably because she saw I was blind, I don't know..."

"Wait, you killed her?" I asked, confused. "But, you said she was giving orders—"

Puck snorted softly. "Please. No. Those blades aren't meant to kill, and I hardly knew how to use a knife when I could still see. No. I just caught her across the arm. Deep enough that I could smell blood, but I doubt I did much damage."

"Then why—" I began.

"I used those blades to excise boils from critically ill patients," Puck said, in a low, dark tone.

I slowly put a hand over my mouth, staring in shock across the fire at the fox. The small man looked anything but triumphant at his admission. In fact, if anything, he looked somewhat ashamed. But resigned.

"Holy hell, Puck…" Ransom muttered in an exhaled breath.

"You infected her?" Grant said, disbelievingly.

Puck gave a long, haggard sigh, closing his eyes. "Please don't lecture me. Trust me. You won't tell me anything I haven't already been torturing myself with for the last few days. I know it's contrary to everything I—"

"Puck, are you bloody kidding me?" The coyote suddenly cut in, giving a snarling huff. "Fuck them! They deserve t' rot in a filthy pit, just like th' people they've been slaughterin'. You did good."

"I'm sure it wasn't intentional—" I began to say.

"No, I knew exactly what I was doing," the fox cut me off, stoically. "I just… I knew they were going to kill us. I knew they were going to kill my patients. I didn't see a way out. I wanted to take her down with me. I didn't think of the Len'sal until sometime afterward, while Rourke was…" He trailed off, at that.

"It was justice, Puck," I said, emphatically.

"No, it was a mistake," the fox sighed, raggedly. "I spread a highly-infectious disease. This region's already dealing with an outbreak. That woman's carrying one of the worst strains of the Fever this land's ever seen. The outbreak in Serahaven was a particularly fatal, stubborn flavor of that disease, based on the few other cases I've heard of."

"But are we certain she's infected?" Grant pressed. "I talked to a Physician or two about the Seer's Fever myself, when we first thought it might be important. Everyone I talked to said it's like the pox. It's nearly unheard of to get it twice. You said yourself you were fairly certain Rourke's suffering the aftereffects, which means he was infected at some point. Couldn't she—"

Puck just shook his head. "The reason I was almost certain Rourke's madness was due to the fever was because of the lack of precautions he was taking in that town. He didn't wear gloves when he was torturing me. He used his bare hands."

I saw Ransom's lip curl and quiver, flashing his fangs. He looked away as Puck continued to speak.

"And he wasn't covering his muzzle at all," Puck said, pointedly. "The rest of them were, including Shadow. Bandanas, I think. Similar to what your men wore. It's a common misconception that the disease can be spread by air. It can't, but... I don't think they know that."

"So if she's never been infected, what are the chances of her being infected now?" I asked.

"One hundred percent," the fox stated. "It's a certainty. And she won't have an easy time of it. I only used those tools on the absolute worst cases."

"I can't believe her and her men haven't been infected already," Grant remarked. "All the villages they've destroyed, all those sick people..."

"The disease is easier to avoid than you'd think," Puck said. "They've been getting a few things right. Enough that I suspect some of them must have been through an outbreak before. They burn the bodies, they burn all the textiles and destroy all the food. Unless during the attacks they get punctured somehow by weapons the villagers carry, and their blood or diseased fluids somehow mingle," he shook his head, "it would be a rare occasion to be accidentally infected, the way they've been going about it. It explains a lot about the attacks. Really, the only way to be infected by the disease is through more casual, intimate contact. Sharing a home, sharing food, maybe drinking water? I never isolated exactly what was doing it in Serahaven. But I suspect it's something mundane. And after the initial infection to a few people, all that's required for an outbreak is for others to be in physical contact with them. That's why healers are so afraid of treating this illness."

"But you avoided it somehow," I said, mystified.

The fox sighed. "No. I didn't."

I'll give Ransom credit for one thing. The coyote was the only one amongst us who didn't move or lean back, at the fox's comment.

"I'm fine now," the fox insisted, especially towards Ransom, who was glaring down at him like he'd been betrayed. "I passed the illness rather quickly, the first few days I was in the Mill treating them."

"You told me you weren't gonna get sick!" the coyote snapped.

"It wasn't an accident," Puck grated out, irritated. "I purposefully infected myself almost as soon as I got inside. I knew I'd get it eventually anyway, in such close quarters."

"Why in the hell—" the coyote riled.

"Because it's safer to infect yourself in a controlled manner than to contract the disease accidentally," the fox attempted to explain. "It's called an inoculation. They used the method to protect people from the pox in Arbordale, a decade or so ago."

Grant blinked. "Oh, hell… I remember that. The Scarring Pox? It was all over the slums when I was young. The priests came through to treat all the children. Only reason we could afford it. Little ones hated it, though. They had to cut you."

"I heard about the method from an Apothecary in Millbrook, a few years ago," Puck said. "I thought the same concept might work on the Fever, since it spreads the same, and I turned out to be right. Although I'm not entirely certain it will work as well on others as it did for me. And it was still extremely unpleasant. I'd really need to perfect the method before I applied it for use on patients."

"You stupid little bastard," Ransom growled. "You swore t' me you'd come outta there alive!"

"And I did!" the fox fired back.

136

"You didn't even know it was gonna work!"

"I…" the fox stammered, "I trusted my knowledge, and my experience. And I was right. It's no different than what you do every time you go hunting something dangerous. I trusted my life on my skills."

Ransom bit back on something he was going to say, and I chose that moment to cut in and avert yet another runaway argument. Some things between the two men had clearly not changed—always so dramatic.

"But if all you essentially did to get through this disease so easily was cut yourself," I pointed out, "doesn't that mean she'll just as easily endure it as you did?"

"First off, I began treating myself even before I was exposed," Puck informed me. "I started taking herbs to strengthen my resistances before I even arrived in town, and throughout the time I was sick. I drank water, constantly, and I made certain to expose myself to the disease at its weakest, from the saliva of patients who'd nearly beaten it already."

"egch…" I heard Grant mutter from behind me.

"And besides all of that, I'm extremely resistant to disease," Puck stated. "I've dealt with disease my whole life. My body might not be strong in the way yours is, but there are different kinds of strength. I rarely get ill any more. I was able to fight off the disease in a few days, and the worst I suffered was a general inability to keep food down. It wasn't pleasant, but I never got the boils, or the fever."

Ransom took a deep breath, and slowly let it out, before putting his hand back on the fox's, and looking down at him sternly, but with visible respect. "Puck, you're the cleverest damn fool I've ever known. I get that yer smart and all, smarter than me, fer sure… But next time, you tell me before you're gonna do somethin' that bloody stupid, so we can at least do it t'gether."

"I'm actually impressed you haven't contracted it," Puck said, confused. "Shivah said you went into the Mill while it was on fire. That you jumped out a window, got cut up and burnt in there. Considering how much in there was exposed, I'm shocked you didn't accidentally catch it. I was afraid we'd find you dying from a combination of the fever and your own stupidity in the mountains."

Ransom looked like he was about to re-start their argument, when I spoke up. "All of this aside," I said, "even if we take for granted that you're right, and she was never infected before. Puck, you said yourself this disease is survivable. Even if she's ill, she could recover. She could just get better, and go right back to doing what she was doing before. We still need to stop her."

"I'm rather hoping they apply some of their own ideology," Puck said, in a hard tone. "Or that the otter turns on her, or her men turn on her, once they realize she's sick. She's the head of the snake. I'm convinced if we just leave them be, this thing will work itself out."

"And I think that's wishful thinking," I stated back. "Puck. We have to go after them even more now. You know that. This is going to make them desperate. And they could spread it."

The fox looked down, sadly, and slowly put his head into his hands. No one said anything for a time, but Ransom eventually reached over and wrapped his arm around him.

"It's good that you told us," I said softly. "And for what it's worth, I understand why you did it. This might actually slow them down. Finally give us a chance. You might have saved a lot of lives."

"Or cost more," the fox said quietly.

I narrowed my eyes. "We have to make sure that doesn't happen."

Puck only nodded slowly, finally relenting. I didn't think for a moment that he honestly agreed, but he'd at least given up on fighting us.

Ransom squeezed the fox's shoulder, and gave a wry chuckle that seemed only a little forced. "Damn, fox…" he muttered. "Remind me to never piss you off."

We weren't able to make the journey down the mountain until two days later, when Ransom was really able to travel. And even then, despite the coyote's insistence, it was clear he might not have been ready. He put up a strong front, but his body was still weak, and it seemed to be frustrating him more than anyone else. We took several long breaks throughout the day and encamped early that night.

By the time I'd managed to shoot anything for dinner, and we'd eaten what remained of our meager trail rations, it was late and I was tired. Grant had done me the favor of setting up our tent, and I crawled in to join him only a few minutes after he had.

It was strange how, in only three days, our nightly rituals had become almost routine. I was rather enjoying the fact. It made our tiny tent feel almost like home, despite the fact that we had to pack it up and move it every day.

I helped the husky out of his gun-belt. I'd discovered by now that I rather liked undressing the man, in the same way I rather liked playing with clumps of moss and batting at falling leaves. He hardly seemed to mind, since my playful nighttime antics more often than not led to activities he greatly enjoyed. And no matter how tired I was, that was still happening tonight.

"I need to groom myself…" The man muttered with a sigh, as he shouldered out of his shirt.

"I need a bath," I murmured, sympathetically.

"I like the way you smell right now," Grant said, with a half-smirk.

"What, like you?" I asked dryly, as I tugged the man out of his pants. He finished the process with a grin.

"Yes. Call me possessive," he affirmed.

"You're deluded, is what you are," I countered, with the barest hint of a smile. "If anyone owns anyone here—"

The husky leaned forward and kissed me, and I closed my eyes and let him linger a long while, before allowing him to pull back. When he did, he murmured against my muzzle. "If you want me, Shivah, I'm yours forever."

I sighed at the man's flare for the dramatic, and just shoved him down, moving over him. He gave a rumbling chuckle, and let me. If I'd had a longer tail, it would have been lashing.

"Just tonight's fine," I muttered, setting back to kissing him.

Something stilled the man while we were in the midst of our affections, though, and I felt him pull away from me a bit as I attempted to deepen our kiss. At length, I opened my eyes and looked down at him.

"What's wrong?" I murmured.

"I just realized," he said with a soft sigh, "I think it's the twenty-fourth."

"The what?" I blinked.

"The date," he said softly, looking sad for a moment. "I think it's Anna's birthday."

"Who?" I asked, curiously.

He sighed. "My youngest sister. My youngest sibling, actually. She'll be twelve. If she's not already. I lost track of the days." He looked regretful for a few moments. "I was supposed to be home for it. We were supposed to have been back in Arbordale a few weeks ago, but then we caught that lead, and everything that followed."

I looked down on the man, suddenly struck by a pang of guilt. He'd become such an integral part of my life of late, I'd forgotten there were seven other people out there in the world that loved him and depended on him.

"You don't..." I said with some difficulty, "You don't have to come with me, Grant. All that, about my taking charge of this. You aren't actually in any way under my command. I know you have family, and I don't want to keep you from them if you need to be with them."

His blue eyes snapped back into focus at that, and he shook his head. "No, no, Shivah. I'm committed to this. And I swear, it isn't just because of you. I made a promise to the people of this country, which includes my family—"

"You were relieved of duty, legally," I said softly. "They're... They're not even going to pay you. I know you wanted to move your family to a better home."

The husky glanced away, his expression conflicted. I said nothing while he thought, even though my heart was screaming for me to say something, anything, that would keep him with me. I needed his help. I only barely had Ransom and Puck's help, and I couldn't do this alone.

But I would, if I had to. I wasn't going to force any of my companions to undertake such a terrible task. They had to make the decision for themselves. Even if part of me knew I was still applying pressure on them, without words, just by being their friend and putting myself in harm's way.

There'd be time for guilt later. Right now, everyone had to do what they felt was right, and even if I was the catalyst for it all, I knew our quest was righteous. If they chose to help me of their own free will, it was their choice.

"Somewhere out there," Grant murmured, after a long while spent in silence, "there's a family who lost their parents, just as we lost ours. And they're trying to survive, the same way we struggled. And they deserve a chance. I can't imagine how cruel—how unfair it would have been, if atop losing first my father, then my mother... our home had been attacked, and someone like Rourke had slain my brothers and sisters in front of me."

He looked up at me, running his palm along my cheek. "Someone needs to stop them. And if we've even the smallest chance, it's our duty. Because we might be able to end this now, before they kill more children, or destroy more families." He shook his head, slowly. "Shivah, I couldn't live with myself if I didn't help you. It doesn't matter if the State doesn't want me anymore. When I joined the force, I wasn't thinking of the State when I took my vows and received my badge. I was thinking of her..."

He reached down into the pile of clothing he'd left beside our bedroll, and pulled something out that I'd seen many times before, but never really looked at. The small, tarnished locket he always kept in his pocket.

I took it from him when he offered it, and gently opened the worn latch. It was a simple silver locket, and not real silver, I was all but certain. Inside, there was only a small, folded piece of paper. I glanced up at him, for permission, and he just smiled.

"My girl back home gave it to me, before I left," he murmured. "Go ahead."

I opened the piece of paper carefully. It was folded through the middle several times into a small square, and when laid flat, was barely larger than the husky's palm. It was a bit ragged, and looked to be torn from a book of some sort. I couldn't read the writing, as it was in Otherwolf, but when I turned it over, I saw what was of real value.

Someone had drawn on the back of the paper, in charcoal. The picture was amateurish, but probably better than I could have ever managed. I could tell at least that one of the faces was meant to be Grant, by the diamond on his forehead, and the other looked to be a smaller husky like him, with far more white around their eyes. And they were much smaller.

"Anna's quite talented, for her age," Grant murmured, sounding proud. "See how she draws my head from the side? The church women who taught her and the boys how to write said that's very advanced, for a girl her age."

I swallowed, as I looked down at the hand-drawn picture.

"You should go home, Grant," I said quietly.

"I will," he said softly, reaching over to cup my chin and turn my eyes back towards his. I'd had trouble looking away even when we weren't close. Nowadays, it was almost impossible. "And you'll come with me. When this is all over. I want you to meet them."

"I'd like that," I said at length, as I dropped my eyes back to the picture. The amateur drawing of the little girl stared back at me.

I respected Grant's resolve, and I understood it. The same as I understood Ransom's desire for justice against the people who'd nearly killed Puck, and the fox's desperate act in what he'd thought were his final moments, to avenge himself against an enemy who'd killed his patients, and meant to kill him.

But as much as I understood everyone's reasons, a fear was beginning to creep into my mind. I'd already lost everyone I'd once known and loved to Methoa, and these raiders. And now, everyone left in the world whom I'd come to care for were throwing themselves right back into the path of the very same enemies who'd once stolen all hope of happiness from me. It was hard not to question my own reasons, any more, let alone theirs. Puquanah might have been right.

I expected in my time of doubt, I would have been visited by Crow. In my dreams, if not my waking life. But he never appeared. And his absence was almost more frightening.

Returning to Crossroads was almost surreal. I suppose in some ways, I'd come to see the settlement as the focal, central point of my life over the last few months, rather than the valley where I'd been born. That realization alone was so strange. So much in my life; my priorities, the things of value to me—even the people in it—had changed so much, this season.

And I was finding, increasingly, that I welcomed the change. It's not that I wanted to remain in the overcrowded frontier town, or that the bustle of the Otherwolf settlement even really appealed to me. I was just so glad to wake each day, not knowing for certain that my life would be a routine of disappointment and unhappiness. My life before all of this had grown as stagnant as marsh water, and in retrospect, seemed just as fetid. It was only when I'd finally stood my ground against Methoa that, even if I hadn't prevailed, things had changed. And even if many of my days now could be equally terrifying or saddening, there were days of hope, as well.

Only a few months ago, I'd been scared at what lay beyond the mountains. I'd been scared of the lands and the way of life of a people I didn't know. I'd been frustrated that I would need

143

to venture into them to chase after Methoa. I could even remember how overwhelmed I'd been by the Trade Post, upon first seeing it, and it had been so small compared to Crossroads... Which was apparently small in comparison to the Otherwolf cities.

I'd been scared of Otherwolves. They were as unknown to me as the moon, and I'd had wild ideas fed only by tales and conjecture amongst my tribe of what sorts of people they truly were. And now I slept beside one every night.

So as we headed into the darkening, yet still crowded streets of the settlement once more that night, I tried to be optimistic. Yes, the time ahead was uncertain. Our enemies were, as always, an unknown. They could be near or far, they could be preying upon the weak even now, perpetrating their crimes even as we wearily looked for a place to sleep.

Or perhaps their luck was finally running out. Perhaps Puck's parting gift had had some effect. Even if it were small, even if the disease had little impact on the vixen, I would take any advantage we had right now.

There was also the fact that, according to Ransom, Magpie truly had burned their supplies. That included their canoes, and that meant their transportation would be limited. They'd always traveled by river before. If they were looking to beat a hasty retreat now, that option had been cut out. They could, of course, simply steal more boats, or horses. They could easily resupply if they took out another town, or even just a trade post. But none of those were a simple undertaking.

It was satisfying to think we might have them running, and I wanted to think there was a chance. The raiders had been such an enigma to us for so long now. Never seen, never even glimpsed, always three steps ahead. Continuously, we found nothing but their wreckage. It was hard to think all of our efforts, and small victories, might in the end boil down to little more than an inconvenience to them. And we might be just as lost in finding their trail as we'd been before.

The fact was, none of us really knew where to go from here. But I was still looking forward to renewing the hunt in the morning. A good night's sleep in the comfort and warmth of an inn—which I had to admit, I'd very quickly gotten used to, after spending only a short time in one—would do us all a lot of good. And tomorrow would bring with it new chances.

The mood amongst my companions seemed to be good, and I suspected they all felt as I did. It was hard not to return to such a lively place without lifting one's own spirits. And the return to Crossroads represented one victory entirely. We'd escaped the mountain, and we were all alive. Some of us were a little worse for the wear; mostly Puck and Ransom, who were still both injured; but we were all together.

Except for Crow. He remained absent from my life. A week ago, up on the mountain, I'd prayed for him to return to me, but I'd still gotten no response. Not even vague symbolism. Just nothing.

I'd had some nights of doubt and worry along the trail, but in the end, Grant's amusing, comforting presence had made it impossible to brood for very long. It felt like every time I was beginning to slip back down the slopes of anger and obsession inside me, the husky would do something to snap me out of it—even if that something was just a smile.

It was hard to spiral into thoughts of vengeance when your bed partner was lazily wagging and 'wuffing' under his breath in his sleep.

So, optimism. I was giving it a try. And honestly, it felt fairly good. I hadn't a clue what the morning would bring, but I was glad to make it back to the settlement, for now. I think we all were. Even Puck.

A lot of that probably had to do with the fact that we were all starving for good meat, and some place to sleep that was sheltered from the still-cold early spring winds. I know it was almost all that was on my mind. We headed for the boarding district right off. Even Puck was murmuring excitably about ordering every type of sausage on the menu at a particular inn and tavern the two men said would make for a good place to spend the night. Honestly, the conversation alone was making my mouth water. I was already planning out my evening, when we made it there. Some place called the 'Cooked Goose'. As we headed inside, we were happy, chatting and laughing, and the last thing on my mind was Crow, or the trials we'd have to tackle in the morning.

As it turned out, there was a whole different sort of trouble awaiting us inside. A more mundane, but unfortunately, also far more common kind.

The Cooked Goose was a lively, raucous place, like most of the inns in the district. As soon as we entered, I was assaulted with smells both foul and inviting, of fur, dirt, musk, leather and trail dust, but also bread and cooking meat, the ever-present, permeating smell of ale, beer and other poisonous drinks, as well as tobacco. The place was smoky and crowded, and it was difficult to hear oneself think over the din, but a small nook near the staircase that led upstairs to the rooms provided a bit of shelter from the noise.

A weathered-looking, pear-shaped, middle-aged Otherwolf woman sat behind the desk, her black fur showing her age in patches of silver across her muzzle and the tips of her draping ears. She wore a cleaner apron than most of the servers I'd seen through the divider that led into the dining area, so I could only assume she was the hostess. She looked up as Grant headed towards the desk, a brief frown creasing her features, for some reason. I remember thinking it odd, because Grant almost always evoked a friendlier greeting from complete strangers, women most especially.

But her frown hadn't been directed at him.

All the same, she stood and smiled when he made it to the desk, addressing him in a courteous tone.

"Looking to book a room then, sir?" She asked, and I realized with some small amount of pride that I'd actually understood every word. My 'Amurescan' was getting better. To be fair, I'd had little else to do during the countless hours I'd spend traveling but learn it from my various companions. It was bound to have stuck eventually.

Also, Grant tended to slip into it very frequently when we were together, a fact which had failed to bother me. It was forcing me to pick up on the language more, and atop that… I have to admit, I found it strangely alluring. I can't really say why.

I moved up beside the husky as he dug into his pocket for some coin. Again, I really wanted to be contributing to all of this, but I knew better than to bring that up here. He seemed to sense my concern, though, and just put his free hand on my shoulder, making it clear I was with him. Ransom stepped up behind him and palmed a few silver coins from his own pack, passing them along for he and the other two tribesmen.

The woman eyed our coin and looked up to our group, clearing her throat, "It's a half moon apiece for yer room and vittles, dinner an' breakfast in th'morning."

"We'll only need three rooms," Grant said, as he sifted through the coins in his pocket to produce a few of those same silver coins Ransom had handed him.

The woman looked between us all, uncertainly. "Rooms ain't got but one bed. This ain't a flophouse. You boys can buy yer own rooms or find someone else's floor t' sleep on."

I heard Ransom sigh in annoyance from behind me as he dug into his pocket and slammed another coin down onto the table. "Fer me 'n the fox there," he muttered, clearly biting back any comments beyond that.

I felt for him, in that moment. I knew for a fact the two men would just end up sharing one of their two rooms, anyway, but they couldn't tell the woman that, of course. They couldn't admit their reasoning for buying one room together had nothing to do with saving coin.

And they'd never really be able to, for as long as they lived. Puck had talked to me about the need for discretion before, about how he and Ransom would have been perceived by the Otherwolf society, was their relationship ever known. But this was honestly the first time I'd ever seen it playing out.

And on their first night together in town, after all that had happened… I'd really hoped at least the most basic of things could have gone right for them.

"Fine. Yes. Let's just get our keys," Grant sighed, clearly not wanting to make trouble on the coyote's behalf.

"Not until you pay up for the bushcat there," the woman stated flatly, looking past him towards me.

Grant glanced briefly back at me, before gesturing up the stairs beside us. "She's staying with me. We'll pay for her meals separately—"

"This ain't a brothel, either," the woman said, flattening her ears back. "Separate rooms for y'all, or you go elsewhere."

"Excuse me?" I said disbelievingly, instinctively speaking in my native tongue. I was too offended by her insinuation to remember she wasn't speaking Katuk.

Grant squeezed my shoulder softly, and tried to diffuse the situation before it got worse. "She isn't…" he made a frustrated noise in the back of his throat, and I saw his fur prickling past the edge of his collar, but he was keeping remarkably calm. "She's my girl," he said, at length, "not a… worker."

"I don't care what you're callin' yer little native," the woman snorted, "I'm fair certain she ain't yer wife. I won't have any o' that un-Godly behavior under my roof."

Grant opened his muzzle to say something, and only managed an offended, frustrated-sounding sigh, before I cut him off, remembering something Ransom had taught me a very long time ago.

"He is my husband," I said, insistently, in Amurescan. Ransom had told me ages ago, when we'd first met Jack, the importance of pretending to be claimed in these lands. And I didn't care if I needed to lie to the woman. I was just getting tired of this. Grant was trying not to look shocked at my lie, and doing a decent job of it… but the brief look he shot my way said something along the lines of 'we are talking about this later'.

The woman seemed surprised as well, but more likely it was because she'd only just realized I'd been understanding the fact

148

that she'd been insulting me for the last few minutes. I knew enough Amurescan by now to know 'bushcat' was a derogatory term they used for native felines. Eventually, though, the surprise faded, and she gave a soft snort. "Well, you can teach a parrot to talk, I suppose," she muttered, then sighed, turning and fishing a few keys off the wall, speaking with her back turned. "You're still payin' full board for the native. I don't care if y' said yer 'vows' or not, it ain't right with God, and this house is right with God. You'll have separate rooms. If y' act in a sinful manner, after that," she put up her hands, "it's outta' my hands."

I was biting back a snarl when she looked my way, and of all things, her expression turned sympathetic. "I want you t'know, darlin', I don't blame you." Then her eyes moved back to Grant, more condemning. "It ain't her fault she's ignorant, but you oughta know better than t' prey on the simple-minded, boy. You ought t'be ashamed of yourself."

"Alright, fuck this," Ransom suddenly growled from behind me, and strode forward to scrape his own coin off the table, back into his palm. "Place smells like piss, anyway. You can keep your sodding rooms."

"Agreed," I growled, leveling an acidic glare at the woman. "And I am not simple-minded—" I began, flashing fangs as I prepared to tear the woman apart verbally, at least as well as I could in a second language.

This time, it was Puquanah who kept things from escalating, in his usual, soft-spoken, subdued way. I felt his paw on my arm, and he murmured, "Shivah, come. Let's go."

I growled, and looked back once at the woman, who now seemed more than a little uncomfortable. Perhaps even scared. There were so many things I wanted to say—so many justifications, so much I wanted to nail into her head somehow, to make her see how ignorant she was acting. A simple-minded person was the sort of person who'd turn away five paying patrons for no reason other than whom was bedding down with whom. Something along those lines. Maybe more scathing.

"You can't argue with religious rhetoric," Puck whispered quietly, stroking my arm. "Come on. Just let it be."

Even Ransom didn't look to want an argument with the woman, and Grant just looked dismayed, but resolved. Laesom was quiet as ever, but even he didn't seem surprised by the turn of events. It seemed to me like every person I was traveling with was accepting this, and that just frustrated me more.

But I wasn't going to fight it out when everyone I cared about clearly just wanted to leave. And in the end, that's what we did.

"Y' know," Ransom sighed and lit a cigarette as we stepped back out into the cold night air. "I hate to say this, but we might run into the same sorts of issues at mosta' the inns on the strip. Might actually have to settle for eatin' dinner at an inn and sleepin' in a flophouse."

"Ransom and I have done it many times in the past," Puck said, calmly. He was still holding my hand, and I could tell by his tone he was trying to make me feel better. But this outrage was fresh to me. He'd had years to get used to it. It's not that it bothered me any less that it happened to him and Ransom as well, I was just now personally very angry.

"I didn't realize just finding a place to sleep would be so difficult," Grant admitted, at length. He looked down to me, and gently wrapped an arm around my waist. "I suppose I should have."

"Some places don't take issue with Ransom and I sharing a room," Puck said, "because a lot of travelers do, to save money. But I suppose when it's a man and a woman…"

"Sorry, sweetheart," Ransom murmured sympathetically.

"No one would bat an eye if she were canine," Grant said quietly. "This isn't about what we do behind closed doors. It's about what we are."

The way he said it… I could tell that none of this had really entirely surprised him. Just confirmed concerns he'd clearly already had.

"Well… to hell with them, then," I said, speaking up. "I know where we can go where no one will judge us."

It was odd, but as we took the steps onto the red-lit stoop of the Cock and Barrel, I was almost looking forward to stepping inside. The sound of the piano, the jovial voices of women laughing, mingled with the conversation of men, the gaudily-colored interior. A month ago, when I'd first come here, the place had seemed almost revolting—a lot of which I equated to what happened inside, to be honest. But that all seemed to pale in comparison to everything else I'd seen people capable of, of late. It seemed petty to judge women for laying down with men for money, when others led groups of murderous raiders and slaughtered the innocent, or held such strong prejudices, they barred weary travelers from their places of business just because they deemed us unworthy.

I was almost ashamed of myself. In a month's time, I'd gone from judging these women for what they did for a living, to being judged for the man I chose to bed down with. Being on the other side was humbling.

Ransom seemed nervous as we approached the door, and with good reason. Veronica had banished him from the establishment only a few weeks ago. Even if she'd done so gently, there was always the chance we'd be rejected here just as we had been at the last inn. And I doubt he wanted to be responsible for that.

But as soon as we stepped inside, Grant, as always, leading the pack, my concerns dissolved. The first two women who saw us were the spotted canine twins, who almost literally squeaked when they saw Ransom moving in behind Grant, and bounded for the door.

The husky and I stepped out of the way and let the two girls through, to enjoy their reunion. I'll give Ransom some credit, the man kept them mostly at-bay, while Puck did his best impression of someone who didn't care that his friend was covered in women. The fox hadn't objected when I'd brought the place up as a possible inn to rest at, so I could only assume he and the coyote had talked about... well, everything. They had a lot to work out. I was hopeful, though. Ransom had visibly turned the corner, at least insofar as he'd been less afraid to be affectionate with the fox when we were in the relative safety of our camp. Even around the other men.

Here in the settlement, well here I couldn't blame him for keeping some distance. But even still, he lingered close to Puck at all times. It was nothing like the canyon's-width distance he'd given him before.

I spied Veronica before long, making her way towards us from the bar. She'd probably noticed us as soon as we'd come in, and her expression didn't seem unpleasant, so I was hopeful she wasn't just coming over to ask us to leave.

"Hey, Ver..." Ransom said, nervously, as the woman stopped a few paces from us, and crossed her arms over her ample bosom, looking our small group over.

"How're you feeling, 'yote?" The cougar asked, enough of a note of concern in her voice that it seemed to put Ransom at ease.

The coyote looked down for a few moments, before clearing his throat and replying, "Better. I think. A little better."

The woman nodded, then stepped forward and offered an arm. The coyote seemed surprised, but he accepted the embrace. For some reason, despite the fact that I knew what the primary connection was between the two of them, I couldn't help but find it touching. I suppose in some way, the women Ransom came to see here were amongst the very few people in his life that he'd really let in close. Them and Puck, and now me.

Puck was quiet, but he made no move to interrupt, nor did he seem particularly upset. All the same, Ransom didn't linger long, just as he hadn't with the twins.

"You know I still can't let you overnight with the girls," the cougar warned good-naturedly, as she pulled back. "Some of them aren't quite as resilient as I am."

"Ah, no, that's fine Ver," Ransom said, clearing his throat uncomfortably again. "I wasn't looking to. Actually, we just really need a place to stay the night, and somethin' to eat that ain't hard tack. We don't need no services."

The cougar gave a soft sigh, glancing past the coyote at Grant. "Now that's a pity," she murmured.

"You don't care who shares a room, do you?" I asked, making my meaning clear by resting a hand on the husky's hip. And emphasizing that meaning by flattening my ears and rumbling a warning at the other feline woman.

Veronica actually laughed. "Oh, I like her. Ransom, you're going t' have to more formally introduce me to your friends."

The hour that followed was a blur of food and…more food. We were all still a bit weary from the trip, but the last two days had mostly been over easy terrain, so more than anything, we were hungry. Our supplies had dwindled to almost nothing near the end of our trip, and other than a few fish we'd managed to catch during the short stretch where we'd be along the river, we hadn't been surviving on much. We ordered a little bit of everything the Cock and Barrel's kitchen was cooking up that night, and dug in until we could barely move. The mood was, for once, light and happy. Good food could do that, especially for people who'd not had any in a long time.

The night bled away into conversation and relaxation, and eventually, most of the other patrons began to filter back to their rooms or just left the place for the night, and we had a bit more privacy. Veronica was clearly in no rush to have us out of the main area, she and some of the other girls spent much of the night lingering near our table, or taking part in our conversations. Nothing of importance was discussed, but I seemed to be the center of attention more often than not. Apparently the fact that I was a traveler, a warrior, and a woman was unusual enough to warrant a lot of curiosity, and even admiration, from several of the women. Veronica included.

I'd never really taken the time to just talk to any of them, when I'd been staying here before. But now that I was taking the chance, I found I'd missed speaking with other women. Even if they were mostly foreigners, and I didn't entirely understand their way of life... I'd missed female company. It had been a long time since I'd had anything but men as companions.

Whenever all of this was over, I was going to have to remember to return here—perhaps especially to speak with Veronica. The woman claimed to have been a sharpshooter when she was young, on her father's farm. Apparently her skills with a rifle were well-known in the area, a reputation which had served her well in keeping her house orderly and safe for the women working here. Even Grant knew about some infamous incident when she'd held off a group of armed men who were trying to hold the place up, until the local Sheriff and his men had been able to get in and put them down. Veronica insisted the shot that had taken down the ringleader had been hers. I believed her.

At some point, Grant had gone off to check on his horse, and when he'd returned, he'd brought something back with him. Something he'd left at the cache where we'd stowed the things we hadn't the room for on the trip up the mountain, his guitar.

A significant amount of goading and free drinks later, we'd all managed to convince Ransom to sing. The man insisted he hadn't sang in front of a crowd, even a small one, in ages, but when Veronica opened a fresh bottle of what was apparently very good whiskey, I knew his resolve wouldn't hold out long. And it didn't.

One of the men who worked here, a red fox in a clean white serving shirt and black trousers, saw Grant tuning his guitar, and made for the piano near the stage. I happily and somewhat excitedly settled in beside Puck and Laesom, and about seven of the women who worked here, as the men all gathered around the edge of the stage and readied to play. Grant pulled up a chair near the piano, and Ransom just leaned up against the stage, murmuring something to the fox seated at the piano, which I didn't catch. The fox nodded and set his fingers to the keys, beginning a familiar tune.

I leaned my chin against my palm, pulling my knees up to my chest as Ransom began to sing. I'd heard him sing several songs that night a week ago, when he'd first sung for Puck again. But this one in particular, I remembered, *The Beaten Path*. It seemed to be one of his favorites.

It was nothing like tribal music, this Otherwolf way of singing, but it was, in its own right, very soulful, almost spiritual. I wasn't even sure if their music was meant to call to the spirits or the gods, but it called to something in me. Perhaps their music spoke more to the souls of people in the world, rather than those in the spirit world.

It was hard not to look at Puck while Ransom played. The fox was entranced, and he looked so happy. I wished that he could see that Ransom was looking at him, was singing for him, because I could tell. But then, maybe the fox could tell, too.

I'm not certain how long we sat together, gathered around the piano, the three men playing and singing to the small audience of weary souls. I'll always remember it as one of the most peaceful evenings of my life. I'd reflect on it many times, throughout my remaining years, and wish I was there again, sharing in the moment with all of my friends. Listening to the men play. Remembering what it was to be happy again.

We barely noticed when a small group of men filed in through the doorway. I vaguely saw Veronica stand and head off towards them, and was just beginning to wonder why the place was getting fresh customers so late at night, when I heard a familiar voice that very quickly dissolved the feeling of ease and comfort in the room.

"Wickham," the gruff Otherwolf spoke, and I whipped my head around, my fur prickling along the back of my neck,

155

defensively. Of all the people I'd thought I might see in this place… Connall had not been one of them.

But there he stood. He was standing with the aid of a brace on one of his legs, still, but he looked to be on the mend. He was flanked on two sides by very obviously armed men, both of which I recognized as being on Grant's squad when he'd still been in charge. Both Otherwolves, of course. Laesom had said he'd purged the unit of anything but.

I hesitated before I drew a weapon, assessing the men, the pit bull included. Despite being armed, they had no weapons drawn, and Connall's paw wasn't even resting on his hip, which I knew he had a tendency to do when he was on the offensive. One person in the room had armed themselves, however. Lingering behind them, near the door like any good hostess, was Veronica. And just as she likely relied upon, the men were ignoring her. But I saw the rifle she had hidden behind the hostess stand from here, and her slow nod at me across the room told me she'd sensed this could go wrong.

I stayed silent and averted my eyes from her, so as not to draw attention to the woman. Connall's gaze was on Grant, but his two men might notice her.

"We need to talk, boy," the pit bull said, his tone grave.

Grant put his guitar down slowly, and maintained a remarkably easy demeanor, despite the tension in the air. At length, he actually shrugged. "I actually don't think we do."

"Outside," the pit bull said, firmly. "Don't make me do this here."

"Do what, exactly?" The husky replied, his tone growing slightly more serious. "If you're going to arrest me, you need cause."

"Are you honestly telling me I don't have cause?" Connall replied. "Don't take me for a fool, boy. I knew as soon as one of the boys told me you were here that you'd come back to do something foolish. You should be halfway back to Arbordale by now, to be reassigned."

"You took away my badge."

156

"And told you to go back to Headquarters," Connall snapped.

"First off, you can't order me anywhere, you could only take me off payroll," Grant said, standing and beginning to cross the space between them. "Which you did. Second of all," he raised his chin, "I quit."

"You know, I knew when they picked you up that you were naïve," Connall growled, "but I never thought you were this bloody stupid, Wickham. You're far beyond your depth on this, son... You always were, and I'm telling you this for your own damned good... You need to go home. Now." His eyes swept over all of us, including both Ransom and I, unperturbed by our scathing glares. "All of you. This isn't a civilian matter. I could have you all tossed in the stocks for pursuing that woman and the otter. There's a reason we terminated the bounty. You're going to get yourselves killed, for no bloody reason—"

"You can't prove that's why we're here in the settlement—" Ransom began, obstinately, but I cut him off sharply.

"How did you know Shadow was a woman?" I demanded, standing slowly.

Grant glanced back at me, confused. "The same reason we..."

He went quiet, and I shook my head. Then we were all staring at the pit bull—every set of eyes in the room.

"Puck is the only one who was there when they burnt the town, the only one that heard her voice," I stated, flatly. "And he only told us long after we'd left Serahaven." I narrowed my eyes at the pit bull, accusingly. "You've met her."

Connall's muzzle twitched, and he let out a long sigh. "We... made contact with her, a few days ago..." He muttered. "She posed as a defector—"

"I don't believe you," I growled, and I meant it.

"Damnit, just listen, woman," Connall said. "She came to us. She was at death's door. We thought we'd get information out of her once she was well again, but in the end, she just used the chance to play on our sympathies to get medical treatment. Apparently at some point in Serahaven, she contracted the Fever."

Puck's ears perked at that.

"She escaped our custody a few days after she turned herself in," the pit bull muttered, irritated. "The men went lax on her guard. We thought she was still in dire straits, but she must have been feigning a lot of the illness near the end, there."

"You had her and you lost her?!" Grant suddenly spoke up, and he sounded angry. "And you fired me for incompetence?"

"I fired you for taking unnecessary risks!" Connall barked back at the man, his posture just as defiant as ever, despite the mens' height differences. "Serahaven was a pointless gamble! We weren't ready, we didn't have enough information! We essentially just put ourselves in their path, to be divided and conquered, and that is exactly what happened! And I told you it would!"

"We saved almost thirty lives in that town," Puck, of all people, spoke up in defense of the husky. "Begging your pardon sir, I don't mean to be telling you how to do your job, but... I'd say you did exactly what you were supposed to do, in Serahaven."

"Our job is to find Rourke!" the pit bull snapped. "Not play watchdog to whatever town we think he might attack."

"He did attack Serahaven!" Grant insisted. "We've been trying to anticipate one of his attacks for years now, and when we finally do, and we save the people in town, we have done our job!"

"We lost seventeen men protecting that sodding place!" The pit bull roared, and even Grant winced back. "Most of which were conscripts from the local garrison! I had to tell their families, Wickham! Do you have any idea how hard it was to look them in the eyes? Tell them their boys died well, when I bloody well know they didn't?! Most of those boys died in a panic, trapped in a gorge, with no escape. All because we got caught with our britches down, by the same sodding bastards who've been making a mockery of us for three years now!"

He crossed the remaining space between he and the husky with a noticeable limp, and it was hard, despite all I'd ever had against the man, not to feel some pity for him in that moment. "Do you think I like being made a mockery of, Wickham?" Connall growled. "Do you think I honestly enjoyed spending these last three years, chasing our tails, accomplishing nothing? Do you think I enjoy being in these piss-water settlements, on the edge of civilization, surrounded by lessers and degenerates?" He gestured at the women in the room at that, and I saw more than a few hackles raise.

"Then why accept the mission?" Grant pointed out. "You were a senior officer. You could have turned it down—"

"My seniority is why I couldn't turn it down!" Connall snapped. "I got into this line of work for reasons you could never appreciate, boy. I serve because I love my country! I've never cared about rank, I've never cared about doing something grandiose with my life. We aren't trying to be heroes here. We aren't protectors, we are civil servants who do whatever is necessary for the good of our nation! And if sometimes that involves putting the overall mission over a few innocent lives, we do that, because we must."

"That isn't what I signed on for!" Grant insisted.

"That's because you're ignorant," the pit bull growled, flatly. "You haven't any broader perspective on our work. And it's not even your bloody fault. You're uneducated, boy. You're simple. I thought at the very least you'd listen to me, and this would all work out. But you were stubborn. You were obstinate. You didn't listen. And you're not listening, even now."

Grant's ears had fallen back, and he looked torn somewhere between doubt and anger. "I'm not..." he stammered, but the words fell off, like he wasn't really certain what to say. I was about to jump to his defense, spitting angry, when the husky spoke again. "Is this because of where I grew up?" He demanded, suddenly.

Connall gave a disgusted snort. "Boy," he muttered, "you're thinking in reverse. You're not ignorant because you grew up in the slums. People like you live in the slums because you're ignorant."

I saw Grant's fist ball, and my hand went to my quiver all but instantly. I knew if this erupted into a fight, they had us out-armed, if not outnumbered.

But the husky wrested control over his anger, with visible difficulty. His hand slowly uncurled, and I didn't miss Connall's sharp eyes taking stock of the fact. He looked disappointed.

"I guess I'm not that simple, after all, Connall," Grant growled, after a long silence. "I'm not giving you cause to arrest me."

The pit bull's brows came together, and for a moment, I thought I saw real concern there. "Damnit, man," the canine said, exhausted, "why can't you see I'm trying to help you?" His eyes swept the room, and settled, of all places, on mine. "All of you," he said, firmly. "Please. Stop. No one else needs to die to these people. Let us do our job."

"Let us help you, then," I tried to emphasize. "We can work together again. Let bygones be bygones. We both have the same goal here."

Connall shook his head. "You want to see these people brought to justice?"

"Of course!" I said, frustrated.

"Then you need do nothing more," the pit bull informed us all, raising his voice. "We've discovered where they're encamped. We'll be closing in on them within the week. "

"What?" Grant and I both said in unison, shocked.

"You heard me," Connall stated. "You needn't do any more. We have them in our cross-hairs. They slipped up a week or so back. Raided a trade post and left survivors. Big mess, but we were finally able to catch their trail."

"Was there an outbreak at the trade post?" Puck spoke up from where he sat, his attention as rapt on the conversation as any of us.

160

Connall barely seemed to hear the fox. "We think they raided it for supplies only. It wasn't a well-organized attack."

"Of course it wasn't," I said, crossing my arms over my chest. "You still had Shadow then, didn't you?"

Connall's eyes flicked back to mine. "Indeed, we did."

"It's possible she's back with them, by now…" I murmured. "Do you know if any of the other men got sick? It's so easy to catch."

"We got very little out of her while we had her, but we got enough," Connall said. "I assure you, we have the information we need now, and none of it is your business. We'll handle this."

"Where are they encamped?!" Grant suddenly demanded, in a tone verging on anger and desperation. "If you won't tell us, at least let us help you! I'll go in under your command—"

"I don't have the authority to deputize another Marshal—" Connall began.

"Then re-hire me, damnit!" The husky insisted.

"And put you back in command?" Connall scoffed. "No, Wickham. I have finally made some headway, and I assure you, I do not need your help, or the help of any of your… native companions," he muttered, not looking at any of us, but the derision was evident. "I came here in hopes I might talk you all down from doing something foolish by assuring you that the situation was well-in-hand."

"Your men ain't hunters!" Ransom shouted, across the room. "I've seen 'em in the field! These people know how to fight like natives. Your boys bumble through th' forest like sodding cattle. They'll hear you a mile away!"

"I've enlisted the help of several mercenaries," Connall replied evenly. "But as I said, it isn't your business any more. I don't need to explain my tactics to you, and I don't plan on it."

"You're hiring mercenaries, but you won't hire me?!" Grant said, aghast. "My God, man! What in the hell did I do to lose your respect like this?"

"I think I already answered that question," Connall stated, coldly. "Don't make me repeat myself. I don't think you're incompetent, Wickham," he said, before Grant could shout something back at him. The husky was literally shaking. I wanted so badly to hold him, but I knew right now, he needed to stand alone. "I want you to know that," Connall said, more quietly. "I just think you're young. You're inexperienced. And you don't appreciate the full weight of this situation. None of you really do. It's not your fault. You're just not capable of handling this properly. You never were."

"Then why in the hell did they give this mission to me?!" Grant demanded, his voice going hoarse in his desperation, on the last word. "Why was I hired?"

Connall sighed, and reached down, which briefly made me bristle, until I realized he was only rubbing at his injured thigh. He was quiet for a long while, and I knew the signs in a man who wanted to say more than he was.

At length, he just shook his head and turned, gesturing at the two men flanking him to follow him.

"We aren't done here!" Grant shouted after him.

"You can't understand the whole situation, Wickham," Connall said, as he walked slowly towards the door. "So there isn't any more I can say."

He turned as he reached the doorway, passing Veronica on the way. At this point she had her rifle out and visible, and made sure the men knew it as they left.

"Please listen to me for once, boy," the man called to Grant, before opening the door. "Go home."

And then the men left, and Connall slammed the door behind him.

Grant slammed the door behind us when we at last turned in for the night some time later. A drawn-out, intense conversation had followed Connall's exit from the inn, and in the end, the only thing the five of us could concretely determine was that we were all frustrated, but no one knew exactly what to do to get the facts out of Connall.

"We could follow him, somehow," Grant muttered distractedly, dropping his rucksack down heavily on the floor and shoving it unceremoniously up against the wall with one big footpaw. "We should follow him somehow. I just don't know how."

"We don't even know when he's leaving, Grant," I said softly, sitting on the edge of the bed and setting my bow and quiver down on the nightstand. "Let alone where from. He may not even be at the garrison any more. And if he is, how on earth could we possibly follow him from there without being noticed?"

"I- I don't know," the husky said with a long, ragged sigh. The man undid the buttons down his vest and shucked it off, rumbling his discontent as he threw it on a nearby chair. It wasn't like him to be so careless with his clothing, so I knew this wasn't just something that would pass easily for once. It was so uncharacteristic to see the husky this upset and be so calm, myself.

I couldn't really say why. But this whole development with Connall didn't upset me. For some reason, I didn't doubt that we'd find a way to be involved in taking down the raiders. Maybe I'd just been calmer lately. Maybe Crow was giving me confidence. Or maybe, I at last had some confidence of my own.

"Grant," I said soothingly. "Don't let him bother you. Nothing's changed, for us. We need to rest, and then in the morning, we'll all be refreshed and ready to tackle this. And we will. Together. We don't need him."

The man struggled to maintain his composure, and let out a long breath, heading over towards me and stopping at the foot of the bed, near where I was seated. I shifted to my knees on the bed and put my arms gently around his waist, lifting myself up against his body.

"He knows…" he growled helplessly, averting his eyes from mine as he continued his bitter thoughts. "He knows, and he won't bring me in on it. I know I don't have the man's experi-

163

ence, but was I really that incompetent, to him? I tried, damnit. I committed three years of my life to this. I shouldn't be barred from helping him end it. This is—" he stopped himself there, his ears flattening, his whole posture slumping, "Was... my job."

"Grant," I said the man's name quietly, but with a bit more emphasis, so as to break him from his defeated thoughts. I reached up and took hold of his chin, tilting it down towards me. "I am glad to have your help. The people in Serahaven were glad for your help. You have been doing your job. Don't let one man's biased opinion sour your resolve. Your confidence was one of the things that attracted me to you. And I've come to rely upon it."

The husky's brows lifted some. "Really?"

I nodded, wrapping my arms around his waist and leaning up as high along the man's body as I could on my knees, kissing him softly along the neck, where his collar was open.

"You're firm. Reliable," I said, looking up into the man's eyes. "So few other things in my life are. Don't start doubting yourself now."

"I'm not," he said, as if affirming it for himself. "I know I've done as much as I could."

"You did," I nodded. "We all have. We gave everything we had. And we'll keep doing so, until we find them."

"I just wish he would do the same..." the man rumbled, unhappily.

"Sometimes you just have to work around stubborn, uncooperative people," I murmured, as I reached my hands down to his waist and undid the buckle on his gun belt. I threaded the leather strap out and pulled the heavy weight of it carefully off of his hips, before laying it down on the chair nearby. He let me, as he had many nights for the last week. He didn't even fight me when I began unbuttoning his riding pants. It had become enough of a routine now that he hardly noticed. He just sighed and undid the buttons along his cuffs, before working himself free of his shirt. I'd already undressed almost entirely while he was ranting.

164

"The beds here are nice," I said, off-topic, as I wiggled my toes against the soft comforter. We'd opted for a more normal-sized room for he and I, and the bed was enormous by my standards, but it would be a welcome change from sharing the tiny tent that had been our home for the last week.

"I don't know how he expects to find their camp without trackers, in any case," Grant muttered bitterly, as he tugged his shirt off entirely and tossed it on the chair with his vest. "Or maybe that's what his 'mercenaries' are for. Bloody hell. Mercenaries..."

He was clearly having a lot of trouble letting go of this. I suppose, considering the fact that he'd spent so much longer working with Connall, it felt like far more of a betrayal, or a humiliation. I cared far less what the pit bull thought of me, and I was convinced our task could be done under our own steam. I didn't need his help. We'd handle this ourselves. A lead would have been nice, but—

I swept my eyes back up Grant's body, intending to say something placating that might calm the man down enough that he could at least rest tonight, but I found myself just stopping to look at him for a while, instead. In all the chaos of the last hour, I'd forgotten that this would be our first night together in slightly more tolerable living conditions. And more importantly, it was the first time I'd ever really seen him like this in any kind of light.

I ran my paws softly up his chest. My staring hadn't caught his attention, he'd still been too wrapped up in his thoughts, but the touching certainly did. He glanced down at me, murmuring, "Shivah?"

I gave a soft, breathless chuckle, pressing my nose into the soft white fur along his chest, almost honey gold in the candlelight. "I'm sorry, you're just so gorgeous..."

The husky's expression softened a bit, and he reached a paw down to thread his fingers through my mane, as he so loved to do. I tugged him down enough to kiss him, and soon I had him beneath me in bed, with no resistance. With the soft light

165

flickering throughout the room, the reds in his fur shone in fiery, rich shades of sharp orange amidst the darker rust, and I traced the border of nearly every marking, committing the man's body to memory. It probably wouldn't be often we'd find any place in Otherwolf society where we could bed down together at night in a lit, warm room like this, and truly see one another.

When I unwrapped my chest and leaned down over him to kiss him again, he made me stop, and ran his own paws gently up my body, likely doing precisely what I'd been. He looked on me reverently for a time, and I found that I didn't mind. Something had certainly shifted between us, ever since I'd let go of my fears of being with him like this. Or maybe it was just a shift within me. It was hard to say. But I didn't feel afraid that he saw me like this. And a year ago, I never could have said that, about any man.

"Shivah," he said at length, his eyes moving to mine. I knew by his gaze that he was going to say something important. I didn't interrupt him.

"When you told that woman today that we were married." He murmured. "Would you ever? I mean, I don't mean soon. I just—"

"Does it bother you to be with me like this, outside of that sort of commitment?" I asked, quietly.

"No," he shook his head. "That's not it at all. I just mean, I don't think the title matters much. And it would be hard. We come from two different worlds, essentially. But I," he let out a breath, "I really love you. So much. I think I have since I met you. I'll wait a lifetime for you, if that's what you want. But would you ever truly want to be with me?"

I averted my eyes. I'd known, of course, that whatever it was we had, it meant more to the husky than it currently did to me. But that wasn't because I didn't care for the man. And it wasn't because I thought I never could. It's just that the thought of loving someone—of loving a man, romantically, and not just as a friend—it was hard, for some reason.

166

"I'm not saying no," I said softly, which seemed to give the man some hope. "But would you give me some time?"

Grant nodded, wrapping his arms around my waist and leaning up to kiss me. "Like I said, Shivah," he murmured, "I'll wait a lifetime, if that's what it takes."

I ran my hands softly over the scruff of fur along his cheeks, and up over his ears. I leaned in close, and nosed him gently. "I won't make you wait that long. I promise," I said with a slight smile.

He smiled as I kissed him again, and when I pushed him back down onto his back, he didn't fight me. Nor did he resist when I got us both entirely undressed, and bore him down beneath me. He certainly didn't argue when I pressed our bodies together, fur to fur, and rubbed my hips against his, until he was firm enough that I could take him in my paw. And that hardly took long.

The only point at which he gave a hitched breath and began to say something that sounded uncertain was when I pressed his broad tip against my nethers. But before he could stop me, I did as I'd convinced myself I needed to do, and needed to do all at once, lest I lose my nerve and sunk down atop him.

And gods, it's a good thing I'd done it all at once. Slowly would have been torturous for both of us. As it was, I was seeing white when I closed my eyes for nearly a minute, and we were both shaking, and adjusting, and overwhelming really wasn't a substantial enough word for how it felt. Satisfying was closer, but it still wasn't entirely adequate.

I kissed him, for lack of knowing what else to do, and wrapped my shuddering arms around his shoulders. And he held me close, and we just sort of rocked for a bit, his paws shakily running down my back and over my hips. There really weren't any words that were right for this, like I said, so neither of us said anything. We just did what felt natural. For the first time in my life, this felt natural.

As much as I loved being atop the man, eventually, we were both panting into one another's muzzles and I knew we both wanted more, and I just wasn't able to take us there, the way we were. So I leaned up and nipped at his neck, needfully, and somehow even without words, he seemed to know. He turned me over onto my stomach, and moved over me, and I could have cared less in that moment what had or hadn't happened to me in the past. The second he sunk into me again, it felt like taking a breath. Like it was exactly what I needed in that second, and this was the way it was meant to be, and Methoa could rot in hell, because I'd never been the one who was wrong.

After that, it was too blissful to last, and I think we both knew it. Every motion felt so good, so right, and it was over-whelming in the best of ways, but there was no drawing it out. I was no less thrilled when my body gave in, even though it seemed far too soon, although I was somewhat shocked by how much I lost control of myself in those last few moments. I'd discover later I'd clawed up the sheets.

But Grant was no more restrained than I. I was in a haze when I felt him stiffen, and he flooded me with warmth, but I think he literally howled. If he hadn't been so breathless, he'd have woken the entire Inn.

We collapsed into a tangled pile atop one another, the both of us panting for breath. Amidst the haze, I was starting to come to terms with the physical reality of what we'd done some. I found, shockingly, that there was no hint of the revulsion, or pain, that I'd once felt. Some discomfort, but it was far outweighed by other, more pleasant sensations.

The husky was still shaking, even long after we'd finished. Or I was. It was hard to say. But I leaned up at length and planted a soft kiss on his muzzle, and waited for him to open his eyes to look at me. And when he did, I smiled.

"God," the man muttered, "I think I've been doing that wrong, until tonight."

"Me, too," I murmured softly.

As it turned out, we'd use much of the evening to practice. And I'm fairly certain we got better at it as we went. Being with a canine had its interesting bits, but for once, I was enjoying learning more about my lover. I enjoyed every second of it we spent together, honestly. Even those spent in bumbling, over-whelmed awkwardness, or amusement at our own shared over-eagerness.

I'm not sure when we eventually fell asleep, but neither of us woke when, at some point during the night, a piece of parchment was slid under our door.

CHAPTER FIVE
THE CONFRONTATION AHEAD

I woke, my every sense dominated by the man in bed beside me. My body was warm against his, my fur was crushed softly into his, his deep breathing rousing me slowly, hazily, as my vision adjusted to the bright sunlight streaming in through the window behind us. I was enveloped in his arms, as I'd become accustomed to being when we slept together like this. His muzzle was just slightly over my shoulder, cascading his warm breaths down the nape of my neck. He looked so serene.

I watched him sleep for a time, as my mind slowly came awake. But I was in no hurry to move. In earnest, I could have stayed right where I was, listening to him breathe, all day. It was amazing to me that something this simple, something as normal as a quiet moment beside someone I cared about, could give me such peace. It was a peace I'd been missing from my life for a very long time.

For the first time since all of this had begun, I considered giving up. It was strange. I finally had the support of friends, a lover, and companions, all of whom were competent people with a vested interest in my quest. Less than a year ago, my chances at pursuing my goal had seemed a pipe dream. An impossibility I couldn't even comprehend an answer to. But I'd endured. I'd made friends. I'd allowed myself to open to those friends in ways I hadn't since I was a child. And I'd earned their trust in kind.

And now we were poised at the tip of a blade, closer than we'd ever been before to achieving our goal, and I had the help I'd need to pursue it—to finish this. Why now, after all I'd endured to get this far, did I want to give up the chase? But there was no denying it. I'd been feeling doubtful about my convictions for weeks now. It just seemed like there were other things happening in my life—in my world—of more importance than the vengeance I'd clung to for so long. Without even a thought, I'd put the chase to save Puquanah, and then Ransom, over my goals. I could have pursued the raiders then. They'd been so close. But I hadn't even considered it. My friends were more important.

And now I had... I looked up at the sleeping canine. I wasn't even really certain what I had with Grant. But I didn't mind the confusion, for once. It felt more like a good unknown. What lay ahead of us was a new frontier, and one that I was certain would not be easy. But I wanted to walk the path with him, find what could be found. Maybe someday, I'd love him as he loved me. Puck and Ransom had certainly overcome many hurdles to be together, and were still. If they could find a way—

The husky stirred, and I saw two stunning slits of blue between his pale eyelids as he slowly awoke. He looked down on me drowsily for a bit, before a soft smile tugged at the corners of his muzzle.

"Good morning, beautiful," he murmured, in a voice thickened by sleep.

I couldn't help smiling back. The man had never apologized, in all the time I'd known him, for his overly charming demeanor and way of speaking. But the more I'd gotten to know him, the more I'd come to realize that, defying all logic, it simply wasn't a show. It was just who he was.

So I just said "Good morning," in return, and leaned up to nuzzle him, giving a genuine purr.

He gave a content rumble, pulling me in a bit closer. "I want to wake this way every morning, for the rest of my life," he murmured, stroking a hand up through my mane and curling a braid around one of his fingers, while he stroked my cheek with his thumb.

I gave a slight smirk and rolled the man easily onto his back—he always gave way for me—and nipped gently at his neck, while our legs entwined.

"You wouldn't rather I wake you in other ways?" I asked, feeling emboldened by the night we'd had, and everything it had entailed.

Grant gave a deep chuckle. "As soon as I wake? You are a demanding woman."

"If you must know," I murmured, nipping at the soft edge of his ear, "I think I'm in heat."

"Lord," the man uttered, as I ran my hands down his chest. "That explains a lot."

It was only after we'd finished making love, I was finally beginning to understand why the Otherwolves called it that, and I much preferred it to the term 'mating', that our playfulness in post-coital bliss brought something critical to our attention.

Grant was trying, to no avail, to get out of bed and make it to his brush, which he insisted he needed, and badly. He wasn't wrong, but I was determined to keep the man in bed until someone came looking for us and possibly ignore them even then. I was winning the battle with the aid of a few dirty tricks, when I caught sight of the folded, weathered piece of paper lying a foot from the bottom of our door.

I released the husky, who seemed more bemused than anything when I sat up and climbed off of him, and called after me as I padded across the room.

"Shivah," he said with a breathless laugh, "get my brush while you're up."

I leaned down slowly onto my haunches and looked at the strange, unsigned piece of parchment. It was sealed with a smear of dark wax, and lay just far enough from the crack under our door that I knew someone had slid it beneath. It certainly hadn't been here when we'd come in last night.

"Grant…" I murmured, quietly, and hesitantly reached down to pick up the piece of paper. It felt heavier than it should have, for some reason. I lifted it slowly as I stood, and held it in both hands. I saw the husky turn to regard me, and then he stiffened and sat up, his own blue eyes as pinned to the letter as mine were.

"Who?" he queried.

I shook my head, turning the paper over slowly in my paws, so that my thumbs rested against the wax seal. I don't know why I hesitated. Thinking back, I believe it must have been because I knew, knew without a shadow of a doubt,, that the letter would contain something of importance to my hunt. And what I would have fought, killed for, in the past, now seemed unwelcome.

But at length, I cracked the wax with my claws and the letter popped open... As I unfolded it, I saw exactly what I'd simultaneously most hoped for and most feared.

A map. It was crudely drawn in charcoal, and red ink to indicate the roads, but I knew the area well enough to recognize that it covered the surrounding countryside. A large red blot must have signified Crossroads, based on the way it connected to the roads, and past the river, past three settlements and a small lake we'd once taken a road by there was a jagged X drawn in charcoal. It lay amidst a largely unsettled area of forest.

And there was writing. Scrawled and unrefined, but written in bold, large letters, in red, over the entire lower third of the paper. I slowly crossed the space towards the bed, where the husky sat silently, and gingerly lowered the paper towards him.

He took it, uncertainly at first.

"Can you read?" I asked softly.

"I can," he said, and it was hard to miss the pang of pride in the man's voice. I imagined where he came from, where he'd grown up, not many could.

He looked down at the paper for a moment or so, and I saw his body go tense.

"Grant... ?" I said.

He seemed to be re-reading it a few times, before at length, his eyes slowly rose to mine.

"It says 'Dusk. Tonight. They need to die.'"

I rapped on Puck and Ransom's door for a full minute or so before I got any kind of answer. And when I did, it wasn't even really a direct one. I heard the men inside, talking in hushed voices. I couldn't make out what they were saying, but Puck seemed to be arguing something quietly with the coyote.

"I'm sorry to wake you!" I called through the wooden door. "But we need to talk. Please. It's extremely important."

Another long pause, and then Ransom's voice called out loudly enough to be heard, "Sure, c'mon in."

I heard Puck snap something at him as I went for the handle. The doors here didn't lock. Apparently it was a policy of the Inn. I suppose I could understand why. There was just a 'knock first' sort of rule for the place that everyone seemed to follow.

When I stepped inside, I was only momentarily disconcerted by the sight that greeted me. And that said something about the direction my life had gone, of late.

The two men were lying in bed together, nude, and unashamedly so, in Ransom's case… Puck was tucked up against the coyote with his back to his chest, Ransom's arm and one of his legs draped lazily over the now irate-looking fox.

"What's happenin', cat?" The coyote asked, stroking his claws over the still-white fur along Puck's hip, tracing one of his tattoos. I swear, the fox nearly slapped his hand aside.

"This couldn't have waited?" Puck asked, sounding uncomfortable and impatient.

"She said it was 'extremely important'," Ransom said, pointedly, then looked up to me. "Seriously, kitten. It better be."

"It is," I said, holding out the paper. "Here, come take a look at this."

"Uh…" The coyote glanced awkwardly down at the fox, who just shot him an irritated glare.

"Well go ahead, Ransom," the fox said, dryly, "go on over there."

174

Ransom gave a hoarse, embarrassed laugh, and then let out a sigh. "Sh-nhh... darlin', I'm sorry, but you're gonna hafta' bring that over here. I ain't budgin' for a little while, here."

I just blinked at the man, confused.

Puck sighed. "Shivah, remember how I was saying there were some gaps you didn't want me to fill in, concerning my relationship with this bastard? Certain things you really don't need to know?"

"I—oh," I murmured. "Gaps. Right. You did mention those."

Puck sighed. "This is one of those. Just bring the paper here."

He held out a hand, and I headed over to them and handed it to him. He held it up for Ransom, who looked at it for a few moments, his eyes narrowing.

I crossed my arms over my chest, arching an eyebrow at the two of them. "Honestly, you could have just asked me to wait," I muttered, as Ransom puzzled over the map.

"That's what I said!" Puck said, exasperated.

"And for your information, this isn't exactly a 'gap' for me, anymore," I murmured, a bit awkwardly. "Grant is canine. I learned a thing or two about... 'tying'... already."

"Definitely gonna have 'that talk'," Ransom muttered, as his eyes scanned the map. At length, he looked back up at me. "Well that's somethin'. I can't read most of it, but I got the jist. Someone wants us in on this attack."

"What?" Puck asked, running his fingers over the parchment, to little avail. The charcoal hadn't left much of an indent in the paper. "What is it?" He asked, frustrated.

"A map," I informed him, seriously. "I think it's the location of Rourke's camp. The one Connall found. It's in an unsettled area, between two of the fringe settlements. It's close, but completely unremarkable. We passed it along the road on the way to Serahaven. I think you mentioned there were a lot of old mines in that area, Ransom."

He nodded. "Yeah, woods're thick there. Rocky soil. Real uneven. Bad place to settle. They thought they found gold out there five years back or so, but mosta' those mines are abandoned now. Damn," he swore, "good place to hunker down. Tough for us. I'm guessin' they're near one of the old mines, which means they're probably dug in real well. Them places were death-traps even without a buncha' bloody murderers usin' 'em to hide."

"What do you mean?" I asked, listening intently. I knew what the basic concept of a mine was, but as to the specifics, or how they could be used against us...

Ransom sighed. "Well obviously, if they're near an entrance, they got an escape route. Might not go far, or they might've been clever enough to pick one that empties out in more 'n one place. Probably hidin' their supplies underground, so we ain't gonna see a lot of signs they're settlin' there. Best bet's to look for fires, smoke—"

"The letter said dusk," I nodded.

"Smart," Ransom nodded, "they might douse the fires when they sleep, but they gotta light them to cook their grub, at th' very least. Boil water. We catch 'em at dinner... It's a shot." He shook his head, looking up to me, "But it ain't just findin' them that's a problem. Those areas're full of sink holes, or shafts the miners dug up fer air, or just exits. You put any sort of effort to it, and you've got terrain ripe fer pit traps, not to mention a lotta loose rock, so creepin' about ain't gonna be easy."

Puck gave a sudden, muffled groan and buried his nose in the bedsheets, grumbling something under his breath in his native tongue that I couldn't make out. I was about to ask him what was wrong when I saw Ransom shift back up into a sitting position, and I averted my eyes, so the man could... settle... himself. He opted to just grab his trousers from where they were unceremoniously draped over the foot of the bed, and pull them on while I continued to stare intently at the wall. I didn't ever need to see that man's bits.

I cleared my throat. "Maybe if we're lucky, Connall's men will attract so much attention, we'll be able to make it to the camp unnoticed."

176

"I don't buy that man goin' in unprepared," Ransom muttered. "He's an asshole, but he ain't stupid. He's got a plan o' some sort, if he's doin' this at all and he ain't just yankin' our chain."

I looked back at the coyote as he tugged up his suspenders, and I knew we were both thinking the same thing.

"You think all o' that last night was just an act?" Ransom said it first. "You think this was his plan all along? Let us do the bits he can't?"

"The question is why he'd do that…" I murmured. I'd considered the possibility it was the pit bull who'd slipped us the message, of course. I'd suspected since everything first started going wrong with Connall that he was hiding a lot from us. Maybe what he was hiding was simply that he knew he couldn't handle this without our help, but didn't want to admit to it.

"It'd spare his pride, for one," Ransom snorted. "But maybe it's more 'n that. Maybe it goes up the chain o'command, or somethin'. Otherwolves wantin' this solved by Otherwolves. Maybe that's the real reason he got rid of yer husky. Wouldn't look too good for the Marshals if Rourke were brought in by a buncha' bush folk like us, when they've had their boys on it fer years. Grant didn't give a damn about who got the credit of it, but men like Connall," he shook his head. "I could see him carin'. A lot."

"I don't care who gets the credit," I growled. "What a stupid reason to cause so much trouble."

"Otherwolves're real wrapped up in this 'higher species', 'lesser species' bullshit, sweetheart," Ransom said derisively. "Part o' their whole identity. Their religion, even."

"I don't know," Puck murmured, his muzzle still mostly buried in the sheets. He had yet to budge, save to wrap his tail around himself. "There wouldn't have been much reason to make such a show of things in front of the women at this place. If he'd wanted to subtly ask for our help, but he didn't want to seem it. Why bother putting on that performance for a small audience of burlesque dancers? I think he honestly doesn't want us involved in this." He flicked his ears at Ransom. "And he's not entirely wrong, you know. This really isn't a civilian matter."

"We ain't talkin' about this again," Ransom said with a sigh.

"Clearly not. No one is willing to listen to me," Puck muttered.

"Even if Shadow got treatment," I said to the fox, "her men could have caught it, Puck. I thought we agreed we needed to do something about this. Even you agreed."

The fox opened his eyes to slits, and the guilt I saw there made me hurt. I hadn't meant to reinforce my point by making him regret what he'd done, again. I had no doubt he'd been regretting it every second since he'd woken from the Len'sal.

But regardless how he felt about it, his actions had driven Shadow to seek treatment, and even if she'd outwitted Connall in the process, the fact that she'd been away from her men was why they'd slipped up and done something foolish enough that we had their trail again. I was certain of that. It couldn't be a coincidence.

And it was likely what had tipped off whomever had sent us this note. And whoever they were, they clearly wanted us to help them wipe the men out. The words 'They need to die' were lodged in my mind, repeating again and again. The conviction in the statement was reigniting my own. Once more. We'd hunt once more. And then after tonight, it would all be over. This had to be fate.

"Could be the rat…" Ransom suddenly said, as he sat and pulled the long metal rod from his rifle, inspecting it for a moment before he reached into his bag to get the things he used to clean the firearm.

I bit my lip. Magpie? I hadn't even considered him.

"What makes you say that?" I asked, now rolling the possibility over in my own mind.

"Rat liked to work this way," Ransom said, not looking up from his rifle. "Sneaky. Subtle. And I still don't buy that he's the one who sold us out. Might be he's been skulkin' around the area, lookin' to clear his name. Huntin' those bastards."

"You think so?"

The coyote looked up at me. "It's what I would do."

"It all but has to be one or the other," Puck murmured, sighing. "Or just one of Connall's men. No one else would have a vested interest in this."

"Well it don't matter who it was," Ransom snorted, and spit on his rifle, scrubbing one of the rings. "We wanted our chance, and we got it. Don't look a gift horse in th' mouth, right?"

"I wish we knew what Connall's plan was…" I said, crossing my arms over my chest. "I don't like going in blind."

"We won't," the coyote said, raising his sharp gaze to mine. "We do this right. Smart. Like huntin' any game. Scope the land, get our bearings first. Watch our prey." One corner of his muzzle turned up, revealing a sharp-toothed smirk beneath it. "G'won in for the kill when we know we've got 'em in our crosshairs."

"What about Grant?" I asked, pointedly. "He won't want to be left out of this, but I'll be honest… the man isn't much of a hunter."

"He's got brass ones, though," the coyote replied. "There's always a place fer men like that. I think I got a thought on how t'go about this. Granted, we don't know the layout yet, but we can adapt it, ah think…"

I nodded. I was entirely willing to defer to the coyote's superior knowledge and experience in fighting and killing men. He'd been doing it far longer than I.

"Get dressed, and let's all sit down and have a talk," I said.

By midday, we had set out into the wilderness again. This time, the lands themselves weren't so much a danger, we may not have been taking roads where we were going, but the woodlands here had been settled and cleared of most threats.

What was most dangerous, looming before us like a great thunderhead, dark and broiling a storm we could not know the strength or ferocity of, was our destination.

We'd bid Laesom farewell in town, the old wolf agreed with our assessment that it was better he remain at Crossroads. The man had never been a warrior, even in his youth, as I'd long suspected. He was primarily a traveler and apparently, a lore-keeper. What some might call a 'storyteller'. I was learning things about the man in bits and pieces, but his story was a long tapestry to unravel that, unfortunately, I knew I would likely never know the full extent of. But perhaps when all of this was over, he'd tell me some of his stories.

I wanted Puquanah to remain in town as well, but he'd stubbornly resisted, claiming if we could all put our lives on the line, we would have to accept that he would, too. I couldn't argue with the fox's logic, but if he insisted on actually joining the fray, I would have to put my foot down. He was walking without much assistance now, but he was still recovering from his injuries, and blind besides.

Puck assured me he wanted nothing to do with the melee early on in our journey, though, and that he was coming along purely to treat our injuries if and when we sustained them. And apparently, he had other preparations I was unaware of.

For a short portion of the trip, we were traveling along the river. It was when we neared an alcove of birch and an ancient, draping willow that the fox stopped, and murmured something to Ransom I didn't catch. I paused in my own tracks, Grant and I looking back at the couple as they spoke lowly, until the coyote nodded, then looked to us.

"We're going to stop here for just a bit," he stated, unshouldering his rifle and bow.

Grant glanced out over the river, holding a paw up over his eyes to look towards the sun. "Are you certain?" He asked. "We need to make good time to get there early enough, if we're going to—"

"Trust me, this is important," Ransom said, unbuttoning his shirt.

I arched an eyebrow. Puck had knelt beside the water, and was sorting through his herbal pouch, pulling a few things out. I couldn't imagine exactly what it was they had in mind.

"You're bound up, right?" Ransom asked me, as he draped his shirt over a nearby tree bough, and unbuttoned his leather pants.

"I… yes," I said, looking at the man curiously. "I always bind myself back if I think I'll be shooting."

"Good. You're gonna need to strip down to yer smallclothes them, sweetheart, or whatever y' got on," the coyote informed me.

"Um…" I heard Grant beginning to object from behind me.

"Oh," I paused, as I smelled something familiar, harkening back to memories from my life amongst the Anukshen. Puck was mixing it in a small clay bowl, adding water as he went. The crimson paste had a distinct scent to it, and though I'd only seen it used a few times in my life, it was hard to forget.

I put a hand on Grant's shoulder. "It's war paint," I informed him. Then I looked to Puquanah, who was focusing on the task at hand. "Puck?" I asked inquisitively, "Are you going to perform a ritual?"

"Do as Ransom says," Puck muttered, "if you want to be involved. If not, it's fine."

I tried to hide the slight smile tugging at the corners of my muzzle. Puck was acting uncharacteristically abashed. I honestly wasn't certain if this had been his idea, or if Ransom had asked him to do this for us, but either way, I was intrigued that the fox would even consider it.

Not to mention, I was somewhat proud that I'd even be considered to take part in a war ritual. Such honors were reserved only for men, in my tribe and most any I had ever known. I began to undress to my undergarments without any further hesitance. Today of all days, we needed the aid of the spirits.

"This is… religious?" Grant asked, uncertainly. He looked a bit lost.

I nodded, looking to him. "Puck," I paused, "Puquanah is going to call upon the spirits of war and pray for their strength, and their guidance in the coming battle. If our prayers are answered, the paint will mark our bodies as vessels for their souls, temporarily. We will gain their ferocity, their resolve, and be elevated beyond our mortal abilities."

Grant just looked down at me, brows raised. "Intense," he said at length. "So," he murmured, "you're going to be inhabited by an animal spirit? Do you get to pick which?"

I shook my head. "They choose their host. And we cannot know which spirits will heed our call."

"The Knights from my homeland used to do something similar," Grant murmured, scratching his chin. "In the holy book, it says great holy warriors might sometimes channel the power or protection of angels."

"What's an angel?" I asked, mystified.

"A servant of God," Grant said, gesturing to the sky. "Beings who dwell in His Kingdom. The final resting place for all Elevated Souls. Those whose bloodlines are the most pure, who have lived exemplary, good lives, eventually are allowed to escape the cycle of rebirth, and join Him. Some of them choose not to rest, and they become angels."

I smiled. "Would you like to pray to your angels for their help?"

Grant gave a soft smile back. "I pray every night," he said. "I thank God for the life I've been given, and the many good things he's sent my way." He stroked my cheek softly at that.

"It sounds like you've actually had a very difficult life, Grant," I murmured.

"Do you know what the chances are that eight kids from the slums would all survive their childhood, and go on to make lives for themselves?" Grant pointed out. "No. I've been very lucky. I'm grateful for it every day."

"I thought your church didn't think very highly of your kind of people…"

He shrugged. "What man thinks, and what God thinks are not one in the same. I choose to believe God wouldn't judge me for how I was born, and that I've just as good a chance at reaching His Kingdom as any Pedigree." He smiled. "Just don't tell the Pedigrees that."

"Would your God frown on you taking part in our ritual?" I asked, uncertainly.

Grant chuckled. "That's sort of a gray area. I honestly don't know. But maybe it's best if I just pray in my own way. If that's alright with you."

"Of course," I said with a soft smile, and leaned up to nuzzle him for a brief moment or two, so he knew it honestly didn't bother me. I smiled as I pulled back. "Although I'll admit… I was looking forward to painting you."

Grant smirked. "Maybe someday just for fun," he promised. "What would you paint on me?"

I leaned up and kissed him softly, and murmured, "Wings. Of course."

I helped Ransom prepare a fire while Puck readied the few things he'd brought that were necessary for the ritual. Strong-smelling bundles of incense, made from herbs I didn't know, a fan made from the red tail feathers of a hawk, and the crimson red war paint, which by the look of it, he was mixing with his own blood. I remembered that it meant more if the holy man who called upon the spirits added his blood, because of his holy bloodline. It made me curious enough to ask something that had been nagging at me, though.

I lingered near Puck as he finished his preparations, while Ransom got more kindling for the fire. "Puck," I said softly, "do you believe in what you're about to do?"

Puck was silent for a time, tightening the knot on one of the bundles of incense. He took a little while before responding. "It doesn't matter," he finally replied. "If the spirits are real, what should matter is your belief in them, not mine. I'm not asking for their blessing."

"But you are, in a way," I pointed out. "You're asking them to help us…"

The fox turned to regard me, and the expression he wore was complex. He could be hard to read sometimes. Right now, he seemed intense, even determined, but also scared.

"Shivah," he said quietly, "I don't care what you or the spirits, if they even exist, think of me right now. If there is any chance in hell this works, or even just aids your confidence, it's worth doing. I'll take what I can get right now. I just want you two to come back to me alive. You're all I have."

I felt compelled to embrace the fox in that moment, and I did. He didn't reject the offer, just embraced me back, gently, and let me hold him for a time. When we parted, I gave him a smile, but said no more—even though I wanted to.

I felt if he was even considering this, he must have had some measure of faith still inside of him. Even if it was just a last dying ember, even if he barely recognized it, Puck didn't do anything he thought would be useless or a waste of his time. Which meant some part of him still believed. I didn't have to say that. I didn't have to point it out. It just made me happy to know it was there.

Being painted would prove to be the most time-consuming part, but Puck did it with such care, and managed it so well despite his blindness, I couldn't help but appreciate every moment of it, like I was watching art being created. The fox may have renounced his faith, but he remembered his training. That much was clear.

The ritual itself was not a long one, but it did involve chanting, much of which I didn't know. Ransom played the part of spirit caller, and Puck and I the respondents. It was nothing like the rituals amongst the Anukshen had been, in which nearly the entire tribe would take part, but despite that, it felt stronger, somehow, like our small band was calling deeper, resounding in a realm we could not see. I could almost feel it.

No one here was paying lip-service. Our prayers were genuine, desperate, and strengthened by our resolve. If there were spirits here, they would certainly hear us.

Puquanah ran the burning incense down over our bodies, the blackened, smoking herbs washing me in smoke and tingling at my skin. When I breathed it in, I felt it burn its way into my body, but it didn't hurt. It felt like power, pushing its way inside of me, puffing me up, and setting my nerves aflame. This was how the spirits were supposed to enter our bodies... I'd seen many warriors breathe in the sacred smoke before, and I'd seen the effects it could have upon them, but I'd never felt them myself.

I had expected—I wasn't certain. That I might hear the voice of whatever spirits heeded our call; that I might somehow feel their presence inside of me. But it wasn't like that. It wasn't so substantial, or understandable. It was more like a sensation, nameless but empowering, sharpening my thoughts and running down through my body, as though it moved through my blood.

Throughout, I heard Ransom's rhythmic, haunting chanting, and when I opened my eyes to look on the man, I had to blink several times, to clear the ghostly images of the fire that had been dancing behind my eyelids from my vision. I could have sworn I'd seen a black-furred Dyre, standing there beside the coyote, its red eyes glinting the same color as the paint he now wore on his fur. But when I blinked, it was gone.

The coyote turned to regard me, and after a long moment spent staring, he finished his final chant, and leaned down to stroke the fox's cheek.

"Thank you," he murmured to the arctic fox, who only nodded, and tossed the remaining herbs into the fire. Ransom made his way over towards me, regarding me for a moment before giving a confident nod.

"You ready to go kill some folk, Shivah?"

I looked up at him. "Do you think the spirits are with us?"

186

"Your bird is here, sweetheart," Ransom gestured up into the willow. "Look."

I did. At some point during the ritual, a flock of dark birds had moved into the branches of the tree overhead. They might well have just been a flock of birds, resting in the willow's many branches.

But there was no doubting I felt different. More powerful than I ever had. Whether that was just, as Puck had said, a boost to my self-confidence, or whether it was something truly spiritual, I could not say.

But I was ready to end this.

We came upon the vague area indicated on the map about two hours before sunset, and fanned out to locate the camp. I left Grant to guard Puck. We had a carefully-constructed plan, and unfortunately, the husky's part didn't come in until later. And even then I was wary of the role Ransom had in mind for the man. It was incredibly dangerous. But, just as the coyote had said, if there was one thing Grant had, it was raw nerve, and the man had accepted the role immediately. I could hardly argue. We were three people taking on a camp of several dozen. Even provided our mystery note-bringer showed, this would be no easy feat.

I moved through the broken countryside carefully, keeping low in the brush whenever it was available, and moving quickly between trees when it wasn't. If there were mines out here, they were elusive, which I suspected was exactly the danger. It was certainly rocky, broken land, and I happened upon a number of long-neglected game trails that looked like they'd had recent movement upon them. I was leaning down to inspect some horse tracks, when I heard the signal.

A lark, giving their territorial call. I waited several moments, and then I heard it again. And again.

Larks were rare in this area, but I knew their call well. Ransom said he'd use it if he found something. I took off towards the call, cutting through the countryside as quickly as I could while still being quiet. Every second counted, right now.

In my haste, I didn't notice the weak spot beneath my paws until it was nearly too late. If I hadn't been such a light person, it would have been too late.

I heard a snap, and felt the thin layer of brittle boughs give way beneath me, and my leg plummeted through them into the cavernous space beneath. I flung my arms out and sunk my claws into the earthen edges of the pit wildly, scrambling for purchase. Everything beneath me eventually gave way, and then I was dangling, clinging to slipping, loose earth, as the thin covering that had been obscuring the shaft fell into the abyss beneath.

I was almost afraid to shift, once I had a firm hold. I could hear the bits of rock and dirt I'd shaken loose with my paws littering down over sharp rocky edges beneath me… There was a bottom, but it sounded a good distance beneath, and likely not one that would be survivable.

I tried to steady my racing heart and stay calm. The best way to do this, I determined at length, would be to move all at once. It would be like pouncing, except without anything to push off of with my legs. All upper body. My arms were strong. I could do this.

I counted down in my head, and when I neared the end, I gave a silent prayer and mustered everything I had and shoved myself up.

The earth came free of my paws in clumps, just as I'd feared it would, but I'd managed some momentum in the thrust, and used it to strike both hands out further along the ground, digging my claws into the dirt there. And there, it was thicker, and didn't give way.

From there on out I was able to just pull myself to safety. I lay on the ground for a time, panting and terrified, and trying to shake off what had nearly just happened. I couldn't let this affect me. The real fight was still ahead.

Hearing the lark call again steeled my resolve. I forced myself back onto my feet and tried to ignore how badly I was shaking. I began heading towards the noise again, but this time, I did so far more carefully.

"Watch yer feet," Ransom snapped in a quiet but harsh whisper, as I dropped down beside him in the small niche he'd settled into. I hadn't even seen the coyote until I'd been within ten feet of him, but the lark call had led me to where he'd hidden himself away. I couldn't see anyone else from here, but the terrain dipped in this area into a rocky crevasse, where there was doubtlessly a mine somewhere, and probably more of those hidden shafts. That last one had most certainly been trapped on purpose, but they wouldn't all need to be, to prove dangerous.

"I know," I muttered, "I already found one of the pits."

The coyote gave me a concerned look. "Yer alright, then?"

"Just scared the hell out of me," I said, embarrassed. "But I promise you, I learned my lesson."

"Ain't just the pits we gotta worry about," Ransom said, and took hold of my chin, pointing it back into the forest from the way I'd come, towards a clearing of pines. "Look there…"

I narrowed my eyes, looking towards where he was directing me, but I didn't see…

It took me a few moments, but when I did see it, I was shocked I'd missed it on the way here to him. And I'd been careful. Lying, now exposed, but the same color as the leaf litter in the middle of the clearing, was a strange, terrifying-looking piece of metal, clamped down on a thick piece of dead wood, like the metal maw was trying to devour it. It had very nearly splintered it in half.

"Bear traps," the coyote growled. "Ah've found three so far. Nasty pieces o' work. They let 'em rust some so they're brown… blend in. Tripped the ones I found on purpose, but… I dunno how many more they got. You watch every step you take, cat. Thing like that'd snap th 'legs on a wee thing like you clean in half."

"I'll be careful," I promised fearfully, then tried to look through the trees into the crevasse. "Why did you call me? Are they—"

"Look out past that rock face there 'at looks like a kettle," Ransom gestured, and I tried to follow his line of sight. "Gets lost against the white rock, which ah'm guessin' is the point, but if you watch long enough, you'll see it."

I narrowed my eyes and did as he said. And at length, I saw it. Smoke.

"I got in close," Ransom said, before I could ask. "Confirmed it. They're pretty well entrenched there, looks like an old campsite they fell back on, or somethin' of the like."

"What makes you say that?" I asked, curiously.

Ransom shook his head. "Cuz from what little I could see, they ain't organized 'tall. The men're a mess. There's a big'un, a bear, who was barkin' orders now and again, but on the whole, they weren't actin' militarized, or even getting' on well. I caught a' least two spats, one broke out int'an all-out brawl. Coydog and a rat. Coydog won." He shook his head, peering over the rise again, but it wasn't possible for us to see anything of the camp from here. "I think they've just used this spot in the past, and fell back here. They're comin' apart. I didn't see the fox. I think she bailed on 'em entirely." He glanced nervously through the trees. "Or she's about and we just can't see her. Hopin' on the former, honestly."

"What caused all of this?" I asked, mystified. I hardly wanted to question our luck, but there was just too much working in our favor, today. It made me suspicious.

"Puck," Ransom said, firmly. Like he knew something I didn't.

I blinked. "The fever?"

The coyote nodded his head. "I saw a' least seven of them with the boils. Wickham was right, they are damn noticeable. Considerin' they've been raiding plague towns fer years and they clearly ain't fallen apart like this before, my guess is they ain't never had an outbreak in their own band before. I'm

190

guessin' the woman didn't know she had it. Or she hid it. People like that gotta share grub. Probably got outta control b'fore they even realized what was happenin'. Might be why she bailed."

"You think they forced her out?" I asked.

"Who the hell knows," Ransom sighed. "But it works in our favor, either way. Remind me to kiss that fox again when I see 'im."

I smiled. "Well we need to meet with him and Grant before we go in, anyway, so... I doubt he'll let you do this without a send-off."

Ransom's eyes flicked down to mine, and he looked strangely uncertain for a moment or two. It worried me. I knitted my brows, and put a paw on his arm. "Ransom?" I queried. "Whatever it is, speak up."

"Yer husband..." the coyote said, and I felt the fur along my spine prickle beneath my cloak, the chill working its way into my heart. "What's he look like?" The man asked, seriously.

I knew he was only asking me for one of two reasons. Either he'd seen him, or he hadn't. I honestly wasn't certain which I preferred, anymore.

"He's a little less than a head taller than me," I said softly, running the images I had in my memories of my husband through my mind, and trying to remember him accurately, not obscured through the fog that always morphed him into a monster in my thoughts. "Older. His eyes are sunken, his muzzle is lean, his ears are more ragged than mine..." I swallowed, "and he'd have a scar on his face. Over his cheek, and down over his lip." The last few moments I'd spent fighting him for my son's life had been harried, but I remembered my claw catching on his lip.

I'd fought with everything I'd had, then. Which hadn't been much, but I'd tried.

"Just the one scar?" Ransom asked, and his question wasn't one I'd expected. "Because the bobcat I saw was beat to hell and back. Looked like a Dyre's plaything."

"I... think he had a few more," I murmured, confused. I'd mostly closed my eyes during the times he'd been undressed

191

with me. But he had been a warrior. But for him to appear 'beat' from a distance, he must have been in a terrible state. And that wasn't the Methoa I remembered.

"Was he the only bobcat?" I asked. There had been other warriors that had gone with him, after all. I wasn't sure how many, but we'd only caught the one.

Ransom shook his head. "Only one 'at I saw. He looked like you said, though. Older. Real mean eyes. Built like a tribal warrior, but then I guess they'd all be…"

"Maybe he got injured in one of their recent raids," I offered. I rather liked the idea.

"Well whoever he is, he ain't high on the totem pole," Ransom muttered, shifting his legs. "I took 'em for a prisoner, at first. They had'm tendin' the fire, and carryin' in water."

I gave a soft sigh. "It's not Methoa, then. He wouldn't do woman's work."

"Yer husband might be dead already then, sweetheart," Ransom said apologetically. "There's a mess o' fresh graves down there. Four that I could see. Probably lost a few others when they raided the trade post. Prendergast said that didn't go well for 'em."

I bit my lip tensely for a moment, then slowly blew out a breath. "Fine," I said at length, and Ransom looked to me, surprised. "However he died, he's gone. That's what matters. I just want this to be over."

Ransom raised an eyebrow, then sighed, and put a hand on my shoulder. "Me too, sweetheart. Let's get this done, then git on with our lives, alright?"

I nodded.

"And fer the record," the coyote said quietly, "I'm impressed yer lettin' this go so easy. Wish I'd had your discipline."

"None of this has been easy," I replied, somberly.

"Aye," the coyote agreed, and stood stiffly, crouching below the pine boughs and gesturing up the hill. "Let's go find th' others, then. We're burnin' daylight."

We moved up through the steep woodland area, taking care. I tried my best not to let what Ransom had said distract me, but it was inescapable. All I could think about now was Methoa'nuk. His eyes. His smell. His presence. That final fight. Having my child ripped from my arms. The purification ritual.

Methoa hadn't simply been a monster to me. He'd killed my son. Left him to die in the cold night air. And then he'd betrayed his tribe, and my home tribe. My parents. Literally everyone I'd ever known. All… Why?

Even to this day, I couldn't make sense of it. Methoa'nuk had determined I was a disappointing wife, and had made claims that I'd been unfaithful to him. He had blamed me for his unhappiness, and I knew he'd resented my family's tribe, the Katoshen, when things had begun to go wrong between us. But he'd resented them beforehand, if the grievances I'd heard him mutter about throughout the years had been true. Our two tribes had been rubbing one another wrong over territory and hunting rights for generations, that's why we often inter-married… to try to keep the peace. And that was why my mother and father had insisted I marry Methoa'nuk. To do my part, to do, essentially, what I had been born for, to keep the peace for our region. In a way, it had been political. Many of my fellow tribeswomen even considered me lucky. Methoa was an honored warrior, in high standing with his tribe, and was very capable of caring for me and any children I might have with him. We'd not have gone hungry.

When my thoughts on the situation were less clouded by anger and betrayal… I began to see my parents in a different light. I'd always assumed I never mattered to them. How could I have, when they gave me to such a monster—forced me into his arms? They delivered me to evil. They knew he'd had two wives previous to me who had died, or 'disappeared'.

But maybe they'd honestly been as naïve as I was. Maybe they'd been worried that I was growing too old to make any other match. Maybe they'd truly thought it was what was right for me. If so, they'd been as much a victim of Methoa as I.

But why? Why, why, why? The last part, the end of the story, still made so little sense to me. All I had was the one spotty account from the only surviving warrior we'd found at the Anukshen village, and then the later confirmation that he'd been right, that both villages had been hit, both villages destroyed. But destroying the Katoshen completely seemed too far, even for Methoa. Our villages had feuded, but we also depended upon one another. We were part of a Nation. A collection of feline villages, who united in times of war. In my lifetime, it had never happened, but I know it had in the past, at least during Methoa's lifetime. He'd fought beside men from my family's village when our Nation had gone to war in the past. That's why he'd been considered 'honored'.

Was it truly just anger at me that had brought this all about? How had he even found Rourke's men, let alone lured them to our village to do his dirty work?

I heard a whistle from ahead, and Ransom course-corrected, taking us up a rocky incline towards where the other two men must have been hiding. When we neared there, I saw Grant peering around the edge of a massive boulder, gun in hand. When he spied us, he gestured quietly and ducked back behind the rock.

When we reached it, I jumped quietly down into the dip in the terrain where they'd squirreled themselves away. I felt Grant wrap an arm around me and tug me away from the edge when I lingered to look out over the crevasse again, to see if I could see the camp from where we were.

I balked, and was going to object, when Grant whispered, sharply, "They're running patrols. There's a game trail near here."

"That why you moved?" I heard Ransom ask.

"No," the husky jerked his head towards a dense area of leaf litter collecting where the hill sloped down into the boulder we were all hiding behind. "That's why we moved."

I gave a soft gasp when I saw what he'd been indicating. The crumpled figure was dressed in muddy brown-colored leather, and his fur was similarly caked in dirt, so he'd blended in well with the leaves. Now that I was looking, I could see the body clearly, but they'd hidden him fairly well. Although the dirt looked to have been applied on purpose, and the man's smell was coated by the thick scent of pine and ash, which must have been intentional, so he'd probably been a well-trained scout to begin with. He looked to be a coyote, or perhaps a coydog. It was difficult to tell.

"He dead?" Ransom asked lowly, moving over towards Puck, who was hunkered near the stone wall. The fox both looked and smelled afraid.

Grant nodded. "I heard him a ways off, was hoping he'd cut around our hiding spot, but he didn't, so I didn't have much of a choice."

Ransom kicked at the man, as if to be certain, then moved closer to Puck, running a dirty paw over the fox's ears. "You did good, Wickham. Thanks for handlin' it." He glanced at the man once more. "I didn't hear a gunshot..."

"Couldn't. Sound would've carried for miles out here," Grant said quietly.

"Then how—"

"I broke his neck," the husky replied, in a tone that suggested to me that he hadn't enjoyed it.

Ransom whistled softly. "Shit, boy. Remind me not to scrap with you." He spit, running a paw over the back of his nose. "Alright, then. Well this works out fine, actually. We were gonna hafta' wait 'til one of the canines down there took a piss, but this's easier."

Grant slipped an arm around me while we spoke, and I didn't resist. I pressed gently into the husky's side, letting him know the comfort right now was welcome. "You think I'll pass?" Grant asked, eyeing the canine.

"Not fer long, but you don't have to do it fer long. Pretty much as soon as you get in is when we'll start the attack," Ransom stated. He squatted down on the ground, and dusted aside what few bits of leaf litter were there, until he hit the loose earth beneath. He pulled out his knife, and began to draw a crude map on the ground. We all got in closer to watch.

"Alright, so…" he gestured down, "their camp's kind of shaped like a horse shoe, around the campfire. Big stone pit, you don't wanna be crossing it. Now. Same thing that hides 'em kind of bottlenecks 'em for us. There's basically one trail in," he marked one end of the 'horseshoe' shape on the map, "here. Other side's pretty much a dead end. The rock comes up there, nice and sharp. Not exactly somewhere we can use for a perch, at least not without bein' seen, but it means they can't escape that way. They can start comin' up the hill after us, once we start shootin'," he gestured to the west side of the camp, "but it's gonna be hard-goin'. There's a lotta berry bushes in this area, and even if they ain't green this time of year, they dead bits are still thorny. Bad brush to be goin' uphill through. And there's also the fact they're goin' uphill, at all. Lotsa' pine, pine needles're slippery… y'all get the point."

"So the hill's a kill zone," I nodded.

"Right," the coyote flashed his canines, "we take our perches, you Northwest, me Southwest. We pick 'em off easy a' first. Go fer the ones that'll look like they're gonna be quickest, not the toughest. Get the ones that'll have the best chance of getting' to us before they do, pick off the slow ones afterwards. Once any of 'em get to either of us…"

"Well we have to make sure that doesn't happen."

"Good chance it will, darlin'," Ransom said with a sigh, scratching his chin, nervously. "There's still almost twenty of 'em. Two of us shootin'. Gonna be tough."

"Three," Grant insisted, "I'll be helping you from the ground."

"Yer job's to keep them from slippin' us entirely," Ransom reminded him. "They got an escape route down there somewhere. I know they do. They're on top of a mine. I just can't see the bloody shaft. But it's there, somewhere. You find it. You make sure no man crosses that threshold alive. These people are on a damned mission. If any of 'em escape…"

"They'll just start over," I growled. "We don't even know who's in charge anymore, with Shadow gone…"

"I didn't see no otters, either," Ransom muttered.

"What?" I asked, shocked. "Rourke is gone, too?"

"Might be he died, but…"

"Damnit!" I said, exasperated. "I don't like this. The ringleaders are all gone."

"Might be that's the only reason we found 'em like this," Ransom said with a sigh. "But it don't matter. We worry about them when this's all done. There's still twenty some-odd murderers down there. We kill them, we cut the legs off this thing. Ain't much one vixen and one otter can do without their men."

"Shadow might be gone forever," Grant admitted. "But Rourke is noticeable. Most of his people were wiped out in the Southlands. There aren't many giant otters left. And he's mad. Alone, I think we'll find him a lot more easily than we did when he had help."

"Well we're not the ones who let Shadow get away," I muttered, venomously.

"Let's just focus on the situation at-hand," Puck, of all people, spoke up. Everyone turned to regard him. The fox hadn't spoken since we'd gotten back, and he rarely did unless he had something important to say. He was taking out his pack, and sorted through it for just a few moments, before he produced a leather-wrapped package, carefully unwrapping it. Inside were two glass vials, which he must have bought recently. They were both corked and wrapped tightly in twine besides. He handed one first to Ransom, then the other to me.

"This will ensure even your less lethal shots slow them down," he said, "but apply it carefully. I can't stress that enough."

"What is it?" I asked, eyeing the odd paste inside. It looked greenish, and somewhat loose and liquidy.

"A concentration of root paste from western water hemlock, and cottonmouth venom," Puck said, narrowing his eyes, "it won't kill immediately, but its effects should be noticeable

197

within a minute or so. It depends on how fast their blood is moving. Coat your arrows in it, but be extremely careful. I don't have the antidote for this."

"That's unlike you, Puck," Ransom said, surprised.

"There is no antidote for this," the fox replied coldly, "so don't use it unless you want someone dead."

No one seemed to know what to say to that, so the fox just dug into his pack again, and pulled something else out, just as gingerly. Although these looked far more mundane.

"Eggs?" I said, confused. I took the one he offered to me. It felt a lot lighter than an egg would have been, and there was something inside it, almost like a hollowed-out gourd.

"Foxes from the Southlands have been using these at war for generations," Puck explained. "It's delicate, so keep it somewhere safe, but it's a lot less dangerous. If it breaks, the worst you'll have is crushed pepper in your pocket."

"What do I do with it?" I asked, confused.

"If any of them make it to you, throw it in their eyes," Puck replied, simply. "They're fragile for a reason. I used ground black pepper and cayenne, and a few other irritants you really don't want in your eyes. Make sure you don't miss."

I shook my head. "Puck, where did you learn all of this?"

"I've spent almost my entire life learning how peoples' bodies work," the fox replied, evenly. "I don't like to use my knowledge this way, but honestly, these people deserve a little pain. And I want you all to come back to me..."

Ransom slung an arm around the fox's shoulders and pulled him in close, leaning in to press his muzzle between the vulpine's small, round ears. "We're comin' back, baby," he murmured, "I promise. Didn't get this far just to die here."

I turned from the couple, wanting to give them some time alone. We couldn't really, hiding behind the small bit of terrain we had, but at the very least, I could leave them be. I heard them speaking lowly in Puck's native tongue as I walked towards the husky, who was kneeling beside the dead scout now, and beginning to remove his outer garments.

"Grant," I said softly, "are you going to be alright?"

The husky looked uncertain enough that it broke my heart. Ransom's plan for him was incredibly dangerous, but just as he'd said he would, Grant had accepted it immediately. I didn't entirely like that we were relying on the man's good-hearted, reckless bravery to accomplish a task we needed done, but there was no doubt that someone needed to do it.

Ransom and I were best from a range, and Grant simply wasn't. The man knew how to use a bow apparently, but poorly at best, and his accuracy with his pistol was only good at short-range. It was a devastating weapon up-close, to be certain, but it took him nearly half a minute to reload it, and from a perch up in the hills, he wouldn't hit a soul. Ransom and I could fire five or six arrows in the time it took him to fire once, and far more accurately.

And that's if he could even get in close without alerting them, which was questionable. Grant simply wasn't very capable of stealth. His only way into the fight would be beneath their noses, and the only place he'd be useful was amongst their ranks.

What's more, if we relied entirely upon shooting them from a range, we might drop a few, but eventually the bulk of them would scatter and escape. We needed to be certain that didn't happen, and moreover, stall them from getting to us at our perches for as long as possible. That meant picking off any of the men that broke cover and sprinted for the woods.

And finally, they might simply button down, in which case we'd be at a stalemate, and we'd have to close in. And as soon as that happened, we lost our advantage. But a man on the ground, hiding amongst their number, might be able to subvert that.

I wasn't sure how well Grant could pull this off. It required some subtlety, in that he couldn't make it obvious whenever he took down a man amongst their number, lest they realize it and the entire camp turned on him. Once he engaged anyone, he'd have to kill them.

It was a bad plan. But it was the best one we had.

"I know we haven't got a lot of water to spare," Grant said, gesturing at the loose dirt around him, "but if you could, make some mud. I'm going to need it." He began donning the dead man's cloak.

"Grant, wait…" I said, suddenly, and walked over towards the man.

The husky looked up as I closed in towards him, and before he could pull the dead man's hood up, I pushed my arms around his neck and clung to him tightly. I felt him move his own paws up over my back, carefully avoiding my quiver and bow, and he lowered his muzzle over my shoulder.

"Shivah…" he murmured, "we don't have much time—"

"Shut up," I snapped. "We have time for this." I pulled back enough that I could kiss him, and I did so, for quite some time. I squeezed my eyes shut, and tried to keep myself from crying. I broke the kiss before my emotions got the better of me, and looked the confused husky in the eyes, gripping his cheeks. "You listen to me," I said, sternly, "you stick to cover, when we start firing. You don't go after anyone unless you're behind cover when you do, and out of sight of the other men. Do you understand me?!"

"If they're making for the hill—" he began to object.

"You leave them to us!" I said, forcefully. "You! Keep them in that camp, but you don't do anything stupid, alright?"

Grant gave a soft sigh, but forced a slight smile. "Shivah, this whole bloody thing is stupid. That's why I'm the man for the job."

"Shut up," I repeated. I didn't know what else to say, so I just hugged him again, murmuring, "Just shut up."

I held him for a long while, as my other two companions said their goodbyes. I didn't want to consider the facts here. The facts were, we were outnumbered five to one, if not more, and the odds were, in barely a few minutes, someone here might be grieving the loss of someone they cared about. Or we might all die.

I tried not to consider the fact that were it not for me, no one would have been here doing this right now. Everyone had their own reasons for putting their lives on the line. The fact that I'd facilitated this didn't mean it was all on me. But if someone died, I still knew I'd never forgive myself.

"Shivah?" Grant's voice snapped me out of my reverie, and I looked up to him. And for the first time, I saw what looked to be fear in the husky's eyes. It was subdued beneath a mask of other emotions; determination, concern, even his paltry attempt a confidence, in such an impossible scenario.

The husky swallowed and glanced down for a moment, before raising his blue eyes to mine again. "I was wondering…" he murmured, "if you'd tell me something."

"What?" I asked, hoping I could.

The man blew out a soft breath, before asking, "What… what's your name?"

I opened my muzzle in shock. He knew I'd been using a false name? How—

"Laesom said 'Shivah' has no meaning, in Katuk," the husky said softly. "I asked him. I know most of your names have meanings. He said it's the name of a goddess from the Northern Wastes. A goddess of the mountain lion tribes. And I know names are unique to tribes."

I averted my eyes from him. I don't know why, but this conversation made me feel too bare. And considering I was having it with a man who'd seen me nude, that was a confusing feeling. I hadn't wanted Grant to know I'd been lying to him about something so important for so long, but on the other hand, I didn't really know if it was a lie. I'd felt long ago that my previous name had died with my previous life. 'Shivah' lived for my goals now. She was a creature of pure vengeance. The woman I'd wanted to be now, putting the weaker woman I'd once been behind me.

But more and more of late, I'd been remembering who that woman was. I'd found joy in life again. I'd remembered what friendship, what real friendship, truly was. I'd begun to trust

201

again, to let people in with less wariness, less fear that they'd disappoint or betray me. Given time I'd even hoped I might learn to love again. I'd loved my parents, once. I'd loved my son. I still did.

My thoughts came to a sudden halt at that. I did love my son, even now. I had never, and could never consider, not loving my son. Even though every memory I had associated with him now was tainted with pain, and the knowledge of what had happened to him. The pain of having lost him. The anger that had followed. The rage.

None of it had ruined how I felt about my baby. I still loved him. Why had it taken me until now to realize that?

I'd never forgotten how to love. I'd just forgotten that I could, again. No, not forgotten, I'd been afraid to—because I'd had something wonderful, and Methoa had taken him away from me. And that pain was too much to conquer. So I'd become afraid of it, instead. Afraid of reliving it.

I'd never really changed. I'd gotten stronger. But I'd never really lost who I was. I was just afraid to be her, again. Because she had things she was afraid to lose. I looked to Grant, who was looking back at me uncertainly, like he was afraid he'd guessed wrong.

I leaned forward and kissed his forehead, softly. "Come back alive," I murmured, "and I'll tell you."

The man looked into my eyes desperately for a few moments, and then at length, he nodded, firmly. His expression set itself into one of grim determination, and I forced myself to smile at him. I would believe. I would try to believe life could be good, again. For all my talk of 'faith' to Puquanah over the time I'd known him, I think I'd lost a lot, when my son had died. I needed to have it now.

"You really know how to motivate a man," Grant said softly.

"Grant, listen to me," I said softly. "One of the men down there might be my husband."

The husky's ears flattened, and his eyes sharpened, intensely.

"It doesn't matter if he is or isn't," I said, "don't engage him. He'll be the only bobcat. Do not engage him."

"I understand you want a shot at him yourself," the canine said, with a sigh, "but Shivah, I have to, if—"

"I don't want you to engage him, because I know he'll kill you," I said, seriously. "Grant, I don't doubt your skills, but my husband isn't to be underestimated. Even if he doesn't look intimidating to you, that man has killed more warriors than there are days in the fall. Don't fight him if you can possibly avoid it. Ransom or I will take care of him."

I saw the man beginning to object again, so I kissed him again, before pulling back and murmuring, "Please. It would literally destroy me to watch him kill someone else I cared for."

The husky smiled, after a few quiet moments had passed between us, and nuzzled me. "As you say," he agreed.

I bid farewell to both Ransom and Puck, as well. The coyote could very well be overrun on his perch, and even Puck was in danger, hiding in the hills. I knew he'd remain near, in case one of us were injured. And of course, I could die. And then I'd never see any of my friends again.

But we'd all made the decision to be here, and we knew the risks.

CHAPTER SIX
A Good Man

I worked my way down towards my perch on my own. Ransom had cleared as many of the 'bear traps' as he could find, but it was possible he'd missed some, or possible I'd accidentally find another pit trap. I moved carefully, keeping my eye on the trail whenever it was visible between the trees, watching for Grant's figure as he made his way down towards the camp. This entire plan could go wrong if he were recognized when he made his way into camp.

I got to an area where I could watch him safely from cover, making his way down towards the distant figures in camp. It didn't seem like most of the men were paying much attention to the trail head now, which we'd timed on purpose. Most of the men who weren't already sleeping or sitting around camp drinking were gathered around the fire, while grub was being dished out. Whatever it was, it didn't smell appetizing. By my guess, weak broth with whatever they had to fill the stew out. Probably dried meat and vegetables.

I couldn't see any bobcats, but many of the men had already turned in for the night. He could be anywhere. It was frustrating. I'd been hoping I'd at least have that question answered before the fight started.

Something else entirely caught my attention, out of the corner of my eye, as I was following Grant's progress down the hill. Something that wasn't a trap, but was certainly a danger. The glint of something steely, protruding from a hedge of young pines just a few meters down the hill from me.

I didn't want to lose my perch, but that glint of something steely was leveling towards Grant, following his path just as I'd been with my eyes, and I'd seen enough men aim rifles to know what was going to happen if I didn't act fast. There wasn't any time for my bow.

Praying I would be able to get to the scout, or whomever it was, before they aimed a shot, and still, impossibly, be silent about it. I leapt. Luckily the gunman was downhill, so with two bounds, and the aid of gravity, I was quite literally atop him, bulling into him with all the strength my small body could muster, and plowing the heavy man into the dirt. I landed on his back and he collapsed atop his own rifle, so the chance he'd fire it was averted for now, but I still had to contend with

I literally choked in surprise when the man swung an elbow backwards into my ribs, but not because he'd hit me. The strike has been cut-off, averted before it could do any major damage, for the same reason I was so shocked, I could only imagine. The canine had turned around partially to swing at me, and we'd both caught sight of one another. I was staring at Connall.

"What—" I began, but at that point the pit bull's head snapped around towards the camp, where two of the men seemed to have heard the ruckus we'd created and were looking up from where they were skirting the perimeter. Connall's thick paw slammed down atop my back and shoved me flat on my belly, back behind the boulder he was using for cover. And for a few tense moments, the two of us stopped moving, stopped breathing, stopped thinking... and just remained entirely still.

The two men eventually lost interest, and muttered something to one another, before going back to their half-hearted patrol. They hadn't even noticed Grant moving into camp. Beneficial timing for us.

"Damnit, you miserable cunt..." the canine whispered fiercely. "You just nearly blew this thing to hell. What in God's name are you doing here?! I told you—"

"Stop it with the act," I snapped, and decided to bluff like I was certain and test a theory, "we both know we're only here because of the map you slipped us. Whatever your reasons, I don't care. We don't need any credit for this. We're here to help. When this is all over you can go home a hero. Just like you wanted."

"What?" the pit bull continued whispering, incredulously. I knew instantly by the man's expression that we'd guessed wrong. "What the bloody hell are you talking about? I told you specifically not to get involved in this! What map?"

"It wasn't you?" I said, then glanced back towards the camp. Grant had moved in, and very few of the men had even taken notice of him. So far so good. "Then maybe Magpie..." I murmured.

"The rat?" the canine still continued to look dubious. "No, that doesn't make any sense, he couldn't have known about this..." He was silent for a few moments, his muzzle twisted up, eyes narrowed in deep thought. Then suddenly, his brows lifted, and he reached over and grabbed me by my cloak. "Who else is here?" He demanded. "Did you bring all your bloody friends?"

"Everyone except Laesom," I said at length, deciding it was better if he knew, no matter what. No matter our animosity, we still seemed to be on the same side here.

"I don't give a damn about the wolf," Connall growled, "or your two native heretics. Where is Wickham? Did you at least leave him out of this?"

I gestured down into camp. "The one with the brown cloak," I said quietly. "The one you nearly shot."

"You bloody she-devil!" Connall nearly spat at me, his eyes blazing. He was still keeping his voice low, but every hair on the man's body was on end, and snarling this close to me, he made me feel like prey. "That man has a family! I have been trying to keep him out of this!"

I shoved his hand off my cloak, baring my fangs at him. "He's his own man," I growled, "and not yours to command. And this matters to him."

"All of your friends are going to die, because you didn't listen to me!" the pit bull snapped.

"Less people would have died if we'd worked together and communicated better from the beginning," I responded, angrily. "I don't care what you think of me and my people, right now, we need to work together—"

"This isn't about you or your people," Connall said, shoving me aside as he went for his rifle again, checking the flint. "It never has been! But you're such an arrogant, selfish woman, you couldn't listen to a few words of wisdom, no matter how much I pleaded." He turned at that, narrowing his dark eyes at me, and his voice sunk to a level so low, I could barely hear it. "Do you want to know what I really think of you, woman? Because I don't bloody care enough to be polite anymore."

I curled my lip at the man in response.

"I think your people are Godless, ignorant and backwards," Connal said, bluntly. "You worship rocks and feral animals, you live in the dirt and smell like it, your men act like wild elk in rut, and your women have no concept of modesty or shame for their bodies." He stared down the sights of his rifle into camp, before turning back towards me, some of the bile leaving his voice. "But I don't bloody blame you for the way you are. We are how we were made by God, and there is a place for people like yours in the world. I don't want your people to die… I never have. You were of great aid to us in the war. Your men fought bravely, in their own way. We wouldn't have won without your warriors."

I blinked, confused. That had almost been a compliment.

"Your people deserve to live on this land as well as ours," the pit bull continued. "You earned it. I respect any right earned through bloodshed. And I hold no vain hopes of conversion for your masses, or any thought that you might civilize. You have your bloody place, and it's separate from us. So long as that barrier is respected, the world keeps functioning. There have to be lessers in order for there to be chosen."

I wanted to point out how conflicting the man's statements had been, but every few seconds, I was looking back into camp, waiting for Grant to give the signal. He was moving around now, likely trying to get the lay of the land first. Any longer and he might get noticed, though…

"That's why you wouldn't accept our help?" I said instead. "Because of this idiotic importance you put on being separate?"

Connall snorted. "No. That's why I purged the mink and the wolf Wickham hired from the squad. But that was a personal preference. We don't work well with them. It's just a fact."

"I travel with a fox, a coyote, a wolf, and one of your people," I pointed out. "And I've never felt so close to a group of people."

"You know..." the pit bull murmured, sounding honestly saddened, "Wickham's a good lad. Had a good future ahead of him, before you all came along and ruined it for him. But this is what happens when our peoples mix. I tried to tell him that. Apart, everyone knows their place. It's how breeding works, it's how life works. Muddy the waters, and people get confused."

"You mean they start aspiring to be more than what your god says they can be?" I snarled.

"A worm might dream of flying," Connall stated. "But its place will always be in the ground. Drop it from a mountain, and all it can ever do is fall. It only thrives in the dirt."

I stared the man in the eyes. "Have you ever seen where butterflies come from?" I asked quietly.

The pit bull arched an eyebrow, clearly not understanding. He wouldn't have, of course. I doubt the man had ever sat and watched a cocoon hatch, or seen what the beautiful insects were before they transformed. But a girl from the mountains, who saw freedom in their multicolored wings...

I saw Grant sit down, over the pit bull's shoulder, and I moved slowly back away from Connall, looking up the hill back towards my perch.

"Where are you going?" Connall demanded.

"To my perch. He's sitting," I gestured towards the clearing. "When he pulls out his water flask, the attack is on. Do you want to end this here?"

"Of course," the pit bull growled.

"Then you don't have the time to force me to leave," I said, pointedly. "Let alone Ransom. So work with us. You don't have a choice."

"You're all dead, anyway..." Connall replied, stone-faced, with a certainty that unnerved me.

"You said you had a plan," I pointed out. "Don't tell me this was a suicide mission."

The pit bull's silence was telling.

My eyes widened. "But," I stammered, "you said you had mercenaries. Other men. What about the other Marshals?"

"I left them all behind," Connall replied, evenly. "That's why I hired the mercenaries. I don't want any more of the State's men to die for this. Too many have already. But I don't give a damn about sell-swords."

"How many men do you have set up?" I demanded.

"It doesn't matter," the pit bull muttered. "No one's going to leave this place alive."

"Speak for yourself," I growled. "We have a plan. And if you're smart, you won't ruin it." I turned, and began to make my way back up the hill, glancing briefly back at the pit bull as I did. "Wait for the signal," I reiterated, "if you really want this to end here, our attack needs to be coordinated."

I was clambering back up the rocky slope, when I heard the man give a soft whistle to get my attention, once more. I glanced back down at him. The canine looked as dour as ever, but slightly less angry. There was even a hint of what almost seemed like concern there.

"Shivah," he said, shocking me by using my name. Usually it was 'woman', or some other choice phrase that demeaned me, somehow. "Watch your back," he said, sternly. "Never drop your guard. Do you hear me? Never."

I headed back up towards my perch, heeding the pit bull's words despite my dislike for the man. It really wasn't a reminder I needed in this place, though. I was on edge as it was.

When I settled in and looked out over the camp once more, two things caught my eye. For one, Grant was sitting with his elbows draped over his knees, cloak pulled up over his head, but some of the men at the fire were beginning to take interest in him. Most especially the big bear, who looked about ready to get up and go over towards him.

I pulled an arrow from my quiver, praying for Grant to notice. And he did. He took one sidelong look at the men, then began reaching towards his belt. He was either going for his water flask, or his gun. Hopefully, he remembered the plan.

But secondly... a man with a fawn and gray hide, blotted with spots along his thighs and arms, was moving towards the camp from around a large pile of crates and supplies, almost out of sight of me, his figure masked primarily by the fire. Where he'd come from, I wasn't certain, but he looked like a bobcat.

And then Grant drank from his water flask, and I saw one of the men nearest to him pitch forward, crying out and gripping at his neck. From here, I couldn't even really see the shaft of the arrow, but I knew Ransom had struck the first blow.

I targeted another man near Grant, wanting to clear the area around him while we had no men on the hill to worry about, and loosed my own arrow. Unsurprisingly, catching the man from surprise, it struck home. I pulled another quickly and nocked it. From here on out, I knew it wouldn't be as easy.

The camp erupted into panic all but immediately. The fact that Connall opened fire not a few seconds later certainly didn't help. The sound of his rifle crackled out across the crevasse, and I saw the bear's shoulder erupt in a spray of gore. I should have told him to target the ones that could move fast, first.

But Connall had his own plan, I'm certain. The bear had been the one barking orders earlier. The shoulder wound couldn't possibly have killed him, but it did make him stupid. He bellowed in anguish and grabbed frantically at his own bow, wasting a full twenty seconds or so realizing he couldn't pull it back with his injury, before giving a guttural growl and pulling a large knife, instead. He was going to come for us, for Connall specifically, and regardless how slow he moved, it might be hard to put him down.

I remembered what Ransom had told me a long time ago. Sometimes it was better to act quickly than smartly. I pulled one of the arrows I'd put aside, one of the six I'd poisoned, and nocked it. I leveled a shot at the huge creature, aiming for his torso to be certain I hit, since it hardly mattered where I struck him with the poison, and fired. My arrow hit home and sunk in deep. The bear all but ignored it at first, his chest was a mass of muscle and fat, and armored in leather besides, but I trusted in Puck's poison, and picked another target at that point.

I heard the crack of another rifle, off in the distance. Ransom wasn't using his rifle for this attack, so it must have been one of the mercenaries. I couldn't be certain in all the chaos if they were doing us any good, but any additional help now was welcome.

Ransom was doing incredibly well. I saw at least four of them who made the mistake to break cover go down with shafts protruding from their upper torso, neck, even one that pierced a rat straight through the head.

We were doing this. We were really doing this. Six down so far and a seventh poisoned. And they'd made no progress up the hill.

I wasn't going to let my confidence get the best of me, though. We'd known the beginning would go well for us. We had the element of surprise. But now, the raiders were hunkering into cover, loading their own weapons, and readying to either fire on us, or try to slip our notice and make it up the hill. The bear had reached it, despite another shot from Connall at the man. That had probably been intended as a head shot, but looked to have only barely clipped an ear.

But the massive creature was slowing down. I could hear his labored huffs from here, his bellowing growls gone weaker. I waited before I wasted another shot on him.

A bullet winged by a tree near me, and I jumped back, hunkering down further into my cover. I had to be careful how long I ducked out. They were starting to return fire. We had a lot of protection up here, but one of them could still get lucky, and with so many men shooting, the chances were better.

Connall was working in my favor, though. The man was making a far more obvious target of himself with that rifle. His cover also wasn't as well-planned-out as mine. I had an immense, fallen trunk to duck behind, in addition to the obscurement of the living pines still growing near it. Connall had chosen a boulder, which while it made for good cover when he was behind it, had very few trees immediately surrounding it, which meant when he leaned out to fire, he was entirely visible.

Out of the corner of my eye, I caught sight of another battle taking place, hidden amongst the raiders' camp. From my location I could see a wagon, likely one they'd stolen from the trade post they'd raided a week back. Two men were hunkering behind it, Otherwolves both, by the look of it. They were re-loading their rifles, and would have a clear shot up towards where Ransom was. It would be a nearly impossible shot for me until they leaned out to fire, and even then, I'd only get one.

But at that moment, a taller man amongst their number in a dark brown cloak tumbled in behind the wagon with them. All I could really see were the backs of their heads while they were still behind it, but I nocked an arrow and waited. And then, they popped up over the wagon to take a shot, and I saw the taller man stand behind them, pulling a pistol from beneath his cloak and leveling it at the back of one of the men's heads while their attention was turned.

I aimed for the other. It all took place in the few seconds it took the two men to aim. I'm not certain whether Grant or I fired first, but it hardly mattered. I caught the man on the left somewhere above the collarbone, the arrow sinking into his neck and sending him pitching backwards, and Grant blew out

212

the back of the other man's skull, sending him splayed for-
wards over the back of the wagon. Neither man got a shot off.
The husky looked briefly over the wagon in my direction, and
I couldn't see his face, but I wanted to. But then he disappeared
again, back behind cover, likely to re-load his gun and make
for other men.

Connall's men were doing their job, even if I didn't know
where they were or how they were going about it. I knew at
least that one of them had a rifle, but judging by how many
had died to arrow-fire, I was convinced now it couldn't all just
be Ransom. There were others helping us. Probably a few.
There were at least ten dead now, many more injured. We were
going to do this.

We were really going to do this.

I leveled another shot at a wolverine who'd made the
mistake of thinking he could work his way from cover to cover
towards my end of camp, likely to make a break for the trail
head. I had a decent shot lined up...

And then I heard the snap of twigs breaking behind me,
and sucked in a breath, rolling out of the way just in time. I
tumbled partially down the hill, scrabbling for footing, looking
frantically up as I splayed my toes in the earth to find purchase
in the loose soil. A lynx, wearing a similar mottled cloak to the
one Grant had stolen from the dead scout stood where I'd
been. His fur was caked with dirt, but I could see the hints of
blisters beneath it all. His jowls were curled up, revealing yel-
lowed fangs and breath that even from here, reeked of bile and
sickness.

I wondered briefly why, if he was a scout like the other, he
hadn't simply shot me, and then I saw the arrow embedded in
the tree trunk immediately to the left of where I'd been
crouched. My stomach sunk.

That man had taken a shot at me, and I'd been so focused
on the battle in camp, I hadn't even noticed. The lynx was
armed with an enormous hunting knife now, though, and
seemed intent on using it on me. And he was fast.

The feline was on me before I could even think to move again, faster at a spring than even I was, and powerful besides. I rolled when he hit me, doing what little I could remember from Ransom's tutelage to shake him loose and slip free of him once he was atop me. Luckily the man hadn't managed to grapple me, he'd simply tried to drive the knife down into my torso. I twisted my body to the side, then furiously jerked my knees in and drove them up into his stomach. The blow had little effect, but it was enough. I was able to scrape myself out from beneath him, the clasp holding my cloak together snapping in the process. I would have let it tear from my shoulders to escape him, but it had gotten entangled in the strap that held my quiver over my back.

Giving a cry of frustration, I tugged at it just long enough to realize I had no time to free myself of it, and instead went for the small hunting knife strapped to my thigh. The lynx's knife was through my cloak, embedding it into the ground, there'd be no getting free of him so long as we were tangled up this way. I had to fight.

I slashed at the man's heel while he was still trying to tug his knife out of the ground, and struck him in the tendon. He gave a blood-curdling scream and all at once, came off of me. I felt my cloak come free and clawed at the ground wildly with both my hands and feet, trying to get up as quickly as possible. I struggled to my feet, only to feel the man's good foot kick me in the back of the knee, causing my leg to crumple, and my body to pitch down the slippery hillside. As I went, I lost my knife.

I saw him several feet above me, kneeling now that he could no longer stand, snarling and growling low in his throat. He pulled his own bow and nocked an arrow, and I was still coughing up dirt, still empty-handed.

But no one was coming to my rescue. No one would save me but myself. I knew in that split second that my choices were, simply, to give in and die, or do what was necessary to survive this.

214

I had barely a second or so from the time he pulled back the arrow to its release, and even less time afterward. The man was barely five feet above me, this shot would be all but immediate, and he couldn't miss. I couldn't get out of the way in time. I was going to get hit.

But it was my choice where.

I rolled to my side, reaching for my bow and quiver as I did. My back was to him when he shot, and my back was where he hit. The arrow embedded itself in my shoulder-blade, through two layers of protective leather and the Dyre-hide cloak. Pain shot down through my body, turning my world white hot for a moment, but it was bearable. I could endure it without passing out.

And that's all that mattered.

I sprung to my heels, forcing my shoulder to move despite the pain, enough to pull an arrow from my quiver, to nock it to my bow. I endured the agony long enough to pull back the shaft and aim, and then I loosed the arrow into the man's gut as he re-nocked his own.

His body spasmed and shuddered backwards, and his hands weakly released his bow and arrow, sending them clattering down the hill towards me. He heaved up bile and blood, clutching at where the shaft protruded from his stomach for a few stunned moments, before crumpling to his side. He lay there for a time, his body heaving in what must have been horribly painful spasms.

But I couldn't muster any pity for the man right now. I reached around to the shaft protruding from my own back, shakily. It wasn't deep… I could feel it was embedded in muscle, but I was still able to move my shoulder-blade, albeit with a lot of pain. The leathers I wore and, perhaps most importantly, the Dyre-hide cloak, had done their job.

The man's arrows weren't barbed, so I steeled myself, and did what I needed to do. I tightened a fist around the shaft, and pulled.

As painful as it had been going in, it had been quick. Pulling out was significantly slower, even though I tried to do it swiftly. It was fairly well lodged, and took two good tugs. Tears were streaming down my cheeks and nose by the time I'd managed it, and all I could do when it was over was toss the bloody arrow aside and crawl on my knees into the nearest brush. I could still hear men down in the camp, which meant someone down there could take a shot at me. As it was, things had to have been pretty bad down there, or someone would have already.

I took a minute or so just to suck air into my lungs, trying not to faint. I hadn't lost a lot of blood… at least I didn't think so. I could feel the hot, wet stain working its way down my back, but that wasn't it. The pain had just been so intense, it was making my body want to shut down. I could fight it. I had to fight it. My friends were still in this, and they needed my help.

I shakily shoved a hand into the pocket along my thigh, pulling out a handful of the dried beans the men in the Marshals boiled to make coffee. Magpie had once told me to chew them if ever I felt in need of 'bodily confidence'. I still wasn't certain what that meant, but I was fairly certain I felt in need of it right now.

I saw Connall beneath me, looking my way. He gestured with one arm, staying behind the boulder for now, despite the fact that the clearing had gone quiet. Everyone, it seemed, felt it wiser to remain behind cover at the moment. I wasn't arguing with the reprieve.

Mustering the strength not to appear as pained as I felt, I crept down towards the man, keeping low in case any of the remaining raiders got bold and decided to take a shot at me. I eventually reached the pit bull, who was risking a glance around the rock when I arrived.

"Something's happening in camp…" the man growled, his eyes flicking back down to the task of hurriedly re-packing his gun.

"What do you mean?" I asked, trying to hide the wince in my voice. I leaned around the rock as well, trying to see what

I could, but all I saw was an empty camp. There were a significant amount of bodies lying about, though... and none of them looked to be Grant.

I didn't like that I couldn't see him, though. It made me very afraid.

The man glanced briefly back at me, then his head snapped around and he outright stared. "You've been hit!" he snarled.

"I'll be fine," I said through grit teeth. "What... is going... on?"

The pit bull either respected my toughness, or didn't care, because he didn't press the issue. He just worked his rifle up over the boulder, setting it cautiously and looking out over the camp. I stayed where I was, looking for anything... any sign of the raiders. A head poking out, a tail... ears...

"They all started breaking cover a little while ago," the canine said, lowly, "all moving the same way, towards where their supplies are piled up over there."

I looked towards the spot he was talking about. It was a blind area for us. The raiders had stacked crates and barrels high enough that they created almost a wall, about twenty paces long and ten paces high. Some kind of blind for them to hide behind?

"It's up against the damn cliff," Connall spat, "they ain't got nowhere to go, but gettin' at them's gonna be tough. Maybe they're hoping to bottleneck us."

"No." I said suddenly, my fur prickling along the back of my neck. I had a bad feeling about this. "No, that's the only spot we couldn't see..." I cursed in my own tongue, pulling free an arrow and standing.

"Get down!" Connall insisted, grabbing at me.

"They're running!" I shouted, to the canine beside me and anyone who would listen. "There's a mine somewhere in that crevasse. They must have hidden the entrance!"

I heard the pit bull issue a curse of his own, and I began to take off down the hill. Connall called after me, but I knew the man's leg was still in no shape to follow me down the slope at any speed that would prove useful.

I didn't care. If they were retreating, Grant would try to stop them. And he'd be alone.

Just as the thought crossed my mind, I heard a pistol shot ring out. I gasped, praying for my legs to take me faster, skipping feet at a time as I slid down the loose, sharp-rocked terrain of the hillside. I bounded over another large, flat boulder, and then my feet hit the beaten dirt of the campsite, and I was jumping fallen bodies and debris, making my way towards the obscuring pile of supplies.

As soon as I got near, I heard the melee. There weren't many men left alive, but the few that were were desperate. Someone fired a rifle in close-quarters, and all I could do was pray it had been as inaccurate as it should have rightly been, fired in a panic.

When I rounded the crates, I saw a scene of pure chaos, but just the fact that they were still fighting meant he was still alive.

There was a large dug-in area behind the piled supplies that dipped into an entrance cavern deep beneath the rocky side of the mountain. It had probably been a natural depression or cave at some point, widened by the Otherwolves who'd mined it. The only entrance to the cavern was deceptively small. I dropped down through it, falling almost five feet into the darkened recess, the sounds of confusion, anger and violence echoing off the stone walls.

I'd had an arrow pulled and held against my bowstring the entire time I'd run, and after my eyes had adjusted to the near-darkness just enough that I could make any of the figures out, I pulled it back and took aim at the first raider I saw. A feline of some sort was grappling with the far taller figure of Grant, trying to force his blade into the husky's chest. I tried to aim carefully, fearing I'd hit Grant, and settled for a shot to the back.

My eyes were still adjusting and my aim was poor. The shot skimmed the man's rear, but little else. It was enough to get his attention, though, which was all it took for Grant to get the upper hand. The husky used his superior size, and presumably strength, to bodily lift, shove, and then throw the man away from him by his grip on his forearms. The much smaller feline went tumbling across the stone floor, and Grant advanced on him, but that was all the offensive he could manage before another man, a stoat, by the look of it, literally leapt on his back and bit him.

The husky howled and pulled the knife from his belt, jerking it up wildly towards the stoat's muzzle. He easily caught him, clamped on as he was, but the man fell back with his knife embedded in his cheek, disarming him in the process.

I hastily nocked another arrow to my bow, the pain in my shoulder a distant memory now, all of my focus on the scene in front of me. The short feline who'd first been trying to stab Grant seemed to be weighing his options from the sidelines now, his gold eyes catching in the dark and glinting as he noticed me. He looked on the verge of flight, so I chose instead to focus on one of the two remaining canines, who was arming a strange horizontal-bow that seemed mounted on something more similar to a gun. The final canine was badly injured and, by the look of the way he was walking, poisoned, which meant he'd be dead soon enough on his own, anyway.

I aimed as carefully as I could while still beating the man to his own shot, and fired. Grant was struggling to his feet, clamping a hand over a badly chewed-up neck, and he was an easy target. This needed to count.

This time, my arrow struck home, piercing through the man's back deep into his lung. He choked and pulled the trigger on the strange bow he held, but his arm had already been dropping away when he did, and the short bolt embedded itself several feet away from Grant in the ground.

That seemed to do it for the feline hunkering in the corner, and he took off into the darkness. I wasted no time in getting to Grant. The stoat was still very much in the fight, despite having a knife embedded in his cheek. The creature was giving a shrill, feral scream that sounded nearly mad, and he may well have been. He was covered in blisters, as well.

And he was armed with a knife and a gun, but using neither. The man was fighting on pure instinct and madness.

I grabbed something from my pouch, and met the creature halfway into his charge, throwing and shattering the egg I'd stowed away in his face. The stoat screamed in agony, bending double and clamping his paws over his eyes. Grant seized the opportunity to bull rush the man, hiking a knee into his gut and slamming him against a wall with it, before reaching up to yank his knife back from the man's face and burying it in his chest—several times.

Until at length, the frenzied creature stopped moving entirely, and the husky pulled the knife out with a sickening pop. And then all there was in the cave was the sound of our heavy breaths and the moaning of the poisoned canine in the corner, who'd fallen prone and was beginning to show signs of his body seizing.

"We should finish him quickly—" I began, making for the man. But at that moment, Grant grabbed my arm, his paw slick with his own blood, and looked me in the eyes, his own blue orbs intense.

"Shivah," he said between rasping breaths, "that last man was a bobcat…"

My eyes widened, and my heart stopped. I'd really begun to think that I'd just imagined seeing him, earlier. That Ransom had imagined seeing him.

"Stay here!" I commanded the husky, turning to take off towards the blackness down which the feline had escaped.

"Like hell," Grant growled, right on my heels.

"I don't—"

"One of these days, Shivah," the husky panted, "you're going to have to accept that it's not shameful to accept help! Let me go ahead!"

Grant always wanted to go ahead. It wasn't just that he was fast at a sprint, it was a strange habit he'd always had, which right now, I wanted badly for him to forget.

But I couldn't outrun the male bobcat, and I knew it. And there was no time to argue. If that shadowy man was truly Methoa he was getting away. Just as he had been for months now. Eluding me. Escaping me. No more.

My pride, my anger, my vengeance be-damned. Grant was here with me, and he had skills that would help me finish this. I could be a one-woman army another day. What mattered now was that that bastard didn't get away again.

"Run him down," I growled to my companion. "I'll be right behind you."

The husky gave a thick, predatory growl and sprung ahead of me, taking off down the dark tunnel faster than I ever could have. And faster than Methoa'nuk could hope to outrun.

I could hear the feline ahead of us. It might have been pitch black down here, but he couldn't be quiet at a full-sprint. I saw distant shafts of light, likely from places where the ground opened up into sinkholes or drop shafts into the mining tunnels, but most of them were small and fleeting.

Until we turned a corner, and I saw what had to have been a full-sized exit. An escape route. Ransom had been right. They'd had this planned out. The feline clearly knew the way.

He didn't make it, though.

They were about five feet from the wide circle of blinding light that opened out into the forest beyond when Grant tackled the man from behind, and tried to bring him down in a pin. The feline was fast, though. Fast, and still armed. The smaller man twisted as he fell and I saw the blade he held so certainly, with such experience and concise, battle-tested confidence, as though he'd done this exact maneuver several hundred times before. The men in my tribe did, after all. The warriors trained with blunt, wooden weapons frequently. I'd seen Methoa best every other man in my tribe.

And I knew in that moment, with a heavy pang of fear, that now would be no different. Grant never saw it coming. He fell on the blade, the cloak obscuring everything about the moment of impact between the two men. I screamed. Not either man's name. Just a primal scream.

But then, impossibly, the husky was rolling off of him and forcing himself to his feet, putting distance between his body and the blade. Even from the ground, the feline man was dangerous, already swinging the blade out again in a short, deliberate arc at the canine's midsection again.

I caught up to Grant as he backpedaled away from the man, his paw clamped over his side. He pulled his hand away after a moment, panting and looking down at the thin line of blood, and the equally short scrape along the side of his torso.

Methoa had missed.

And now, I was certain. The man was barely ten feet from us, standing in the bright circle of fading sunlight, the last orange rays of the day, casting a halo around his figure in deep, burning hues. My eyes were again readjusting to the light, but I could have seen nothing but his eyes, and I would have known him. He was not the man I remembered. And yet he was.

In my mind, in my past, my husband had been a hulking, indomitable, terrifying figure. Larger than the mountains, dominating every horizon when he was near. His power over me had been so absolute, so suffocating; I'd seen him as simply that. All-powerful. Like a great monster, whose very presence reduced me to weakness. He was a dark and dreadful god to me then. But now...

Now, he looked like a short, spiteful, aging creature. And he was in terrible condition, besides. He looked malnourished and weak, his hide pockmarked with some of the feverish boils so many of the other men here wore, his fur unwashed and patchy from lack of grooming. His mane was in knots, none of his turquoise beads remained, and he wore nothing but a breech-cloth. He seemed to have been stripped of all of the adornments he'd once prized so much, if not his dignity in its entirety. His pelt was a road map of fresh scars, just as Ransom had said. He looked like a beaten, abused animal.

But that defiance was still there. That hateful, spiteful gaze. Everything that he'd once been remained still, in his eyes. And looking into those eyes was all it took to remind me of everything. Every last cry I'd heard my son give, when he tore him from my arms. Every rock that had struck me. Every assault I had endured, when I'd been trying so desperately to be a good wife for him.

Every moment of peace I'd felt since I'd left the valley melted away, and that aching, burning rage screamed to life inside me, filling my chest with fire. I could hear Crow scream ing, somewhere distant, or perhaps very near, in my heart. It was like a victory cheer, the spirit infusing me with the power to achieve my purpose, at last.

If I died here—if Crow truly did take my soul—it would be worth it. As long as that man died. As long as I never had to see those eyes again.

I could end this pain. Finally. I'd never have to feel it again. He just had to die.

"Spirits…" the man suddenly spoke, his eyes focusing on my face for the first time. His voice sounded like evil and torment, just as I remembered him. And then he gave a low, unhinged chuckle, bubbling up into a full-throated laugh. He spread his arms wide, looking to the skies. "or specter, or illusion. Gods above, I am truly your plaything of late. What cruel demons conspire against me now?"

"I am not a spirit, Methoa!" I snarled. "Nor a specter, nor illusion. I am your wife." I reached into my quiver, pulling an arrow and nocking it to my bow, and pulling it back. "And I'm here to send you to the next realm."

"My wife is dead," the man replied evenly, his tone maddeningly unafraid. I wanted him to quiver. I wanted him to grovel. Beg for his life. "She was a whore," he continued, unabashedly, "and we slew her like one."

I heard Grant give a deep, guttural growl from behind me, but Methoa was still armed, and even with a bow pulled on him, I knew better than to believe we had him at our mercy. The bobcat showed no concern for the weapon I had drawn on him. Perhaps he underestimated me. Perhaps he truly thought I wasn't real. Perhaps he was mad. It hardly mattered. Weak or not, the man was a seasoned warrior. If the shot wasn't placed perfectly, he'd still be able to come for us. He was still armed. He was still deadly.

Besides, I didn't want this to be over so soon. Not until I'd had my say. Not until I'd gotten the answers I came for.

Methoa's scarred muzzle turned up in a grim, humorless grin. "I guess I didn't bury you deep enough," he said dismissively. He spit out a glob of blood, still maddeningly calm, like he simply didn't care. I knew he could feel the anger coming off of me. I knew he could see the rage in my eyes. He knew what he'd done to me. To our son. To his entire tribe.

And still. He wasn't even cognizant of what he was, or the evils he'd committed. No shame. No remorse.

"End it, then," the man said, evenly. "You came a long way to die again, woman, but I suppose it's one more thing I must do for you, since you hadn't the honor to accept your shame willingly. You are making your ancestors weep."

"I've a bow drawn on you," I said with a snarl. "If anyone dies today, it is you!"

Methoa gave me a long stare, and responded, simply, "I don't care." In his apathetic gaze I saw the same pride, the same defiant disregard for me as I'd ever seen. I'd pulled myself out of hell, become strong, turned the tables on this man. And he still acted as though I didn't exist. Forever righteous in his ignorant superiority. I could kill him here, and he would die thinking of himself as a great man. He would never understand what he'd done.

And that made me feel cold. What had this all been for?

"I've borne your shame for you, woman," the man said with a sneer. "And now I understand why. The honor of my name needed be reclaimed, sullied as it was by a woman like you. I've endured great suffering, because you weren't willing to."

"Your hatred was for me, Methoa!" I screamed, desperately. "How could you bring our tribes down with us? They had no part in this!"

The bobcat stabbed a finger at me across the clearing. "It was your shame that brought that vile woman's wrath down upon us! I wondered until now what we might have done to anger the gods, but now I know! You were meant to die!"

"You led her into our village!" I said, incredulously. This was beyond the pale. He was blaming what had happened to our villages on me for surviving?

"To trade, you wench!" The man snarled. "As I have for five years now! We traded meat for thundering weapons with those outsiders, every year! Only this year they wanted more. More than we could possibly give."

"They just wanted food?" I said, disbelievingly. And yet for some reason, it made a horrid kind of sense. Our village hadn't been sick. And how else could Methoa have happened upon the raiders, unless it was pre-arranged? Why else would they have done all of this, unless they needed something out of it?

They hadn't been working for him at all. I'd just made him into such a monster in my mind, I hadn't considered the obvious, more mundane reason.

They were raiders. It had been a raid.

"I tried to convince the elders we could aid them in a raid of your worthless village, instead," the man said with a disgusted snarl. "But they wanted everything we had. When the elders resisted, the otter shot and killed them. All of them."

"It was your job to protect your people!" I screamed, angrily. "How could you join them?"

"They were inside our walls with two score men with thundering weapons," the man said dismissively, as though there was no possible blame that could fall on him. "I told the warriors not to resist, but the women panicked when they began taking our winter stores—"

"They had babies to feed!" I cried hoarsely. Now he was blaming the wives?

"These people are not our people!" The bobcat replied, in stark defiance of his responsibility. "They have no compassion for our young, for our lives… even for the lives of their own. They could not be reasoned with. I saved the few I could."

"By joining in the massacre?" I demanded. "By helping that woman murder innocents in all the time since?"

"You think I serve her willingly?" Methoa spat. "A woman? This is the greatest humiliation I have ever endured! Every scar marks a time I resisted! She keeps us like cattle. Like playthings, for her amusement. All we've done is labor and endure her cruelty. Death will be a release!"

He was advancing on us, and I tightened my hold on my arrow, readying for the moment he would spring. My arm was shaking with exertion and pain, though. If I missed, it could all be over. He was a bare few feet from me, but I knew better than to be overly confident. I quickly surveyed the space between us, and noticed something I was all but certain my husband hadn't.

"I will not be judged by you, woman!" The man roared, continuing his rant. "You who brought this on your own people! If you had accepted your fate and gone quietly, none but you would have suffered! You brought shame on my village, and shame brings ill times! Your sins brought these people to our door!"

The man sprung forward at that, and when Grant tried to move to meet him to protect me, I released my hold on my arrow, and flung an arm out in front of the husky's chest instead, halting his charge, and losing my shot.

But it didn't matter.

Methoa ran directly into the bear trap he'd been too focused on his self-righteous proclamations to notice, and the massive, rusted metal jaws snapped up and slammed over his leg with a sound like cracking wood. My husband screamed in shock and agony and plummeted forward, the chain of the trap going taut as he pulled it with his fall. The thick metal teeth peeled flesh from muscle as he fell, and I smelled bone marrow in the air.

The man lay shaking on the ground, the trap firmly locked around what remained of his leg. He curled into a near fetal position as I slowly approached him, and drew my bow on him again. His breaths were ragged and hoarse, weak, pained cries escaping him on every exhalation.

I turned his head over with my foot, forcefully, so he'd be looking up at me.

"I want you to know something, husband," I said quietly, "before you die."

Methoa's eyes were clouded with unshed tears of pain and shock, and I wasn't certain if he could truly hear me. But I needed to say this.

"I bore you a son," I said softly. "I have no reason to lie now, and I wasn't lying then. Tale'nuk was your flesh and blood, Methoa. Your only child. And you killed him."

I pulled back my bowstring, slowly, and watched Methoa's eyes sharpen with some clarity. Perhaps in his final moments, even if he would never regret what he'd done to me, he might regret what he'd done to the boy who bore his own blood. The little creature who'd been a piece of him.

"Did he cry?" I asked softly. "When you left him out in the cold? Did he cry out for his father?"

A tear slid down the man's cheek, and he squeezed his eyes shut. I would never know if he'd been crying for our boy, or his own suffering. Even if the man truly had regrets he never would have told me.

I released the bowstring and the arrow struck his chest with a dull thud. The man went limp all but instantly, and with an anticlimactic, final sigh, he was gone.

And then I didn't know what to do. I was still breathing. My heart still beat in my chest. The aches in my body began to return, and the fires began to dim inside me, leaving me with little more than a thick, heavy coldness, seeping down into my limbs. My arms fell at my sides, and I stared down at the dead man at my feet.

There was no jubilation. There was no relief. There was no satisfaction. There wasn't even regret. This wasn't how this was supposed to end.

"Shivah…" the husky murmured from behind me, and quietly stepped up to my side, wrapping an arm gently around my body. I let him, but did nothing to return the gesture.

The husky seemed to notice the blood stain down my back, and looked momentarily panicked. "God," he moved a hand up to cup the wound and put pressure against it. It hurt, but I didn't care. "Shivah, we need to get you back to Puquanah.

228

That looks bad," he insisted, trying to look me in the eyes. He tipped my chin up to face him. "Are you faint? How do you feel?" He asked, concerned.

I continued to stare down at my dead husband.

"I feel…" I mumbled, softly, "nothing."

"I knew someone else was firin' shots," the coyote growled, wincing and closing an eye as Puck applied a salve to the bloody wound he'd suffered to the shoulder. Someone had managed to take a shot at him when he'd broken cover to fire, and he'd been lucky enough that it had only clipped him. Still, it was a rifle shot, and had carved a nasty gouge through the muscle there. He looked to be in a lot of pain.

"Aye, they were going down fast. I noticed it even from inside the camp," Grant agreed. "Unless you two were exceptional shots…"

"Not to mention there was rifle fire," Ransom said, around another wince. "Confused the hell outta' me 'til I realized they were on our side. I was worried about you, kitten."

I didn't reply, even when the coyote looked my way. I just shrugged out of my leathers carefully, with Grant's help, so Puck could get to the wound I'd endured when he was done with Ransom.

"You're certain it was Connall?" Grant asked me, his tone quiet and soothing. He'd been nothing if not attentive since we'd returned.

I nodded stoically. "I didn't just see him from a distance," I said softly, at length. "We spoke."

"Hell, well," Ransom snorted. "I wish the bastard had stuck around, but I guess he's gotta rush off and take the credit. Whatever," the coyote muttered, derisively. "Fact is, we probably wouldn'a had this without 'em, so it worked out fine. Them mercenaries musta' cost him a fortune, but they was worth it. Dunno how much the other rifleman did, but there was a sharpshooter somewhere on a rise a few hundred yards from me that was pickin' em off like flies."

"How can you be certain?" Grant said, defensively. "You and Shivah must have dropped half the men in that camp…"

Ransom shook his head. "Ain't you taken a look down there, yet? A lotta them kill shots was done with black-fletched arrows. Beetle black, like from a cock, or a cayuga mallard or somethin'. Shivah and I use goose feathers. Gray."

"It doesn't matter how they died, or who did it," I said, stonefaced. "They're dead. We accomplished what we came here for. Let's just go home."

Grant looked to me, concerned, but Puck was the first to speak again. "Not until your injuries are treated. Wickham, don't touch her wound, damnit."

Grant paused, halting his hand where he was about to apply pressure to the bleeding puncture again.

The fox got between us and pulled something from his belt, uncorking it and pouring it gingerly over my wound. It stung enough that even in my state of dumb shock, I hissed and squeezed my eyes shut.

"I'm sorry," the fox apologized, "but it's an open wound. And Wickham, it's all but a certainty you're infected. We need to start you on treatment for the Fever, now."

"I thought there might be a good chance," the husky said with a ragged sigh, rubbing his paw up over his neck wound, which probably wasn't very dangerous, but it looked like a bloody mess. "Especially after this. H-how would I feel, if I were?"

Puck shook his head. "You won't feel anything right away. We'll know by tomorrow morning."

Grant cast his eyes aside, looking mildly frightened at that. I couldn't blame the man. We'd seen what this illness did.

"It will be alright," Puck tried to say as confidently as he could. "You're a young, strong man, and I know how to keep it from escalating to a deadly level. You're just going to have to do what I say, alright? We'll get you through it. It's not going to be pleasant, but you'll live."

The husky nodded, flicking one ear back, nervously. "I…" he sighed, and continued on, guiltily, "I already touched her wound once before…"

"Then we'll treat both of you," Puck said, unfazed. "It doesn't matter. I can treat two people as easily as one."

Ransom suddenly went tense and twisted his head towards the woods, his hackles raising. I saw Puck jump almost as soon as the coyote did, in response to the man's sudden alertness.

"What?" Grant said, glancing around. "What's is something—"

"No, I don't…" Ransom sighed, relaxing some. "I'm just real nervous here, 's all. Lotta' death on the wind."

"That's fine. We should move on anyway. We need water," Puck sighed. "You've all lost blood."

"There's a stream not far," Grant said, hefting his pack. "Mountain stream. Cold waters, good and clean."

"Good, you can wash up before I treat those," Puck nodded, gripping his walking stick and helping Ransom up. The coyote had lost a lot more blood than the rest of us and was somewhat unsteady on his feet, but together, the two men seemed able to walk.

"I'll scout ahead," I murmured. It was something of a pointless gesture now. We'd killed every threat in the area, but there was always the chance we'd stumble over more traps, or something of the like. And it was getting dark, besides. There were other dangers in the woodlands besides raiders.

We traveled for about an hour, Grant hanging back closer to the two men, while I surveyed the trail ahead. The time spent moderately alone was neither of help or nuisance to me. I couldn't make sense of emptiness, no matter how hard I tried.

And that's what this felt like. Emptiness. I'd been waiting for some great conclusion to this personal tragedy of mine. Some final, epic battle between my husband and I, that would exalt me either into peaceful rest, or a triumphant catharsis that would free me from the shackles of the memories he'd given me, the pain he'd caused me.

But those memories were still there, and that pain, if anything, was freshened by the confrontation with the man who'd caused it all. The moment my son had been taken away, the moments leading up to the stoning ritual, the imagined visions in my mind of how my son must have died. And now, added to that, I would forever remember the moment my husband had died. It did not make me feel triumphant. It just made me feel sick.

I'd sought peace. Resolution. Instead, all I had was one more painful memory.

Even Crow was vacant from my heart. Was Puquanah right? Had I truly imagined him all this time? An aberration of my thoughts, who rose only when I was most angry, most desperate?

I heard Puck call out to me that the river was near, and I stopped along the trail as Grant jogged to catch up with me. He huffed as he got close, and gestured back towards the men. "It's just down the rise there. Do you want to help me get water? The boys are going to start setting up camp. Ransom won't make it back into town tonight. The man needs to rest badly."

I nodded silently, and began to follow the husky. We collected the water skins and began making our way down towards the distant brook. I could see it sparkling in the final fading rays of daylight, down a steep ravine and across a small stretch of open woodland, where the trees made way for a small field of boulders and mosses. The terrain almost reminded me of the beautiful glen we'd found in the mountains, but I was in no mood to be nostalgic right now.

"Shivah," Grant said softly, once we were alone. He was careful not to touch me again, but he walked closely beside me, instead, his compassionate blue eyes looking down on me. "Talk to me." he pleaded quietly.

The husky was the only one amongst my companions who knew what had truly transpired for me, down in the raiders' camp, down in the mines. When I'd returned, Puck and

Ransom had been so glad to see I'd survived, they hadn't even thought to ask about my husband. Grant had told them that we'd hunted down and slain the last of the raiders, but that was it. He'd been silent about my final confrontation with Methoa.

The fact was, I didn't really know what to tell them. I would tell them what had happened in time, but I wasn't really certain what I'd accomplished. What it had all been for.

"This wasn't how it was supposed to be," I said softly, at length. Grant continued to look down on me, and I could tell the man wanted to hold me. Badly. But he resisted. There was still the chance I'd not yet been infected.

"How was it supposed to be?" The man simply asked, instead. He was good at boiling things down simply.

I looked up at him, stopping where we stood and really considering what he'd asked me. What had I expected? That some great, righteous fire would swallow and surround us both, the moment I pierced his heart... That I'd see his soul sent to hell, and embrace my afterlife with the vengeful spirit I'd been so reverent of?

"I thought at least," I murmured, "I'd feel good about ridding the world of him. Satisfied, that I'd..."

The husky's brows arched. "Taken his life?" He filled in, softly.

I nodded.

"Shivah," the man said with a soft sigh. He turned entirely to face me. "You just haven't got that inside you. Only a certain type of person can feel good about inflicting death, and you should be proud you aren't so far gone. That it still bothers you means you're still a good person." He put a hand on my arm, where my sleeve covered me, and I felt the heat of his paws through the leather, giving me that small sliver of comfort.

"I don't feel good about what we did today, either," the husky said. "I killed a lot of men today. That it had to happen doesn't mean it's not still sad. You can't right pain by inflicting more pain. You can stop men like that from inflicting it again, but... You can't ever undo what's been done. They still left a lot of sadness in their wake. Real satisfaction in justice comes when you mourn the loss of life, but you do what needs to be done, anyway. The day you start enjoying it is the day you'll start seeking it. And that's when we become them."

I looked down, swallowing back the pain in my throat and wrapping my arms around my chest. "I'm still," I said softly, choking, "so sad…"

Grant leaned forward and put his forehead to mine. I wanted to reach up and put my fingers through his fur, to hold myself close to him.

"It's alright to be sad," the man said, softly. "It means what has passed mattered."

I closed my eyes, unable to fight back the memories of my son, in that moment. The pain now felt sharper than even the day he had been taken away from me, like I was truly allowing myself to feel it for the first time. And it was terrible, deep, and aching. I missed him so much.

I'd wanted so badly for this all to fade. But I hadn't even let myself feel it until now.

"Grant…" I said softly when the man parted ways from me and began to move forward towards the clearing beyond.

I gave a frustrated huff, pushing my tired body to try and keep up with him. But he was doing it again. Insistently walking ahead, as he always did. Even when it didn't matter.

"I have shorter legs than you," I said breathlessly, as I jogged to catch up with him. "It isn't fair—"

My words trailed off when I saw him stiffen and shudder backwards to a stop, a few feet into the clearing, like he'd seen or smelled something. I stopped in my own tracks, looking out over the empty, small field. I saw nothing. Smelled nothing.

"Grant, what—" I began to say, stepping out onto the field of lichens and moss.

He gave a hoarse gasp, and breathlessly uttered, "Get to cover…"

I was going to demand why, but at that moment Grant turned somewhat, as he stumbled backwards on suddenly unsteady legs, and buckled to his knees.

And I saw the arrow protruding from his chest.

"Get to cover!" The canine screamed, desperately.

But I couldn't. My body was beyond my control, running to his side, and all I could see was the black-fletched shaft buried in the man's chest, so close to his heart. I flung my arms around him, trying to pull him to his feet, but he shoved me off of him and I was no match for the man's strength. I went tumbling back down to the ground, back the direction I'd come. Everything seemed silent, but I saw another arrow bury itself in the ground, right where I'd been not a second before, beside him.

I screamed his name and tried to struggle back to my feet, even as I went for my bow. But my hands wouldn't work, my grip shook where it took hold of an arrow, and I dropped the first, tears beginning to cloud my vision.

The husky was still there, on his knees, in the clearing. And he was pulling his pistol from his belt, and gripping his shaking arm by the elbow to steady himself. And then thunder crackled out across the clearing, surrounding him in a thin veil of smoke as he fired the weapon.

And then for the first time since we'd been chasing this specter across the country, never even knowing who or what we were truly chasing... Only then, in that moment did I see her.

She fell from the branches of a nearby pine, her cloak tangling in the boughs as she tumbled down through them. When she at last hit the ground, she still managed to do so with some grace, rolling several times to soften the impact. The crumpled, dark, distant figure was still for a few frozen seconds in time, and then she lifted her head, slowly, and stared at us across the clearing.

All I saw beneath the cowl were green eyes, amidst a dark vixen's face. Her arm was hanging limp at her side, so Grant must have hit her. But she gave me little time to see any more, before she took back off into the forest.

I didn't care. I ran to the husky's side as he weakly let his legs give out, and leaned back against the nearest boulder. I desperately wrapped my arms around his midsection and lifted, but all I managed was to lift him to a sitting position against the rock. He was so heavy, so impossibly heavy.

"We have to get you to Puck." I said insistently, trying to steady my voice. I gripped the husky by the cheeks and forced him to look me in the eyes. His breaths were coming slow and ragged, and his gaze seemed hazy. "You have to help me lift you," I said desperately, tears stinging at my eyes. "I can't do this alone, Grant! You have to stand!"

The man tried to move, I could see the effort he made. But his legs barely shuddered.

"I can't…" the husky said, fear creeping into his voice.

"Yes you can," I said, harshly, wrapping my arms around him again and trying with everything I had left inside me to lift him. He had to get to Puck. We had to get the arrow out, and I couldn't do it alone.

"Puck!" I screamed, as loud as I possibly could, hoping to whatever gods still heard my prayers that he'd hear me up on the rise.

"Shivah," Grant murmured, his voice gone weaker than I'd ever heard it, before. "Something is wrong inside me…" he mumbled the last part, his eyelids beginning to droop.

"Do not close your eyes!" I shouted, furiously shaking the man's shoulders until his eyes snapped open again. I stared into the blue orbs, nearly muzzle-to-muzzle, forcing him to look at me. "If you're going to die, Grant," I said, my voice shaking, "you are going to look me in the face when you do it. You are going to tell me you've lost the will to live. Do you want to disappoint me like that?"

"No…" the canine said hoarsely, swallowing and trying to reach for me, with one of his hands. I took it, wrapping my fingers through his, tightly. I tried to look strong, for him. I

236

didn't want him to be afraid. Maybe he could will his way through this.

"I don't want to die…" the man insisted, softly.

"Don't be afraid," I said, nuzzling him, and hiding the fact that I was crying. He was, too.

"Not afraid… to die…" the man mumbled, quietly. "Sad…"

I squeezed my eyes shut tightly, giving a shuddering sob I couldn't hide.

"I wanted more time with you…" Grant said, his voice fading.

I stroked my fingers through the husky's thick fur, pressing my nose into the scruff of his neck. I could still hear his heartbeat, but it was so slow. I inhaled his scent, listened to him breathe, felt for every heartbeat, and tried to remember every second that passed.

I leaned up and kissed him softly. The man pressed against me as much as he possibly could, with what little strength he had left. I don't know how long we sat like that, but when I pulled back, I looked him in the eyes, and whispered, "Alongsaa."

The canine's brows lifted, and he blinked drearily, murmuring, "What?"

"My name," I said, swallowing back another sob. "I promised you I'd tell you."

The husky smiled at me, for the last time.

"That's beautiful," he replied, quietly. "It suits you much better…"

I felt his heartbeat fading, and I screamed for Puquanah again. And again. And again.

And I talked to Grant. I told him things I wasn't even certain were true. I held him, and I talked, and I pleaded with him,

long past the point that anything I said mattered.

CHAPTER SEVEN
A Deep, Unseen Sickness

Fire blossomed outwards in a tremendous explosion of cinders and ash, amidst a dark black void. It flung glowing bits of light throughout the sky, cascading in wild, irregular patterns, like stars.

I felt lost in it. Freezing in the void, yet burning inside. Was I one of the cinders? Was I a star, amidst a sea of stars? Was that not what we all were? Ultimately alone, separated by worlds of distance. Our own singular entities, ever in sight of others, but never able to cross that void.

"Every soul is a star," a familiar, omnipresent voice spoke, fire popping and crackling between its words. "Separate yet woven together into one great tapestry. Some burn brighter than others. But all eventually die off to fading cinders when they've consumed all the time they have."

"I remember the elders telling me," I heard myself saying, almost by rhetoric, "that many generations ago, one of the greatest stars in the sky burst. It glowed brighter than every other star for several days and then it faded, and ceased to be. She was the eye of the…"

I went silent at that for a moment, realization dawning…

"Crow," I said at length. I looked out into the void, but I could only hear him, feel him. I could not see him.

"She was my only kindred soul. The only being who ever understood me," the spirit said, his voice echoing across the cosmos. "We were as one. We lived as one. We burned for one another. But she could not endure it as I could. She began to crack apart, like an ashen log. When her fire consumed her, she left me behind. Alone again, as I had been before her."

The distant memories of fireside stories, of myths heard in my childhood, flitted through my mind like the flashing embers that still danced through the void around me. I remembered the legend of the Eye of the Crow. It had been a star, once. And then it had ceased to be, in three brilliant nights. It had lit the night sky nearly as brightly as the moon, and then it had been gone forever. It was said when it died, the great Crow spirit in the sky had died, and had taken much of the magic in the world with her.

I'd never heard a story of another spirit—a kindred spirit to her—who'd been left behind. But even the spirits loved. Was my Crow this once-great spirit's lover? Or family?

Or was my mind creating explanations from stories I'd heard in my youth? Was I dreaming this? Where was I? What had happened?

Fleeting glimpses of the last memories I'd had began to flicker in the peripheral of my thoughts, and with them came stabs of pain, distant as they ever were, in this dark place where Crow spoke to me, but a powerful reminder of the last moments I could remember in the waking world.

"What do you want from me, Crow?" I demanded, my exhaustion and my aching pain returning to me in hard, unrelenting stabs. Try as I might, I couldn't deflect the blows. It was consciousness, catching up to me. And this time, I didn't want to return, but I could feel Crow pushing me back towards it.

"I've done what you asked," I cried into the void. "Isn't it supposed to end now?"

"*It never ends,*" the spirit replied.

"You said it would end when my task was complete!" I cried. "I can't endure this anymore. When will it be over?"

"*You live for vengeance, now,*" the spirit stated. "*The cycle of vengeance is never-ending. If it ends, you are of no use to me. You will burn. Forever! As was your oath!*"

"You promised me peace!" I sobbed.

"*I promised you power,*" the spirit countered. "*Fire. Life. You have your life, and you have power, now, and you will continue burning! There is no peace for souls like ours!*"

"This wasn't what you promised," I said, weakly. "You tricked me. This hurts. It still hurts. I want the pain to stop. I want peace—"

"*No peace!*" The spirit roared, two blazing eyes burning to life and dominating my vision. "*We made a pact!*"

"You abandoned me!" I said, angrily.

"*You abandoned me!*" The spirit roared back, his breath like a great wind through the void, causing the stars to swell and glow as he spoke. Like fanning embers.

"You were supposed to give me the strength to beat these people!" I cried back. "To fight Methoa, and right the evils he's done! They have hurt SO many more people! People I cared about! Where was your strength, then?!"

There was sharp, cawing laughter. "*Fire is not precise!*" The spirit rasped. "*I told you to avoid distractions! You are a pyre! You will burn all whom you surround yourself with, until the day you die! And then we will burn out together, as I should have with her!*"

"Why do you want her fate?" I asked, wildly. "Why do you want to burn?!"

The spirit was silent for a time. When he at last responded, his voice was low, and distant. Reminding me of when I'd first heard him. "*Why do you?*" He countered.

My eyes snapped open. There was no rush of fire escaping the void this time. No final threats or promises from the spirit. I just came back to consciousness, all at once. I felt warm, and smelled canine fur. For a moment, I thought everything that had come before had been the dream. That we'd never received a letter. That we'd never gone to the camp, never found Methoa. That I'd simply fallen back asleep in my room and slept in, beside Grant, and now I could re-do the day. Tear the map in half, toss it in the fire before Grant woke.

But the arms that were holding me were thinner, and his fur smelled wrong. Familiar, but not the husky.

I blinked bleary eyes up into the two gold ones looking down on me. He wasn't Grant, but I was still glad to see Ransom. Maybe he could tell me I'd imagined everything.

"Hey, sweetheart," the coyote murmured, softly. "Why don't you just go back t' sleep? I've got you."

240

His comment snapped me back into focus, and I jerked awake in his arms, trying to make sense of my surroundings. We were in a tent. He was sitting, and I was half-lying, now half-sitting, in his arms. It was dark out. The sun had been going down when…

I struggled against the man, but he didn't let go. "Grant!" I insisted, my voice weaker than I remembered it, so hoarse as to be almost unrecognizable now. "We have to—"

"We got him," the coyote murmured. "Brought 'm back to camp. Don't go outside, honey. Please just wait 'til Puck's done."

"He's hurt!" I persisted, my voice cracking. I saw the coyote's features twist into something more painful, perhaps because I was struggling against his bad arm. Perhaps other reasons. I needed to get to the husky. That's all that mattered. "Let me go!" I struggled. "I need to talk to him—"

"Sweetheart…" the coyote released me enough that he could look me in the eyes. He gripped my shoulders, turning me to face him. "Listen to me, alright? You can see him later. But honey… He is gone. He was gone when we got to you. There weren't nothin' Puck could do—"

I yanked out of his grasp entirely and struggled to my feet, shoving open the tent flaps and stumbling out into the night. There was a low fire lit, and I saw the figure of Puquanah across it, leaning over…

My heart stopped.

None of it had been imagined. Everything in that field, every final, excruciating second, had been real. The husky's still form lay across a bison hide, an excised wound in his chest that wasn't bleeding. The fox was kneeling beside him. He held the very arrow that had been buried in Grant's chest in his small paws, the stained steel tip glinting in the low light of the fire. And Grant was far too still. He wasn't breathing.

Puck's ears flicked back towards me, as he slowly set the arrow down, a surgical blade in his other hand, just as bloody. "Ransom," he murmured, softly, "she doesn't need to see this."

I felt the coyote arm's close around me again, pulling me against his chest. I screamed and struggled, not with any real strength, and not with any words that mattered. But even injured, I couldn't really get away from the coyote when he put his mind to it. He yanked me back away from the campfire, towards the treeline. And that's when I was able to breathe between my gasps, and I smelled death. Fresh death. It was an all-too-familiar scent in my life, now. But to have it mingled with the scent of the man I'd cared for—the man I'd shared a bed with for the last few weeks…

I felt my legs giving way and darkness spinning into my mind again, seductive and clawing. This had happened once already, while I'd been in the field, when I'd realized I could no longer hear his heartbeat.

Ransom's arm tightened around my waist and held me up as I slumped and nearly fell to the ground. The jolt of the man's grip keeping me from falling was enough that I didn't pass out again, but I wish I had. All I wanted to do right now was go back into that void. Beg Crow to take me, as he'd promised.

How was I to be expected to suffer like this any longer? How could the spirit be so cruel?

"If you're goin' back into the black, sweetheart, I'm getting' you back into the tent," Ransom said, softly. I could tell he was trying to look me in the eyes, but I could barely lift my head.

The coyote, instead of holding me up, slipped down to my level, lowering himself slowly into a kneeling position and letting me down gently as he could, until I was on my knees in the dirt. I didn't know what to do other than remain there, staring at the ground.

Ransom was silent for a long while. The silence suited me fine. The fierce melee of twisting, confused, tortured thoughts in my head was becoming too much to bear. It felt like it was all colliding and knotting around itself into a web of pain too complex to even consider unraveling.

My entire life. A tangled tapestry of grief, punctuated by moments of hope and happiness, just grand and wonderful enough to decimate me that much more when they came to a terrible end. Parents, childhood, strangers, marriage, rape, humiliation, my child, my love for him, betrayal, loss, death and rebirth, rage, survival, friends, a renewed hope… and then loss returned, like a buzzard circling my dreams.

That was my life.

I had endured it all once, through fury. My anger had given me the strength to carry on. But that anger's purpose was to extinguish the man who'd caused me so much pain. And even when I'd done so, the pain remained. Killing Methoa'nuk had not stopped tragedy from reoccurring in my life.

What had it all been for? I'd committed everything I was to the hunt for him, in the hopes that removing him from the world would make up for the evils he'd done, and prevent any future pain in my life. And it had done neither! I still hurt! I still lost someone. Again!

Was this all my life would be, from this point on? Anger, and hurt? There was no healing what had been done, I knew now, and there was no preventing future pain. The world was cruel and unforgiving, and nothing I'd accomplished had mattered. It never would, would it?

Perhaps this was the true bargain I'd struck. It wasn't that Crow intended to kill me. But he had taken my life. This was no kind of life.

I couldn't live with it. But I couldn't end my life. I couldn't hurt my friends the way this was hurting me. I just had to continue. And accept it would always be this way. That was all that could be done. All that I could tell myself, to bear it. All at once, like some door inside me had shut, the tangled web of pain disappeared. And everything got very quiet.

Ransom was not the sort of man who said placating, false things. He only spoke if he thought he had something of value to say—especially when someone was angry, or upset. Instead, he merely held me, and watched over me. And when my shaking at last stopped, and I slumped against him, he was there for me, holding me up, silently. There was nothing the man could have said that would have given me any peace, anyway, and I'm certain he knew it. Holding me was all he could do.

The gesture didn't give me any comfort, I was finding. It would have, before. But now I just didn't care.

It was the best I could do. When he died, or left me, at least it wouldn't hurt.

"How did he die?" I asked quietly, at length. My voice sounded so calm, when I finally managed it. So much so that it seemed to unnerve the coyote.

"Puck said... he bled out on th' inside," the man spoke, quietly. "Wasn't nothin' anyone could've done. He was dead as soon as that shot hit him. But Puck tried, honey," he insisted, his voice hoarse and pained, "He really did—"

I nodded, silently.

The coyote swallowed, and looked down intensely into my eyes. "Tell me you saw who did this, sweetheart. Please..."

I finally looked back at him, and spoke the name that would next consume my life. The next hunt. That was all I could be, any more. A hunter.

"Shadow."

Ransom stiffened and lifted his muzzle to the wind, his eyes darting through the dark trees around us. "That woman is here?" He said, alarmed. "How... why... ?"

"I don't know," I said, standing. "But she won't be hunting us again anytime soon. Grant shot her before he died, and I can only imagine it was bad, or she wouldn't have fled."

This time the coyote didn't stop me, but he followed me at a close distance as I headed back into camp. When I made it back towards the campfire, Puck was covering Grant's body in one of our blankets. The fox was shaking slightly as he put away his tools, and when he heard us, he turned towards me, his ears falling flat against his fur.

"Shivah, I'm sorry," he said with a shuddering breath, blinking forcefully and running his arm over his eyes. "I-I tried... The shot was too close to his heart, h-he... bled... inside. He was already gone when I got to you."

244

I wrapped the fox in an embrace, because I knew he needed me to. He buried himself against my chest, and cried. Even Ransom cleared his throat thickly where he stood beside us, the tall man having trouble remaining stoic.

I didn't cry. I was done crying.

We spent almost the entire following day burying him in the dense, rocky earth of the forest the raiders had chosen to take refuge in. For all of its foreboding, dangerous terrain, it really was a wild, beautiful place. And one the Otherwolves would likely never be able to settle. He would remain undisturbed, if nothing else.

We decided to bury him where he'd fallen, near the lichen-covered boulder in the field that led down towards the brook. The part of me that couldn't entirely let go of what I'd felt for him realized, I suppose, that there was some symbolism to the place. It was on a field like this, high in the mountains, that I'd first realized I might care for him, and I'd first begun to open my heart to the man.

None of us knew any rites in his religion, but hopefully his God would heed our prayers as he would any of his people. It was all we could offer. We couldn't return the man to Crossroads. We hadn't come on horseback, and it was nearly a day away. This had to be his resting place.

Ransom sung. I'd never heard the song he sung that day before, and I honestly hoped to never hear it again. I'd once felt joy at the upswell of emotion the man's voice could bring, but right now, I didn't want to feel anything.

Even Puck prayed for the man's soul. I wasn't certain where his faith lay any more, but I'd never seen the fox so earnestly chant, before.

I hoped the spirits, or the gods, or the Otherwolves' One God and his 'angels' would hear us. Any beings above. Anyone. I didn't care what lay beyond. Heaven or Hell, the spirit world or rebirth of a new soul. Whatever followed all of this.

245

Grant deserved better than this world had given him. He'd been too good for it. The only justification I could imagine was that. Wherever lay beyond, it had to be an improvement on here. And I hated hated the world... for being so terrible a place, we couldn't be happy together here. But maybe what was beyond was better. Maybe he was there because he deserved to be.

He certainly deserved better than I'd been able to give him. I'd ruined what time we'd had together with my anger. My 'quest'. I never should have come into his life. I burned everything I touched. I regretted everything. Absolutely everything.

My paws were raw from digging, my body caked in dirt, my limbs aching. I stood over the grave for several hours. We all did. I welcomed the pain the labor had brought. It felt right to hurt right now, and I couldn't hurt any other way.

I'd taken his locket. I held it in my hand even now, the tarnished metal growing warm in my palm. It was the only thing on his person I could find that was uniquely his, some memento of the man. But not for myself. Someone had to tell his family.

"I found this in th' field," Ransom said quietly, in the midst of the long silence following our prayers. He stepped forward and handed me something, wrapped in buckskin. I didn't need to unwrap it to know what it was. The weight and shape alone was enough. His pistol. He'd dropped it after he'd fired at her.

"Maybe we should have buried him with it," I murmured. I don't know what I'd ever do with the man's gun.

"It's valuable," the coyote said, clearing his throat and dragging a breath in through his nose, like he had been all day. "His family's poor. We ought to bring it back to 'em... Let them decide what t' do with it."

I just nodded.

Puck turned his muzzle towards me, trying to look at me. I felt the fox's paw on my arm. "Shivah," he said, his voice somewhat raw, "it's alright to cry..."

I pulled my arm away from the fox, lowering my brow and staring him in the eyes, even though he couldn't stare back. "Just say it, Puck."

The fox looked confused. "What?"

"Say you told me this would happen," I snapped. "Stop holding it in for my benefit. You were right. I got him killed."

"No—" the fox insisted, shaking his head. He looked like he was going to cry again.

"Everything that's happened to all of you has been because I wanted to pursue these people," I said in a hard, unyielding tone, "you didn't want any part of this from the start."

"We're still alive," Ransom pointed out. "Grant died doing his job. He was a bloody Marshal, Shivah. A lawman. Lawmen die doing their job sometimes. It's a dangerous line o' work. I'm sure he knew that and accepted it."

"Stop placating me!" I cried, angrily. "Just blame me! This is my fault! Get away from me, before this happens to both of you!"

Puck winced back away from me, curling his tail around his legs. I shoved the gun into my belt, and made to leave, but at that point, the coyote grabbed me by an arm and yanked me back over to the grave. When I resisted, he yanked both of my arms behind my back and held me there, in an iron grip, forcing me to stare at the upturned dirt.

"Look at him," the man demanded. "Look at his grave, damnit! And show some bloody respect for the dead! D'you honestly think that man would want us fightin', right now? Over him?"

I bit my lip until it bled, forcing my gaze away from where we'd buried the man I'd cared about, just hours earlier. Ransom was holding my arms tightly enough that it hurt. I couldn't rip away from him even if I tried.

"That boy cared about you!" Ransom said, emphatically. "Least you can do is treat his death with the respect it deserves. Make somethin' outta the time he gave you. Don't just discard it like it meant nothin'! He's watchin' you, somewhere, right now. You really think he wants to see you miserable over him?"

"He died because he walked ahead of me," I said, weakly. "That's the only reason she shot him first."

"He died tryin' to help other people. That's ALL that man was about," the coyote said. "D'you know how bloody rare that is?! There're men like me, a dime a dozen in th' world, who don't give a damn about anyone but them and their kin. When we do somethin' fer others, it's a bloody accident. That boy was better'n all of us. And you ain't showin' him any respect by takin' the credit for everything he did. He made his own damn choices, Shivah. And he made them because he was a good man. Not because of you!"

He released my arm at that, and I stood where I was, limply. I hadn't been able to look down at the grave, while he'd been speaking. But now, I couldn't look away.

"And it is alright to cry," the coyote said, dragging in a deep breath through his nose and fiercely running his arm over the back of his eyes. "Ain't nothin' shameful about it..."

Silence descended over all of us again. I stood there, my paws in fresh earth. It was almost a feeling of disbelief... Knowing that beneath the earth lay a man that yesterday, I'd been able to touch—talk to—feel his eyes on mine, when we walked...

He couldn't be gone.

I wanted to feel something. But that door had closed, and I knew what opening it brought. I knew I couldn't sort through what lay beyond. This was easier.

But I couldn't pretend to feel what I wasn't allowing myself to. So I just stood there and stared at the grave, in silence.

The question following that terrible day was where we went from here. And no one really seemed to know the answer, but the short-term solution was Crossroads. Ransom's injury was worse than mine, he needed to rest somewhere safe, and someone from the local authorities had to be appraised of what happened at the mines.

We were also still missing the vixen, and the otter, but not a soul mentioned that fact. Honestly, I think as far as Puck and Ransom were concerned, this was the end of everything concerning the raiders.

And it probably was. Shadow, wherever she was, was badly injured. We'd found a lot of blood near the pine where she'd fallen, and no bullet, which meant it was lodged in her when she'd fled. Ransom educated me a bit about gunshot wounds, and apparently, that could be a very bad thing for her. She might have even bled out and died, somewhere in the woods. There was simply no way to know.

It hardly mattered. Alive or dead, I would hunt her down. I didn't even know how, at the moment, but it had become who I was, and it was all I had left. My life literally took no other direction from here.

But the raiders were gone. She could inflict little to no damage on her own, and Rourke, wherever he was, wouldn't get far alone if he were as mad as Puck had said. The raiders were done. Their reign of terror was over.

At least we'd helped accomplish that. It would be something to tell Grant's family, someday.

Ransom and Puck had been giving me some distance. Puck especially seemed unnerved by me, although he'd made incessant attempts to talk to me along the trip home. He seemed concerned, but... I didn't know what to say to alleviate his worries. I thought considering all that had happened, I was holding together well.

He could be concerned if he wanted. That's how the fox was. Empathetic. Caring. Even Ransom I know, in his own aggressive way, was worried about me and trying to show he cared about me.

All the more reason I needed to find a way to put distance between us soon. I could just leave, of course. It's not as though the men never gave me my space. But it wasn't the right thing to do, and I knew it. These two people had saved my life, literally pulled me from a shallow grave, kept me beside them even when I was an inconvenience, and stuck by me through hell. They had earned the right not to simply be abandoned.

I just had to convince them our paths were not the same. I knew Puquanah. He'd want nothing to do with any further killing, especially after everything that had happened. The two men would choose one another over me, eventually. I just had to show them that being around me was destructive.

I hated Crow for this new life he'd given me. And yet, I had asked for it, after all. The trickster spirit hadn't even so much tricked me as given me exactly what I wanted. I'd just fooled myself into believing, over these last few months, that having my comrades, having people who loved me in my life again, meant I got to live a real life.

I'd been wrong.

Fire consumed. And the blaze in me had never gone out. It festered still, even now, stronger than it had been before. Hatred for Methoa. Rage against the situations that had led to so much pain in my life. Bitterness at the world.

But at least there was single-minded purpose in this. Not the twisted knot of indecipherable pain that lay in the recesses of my mind, beyond the curtain of flames. That could stay there. This was what I lived for, now.

We got back to Crossroads the following afternoon, after traveling all day from early morning. Puck and Ransom immediately got a room at the Cock and Barrel, and with little fanfare, decided to turn in early. They tried to persuade me to do the same, but I noticed something, or rather someone, in the dining area of the brothel, and told them I wanted to eat a meal, first.

"You need to eat," Puck said with a nod, gripping my hand and forcing a soft smile. "Go easy. Soup, maybe some bread. You could still be infected, so you need to keep your strength up."

I just gave the short man a dismissive nod. I hadn't eaten since Grant had—well, since all of that—so it was yet one more thing the fox was worrying over. At least now he'd stop bothering me about it.

"If you see Laesom, send 'm on up," the coyote said, flexing his bad shoulder with a wince. "Ver said he's been in and out. I'd like t' talk to the man s'more before we part ways."

The two men made for the stairs, Puck staring in my direction for a bit longer than Ransom, as though he wanted to say more. The look of hopelessness in his pale eyes hurt some, but I shut out the feelings as soon as they hit me, averting my gaze. I was trying to put distance between myself and the two men. Now was no time to be commiserating with the fox. He actually had a life ahead of him.

I waited for them to disappear upstairs entirely before I made my way into the dining area, singling out the man in the corner of the room, sitting alone in a darkened booth away from the women and the general merriment of the establishment. He was smoking something, and noticed me as soon as I got near, cutting my way determinedly through the crowd towards him.

I slammed my hands down on the table and leaned over it, staring the pit bull in the eyes intensely. But he barely blinked.

"What are you doing here?" I growled.

"Waiting for all of you to arrive," Connall replied, evenly. He blew out a cloud of smoke from the thick brown cigarette he was smoking, or whatever it was. He crushed it into an ash tray to his left, matching my stare with an intensely serious one of his own, making it clear he was not intimidated by the icy glare I was directing down at him. "You took your time," he muttered, "I was hoping not to have to wait in this hell-hole any longer than strictly necessary—"

"Grant died," I stated, coldly. "We were somewhat busy... burying him."

"Lord..." the pit bull sighed, disgustedly. "His bloody family. Someone has to tell them."

"He told me where they live," I said, my voice dropping, some. "I plan to find them."

"Yes, because that's just what our populace expects," the man muttered, bitterly, "our law enforcement agencies, sending

251

our men off to their deaths, then informing them via native couriers with only the barest grasp of our language. I'll make sure his family hears of his death," he said forcefully, "properly, and with due honors. There ought to be some consolation pay in all of this for his loved ones, at the very least."

There were a lot of things I was angry at Connall for. A lot of deep-seeded resentment. But on this one point, I knew he was right. The idea of finding Grant's family and telling them of his bravery had been far-fetched from the start. It was probably better if his own people handled it.

"Is that why you're here, then?" I asked, not hiding the bitterness in my voice. "To see who amongst us survived?"

"Partially," the pit bull admitted, unblinkingly. "Do you blame me for wanting to know? You made yourselves part of that offensive. So shoot me if I was concerned."

"If you were that concerned you could have stayed around after we wiped the camp and joined back up with us," I pointed out. "We couldn't find you at all, when it was all over. You or your mercenaries. You didn't even remain behind to ensure all the men in camp were dead. We had to handle that."

"And I knew you would," Connall replied, waving a hand. "I had other matters to manage, miss. Mercenaries to take care of."

"Credit to claim," I said, deadpan.

"Whatever you want to believe," the man replied, sounding in no way offended by my accusation. He also wasn't crowing about it, so... I didn't know what to make of that. "Believe me when I say," he finished, "picking off dying men was not my priority at the time. We actually did return the next morning, to burn the bodies. But you were gone by then."

I narrowed my eyes at the Otherwolf. "Alright, I'm done with this," I growled, "what is your game, Prendergast?"

The pit bull's eyebrows lifted marginally. "'My game', miss... is what it has always been. Protecting this country, at any cost. I gave myself to this country in the border wars with the tribes from the Northern Wastes, I gave fifteen years of my life to the Marshals, I gave up my relationship with my wife and children in service to my country, and I intend to give my life, some day, in the line of duty. My life belongs to this Nation. And this Nation has many troubles. I will do whatever I must to see to it that those troubles do not destroy her."

"Fine, then," I growled, irritated by the man's verbose speech that, in essence, had said nothing at all. "What are you doing here? What do you want with us? How can we possibly be of more service to you than we have been already?"

"Tying up loose ends," the pit bull said in a low tone. "And this visit is purely a gesture of good will, miss. Because I thought you might want to see his through to the end, as well."

I blinked, surprised. "You mean—"

"Shadow," the pit bull said with a slow nod. "That woman made a fool of me, and what's more, she was their ringleader. I don't like that she's still out there. There's always the chance this beast rears its' head again."

"You intend to keep hunting her?" I pressed.

"What I want doesn't matter right now," the man replied. "I want to know what your plans are, miss. If you tell me you're going to give this up here and go on with your life, we have no more to discuss. If you tell me you are still hunting her, however—"

"I will not give up hunting her until the day she dies at my feet," I snarled. "She's the reason all of this happened. She killed Grant."

"She's dangerous," the pit bull countered. "But that isn't going to stop you... is it?"

I shook my head, slowly

Connall gave a long, heavy sigh, and for a moment, I could have sworn I saw regret pass over his features. "Alright, then," he said, at length. "Then I have a few things to show you that might help. I could use a hunter like yourself. Someone who is able to think like a tribesman. Like her."

"What sorts of things?" I asked, leaning forward, suddenly intrigued.

"Possessions she left behind," the pit bull explained. "From the time we had her in custody. I'm hoping they might mean more to you than they do to me. Perhaps give us some clue to her lineage. Where she might return, how she might operate… things like that."

I nodded, but at that point, the man put up a hand. "Let me make myself abundantly clear, though," he stated. "Hunting her isn't strictly legal," he leaned forward, putting his elbows on the table. "She wasn't the hunt I was charged with. So all of this, the fact that you're helping me especially, has to stay between us. Not even your friends can be involved."

"They wouldn't want to be," I said, quietly.

"Good," the pit bull nodded. "When can you start?"

"Now," I said determinedly. The thought of working with Connall after all he'd done turned my stomach some, but this was a windfall. And it fell neatly into everything I wanted right now. Puck and Ransom didn't have to be involved, couldn't be involved, if Connall had his way, and that was just fine by me. And if I had to work with any person in the world to hunt down a deadly murderer, Connall would have been the man I picked. For one, the man was competent, and canny. There was no questioning that.

But secondly, and perhaps most importantly, if he died I would hardly care.

"I left her possessions in a safe box at a fallback location the Marshals use on the outskirts of town," the pit bull said with a nod, standing and supporting his knee with a braced hand as he did. He seemed to be getting around without the cane now, but his leg was still clearly paining him sometimes. It probably always would. That had been a bad shot. "I hope you don't mind if I ride," the man said as we began to make our way back towards the door.

I was about to make some dismissive comment about not minding the walk, when I saw a tall, older wolf duck his way quickly into the establishment through the main doors, ahead of us. We noticed each other all but immediately, and Laesom began to make his way through the crowd towards me. And I knew immediately something was wrong, because he actually pushed his way through several people, which he never did.

"Shivah!" he said, out of breath when he at last made it to me. He looked bedraggled and harried, like he'd been running for some time now. I reached out and put a paw on his shoulder.

"Laesom, what's wrong?" I asked, seriously.

"I think something is wrong at the Physician's," the wolf uttered, panting.

"What do you mean?" I asked, confused.

The wolf gestured out weakly towards the door. "I've been in town gathering traveling supplies, and the Physician here sells clean bandages and dried medicinal teas, but his shop was closed."

Even Connall seemed surprised by that, speaking up from behind me. "In the middle of the day?"

The wolf seemed to notice the pit bull for the first time, and grew somewhat more reserved. "Paymaster..." he said in a wary greeting.

"Are you certain he wasn't just out, Laesom?" I pressed.

The wolf shook his head. "I asked the vendors across the street how long the shop had been closed. I thought perhaps he'd return soon, but they said the shop's been closed all day. And all of yesterday..."

My gut sunk as the possibilities began to occur to me. The Physician could have simply been out of town somewhere, but...

No. This was too coincidental.

"Laesom," I said intently, looking the wolf in the eyes. "Listen to me. Puquanah and Ransom—"

"I was planning to speak to them next," the wolf said with a nod. "And Grant. Where is he?"

I swallowed, closing my eyes a moment. That's right. He didn't know.

"Dead," I said, and I could barely look at the stricken expression that fell over the wolf's features. I just pressed forward with our current crisis. "And no. I do not want you to tell Puck and Ransom. At all."

"But, why—" the wolf stammered, still looking shocked from the news I'd just given him.

"Because enough people have died over this," I snapped, knowing I had to be firm with the good-hearted older man right now to get through to him. He stared down at me, lost, clearly not understanding what was happening, but wanting to. "Just let Connall and I handle this," I said, putting a hand on the wolf's arm and giving it a soft squeeze, and trying to look unconcerned. "It's probably nothing, anyway. He's probably just out of town."

"Ah... I suppose..." the wolf said, uncertainly.

"Good. We'll go to check just to be certain," I said, gesturing to Connall, and looking back at Laesom as I headed out. "Just sit tight. We'll be right back."

We headed out as though we weren't in a rush, but as soon as we made it outside and the door closed behind us, I bounded down the stairs, calling back to the pit bull as he followed.

"I'm sorry to do this to you, old man," I said, "but I'm running."

"I can keep up just fine," the dog grunted, proving it by hastening his pace to keep up with me. "And I am not an 'old man', woman. I'm four and seven years."

"Just watch my back," I called back to him. "If she really is there, we might get the drop on her."

And this time, I was going in first.

It took us nearly half an hour to make it through town, with the midday crowds, but when we did finally arrive, I was no less fired-up than I'd been when we'd started across town. If anything, along the trip, my heart had been tightening in my chest, my nerves were tingling, and I was going over every possible scenario for what lay inside the closed-up shop.

It had been meant as a bluff, but there honestly really was the chance the Physician was out of town. The man might have gone to see a case in a nearby settlement and simply stayed a few nights. Or perhaps he was seeing family. There were a myriad of options for why the man was apparently missing that weren't insidious.

But I'd had no such luck of late. Everything was the worst it could possibly be.

With that in mind, the worst case scenario for this was, I decided, that the woman had been here, gotten what she needed from the man, and left already. Perhaps used him the way she had Connall. It would be nigh on impossible to follow her trail in town, and if she'd gotten treatment, she'd be on the mend that much faster, which meant she'd be a threat again soon.

But she might still be here. And that's what had the fires inside me roiling.

My suspicions were all but confirmed when we reached the front door, and I reached forward warily for the handle, only to realize it need not be turned. The door was actually open by a crack.

I swallowed, trying to peer through the dark crack for a few moments, or listen for anything beyond. The road here was fairly unoccupied this time of day, so there wasn't much noise from the city, but even so, I heard nothing. It was eerily silent inside. Silent and dark. The blinds seemed to have been drawn over all the windows.

I heard Connall pull and check his pistol behind me, snapping the cap into place and moving up close enough to me that I could feel his shadow on me.

"You smell that?" He murmured.

I nodded. I did. And it was a distinct scent. One I'd smelled far too much, of late.

Blood. The copper tang in the air was becoming so regular a part of my life now, it almost didn't evoke the natural panic in me it once had. But it still made me fearful for the Physician, and the nurse who worked for him. This blood smelled fresh. It couldn't be from Shadow.

I pulled and nocked an arrow, and looked back to Connall. "Stay behind me," I directed him, fiercely.

"The man with the limp? Probably for the best," the pit bull agreed with a snort. "But I'll watch our rear. If they're in here, don't shoot to kill. I want them for questioning."

I gave an affirmative nod and slowly pushed the door open with my elbow. I had a few questions of my own I wanted to ask that woman. At knife-point.

We stepped into the darkened office. As expected, nobody appeared to be in the main room. It smelled like I remembered save the blood, though. Sterile and herbal. The odd mixture of his many different medicines hung in the area, along with the sharp tang of the medical alcohol they used to treat injuries. And that blood. I could still smell the blood.

I couldn't smell rot or death. That at least was something.

We slowly moved down the empty, wood-floored hallway, pushing open doors as we went. I found a study, stacked with books and paperwork that looked like it hadn't been used in days. A cold cup of tea sat on the counter. The main treatment room, where he'd tended to Puck, lay beyond that. It hadn't even looked to have been slept in, of late. The supply closet was the first real sign we had of anything being awry. When I opened the door, my foot tapped a fallen glass vial, and as my eyes began to adjust to the dark, I was able to make out many more littering the floor. Supplies had been pulled from the shelves, a roll of bandages lay half unraveled near the corner, some of the large glass containers full of herbal remedies had been left open. It was very obviously in a state the fastidious Physician would not have left it.

Connall had gone to open the door opposite the closet, and I heard him behind me, giving a sigh. "Damnit," he growled. "Come here."

I turned and looked towards the room he was inspecting. And that's when I realized what it was. It was the small treatment room Grant and I had shared, the one night we'd been here. The first place we'd ever slept next to one another. I tried to push back the ache in my heart, reminding myself of my mission. I didn't have time for this. I needed my fortitude to get me through what was happening right now.

I walked into the doorway, where the pit bull was standing, and immediately saw what had caused him to stop. Unlike the others, this room had very clearly been used. It was hard to say how recently, but this was where the smell of blood was coming from. And the sight before us was foreboding in its uncertainty.

The bed was stained in blood, not in one place in particular, but mostly towards the right-hand-side of the sheets. There were blood-soaked, unwrapped curls of frayed bandaging lying about that had clearly been removed from a wound, and loops of rope roughly the circumference of wrists, tied with enough length that whomever had been bound in them had been able to move around, but bound to the heavy wooden cabinet at the far corner of the room.

And there was a massive bloodstain near the doorway, seeped into the floorboards. It scraped along the floor out towards the back, indicating whomever it was, they'd been dragged. And judging by the sheer amount of blood, they hadn't been alive when they were.

It led towards a door at the end of the hallway.

Connall gave me a silent signal to go ahead, and I did, taking the fore as I made my way towards the simple wooden door. I could see a thin beam of light beneath it, and the sounds of birds beyond, which meant it must have opened into a plot behind the Physician's residence. Many of the houses in this town had yards in the back.

When I reached it, I realized that unlike the front door, this one had been closed entirely. So we had to do this fast. I turned the handle first, slowly, until I heard the door click, and then I quickly re-nocked an arrow to my bow, and listened for a moment. Now that the door was slightly open, I could hear…

something. Someone, moving around. The soft crunch of paws on grass, and a slight rustling, perhaps of clothing. Metal. They had metal on them. So they were armed with something.

I thought for a moment that I heard someone upstairs, as well… but I attributed it to nerves. This residence had no second story.

I gave Connall one last look. He nodded at me, his pistol held at the ready.

And then I slammed my shoulder into the door and flung it open, charging out into the yard, pulling back my arrow as I did and aiming at…

My breath caught in my lungs. It was him. It had to be.

He stood slowly, from where he was leaning over a small garden plot at the far end of the very small yard. As he stood, he tilted his head just slightly, blinking two dark, round eyes at me, the corners of his muzzle turning up in a strangely serene smile. His full height was jaw-dropping. Almost the size of a bear, except built lean and sleek, as most otters were.

Rourke.

It had to be. I had never met the man in my life, but I knew the creature who stood before me had to be him. I could all but feel it. He was everything Ransom had said he would be. Massive, for an otter. His body was covered in strange, ritualistic scars and piercings that looked to be made from bone. He didn't carry six pistols, but then, he wasn't even wearing a shirt, at the moment.

"Raise your hands!" I demanded, trying to keep my voice from quavering. Something about this man terrified me. I couldn't even define what it was. I'd seen larger, more physically intimidating men before, but he felt wrong. My skin was crawling, having his eyes on me, looking at me the way he was. Like he was taking me apart with his gaze.

"You are… the one who got away, aren't you?" He asked, in a strangely smooth voice. I couldn't place his accent. It wasn't like any I'd ever heard before.

"Hands up now!" I shouted.

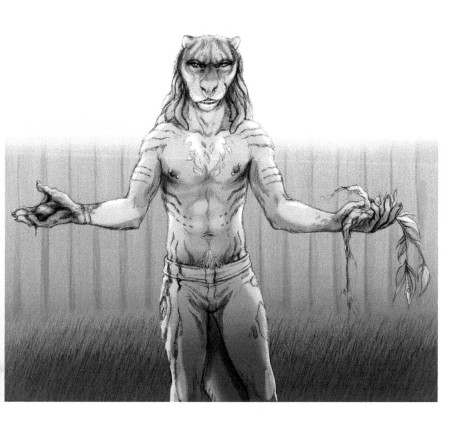

"We don't see the need," the man said, but he did as I bade him to, nonetheless, slowly raising his arms to his side. "No need. We haven't your black wings to take flight."

My heart was racing. It couldn't be this easy. I was waiting for something to go wrong. Anything. I noticed that he was holding something dark in one of his hands.

"Drop whatever it is you're holding!" I growled.

The otter looked mildly amused for a moment, and then he opened both fists. The strange, stringy mass, covered in clumps of black dirt, fell from one of his hands. The other appeared stained, but empty. I was almost too horrified to look down and identify whatever it was that he'd dropped, but when I finally did, all I saw was some kind of gnarled plant root. It looked like it might have been ginseng.

His hands were covered in more than dirt, though. He was stained up to the elbow in dark brown ichor, which I was all but certain had something to do with the stain we'd found in the hallway. But I didn't see anyone out here, alive or dead.

"Where is the Physician and the woman who worked for him?" I said, keeping my arrow trained on the man's heart.

The otter blinked almost drowsily at me, that serene smile still in place. He was silent for a few moments, before replying, bluntly, "Fertilizing this garden."

My muzzle twisted into a snarl. "You sick, depraved—"

"Where is the vixen, Xeli?" Connall spoke up from behind me, his tone calm but authoritative.

"Left. Gone. Left us behind," the otter said with an amused, somewhat unhinged chuckle. "Done with us, I think. Given up on our task. She is following mortal words from mortal mouths, now," his muzzle twitched, and his smile faded to one of disgust. "She will find nothing without our guidance."

The fact that the man spoke in plural was strange enough, but I was beginning to see hints of what Puck had spoken of. Half the things the man said didn't seem to connect, and he often said the same thing in several different ways. I'd never met someone who was honestly mad before. It only made him more unnerving.

"Damnit," the pit bull growled, angrily. "Where? Where has she gone to?"

Rourke's eyes fell on me again, and one corner of his muzzle twitched up into a half-smile. "That woman is making us uncomfortable, Prendergast. We don't like talking while we're uncomfortable. Would you please tell her to put that bow away? Dropping it... much away... would be preferable."

"Like hell," I snapped, tightening my grip on my arrow.

And then I felt the cold muzzle of a pistol pressing against the back of my head.

"Put the bow down, miss," the pit bull said, in a calm, cold tone. "Slowly."

I sucked in a sharp breath, and let it out with a wrathful ferocity. "Son of a bitch..." I uttered, squeezing my eyes shut.

Gods. I'd been so suspicious of the man for months. How had I let my guard down today? I was smarter than this!

I'd walked right into this. And all the signs had been there, for so long now. I'd just been too hopeful that the offer he'd brought today was real to question it. I'd let my desire for vengeance win out over my reason.

"You were trying to get me alone," I said with a shuddering sigh of realization. "That post... on the outskirts of the settlement, where you were going to take me..."

"Drop the bow," the canine said more emphatically, but he still sounded maddeningly calm. He had no reason not to be. He'd won.

I briefly weighed my options. Rourke was still standing in front of me, and I still had an arrow drawn. I could take him down with me. What did I possibly have to lose? If Connall was truly in league with this man—and that certainly seemed the case—that meant he'd been the traitor all along. This went deep.

I wasn't going to leave here alive. I couldn't possibly take out both men. It was highly likely I wouldn't even kill Rourke before Connall's bullet pierced my skull.

A tempest was roiling inside of me, growing stronger with every passing moment. I was white-hot with anger, with indignation and loathing I had never before known. This went beyond one man's personal offense against me. This was betrayal on a scale so enormous, it was almost impossible to comprehend.

My body was shaking with rage, and with it, the grip I had on my arrow. For all of his calm and delirious smiling not moments before, even the otter was beginning to look nervous. And I could feel Connall pushing the muzzle of his gun harder against my head.

"I will shoot you, woman!" The pit bull growled.

"You don't make empty threats, Connall," I snarled. "I know you will. You were going to kill me no matter what today, weren't you?!"

"You put yourself in this position," the pit bull said with the same superior tone he'd use when cutting a man's pay for the day. As if he honestly expected me to blame myself for what he was about to do. "I gave you an out," he said, flatly. "I never wanted you, or any of your comrades, involved in this. I've been trying to keep you out of our dealings from the start. I told you time and time again to leave this to us. I even asked you if you'd give it up, today. You denied me at every turn, even the last chance I flung your way. If you hadn't been so stubborn, you'd have lived a long life."

"For a man who seems so intent on killing me," I said between gritted teeth, "you're certainly slow to pull the trigger."

The pit bull was silent, and I flexed my fingers on my bowstring. "It's the otter, isn't it?" I said, pointedly. "You want him alive. I'll bet it would really piss you off if I shot him right as I died, wouldn't it?"

"An inconvenience," the pit bull replied, and I swear, Rourke looked almost offended. "He's not irreplaceable. It wouldn't even be the first time. Do you honestly think a Tribal Southlander would have an Amurescan name? We kept it after the first one died, just to keep up his reputation. Isn't that right, Xeli?"

"You're a demon!" I said, hoarsely, almost too angry at the man to form words.

"I am a Patriot," Connall countered. "But I won't explain myself to you, woman, and I'm growing tired of this stalemate. Think of me what you will. You couldn't possibly understand what's happening here, and you never will. Your people are too simple to grasp the greater picture."

As he spoke, my eyes had drifted to the sunlit ground beneath my feet for only a moment, as I took stock of my entire environment… looking for anything… absolutely anything… that might allow me to make it out of this alive and best my opponents. But I was standing in the middle of an empty lot, flanked on both sides by the two men, and my arm was getting tired. I was beginning to lose hope...

And then I saw something. A shadow cast from what had to be the nearby roof. And neither of the two men had seen it.

I had to ensure Connall's gun wasn't directly to the back of my head. That would be my only chance.

"Allow me something," I said suddenly, cutting the pit bull off. He went silent and let me speak. "Allow me to pray?" I asked, and I tried to sound less angry than I was. Hopeless. I wasn't much of an actor, but perhaps just the fact that I was a woman would be enough. Men like Connall thought I was weaker than I was.

As a show of good faith, and for my own part, it was an enormous gamble, I let the bowstring go slack, and began to lower it.

There were a brief few moments of silence from Connall in which I worried my bluff had failed, and he was just going to pull the trigger. But then the gun eased away from the back of my head, and I heard him take a step back.

"You may," he said, at length. But I heard him cocking his gun, even as he allowed me to kneel. I laid my bow at my feet and kept my hand over it, and I watched the shadow shift, raising something long and pointed.

I began to pray. I really did. Because if I was wrong...

And then the gunshot came, ringing out through the small yard. But there was no sudden stab of pain. No well opening to darkness in the next realm. I was alive and breathing.

Because that gunshot hadn't been aimed at me.

I heard Connall cry out in shock and pain, and then his heavy body struck the ground, his gun going off as he fell. Wherever the bullet went, it hadn't been anywhere near me. I spun to my feet, pulling my arrow once more and taking aim at the otter, as he froze in alarm and looked past me. I was drawing the string back when he seemed to snap out of it, and began going for the bandoleer of pistols hung over a nearby fence-post. Ransom had said he carried guns, so I could only assume those were his, and he'd know how to use them.

I was leveling a shot for his chest when a shout from the roof nearby caught my attention.

"We need him alive!" The familiar voice called out. "No vitals, Shivah!"

At the last minute, I shot lower, for the man's long legs. I caught him between his thigh and rear as he turned to run, and he cried out and pitched forward into the garden, clawing at the freshly overturned earth as he tried to get back to his feet.

I leapt forward, intercepting him by landing fully atop him.

And then, I was at last able to unleash my anger.

I drove my knee up between the otter's legs to incapacitate him first, and the man proved slow to respond and defend himself, so it worked. The otter went wild-eyed with pain, and was barely able to bring an arm up to try to push me away, before I balled my fist, just the way Ransom had always shown me, and slammed it with all the force I was capable of into his gut.

The far larger man gave a wheeze of breath and struggled wildly beneath me, but he clearly had little to no skill in combat, and I just moved my hips further up his chest when he brought a knee up to attempt to work a foot beneath me and knock me off. I drove my second fist into his nose, and felt something in the fleshy lump rupture, but by that point I was already bringing my first fist up to swing into his muzzle. Teeth cracked somewhere inside, and it felt so damned good to feel every blow shattering something, so I just kept hitting him.

Eventually he stopped struggling, going limp beneath me as I pounded my fists into his misshapen muzzle, again and again... and again...

I grew tired before I really wanted to stop, but it was clear by then that he wouldn't be moving any time soon. He wasn't unconscious, but he was all but sniveling beneath me, just trying to block his head from my blows, now.

266

I leaned my head back and closed my eyes for one long moment, dragging the scent of the midday air, and the otter's blood, into my nose. I should have reveled in that moment, but despite everything this man had done to me, to Puck and Ransom, to the people of this land, I felt no satisfaction. Maybe Grant had been right. If I couldn't find pleasure in this, after all this man had done, would I ever?

I heard the sound of paws striking the ground from a long drop, and finally opened my eyes and looked to where Connall had fallen in the grass behind me. The man hadn't even gone for his gun yet, which meant his injury had to be bad, wherever it was.

And the rat who'd shot him was walking determinedly towards the man, rifle still in hand, and re-loaded.

I stood and walked the remaining few feet between the fallen otter and his bandolier of pistols, hefting it and throwing them towards the opposite corner of the lot, nearer to the building. If the bastard felt like getting up and trying to get to his weapons again, he'd have to get by Magpie and I to get to them.

But honestly, I didn't think he'd be moving again for quite some time.

I headed over towards the black and white rat, who was dressed in the same ragged clothing he'd been wearing when he'd last parted ways with us, and a brown traveling cloak that had seen better days. He looked tired, hungry and dirty, but I had literally never been so happy to see a rat in all my life.

He gave Connall a firm, angry kick to the ribs as he neared him, and forced the man to roll over, sticking the bayonet of his rifle to the pit bull's chest, in a very satisfying reversal of the way the canine had been threatening me not a minute earlier.

"Knew you'd show yer true colors eventually, you miserable sack of shit!" Magpie snarled.

The pit bull seemed to have been shot in the lower back, judging by the pool of blood collecting beneath him. Whether or not it was fatal, I didn't know, but other than being in an extreme amount of pain, he didn't seem to be showing the signs I'd seen in dying men, of late. He wasn't coughing up blood or seizing.

Or growing tired.

If anything, the man was more a spitfire than he'd been before, his jowls pulling back to reveal an equally enraged snarl to the rat's. He was clearly in agony, but it wasn't stopping him from being spiteful.

"Only a bloody ex-convict would have nothing better to do with their freedom than skulk on rooftops stalking men like game," the pit bull growled.

"You set me up, you sonofabitch!" The rat hollered.

The pit bull actually gave a dark chuckle, although it didn't sound genuinely amused. "You made it too easy, you scum…"

"Why?" The rat demanded, pushing the bayonet into the man's chest enough that it drew blood. It was exactly what I wanted to ask. "Why in the hell… just why? We lost so many of our boys that day!"

"We wouldn't have lost a soul if we'd left that bloody village alone!" The pit bull snapped back. "I had to get the men out, or the raiders would have killed ALL of them!"

"They nearly did, anyway!" The rat screamed back. "You led them into an ambush!"

"It wasn't supposed to be a bloody ambush," the pit bull groaned, his head falling back as he squeezed his eyes shut and spoke through grit teeth. "I just needed to keep them out of the damned village long enough. It was the woman's decision to post men at the crevasse. She thought we should take casualties, or it wouldn't look like we'd even bloody tried. I got caught in the damned crossfire, too! It wasn't supposed to happen that way. I never wanted our boys to die in that hellhole. Why do you think I sent nearly everyone away?"

My eyes widened. "That's why most of the guards you left behind were the volunteers from the village…"

"You didn't give a damn about a few rodents' lives, that it?"
The rat sneered.

"They had to die. Everyone in that village had to die," the
pit bull said around another gasp of pain. "Our being there at
all was a bloody mistake. I tried to stop that damned boy from
bringing our men there, but he wouldn't listen!"

"The C.O. was doing his damn job!" Magpie said, enraged.

"His job was to chase his tail for three years!" Connall
rasped. "And to listen to me! If you all hadn't intervened—"

I couldn't take it anymore. I swung a paw out, claws extend-
ing almost unconsciously, and raked it across the man's
muzzle. He gave a sharp yelp and tried to yank away, but I
sunk my claws into his cheek and forced him to look me in the
eyes, as I peeled back my lips to reveal my fangs to the man.

"Grant is dead because of your betrayal!" I cried out. "If I
hear you speak ill of that man once more—"

"What?" I heard Magpie utter in disbelief, from beside me.
The rat's eyes widened in shock and horror. "No..."

I closed my eyes. I'd forgotten that he wouldn't know...

"You son of a bitch!" the rat said wildly, kicking the fallen
canine in the ribs.

Connall gave a rattling cough and took the blow with all
the fortitude I'd expect of the stubborn old man. "No," he said,
hatefully, "Wickham is dead because of you. All of you. But
most especially you, woman!"

I dug my claws deeper into his cheek, but the man didn't
seem to care. "I wasn't the one working with the enemy!" I
said, desperately. I wanted to believe my righteous fury. I really
did.

But too much of me agreed with him.

"I have been trying to keep that man, and every poor soul
under his command, away from the bloody raiders for years,
now!" Connall spat back at me. "He wasn't ever supposed to
come within ten miles of those people, nor were any of my
men!"

"It was his job!" I said, echoing Magpie's statement. "You might not have given a damn about your mission, but he did! He really wanted to help people! He was a good man!"

"He was a child!" Connall roared suddenly, with such intensity that I pulled my bloody hand away from his jaws. "A scapegoat! A figure-head we could blame when the hunt failed! He was hired because he was inexperienced, because he was supposed to be incompetent! He was a bloody Road Warden before his appointment. Do you know what their primary task is? Cleaning dead animals and fallen tree branches from the road, blocking washed-out bridges, looking for lost children— they're glorified civil servants! Do you honestly think the Marshals would put a slum dog with no field experience in charge of a hunt like this?"

I stared down at the man, gape-jawed and horrified. "You set him up to fail?" I said, disbelievingly. "How... Why would you do that? He believed in what he was trying to do! You would have ruined his confidence, his life, his job... For what?"

"Wickham was barely twenty-three years old!" The pit bull said with a derisive growl. "His 'career' could have taken the hit. What were we supposed to do? Destroy a senior agent's name? Someone with a wife and children? He applied at the wrong damned time. That's all. He was convenient. If you hadn't interfered, though, he would have survived. All of my men would have! And he could have gone back to cleaning roads somewhere, and gotten on with his life. You are the only reason he's dead now!"

I'd barely heard anything he'd said from the first few words on. I was stuck on the very first thing he'd said.

"Grant was twenty-three?" I uttered in a hoarse whisper.

I had always assumed the man was far older than I was. In his thirties, at least. He had to have been, to be in such a position of authority. It had been one small consolation, amidst the maelstrom of terrible feelings I'd had surrounding his death.

But this was just one more blow. One more stab in the chest, one more tangled knot to add to the ball of pain I was forcing away in the recesses of my mind.

He'd barely begun his adult life. It just made everything an even deeper loss.

"Why?" The rat suddenly screamed from beside me, and cracked the butt of his rifle down into the pit bull's gut. "Why did all of this happen? I want some bloody answers, now!"

Connall looked like the old dog was finally beginning to weaken, but that wasn't good for us. The repeated blows were taking their toll, and there was still the gunshot wound. He might have even been dying. It was hard to say.

"You aren't cleared," the man said, hanging onto the firmness in his words. Whatever his convictions, they clearly went deep.

Magpie's lip twisted up in a snarl, and he suddenly shifted his rifle into one hand, and gestured with it to me. "Take this," he said, stoically. Something about his expression had just gone very cold.

"What are you going to do?" I asked the rat, uncertainly. I wanted answers from the pit bull as much as he did, but I honestly didn't think Connall could take much more without passing out—or dying.

"Just trust me," the rat said, looking me in the eyes for a moment.

Trust had been in short supply of late. It had only been yesterday that I'd been uncertain whether or not the rat was an enemy, but after what had happened today, he'd earned something from me. I decided I'd give him a chance. I took the gun from him, and watched as he reached into his belt, and pulled out a curved knife of some sort. I'd seen Ransom use it on several occasions when he was skinning game.

I wasn't sure what his intentions would be, but I was worried whatever they were, I wouldn't have the stomach to watch them.

Magpie hunkered down over Connall, holding the knife so that it was visible, but held only in a relaxed grip in one of his hands. I saw the older man's eyes flick to look at it at least once, proving he wasn't entirely immune to fear. No one was, after all.

"So you're in deep with Command, are you?" The rat said, in a low tone. "What? The Intelligence Bureau, I'm guessing?"

Connall said nothing, but the rat just nodded. "Yeah, thought so. They're th' only ones that go around talkin' about 'clearance'. Always thought it was stupid, honestly. Sort of gives away that you're hiding somethin', don't it? But it's not just about keepin' secrets in the end, is it? Some of it, at least, has gotta be about superiority. You like to taunt us peons with your secrets. That's why you really use talk like that. Makes you feel big and bad."

Connall opened his muzzle to say something, and Magpie rapped it with the flat of his knife. "No, boy. You listen to me when I talk. You talk when I tell you to. That's how this works."

"You have no authority to—" Connall snarled.

"You know, I used t' do Intelligence work," the rat interrupted him, scratching his own chin. "Lifetime ago, feels like, but I remember the ins and the outs. I got a lot of training to do what I used t' do, before my career went all tits-up. But you know all 'bout that, so let's not re-hash. If you're in deep, Prendergast, I'm guessin' you've heard of Captain Sigheim? And his Northern regiment?"

That seemed to catch the pit bull's attention, in a big way. His eyes widened marginally, and again, he went entirely silent.

"Yeah, I figured you might have," Magpie said, in an easy tone. "He's not a real well-known man outside our circles, but then… you're in deep in those circles. So you know the sorts of things that man was able to accomplish. The good work he did up in the North, pullin' all those useful tidbits out of the Sok'ta POW's we caught. Ain't easy to torture a polar bear, but damn if he didn't find a way."

"What the hell is your point?" Connall demanded.

"You've seen my dossier," Magpie said, "so I'm guessin' you're already comin' around to my point on yer own. You know I was stationed up at Tokon'etan for a few months, near the end of my last deployment. You know Sigheim and his men winter there. Well, my unit commander," he chuckled, "thought it might make for some good life lessons, if we trained under Sigheim for a bit. Learned the secrets to his infamous 'Creative Information Retrieval' techniques. It was real educational."

At that, the rat leaned in close to the man, dropping his voice to a low, almost slithering tone. "So I guess at this point I don't need to bother explainin' to you what I'm gonna do to you, over the next few hours. Because you're in real deep, aren't you, Prendergast? So you already know them things we did t' those natives that no one was s'posed to know about…"

"Stop," Connall cut him off, twisting his muzzle into a snarl of disgust, and what looked like real fear, for the first time. It was somewhat shocking to see the man reduced to such a pitiable state. But there was real, mortal terror behind his dark-eyed gaze. Whatever Magpie had intended, just the thought of it was enough to shake the canine's resolve.

"It doesn't matter, anyway," the pit bull said, with a shuddering, defeated sigh. "The whole damned country will know soon enough. We weren't ever going to fully stop it. It spreads too fast."

"What do you mean?" The rat pressed.

"We're on the verge…" the pit bull said, swallowing thickly, "of a full-blown plague, the likes of which this country has never seen. And we won't survive it. We can't. If the entire population isn't decimated, our infrastructure will be. Our social structure, our military. This country will crumble, from the inside out. Like a rotting fruit."

I gasped softly. So all of this did have to do with the disease, after all? But why? What did Connall have to do with Rourke? With the raiders?

The whole terrible picture was starting to fall into place in my mind, even as the canine went on, his voice laced with regret, pain, and shame.

"We've been trying to stem the tide," Connall said, his head falling back weakly against the ground, eyes squeezing shut for a few moments. "Quietly at first, taking infected families, then communities, into quarantine. But then it started hitting entire settlements, and it was like wild fire. Like the disease got stronger, somehow. None of the Physicians we hired could make sense of it. It just got more and more out of control. And every time we thought we had a situation contained, we'd miss someone. It would spill over into a new town, somehow."

He balled his fist against the ground, weakly slamming it against the dirt. "Eventually, it comes down. The only way to be absolutely certain that it doesn't leave a settlement is to purge it, entirely. No one really knows when people are clear of it, or how it's been spreading. Sometimes we'd close off a town, bury the dead, and leave survivors who seemed well and clear of the illness, and it would STILL somehow move to the next town over, months later. It was maddening."

"How did it ever get this bad?" I asked, horrified. I'd heard of diseases spreading from tribe to tribe before, but generally they never moved beyond a region. This was… if what he was saying was true, this was unlike any illness I'd ever heard of before.

"We traced it back to a Loyalist plot from the war," Connall said, and I saw Magpie's eyes widen in shock. "Back when it looked like the tribes might ally with us, to push the Amurescans out, a lot of people still sided with the King, and were afraid the natives' aid would help us win the war. They were right. It did."

He coughed, "They called themselves 'patriots', but all they did was dismantle and destroy this country. But resistance militias and sabotaging our troops and ships wasn't enough for them. At some point, a group of mariners from our own ports, who'd been to the Dark Continent and seen this disease began to sell infected grain and cloth to the native tribes. They kept up this plot for years—even after the war ended. Until we discovered it and stopped them. But by that point the damage had been done."

"Bloody hell..." Magpie said, quietly.

"Disease isn't a weapon you can control," Connall said weakly. "In the last century, it's hit our settlements and the natives' equally, and we can't stop it. We tried every humane way first. I never hated your people, miss," he said, his eyes squeezing to mere slits. "We need one another to survive. I wanted to stop this. That's why I agreed to this bloody task. And I have loathed every day of it."

"Puck found a way to treat himself. To weather the disease more easily," I said, defensively.

But Connall was already shaking his head. "The inoculation? It's too much of a risk. And we couldn't treat half of our population with it even if we wanted to. The method that works the best, only the Amurescan Physicians know, and they won't part with it, except to sell it. And it still infects those you use it on, still makes them infectious. An inoculated man needs care for several days, and he's contagious the whole while. And people STILL die from it. It's not a treatment for the masses. We don't even have enough Physicians in this country to treat the population in a city like Arbordale, let alone this whole country. And no one could afford it, besides. Save... Pedigrees, and their men."

"It's the government's damn job to protect its people," Magpie said, vehemently. "Find a bloody way! KILLIN' folk ain't a solution!"

"I'm trying to tell you, there isn't a way!" Connall snapped. "This was the last resort! And it's been holding things off, at the very least—"

"But it's not stopping it, is it?" I asked, deadpan.

"No," the pit bull said, choking slightly on the word. "But it's all we have. And I made an oath to my superiors that we'd keep trying, regardless how we had to."

"That's why you've been letting Shadow and her raiders continue terrorizing the territories?" I demanded. "Why even go after her to begin with?"

"Because we had to look like the Marshals were taking action against them!" the pit bull said. "Wickham was sup-

275

posed to defer to me! Everything in his record suggested he was a follower, who'd listen to a senior officer with more experience. And he was! He did! Until you!"

I sneered. "You could have taken the blame, if you love your country that much."

"None of the men in my position with clearance, myself included, could have failed for so long without raising suspicions at the Senate," Connall said, exhausted. "We needed a fall man. I didn't even make the call! I just did what I was ordered!"

"So what, you've been helping her, and the otter?" The rat said, disgustedly. "How in the hell did you even find these sick bastards? It can't be a bloody coincidence they were out here, doin' exactly what you needed done."

"Rourke's raiders were little more than a group of thieving, murdering brigands who hit wagon caravans and trade posts when we found them," Connall muttered. "But they had a long-standing reputation, and that's all that mattered. We put our agents in place and took them over beneath their own rutting noses, and turned their attacks the way we wanted. We couldn't have government men destroying settlements. It would cause a panic."

"Agents?" Magpie seized on that word, confused.

I took in a sharp breath. "Shadow," I said, softly.

"And Xeli," Connall confirmed, curling his lip, "and trust me, I argued against that one. But she wanted him with her. They always work together. And she pushed for this task. Hard. I don't know. She's got some personal stake in it. The otter proved useful as the front man, at least. Man is raving mad, and he likes to take people apart with his hands. It wasn't hard for her to hide in his wake."

I shook my head. "This disease," I said softly, "is survivable. You've been letting them murder innocent people who could have survived."

"The survival of the country is more important," Connall said, stoically. "And it doesn't matter anymore. You destroyed everything we had in place. What little impact we were making on the spread of it is over, now. If she abandoned the mission, it must be beyond repair. She was more committed than even I was."

"You helped us take down the raiders," I reminded him, still confused by that. "And if you didn't slip us that map, who did?" I looked to Magpie, but he just seemed baffled.

"Map?" the rat asked. "I've just been keeping tabs on him, here in town."

"You didn't take down the raiders when you killed them at the camp," the pit bull said, dismissively. "Your bloody 'shaman' did, when he infected her. By the time she'd realized it and separated herself from the men, they were all infected. We had to take them out. She spearheaded that herself. She never cared about those brigands. Once they were sick, they were just another infection to deal with." The pit bull's face twisted in pain, and he shifted a bit. "Tough gamble, though. We had to kill anyone involved. Hired as many mercenaries as I thought she and I could take out, when it was all over. But she didn't think it was enough."

My heart sank, as I realized what he was implying. "Shadow... She was the one who gave us the map?"

Connall sighed. "I never should have told her you were back in town. She wanted an excuse to take out that bloody fox, anyway. To be honest, I think she just got off on the idea of using you, then killing you. And she would have, too, if Wickham hadn't shot her."

He turned his head just slightly towards the fallen otter, who was still lying on the ground, wheezing through a broken nose.

"Bastard," he growled. "I told him to lay low when she got back to him. But those two are like rabid animals. Any excuse to kill."

"You were going to execute me, to hide your sins," I said, coldly. "You have no moral high ground to stand on."

"I don't revel in it like they do," the pit bull said, strangely quiet, for him. The spite had begun to fade from his voice, replaced with an odd sort of calm. "I've just done what needed to be done. And I feel shame for every single evil I've taken part in. But... God will understand..."

I saw him raising his arm, and it took me a moment to realize he'd pulled something from beneath his coat. Something he must have been lying on, up until now.

"Gun!" Magpie shouted in alarm, grabbing for his rifle. But I instantly knew it had been the wrong move. In the time it would take him to seize it from me and raise it, either of us could have tried to wrestle the man's arm under control, or pull the backup pistol from his hand. I could try and go for my bow, or my knife, but we'd let our guards down around the badly-injured man and made the wrong snap-decision to go for our weapons, and now it was too late—

And then Connall put the muzzle of his own pistol to his throat, and fired upwards.

I had seen a lot of death over the last year, but I had never before seen a man take his own life. The image would stay with me for the rest of my days.

We weren't there at the Physician's much longer, before Laesom arrived with Puck and Ransom. The wolf had apparently not heeded my request to allow me to handle this situation alone with Connall.

Strangely, the two men had barely blinked twice at Magpie's presence. Ransom in particular did not seem surprised at the rat's innocence, nor Connall's guilt. Although we were all equally disturbed, and gave a wide berth, to the pit bull's remains. It was very clear by the way he'd fallen, and the wound in his head, how he'd died, and no one seemed to know what to say about it.

The whole thing was just sad. Even Connall's death, and everything that surrounded this whole bloody mess. It was all so pointless. It was hard to find a villain in it all, and that just made it more frustrating. There was no clear source to vent my anger at. I was angry at Connall, certainly, but some part of me understood his reasoning, even if it had been cold and flawed.

Rourke was insane. Even suffering his grievous injuries, he was still rambling incoherent, disjointed thoughts. Shadow might well have been mad, as well. It was impossible to say. The raiders were all already dead, the government that had tasked Connall with the horrible things he'd done was no one entity we could find or blame...

The real villain in all of this, the only truly guilty culprit, was the illness itself, and the men who'd spread it across the country. But they were all long dead, and the illness was a non-person. I felt like a kettle, with no escape for my steam.

"So. What d'you think we should do with the otter?" Ransom asked lowly, sitting between Magpie and I on the stoop of the back entrance to the Physician's office. Puck had been attempted to speak to Rourke, whom we'd tied to the fence, bound by the legs and wrists.

"I still say we should've killed him," the coyote said with a toothy sneer. The anger in his tone was palpable, and I couldn't blame him. The man who was sitting not feet away from Puquanah was the very man who'd nearly tortured him to death not a month earlier. But as always, the fox was treating him with calm and poise. I wasn't sure what his intentions for the man were, but he'd insisted he wanted to talk to him, to the point of physically holding Ransom back from gutting the otter when he'd first arrived. The coyote still looked like he wanted to.

"I don't know," I said quietly, watching the whole scene with a sort of disconnected apathy. The last few days had all been too much to process. I didn't know what to think of anything anymore.

"Shivah!" Puck suddenly called my name, and my ears snapped up. He was gesturing to me from across the yard, indicating for me to come over.

Ransom stood beside me, hand on his rifle. I put a paw on his arm, "It's fine, he's tied up," I reminded him. "I think he just wants my opinion on something."

Ransom's muzzle twitched and he narrowed his eyes across the yard, but slowly sat back down. I began to make my way over, in trepidation. I couldn't imagine what Puck had been speaking to the otter about, or what he might need me for.

"Here she is," the fox said, in a soft tone. "Will you talk to her about it? She'll understand."

The otter looked up at me warily. One of his eyes was swollen shut, but in the other, I saw through to the fear there. And it wasn't like how Connall had looked when he was afraid, or how my friends looked. This was a more desperate sort of fear. A wildness, like when an animal was caught in a game trap, and didn't understand what was happening to it.

I felt a pang of pity for the man. For all the horror surrounding his name, up close, in person, it was clear he wasn't well.

I knelt beside them, putting my hands on my knees and waiting. I looked to Puck, but his attention was still fully on the otter.

"She speaks to the spirits, as well," the fox said, soothingly. "She is a true believer. You can tell her, can't you? About your mission?"

The otter was silent a further few moments, and then he nodded, giving a broken, but genuine smile. "We knew, we saw wings…"

My eyes widened. "Crow. You've seen crow?"

"Ah, you do know the spirits," the otter said, a sense of peace washing over him. "A crow. Tricksters… Yes, you've been very canny. Many tricks. You nearly beat her at her own game. No one ever has, before. You'll believe me, won't you?"

"Believe what?" I asked, uncertainly.

"Xeli… seems to believe there is a spirit inside him," Puck said, trying to keep his tone level. I knew his true feelings on spirituality, so I was impressed with how gently he was handling this.

"It bored inside this one when I was ill," the otter said, nodding, "back when we was just I. And we reside as one, now.

280

He is this one's guiding hand. He leads, this one follows. Maggot knows where the root of all illness comes from. The heart."

Puck leaned forward, curiously listening in. I just gave the man a distrusting look. "A maggot spirit?" I asked, dubiously. "I've never heard of a tribe that worships a spirit of decay."

"The insects of the earth are the most powerful of all spirits," the otter said, clearly blissful to be speaking on the subject. "All dies. All decays. They consume all. They are all."

I looked briefly to Puck. "Am I mad if I say that actually makes a bizarre sort of sense?"

"Why do you take people apart, Xeli?" Puck asked, calmly. "Can you answer that? Why have you been doing the sorts of things you do to victims of the fever?"

"We are looking for the heart," the otter replied, serenely. "If we bore deep enough, we will find it. And then we will devour it."

"You're eating people's hearts?" I asked, horrified.

That seemed to bother the otter. He jerked against his bindings, snapping defensively, "No! Not people's hearts! The heart of the illness! The root from which it all springs! It infects, it dwells inside, and then it moves to its next victim. If we can find this insidious spirit, we will devour it! We will destroy it, and stop this plague! No more will need to die. No more parents, children, no more tribes!"

His voice went hoarse at that, and he slumped against the fence, blood dripping from his mouth onto his thigh, from the injuries I'd inflicted on him. "Of all, only this one was spared. Forty-three. One lives. We would ask ourselves why, when we was I. And then Maggot begins talking, and we knew our purpose."

"You hear him, Xeli?" Puck asked quietly, and sympathetically.

"He burrowed into this one's mind, to find the illness," the otter nodded. "When the kits died. Youngest to eldest. One, then two, then three then four. When we was I."

I had to look away from the man, at that. He was crying, and he didn't even seem to realize it. He still had that odd serenity to him, but clearly some part of the man remembered the death of his children.

It was too hard to watch.

"How did you come to work with Shadow, Xeli?" I asked softly, adopting Puck's method and using his real name. "Is she like you? Does she see spirits?"

"She is like a weapon, given form," the otter said. "This one was born a shaman. That is why Maggot came to him. She kills. It is all she is, now. Whatever she was before… It is gone. She cares not for spirits, gods, or mortals. She just kills. We would go to villages struck with the Fever, to open the dead. She found us at one such village. She wanted to know what we knew of the disease. Wanted to know if we could protect her from it. We needed to find more dead."

"So you began to work together," I blew out a soft sigh. "That's it, then? You needed her, and she needed you?"

"Not any more," the otter said quietly, his head slumping. "She has discarded us. And we cannot continue our work without her."

I was silent for a long while, considering what I was about to say to the man. It was clear I was at a critical point in my life, and what path I took from here would be meaningful to more than just my life. But for the first time since Grant had died, I felt some clarity of purpose. There really wasn't any question what came next.

"Don't worry, Xeli," I said softly. "I'll continue your work for you."

The otter lifted his head, looking hopeful. "You will find the heart?" He asked, hoarsely.

I nodded. "Yes, Xeli, I will. I will find this 'heart'. I will ensure none of your suffering was for naught. We'll stop the disease, somehow. You're right. Too many people have died."

"We'll both stop it," Puck said, firmly. I looked to the fox. He had put a hand on the otter's arm, comfortingly. How he could muster the courage to get so close to a man who'd nearly flayed him to death, I couldn't even imagine.

The otter seemed grateful, and his body slumped, heavily.

"Then we can… rest… can we?"

"Yes, Xeli," Puck said quietly. "You can rest."

CHAPTER EIGHT
Arbordale

The room I found myself sitting in made me feel woefully out of place. I'd been in many Otherwolf buildings by now, but never one so well-kept, and clearly meant to impress. Where the Cock and Barrel was gaudily opulent, with multicolored tapestries, painted walls, and cheap adornment just about everywhere, everything about the room I was in now felt more subdued, more regal. Older. I'd never even seen some of the things that were hung on the walls… fine swords, an ornately-engraved shield with a picture of a crowned canine striking a warrior's pose, a full-length mirror whose frame was laced with gold leaves.

I'd only seen my first mirror a few weeks ago, and it had been small, at the market, and immensely expensive. I could only imagine how much this full-size one had cost.

The floors were a deep, dark cherry wood of some sort, as were most of the furniture, and the walls were actually painted a color, which I'd never seen before—a light sky blue. It made the room feel comfortable somehow, despite the intimidation of merely being in an estate like this.

The room was inside the largest building in town other than the fort, a house that belonged to 'the Mayor', which I took to mean someone like a chief. He was the man we'd been sent to, after we'd brought Rourke to the local garrison. It only seemed right that the man answer to the justice of the people whom he'd been hurting, and none of us had the heart to carry out executing him.

Well, maybe Ransom. But Puck didn't want him to, and this had felt right. Rourke, or Xeli, rather, needed to answer for his crimes—mad or not. He would likely be executed, and honestly, considering his condition, that was probably for the best. But we'd all decided it was best that we not carry it out in secret. People needed closure, after all. It was no different in tribal societies, when someone committed a crime. The whole tribe, sometimes the whole nation, wanted to be appraised.

The coyote himself had opted to stay outside, as had Puck. Apparently places like this made them nervous. But Magpie had offered to come inside with me at least, and for that I was immensely grateful. I'd have felt even more awkward if I were here alone.

This place was also making it very obvious to me that I was dirty. We'd had no chance to bathe over the last five days or so, and though on average that wouldn't have been a long time for me to go without a bath, the last week had been full of trekking, fighting and bloodshed.

At the very least, by now it was all but certain I'd not picked up the Fever. Puck suspected Grant had simply not had the time to become contagious, and as morbid as it was, I was glad at least that it wasn't one more thing I had to deal with.

I jumped a bit in my seat when I heard the door open, and two large canines pushed their way inside, members of the garrison, by the look of it, or personal guards of some sort. They were followed by an even larger man, who I struggled to realize for a moment was a canine at all. The man was built like a bear.

But his fur was too long, his ears were draping as Otherwolves' often tended to be, and his face was definitely canine, thicker-jowled than a wolf's but not pushed in like Connall's had been. His fur was mostly black, save a blaze of white from his muzzle up to his forehead in a pointed line, and it looked as though his paws were brown. He had very round, brown eyes and an overall pleasant look about him, despite his size. Something about his demeanor was just not intimidating, and set me at ease. He looked like the sort of man who smiled a lot.

Of course appearances could be deceiving, so I readied myself for anything. We didn't even know why we were here. The men at the garrison had assured us we weren't under arrest, but that the man in charge of Crossroads would want to speak with us. They could have been lying, I suppose, but why bring us here instead of to the prison, if they meant us harm?

"Well, now!" The man said in an almost bellowing tone, as he stood before us and crossed his large hands behind his back. "A woman? I must admit, I didn't expect that. But I suppose your peoples need as many warriors as possible to contend with the wilds beyond the range, eh?"

"Uh…" I stammered, not knowing what to say. Was he insulting me or congratulating me?

"Yer the mayor, then?" Magpie spoke up.

"Very good," the Otherwolf said with a grin. "Did the fine suit give it away?"

"It's a very fine suit," Magpie agreed, eyeing the man's finely-tailored clothing. Like his office, he seemed to favor black and dark cherry colors, which honestly did set his fur off well. "But honestly, no. I'd just heard the founding family here were Bernese."

The man gave a hearty laugh. "Aye, I suppose we do stand out in a crowd."

"Look, let's cut through the fat," Magpie said with a sigh. "All we did was turn in a criminal. Are we in trouble here? We're not mercenaries. We're not looking for a bounty."

"Let me cut through the fat," the canine said, "I don't care if you are mercenaries. In fact, I don't need to know a thing about all of you. A man's personal life and trade, or a woman's, I suppose, are their own business." He looked to me at that. "All I care about is that someone finally brought that bastard in. I wanted to meet the man who did. You're a bit of a surprise, miss, but not an unwelcome one. I'll bet it really burnt that man's ass to be brought down by someone of the fairer sex!" He slapped his knee at that and laughed. I suppose to most men, it would be considered rather humiliating to be bested by a woman.

I tried not to get irritated. The man clearly meant well.

"Nathaniel Braxton," the Otherwolf said, sticking out one large hand to me, and startling me a bit. I warily put my own far smaller paw out, and we shook. Magpie followed suit, looking equally baffled, but clearly a lot less worried.

286

"It's a pleasure to meet you both," the man continued, "and I wanted to extend this town's thanks. I'm sure there are a lot of smaller settlements in the area that will be equally grateful, but as they haven't all the pleasure of your company, let me thank you for all of them. This province owes you a great debt. That man was a blight on the land. I've lost track of how many souls we've lost to his brutal band."

"You've nothing to fear from them anymore, either," I promised, quietly, casting my eyes down. "They've been dealt with as well."

"So I heard, through the garrison," the canine nodded, "I got the report in yesterday, from the Marshals. Dreadfully short and to the point, but then that's how they are. There was no mention of Rourke, though, and now I suppose I know why. They let him escape, did they?"

I was silent. I didn't want to tell him how right he was.

The man didn't seem to be delving too deep into it. He was clearly in far too good a mood to suspect treachery. Best it remain that way.

"The Marshals," Magpie said, after a soft sigh, "still deserve a lot of the credit. We assisted them, and they fought very bravely, and suffered great losses."

"Oh?" The 'Bernese' man raised his brow. "Is that so? You know, unfortunately popular opinion about those boys in these parts has been none-too-fond of late. Folks seem to feel this should've been dealt with long ago. Hell, I personally would have committed men and resources to the effort if they'd ever bloody asked. I was all-too-happy to send some boys over to Serahaven when the request came down. I'm glad they were able to do some good."

I averted my eyes. "I'm very sorry. So many men were lost."

"Not your place to apologize," the canine insisted, with a kind smile. "Those boys were doing their duty, and it seems it did some good. I hear the mill down there is operating again. Very important grain producers, those mice. They're responsible for a full third of the bread that comes out of our ovens.

You can't imagine the nightmare losing that settlement would have caused our economy. If bread doubles in price, a lot of families go hungry. And you can't fix problems like that with coin, only people. Those boys knew what they were protecting, and why. It does their memory no service to regret their sacrifice. Only honor it."

I turned my head to look out one of the windows, repressing the thoughts this conversation was bringing up.

"Many Marshals lost their lives, as well," Magpie said, somberly. "I just... I wanted you to know that. Those men did their best, and we couldn't have caught Rourke without them."

"It's very humble of you to share the credit," Nathaniel said, nodding slowly. "I'll make sure the people know of it. Honestly, it will do the public good to know that even out here on the edge, our government sends good men to protect us. It's easy to feel abandoned out here, sometimes." He gave a jowly smile, "But then, that's why my ancestors, and the ancestors of most of the people who live out here came so far to begin with. Freedom. So I suppose it's a double-edged sword."

"What will happen to Rourke?" I asked, quietly.

"There's only one suitable punishment for a man with as many evils in his history as that otter," the canine said, his expression gone serious. "The justice in our neck of the woods is swift and merciless. He'll be executed tomorrow at noon."

"How?" Magpie asked, and I wondered at the morbid question. Did it even really matter?

"Drawn and quartered," the canine said, with a snap of his teeth. "It's some measure of repayment for his sins. I wish we could take enough blood from that man to equal what he's taken from us, but... alas, we'll take what we can get."

Magpie had twisted his muzzle up and looked extremely grim, but he was saying nothing. I didn't understand what the canine even meant.

"I'll have to thank the Marshals later," Nathaniel said, rubbing at his chin. "Do you know the Commanding Officer?"

Magpie looked to me, and I knew he wanted me to say it. I had to steady my voice before I did, I could feel it quavering. "His name was Grant Wickham," I said, struggling to keep my voice firm. Something about saying his full name was so much harder.

The Mayor gave a sigh. "He's amongst the dead, then?"

I nodded, swallowing. "He was the most passionate amongst us to hunt the raiders down," I said with complete conviction. I might have been just as committed to hunting them, but it had been for all the wrong reasons. Grant had honestly just wanted to stop them because it was the right thing to do. He'd really believed in the promises he'd made to his people. And they needed to know it. Someone needed to know.

"Damned..." the large canine said with a sigh. "Did the man have any family?"

I just nodded.

The Bernese was silent for a few moments, before he shook a finger in the air, as though remembering something, then turned and made his way across the room towards his desk. I watched him, perplexed.

"Don't get me wrong... I'm a patriot," the man said, as he dug through his pockets and produced a key he dwarfed in his large palm, before leaning over and using it to open the lowest drawer on his desk. "But unfortunately, I've had relatives die for this country, and I can speak from experience and tell you, the consolation pay for their families is beyond meager."

He dug his arm into the lower drawer, and pulled out a small metal box, hefting it with a satisfied grunt and slamming the drawer shut, before heading back over to us. "The government may have dropped the bounty on that man," he said, as he began to unlatch the box, "but we never did. I figure any man or group who've rid us of that demon deserves our gratitude. And real gratitude is best expressed in coin."

He gingerly handed the box to me, and I took it, alarmed as soon as he released it at how heavy it was. I settled it down in my lap with a rattling thud, and opened it.

I'd never seen so many coins in my life. They were stacked against one another in rows along the interior of the box, tightly packed in together. And they were all gold.

"Take whatever you need for yourselves," the man said with a wave of his hand. "But, if you've such respect for your fallen comrade, you ought to send some to his family, as well. Give them my thanks, too. This province owes you all a great debt."

"Not anymore," Magpie said, gape-jawed as he stared into the box.

"We're very grateful," I said quickly, kicking Magpie's foot. "We'll see that this makes it to his family. I… I have an idea where they live. We'll find them."

"What you all do with the coin is up to you," the Mayor said, good-naturedly. "But you seem like good folks, so I'm certain it will make it to the right people. My family is never hurting for coin, so don't worry. But the people's love, that's a hard thing to buy directly. You've no idea what good putting that bastard to death is going to do for my next campaign." He gave a toothy grin at that. "Besides," he stood, and stepped towards the wall, gesturing to the shield hanging from it, "my family were Knights, back in the old country. The Knights of old worked with any heroic enough to defend our lands on the Kadrush, or the Huudari borders. Rats, felines, canines. It didn't matter to them, and it doesn't matter to me. Out here what you need are people who get the job done, and you've done that. If you two ever need employment, just ask to see me. There's always folks who need killing out here, and I believe in ability over breeding. Or gender, I suppose!"

"I think we'll be moving on soon," I said. "But thank you. I'll keep that in mind for the future."

Work for an Otherwolf? Well, if I survived hunting Shadow, I'd have to make a living, someday, and this had become my one true skill. I'd consider it, at the very least.

"You in particular, miss," the Bernese said, with a smile. "You ask to speak to me direct. I might have a position for you here."

"Uh-huh," Magpie muttered, sounding strangely annoyed. I wasn't certain why. It had been a kind offer.

That evening found us back at the burlesque club, in Ransom and Puck's room, sharing a meal. It had actually been the first I'd had in several days, and I hadn't realized until that moment just how much I'd needed it.

Maybe it was a cold thing to say, but even considering the grizzly method by which he'd died, I had a sense of closure about Connall. While the betrayal had been a hard reality to contend with, I think I'd always known, deep in the recesses of my mind. Not the whole conspiracy surrounding him, certainly, but... I'd never been comfortable around the man, and even Grant had grown to resent him, near the end. And that man never resented anyone.

And I was relieved it hadn't been Magpie. The rat, in the brief time I'd known him anyway, hadn't ever given me a bad feeling. And I'd had a hard time after Serahaven making sense of why he would have done what Connall had accused him of. It was good to know my instincts had been right. Certainly he'd always been mysterious, but then considering his past, I suppose I understood now why he kept so much close to the chest. Honestly, I wish he hadn't. I wouldn't have been as suspicious of him when I'd found out, if he'd just told me from the start.

I had a lot of friends like that.

"Y' know what bothers me the most..." the rat said suddenly, over our silent meal. I looked up to him. He'd barely spoken since we'd come back from the estate. In fact, he hadn't spoken much at all since he'd reappeared that afternoon at the Physician's. He was nowhere near as jovial as he'd been back when I'd first joined the Marshals, but then, few of us were.

"I hate thinkin'," the rat said, bitterly, "that the C.O. went to his death believin' I sold you all out. I'd still be in a work camp if it weren't for that man. He really pulled me outta the fire. Put his faith in me." He narrowed his eyes, "I hate that I let him down."

"Prendergast let him down," Ransom said, dropping a bone on his plate. "Don't you go blamin' yourself. And for what it's worth, I don't think Wickham ever blamed you, Gabriel. I dun' think he bought that tripe fer a minute."

"The last time we spoke, he nearly pulled a gun on me…" The rat said regretfully.

"Only because you had one on us," I said, reminding him. "And because I was there. Grant was very protective of me," I looked down at my plate. "Even though I never asked him to be."

I felt Puck put a hand on my arm, but if he'd been expecting me to break down or cry, he got no such reaction. I simply grabbed up the drumstick on my plate and set back to eating. I needed to keep my strength up, after all.

"I don't think he ever blamed you," Ransom said to the rat. "And I never fuckin' did, if it makes you feel any better. I knew that pit bull was dirty from the start."

"If what he said was true… I suppose he had his reasons," Puck said quietly.

We all turned to stare at the fox, aghast. Puck seemed to sense it, and just sighed. "I'm not saying what he was facilitating was right, but a contagion like this could claim many, many more lives before it fades out. And we don't have any idea when that could be. Diseases like this never last forever, but they do reoccur. And if this plague is bad enough, it could do irreparable harm to the nation—both of our nations—before it dissipates. Or it could the next time it rears its head. He was right about one thing. It has to be stopped somehow, and the government clearly couldn't figure out any other way."

"How are contagions generally stopped?" I asked, mystified. I'd heard of many diseases in the past, but none that could threaten an entire country.

"If it were the pox, they'd inoculate the pockets of people that surrounded infected areas, and treat those who already have it," Puck said, "but the pox doesn't usually kill, except the very weak, young and infirm. This disease is far more deadly, and the inoculations need to be handled carefully, by people who really know what they're doing. Not just snake-oil salesmen or 'shamans' or faith healers. A lot of apothecaries, even, won't know how to treat someone who's enduring the symptoms, won't have the know-how to keep it from spreading. As it is, we only have the most basic knowledge of how it spreads, and I got that from a certified Physician who'd had real schooling in medicine."

"Poor bastard..." the rat muttered.

"He might not have liked getting his hands dirty," Puck said with some regret, "but the man did know the art of medicine. He was honestly knowledgeable. That's painfully rare this far away from the cities, and uncommon even there. Even if the government mass-produced inoculations like they did for the pox, Connall was right. There simply aren't enough people with the knowledge across the territories to use it responsibly. I'd like to say I could travel from place to place and teach people, but..." he sighed, "It wouldn't really matter. Even if I worked with several other Physicians and trained people, with the rate the disease has been spreading, we wouldn't be able to keep up. There have been... What, two outbreaks in this province alone, in the last month?"

We all got uncomfortably silent at that.

"And that's only the ones we know of," the fox said with a soft sigh. "And there are twenty-three other provinces. I could try passing on what I know. Information that valuable travels fast. But I don't know if will outrun the disease."

"What can we really do to stop this thing, then?" Magpie asked, grimly.

"There is something to what Xeli said," Puck stated, catching me off-guard.

"You believed him?" I asked, confused. Even I'd been dubious of the otter's story.

"Not about maggot spirits, or rooting through corpses for a magical cure-all," Puck said. "But the idea of there being a heart to this illness isn't that far-fetched. It's not going to be something physical, though, and we certainly won't find it in a corpse. The heart of an illness isn't in the people it infects. What matters, the root of it all, is how it spreads. Cut off its route to new victims, and you stop it at its source."

"That makes sense," I said, surprised that I'd understood what the fox was trying to say. Normally a lot of his medical knowledge was beyond me. But this I could grasp. "If we could stem the tide, those infected can be treated, and—"

"It ends with them," the fox nodded. "Nothing's fool-proof, of course. Diseases come and go. I'm sure the Fever will never entirely be gone. But we could stop a nationwide contagion, if we at least stop its spread."

"How is it this is so much worse than every other disease?" I asked, still confused about that fact.

"My guess is because it's foreign," Puck said with a sigh. "There are a number of diseases the Amurescans brought over that affect the tribal wolves here far worse than they ever have the Otherwolves. I think it's a matter of tolerance. If someone exists in a population long enough, the people there grow resistant to it. Rather like how tribes like mine from the north have longer fur than foxes to the south."

"The Fever came from the Dark Continent, didn't it?" Ransom said, ominously. "The continent to the south that all the traders are talkin' about bein' heaped in gold, but danger-ous as hell."

Puck nodded. "I think that's why it's so contagious, why so many different peoples are so weak to it. Whatever the indig-enous population is there, they were likely very resistant to it. But we have no defenses like they do, and it's just tearing through us..."

294

"What sort of defenses protect against a disease?" Magpie asked, mystified. "What've they got? Different pelts, or somethin'?"

"It's not necessarily something we can see," Puck said. "The disease is invisible. Maybe the defense to it is, too. I've always had a stronger defense to disease, but there's nothing visibly very different about my body to all of yours. I think it's just like growing a thicker coat. Our bodies know to grow thicker fur when it gets cold. My body is used to being exposed to disease, so my defenses went up."

"Well that's bloody brilliant and all," Magpie said, "but how do we use that t' stop it? Kind of a self-defeatin' process if we've got to parade people around to all kinds of maladies b'fore they're 'strong' enough to deal with the Fever."

Puck shook his head. "No, but I think it's why the inoculation works. The body learns how to fight it, on a smaller scale."

"Yeah, but again, you said that wasn't gonna work for the masses…"

"Shadow is going to a place called 'Serwich'," I stated, catching everyone except Puck off-guard.

"Wait, what?" The rat looked to me. "How do you know?"

Puck sighed. "It's one of the last things Xeli told us before we took him off."

"Never heard of it," Ransom said, suspiciously. "S' it a province? A settlement?"

"It's a colony," Puck said softly, "on the Dark Continent."

That earned a long moment of silence. Ransom looked as though he were slowly putting the pieces together, and Magpie just seemed uncertain, but I think he immediately knew our thoughts.

"Hold up," the coyote said, recognition clicking in his eyes, "nah nah nah… you can't be serious, Puck. Her, I expect t' say crazy shit," he said, gesturing to me, "but you can't be sayin'—"

"If I'm going to find out how this disease spreads, Ransom," the fox said softly, "the best place would be its natural home, talking to the first people who ever had to deal with it."

"You ain't even ever been on a boat before!" The coyote exclaimed. "This ain't like sayin' we're goin' across the country, Puck. It ain't like when we went to the Southlands. And you didn' even like it there."

"I'm not anticipating I'll like this, either," Puck said. "It's not a pleasure trip."

"You can study it or whatever here," Ransom said, pointing at the ground. "It's breakin' out all over th' place right here in the territories."

"I did study an outbreak here," Puck stated. "And I learned a few things, but little more than what the Physician had told me. I still don't know how it even arrived in Serahaven, or how it's been spreading to any of the towns it's hit. There seems to be a link with the river, but in every occasion I know of, the towns afflicted had either been hit by Rourke's men, and purged, or just got through outbreaks with a LOT of deaths. Either way, almost everyone knows to burn or bury the dead immediately and dispose of anything made of cloth, so it's not spreading the way the pox does. Serahaven hadn't even had any visitors before the outbreak there, which means it somehow arrived without people or goods to spread it. There has to be another reason. Something I'm missing..." He said in quiet frustration, dragging his knees up to his chest.

"Xeli said it destroyed almost all of the Southland otter tribes," I said sadly. "His people are on the verge of dying out."

"What in the hell does the vixen want on the Dark Continent, anyway?" Ransom asked, frustrated.

"The same thing we do," Puck said, quietly, "except she intends to get it through any means necessary."

"Xeli said it was always a plan of theirs," I murmured. "If they had no other options. Go to the source of the contagion. Make the natives there tell them how to stop it, somehow."

"How?" Magpie asked, baffled.

"The same way they've been going about it so far," Puck said. "The same way they tried to get me to tell them where the

Serahaven villagers were. Torture and bloodshed, until one of those poor creatures tells her what she wants to hear."

Magpie just snorted. "From what I've heard, the natives there ain't exactly 'people'. She's not gonna get much out of 'em. I don't think they even speak."

"It's not a well-thought-out plan regardless," Puck said with a sigh. "I think she's just at the end of her rope. She didn't even want to bring Xeli... which I can't blame her for, that man wouldn't fare well on a ship, being as he is, but... He might have remembered a few things about real medicine, beneath the madness. I doubt she'd even recognize valuable knowledge for what it's worth, even if the creatures there could give it to her. But that doesn't matter to us," he said pointedly to me, "we aren't going there for her."

"We ain't goin' at all," Ransom insisted, crouching down beside the fox. "Puck... you can't be serious about this..."

"I really am, Ransom," Puck said softly, but seriously. He turned his muzzle towards me for a moment, then back to the coyote. "I don't see spirits like Shivah. I don't really believe in the gods guiding our hands. But I do believe we all have a purpose. I have to, Ransom. Look at what's happened to me."

The coyote went silent at that.

"If someone like me can be born... different, and lose their sight, and their family, and everything they knew and thought their life was going to be," the fox said quietly, "I have to believe there's a reason it all happened. Otherwise everything feels too hard. Too cruel."

"Fox..." the coyote murmured with a sigh.

"Perhaps it's why we've all suffered," Puck said quietly, sweeping his blank eyes around the room. "So that we'd all be here, right now, to do this. Think about it. If everything that's happened to us hadn't happened, if we were all enjoying the easy lives we'd thought we'd have, somewhere in the world, we wouldn't have come together. We wouldn't have discovered the conspiracy, and learned what we have about the disease. And then, who would deal with this? The government can't. Xeli and this 'Shadow' couldn't. I think we're meant to."

"Sounds awful close to 'faith', Puck," I said.

"There's nothing wrong with faith," Puck stated. "But I'll keep my faith for myself, and all of you. I don't need to believe in a supreme being to have faith. I have faith we can fix this, if we follow through and use our skills. I have faith in us."

"Mosta' the 'skills' to heal a plague lie in your court, Puck," Ransom said.

"Puck can't make it across the sea without a guard," I said, firmly. "Especially if Shadow is going to be there, somewhere. We already know she has a grudge against him, and likely all of us."

"And you'd love any excuse to hunt her," Ransom pointed out.

"I'm in," Magpie suddenly said, surprising even Ransom. The rat shrugged at all of us. "What? I ain't got much anymore other 'n all of you. And besides, it's a chance t' see a whole 'nother bloody world. I've never even left the colonies. Hell, you only live once."

Ransom looked to me, desperately. I narrowed my eyes back at him. The coyote knew where I stood on the issue. And even if he chose to believe I was planning to accompany Puck purely to go after Shadow, it didn't change my decision.

The fact was, I'd been looking for purpose. Right now I was just following the currents of anger in my life, and this was the way the river was flowing. It felt better knowing that those currents were sweeping me towards something meaningful. I didn't care how far I needed to go, if it meant I finally accomplished something with my life, other than killing a few souls who needed killing. I'd gotten no satisfaction from Methoa's death. Maybe I'd finally have peace, if I was able to do something useful. I worried for my friends, but I'd never seen Puck so determined as I did now, and I'd be a hypocrite if I tried to stop him.

Besides, going off to try and handle a threat alone had nearly ended in disaster, and not just for me. If Connall had

had his way and I'd died in that yard, the conspiracy never would have been uncovered, and we'd be in no position to help our province, now.

This had grown beyond my own wants and needs, and beyond even the importance of our lives. If Puck was willing to lay his life on the line for this, I had to respect that. At least this time, it was his choice. I suppose it had been Grant's choice, as well…

"Hell," the coyote sighed. He looked down at Puck, his brows lifting. "You know I go where you go, fox. Even if it is halfway across the bloody world."

Puck smiled softly. "Thank you, Ransom…"

"Y'all came up into the mountains t' save me from my own stupidity," the coyote said, smiling back. "I'd follow you t'the ends of the earth."

"Well we still need t' figure out how to get there," Magpie pointed out. "It ain't a hop skip and a jump away. We're gonna need to charter passage on a ship. Well, get to a port city, first."

"I need to go to Arbordale," I said somberly. I glanced down at the box at my side.

"Yeah, what are we doin' with all that money?" Magpie asked, looking around.

"I'd like it if most of it made it to Grant's family," I said. "I know we'll need money to travel, but I think the lion's share should go to them."

I got no disagreement from anyone in the room. Everyone was quiet for a time, before Ransom spoke up.

"Arbordale's a good choice all-around. Huge port, gotta be one or two ships goin' to the colonies down south. It ain't that far from here, either. Few weeks on horseback at most. Hell, I can start gettin' us ready to travel as soon as tomorrow. Just need to get some supplies."

"I'd prefer we not leave until Rourke's been dealt with," I said, firmly. "He's set to be executed tomorrow, and Shadow could still come back for him. I want to watch him die, just to be certain."

"No, you don't…" Magpie said, darkly.

I glanced his way. "Why? I can handle watching a man get executed. I've seen a lot of people die, lately."

"Not like this," the rat shook his head. "Just take my word for it, alright? I mean, yeah, by all means, we can stick around and make sure the act's done, but it's nothin' you need to be seein'."

"How are they executing him?" Puck asked, concerned. Ransom seemed curious, as well.

Magpie closed his eyes a moment. "Drawn and quartered."

"What?" Puck exclaimed, shocking me. I hadn't even known what the Mayor had meant when he'd said that, but the fox clearly did. "That was banned! I-I thought…"

Ransom just gave a thick chuckle. "Bastard deserves it."

Puck whipped his head around to glare at the coyote. "Nobody deserves to die that way!"

"What—" I began, but Magpie anticipated me.

"They're gonna drag 'm through town, tied to a horse, and let the townsfolk beat on 'im," the rat said, "then they tie 'm to the pole in the center square, cut off his bits and disembowel him… y'know… pull out his guts. They usually finish it off with a hangin', or just behead 'm, after that, to make sure the deed's done. Most of the ones I've seen don't make it that far, though."

I gaped at the rat, horrified. "Wh… how could… why would anyone—"

"It's barbaric, it's disgusting, and it's supposed to be illegal!" Puck exclaimed.

Magpie only shrugged. "It's frontier justice. No one from the capital's gonna come out here and tell the locals how to execute their criminals. And it ain't like it's the usual way. Rourke's just…" he sighed, "killed a lot of people. The masses want justice, and this's how they do it out here."

"Xeli is sick," the fox emphasized. "It isn't his fault he is the way he is!"

"He nearly took you apart alive, fox," Ransom said with a sneer. "I ain't got no pity in my heart for th' man."

"Well I do!" Puck said, passionately. "This isn't right!"

"It isn't our call," Ransom said. "I wanted to kill the bastard myself, one shot to th' head, but you said we had to bring 'm to the local authorities. Well, this's how they want to handle it. It ain't our problem anymore."

It seemed like this might become another drawn-out argument between the two men, so I stooped down to retrieve my plate and the box of coin, and began getting ready to leave Magpie did the same.

By the time we'd made it to the hallway, the rat seemed deep in thought about something. I watched him for a few moments, curiously, before asking, "What? What's on your mind?"

"Just reflectin' on how I got here," the rat said quietly. "Hard to keep track of it all. What led me t' this point in my life, how far I've come up, how low I was once." He forced a slight smile. "Whether or not this's really an improvement. Ah, well," he sighed, "at least fer once, this feels important. I dunno how I came from the military to intelligence work to... trekkin' across the ocean to help cure a lizard plague."

"'Lizard plague'?" I repeated, baffled.

"The creatures that live there, on the Dark Continent," the rat nodded. "They say they're lizards. Y' know, like you'd see crawlin' around on trees, but... big. Walk on two legs. I've heard varyin' account of how smart or civilized they are, but just picturin' a huge lizard's a little crazy. I guess we're gonna see a lot of crazy things down there. And y'know... I guess some part of me's lookin' forward to it."

"To seeing huge lizards?" I queried. I wasn't certain I could say the same. That sounded terrifying to me.

"Gettin' away," the rat said, sweeping a hand out as if to encompass the whole province, "from all of this. I feel kind of like... I just keep getting' trapped in circles here. Fallin' back into the same lines of work, the same routines. And everythin' that's the same reminds me of things that've happened, in the past, and that ain't good, fer me. Makes me..."

he glanced down at his black paws, "makes me make mistakes."

"I know how you feel," I said quietly. And I really did. I hated having to relive the past, but sometimes it felt like that's all I was doing, every day.

The rat was silent for a long while, until he finally murmured, "I could 'a sworn that woman had a knife."

I waited for him to say more, but he didn't. He just looked up at me, flicking his ears forward, and reached forward to clap a hand on my shoulder. "But, hey. Let's call this a start to somethin' new. Don't know what, but so long as it ain't what came before, gotta be better, right?"

I nodded in agreement, but it was mostly for the rat's sake. He might be able to escape the demons of his past, but mine followed me even still, and there was no escaping him. Crow would never let me live a normal life. Not until we both burned out. Like dying stars.

I ate breakfast with Laesom the following morning, and we spoke for a while. I knew there was a good chance that once I left Crossroads, I might never speak to the wise old wolf again, and I wanted to hear some of his stories and glean what I could from them. He told me about his tribe, about how he'd come to be separated from them, about his life traveling, his eventual entanglement with Otherwolves, his lover, and his lover's young trainee, Grant.

The wolf acted more broken up over the husky's death than even I was able to show, which in a way, made me feel guilty. Except that I knew somewhere, deeply buried in my mind, the grief was there. I just couldn't contend with it, and I'd been able to put it aside to focus on what mattered, now.

I tried at least to make it clear that the husky's death pained me, greatly, and Laesom seemed to accept that. He might have even known what I was going through, internally. He was a more canny man than he let on.

When we bid each other farewell that day, the wolf heading for the trail once more, it hurt to see him go. I really would have liked to know the man better and hear more of his stories. But our trails parted here, and that's just how life was, sometimes. At the very least, I knew wherever he went in the world, he wouldn't be contending with the same dangers we would be. And it was clear the wolf was not only a survivor, but very fond of life. There was always the chance we'd meet one another again someday.

I headed out to the stable afterward, to tend to Helios. The gelding had been quiet and lacking in appetite ever since Grant had never returned to him. I honestly wasn't certain what to do with the animal. I wasn't sure if horses could grieve, but the poor beast certainly seemed out-of-spirits.

I couldn't imagine selling him, but Grant had always said he didn't take well to anyone else. The horse was wild-caught, one of the plains horses the coyote tribes often tamed, and even gelded, that spirit remained.

We would have to tie him to Molly to even move him, if no one could ride him. And then what? We couldn't bring a horse across the ocean. I would have given him to Laesom, but the man already had a horse, and another would only be a burden for him.

I felt Helios bump my elbow with his nose, and I glanced back at him as I hefted the bucket of water I'd brought and hitched it to the side of the stall. I stepped back so that he could get to it, but he either wasn't thirsty, or didn't want to drink with me here. I sighed and began to head for the stall door, when the horse's broad nose bumped my back again.

I turned around, uncertainly. Helios had never been exactly friendly, but he'd also never been dangerous. All the same, perhaps I shouldn't have had my back to the horse.

The horse looked at me with his big brown eyes, his head hung somewhat, ears flicking. I wished at that moment that the beast could talk. It wanted something from me, of that I was certain. But I wasn't sure what.

"Do you miss him?" I asked softly. I gingerly reached forward and put a palm on his nose, and when I wasn't rebuffed, I stroked the soft, velvety skin there for a bit, then ran my palm up to card my fingers through his mane, and sort out a few tangles. The horse snuffled at me.

"Me too." I said, quietly.

The tranquil moment was broken by the sound of the heavy wooden door into the barn clattering open. I looked over the lip of the stable, but I hardly needed to. I heard the distinctive voices of the two arguing men before they came into sight.

"Are you two still fighting?" I asked the fox and coyote tiredly. Honestly. I would have thought the men would have settled most of their differences by now.

"No, because apparently, what I think don't matter!" The coyote snarled, throwing down a freshly-packed, heavy travel bag beside the stall Molly was in.

"It was the only decent thing to do," Puck said quietly, putting down his own bags.

I looked at the mens' belongings, concerned. "I thought we weren't leaving until tomorrow," I said.

"Yeah, well, that was the plan," Ransom said, angrily, "but the fox here decided my opinion don't matter none, and went an' fucked us! Why d'you even bloody talk t' me about these things, if yer so damned certain you just know better than me all the time?!"

"You're too angry to be thinking rationally about it, Ransom, or you would've agreed with me," the fox said, clearly trying to remain calm.

"Damn straight I'm angry! If you'd let me kill 'm when we first had'm, none o' this would've been an issue at all!"

"What the hell is going on?" I demanded, looking to the fox.

Puck began to say something, but Ransom angrily interrupted him. "The fox here thought that bastard didn't deserve t' have his guts pulled out. Y'know, like he did to... how many other people?"

"So we should mimic him?" Puck said, incredulously. "The man was insane, Ransom! We shouldn't act like insane people!"

"So he went and—"

"I went to the garrison and asked to see him before he was executed," Puck said. "They made an exception since I was a priest."

I got a sinking feeling. "Puck, what did you do?"

"We ain't got time for this," the coyote snapped, throwing his saddle over Molly's back. "They're gonna find that bastard's body soon enough, and they're gonna know it was you, fox."

"I gave him something to end his life peacefully," Puck explained, quietly. "With a bit more dignity. He took it willingly. He even asked me to pray for his soul. I think somewhere inside that man's mangled mind, he understood what he's done, and regrets it. He wanted to die."

"Die drinkin' poison, or bein' disemboweled?" Ransom snorted. "You don't gotta be real moral to make that choice, Puck."

I gave a long sigh. "Puck... I hate to agree with him, but—"

"He didn't deserve to be tortured to death!" The fox said, vehemently. "I don't believe in vengeance! I'm sorry Shivah, I know it's practically your cornerstone, but it accomplishes nothing. All it does is beget more hate. More violence. Hatred's a cycle. Someone has to be the better man, and stop it, or it just keeps repeating!"

I stood there in stunned shock. It wasn't often the fox snapped at me, but in my experience, at every point he had in the past... I should have listened. The man was hardly infallible, but the things that made him angry were usually things that he'd thought over long and hard, and Puck was a very intelligent person.

It wasn't even that I didn't accept that he was right. I'd gotten the revenge I'd wanted on Methoa, and it had left me feeling hollow, not satisfied. But with Grant's death, I simply hadn't been able to really reflect on it. It had all been rolled up into that knot of pain I was ignoring.

This time I was doing what I was doing for the right reasons, wasn't I? Even if hunting Shadow was part of it, I'd committed myself to this trek, because we had to. Not just for the sake of vengeance.

I was doing this because it's all I was, anymore. Because what else was there? That's what Crow had said, and it felt like he was right. Everything good in my life got taken away. The only way to get through it all was to focus on what I was good at. Focus on the hunt, and stop fooling myself into believing there could be anything else.

Or Crow, or the world, or fate, would take it all away again. And it would just be more pain, like all the pain I'd contended with in the past. I couldn't endure that again. I burned everything I touched. So I had to make certain I only chased after those I wanted dead. And if it happened to help Puck with his quest, all the better. It wasn't as though I was only doing this out of anger.

Was I? Gods. Nothing in my life made sense anymore. Why was it so hard to get through every day?

"Hey, cat!" Ransom shouted at me, over the stall. "Can you ride that damned horse? 'Cause we've got to get moving."

I blinked. "What about Magpie?"

"He's out gettin' the last of the supplies," Ransom called back. "We're meetin' him on the trail. He said he wanted t' stop by the brothel first, though, so we're meetin' him up at kettle rock."

I arched an eyebrow.

Magpie caught up to us at the meeting spot about half an hour after we'd gotten there. I'd spent the time trying to get the saddle on Helios adjusted. The horse hadn't bucked me at all on the trip out, and that was impressive, considering I wasn't much of a rider. But the saddle wasn't made for someone my size, not alone, anyway, and there wasn't much that bringing in the stirrups would do for that.

The horse seemed in better spirits now that we were out and moving, at least. I doubted the animal could understand the concept of losing an owner forever, but maybe if I gave him enough apples and grain, he'd be content enough that he'd forget. Focusing on something else was working for me.

The rat seemed in remarkably good spirits when he at last came sauntering into camp. He tossed something Ransom's way as he hefted his small pack of belongings and dropped them into our cart. "Veronica sends her love," the rat said as Ransom caught whatever he'd been tossed. The coyote inspected it for a moment, then got a strangely embarrassed, awkward look and stowed it. I was curious, but didn't pry. Whatever it was had been small, and silvery. Likely a memento of their time together, something personal I wouldn't understand.

"So how'd it go?" Ransom asked, uncertainly. I crossed my arms over my chest, trying not to be judgmental. I'd never figured Magpie for the type to... carouse with those sorts of women in that way.

"Better'n I even thought," the rat said with a chuckle. "Veronica'll handle it. I figured woman like her, wouldn't be hard fer her to get an 'audience' with a man like that, but apparently she already beat me to it."

"What?" I asked, confused.

The rat glanced my way. "The Mistress at the Cock an' Barrel. As it turns out, she's good 'friends' with our local Mayor. She's gonna have a word with him later tonight, about Puck's little pre-execution execution. Get things smoothed out."

"You're damned lucky, fox," Ransom growled. "They could'a charged you with murder. Then where the hell would we've done trade when we came back here?"

"I-I didn't..." the fox stammered. "I didn't think—"

"No, y' didn't!" The coyote snapped, tightening the reins on Molly and turning her. "Fer someone so smart, y' act really stupid sometimes! Yer lucky we got friends!"

I was still confused. I looked to Magpie. "Veronica knows... Nathaniel?" I hadn't ever figured the madame for having friends in such high places.

"If a woman's runnin' a business that profitable in a male-run town, it's usually because she's doin' a' least some of the work on her back, sweetheart," Magpie said, hiking himself up into the saddle with me. Helios gave a disgruntled snuffle and tossed his tail at the rat.

"I... oh," I said, quietly, and with some disappointment. I'd known, of course, that Veronica slept with some of her clients, but I'd thought, like with Ransom, it was all by choice now. She seemed so independent, so strong. "I honestly thought she'd just earned the place, and worked hard for it," I said quietly.

"She did," Magpie said, checking the rifle on his back and making sure it was secured. "Aw, don't get tha' hurt look, Shivah. Woman knows what she's doin', clearly. And if she's gotta grease the wheels with the local politicians, really... Who's usin' who?"

"She just... she should be able to have her own business without having to do that," I said, vehemently.

"She didn't seem ornery at the concept of seein' the man again, actually," the rat said, with a chuckle. "Hell, who's t' say what's between two people? Maybe she's fond of th' man."

I didn't reply, just turned Helios and began following Ransom down the trail. The rat gave a sigh after a few moments, noticing I'm sure, that I still seemed upset.

"Look, it's the way of the world, sweetheart. Try not to stew on it, alright? It ain't our business, and right now, whatever's goin' on there is workin' in our favor."

"You went to her to ask her to do this for us, not knowing they had a pre-standing arrangement," I said pointedly. "You were asking her to use her body."

"I had a pretty damned good idea what kind of a man he was, honey. And I didn't expect she'd do it herself. She's got a lotta girls coulda' paid a housecall or two, and would'a been happy to. The man's the Mayor."

"How could you know what kind of a man he was from one meeting?" I countered.

"Well for one, he came on t' you," the rat said pointedly.

"What?" I said, confused.

The rat sighed. "Shivah, yer gonna have to get a better sense fer this if you're goin' out into the world. When a man says he's got a 'position' fer you at his house, like that, if you accept, he's gonna be expectin' things."

"That's ludicrous!" I said, aghast. "I would never have agreed to that if I'd known that's what he meant!"

"Women out here don't get a lot of choice, especially if they're gettin' tossed favors," Magpie said, "it's just part of how things're done. Universal currency. You mean t' tell me women don't barter sex in the tribes?"

"No," I insisted. "Not until you're married."

"Right, dowries and all that," the rat muttered. "Mnh. Ain't that sorta' the same thing, though?"

I was silent at that.

"Look, hon, I ain't sayin' there's not good men out there. There are," the rat said. "Just be careful, alright? We're headin' thick into colonial territory. We're gonna run into some bad men, and some of 'em won't be nearly as subtle about what they want as the Mayor was."

"I can take care of myself," I said firmly.

"Oh, I know you can," the rat said, clearing his throat. "Yer just a little naïve, is all. I worry for ya."

"Well we've got a three-week-long trip to go over all the colorful euphemisms men use when they want tail," Ransom said from ahead of us, clearing his throat comically. "Lemme get things started…"

ADDITIONAL ART

Healing

I thought I lost you

Let Go